He Remembered Them All Vividly.

Delicious Lisa had happened by accident. But Elizabeth. She had stopped by for coffee. He had left her body in the fountain at Lincoln Center. He scratched his head. No, that was wrong. Elizabeth had been found in the middle of Washington Square Park in a lawn leaf bag. Ah, there was Nicole. Nicki. With her jet black hair and violet-tinged eyes. She had whispered she loved him right before he strangled her. He smiled. Then he frowned. It had all been wonderful. Only Heather Cooper had ruined it. She knew from the start and fought him.

Charlotte Greene in June had been the best. Even better than Lisa. Because she had the same name as Mama. Mama. Suddenly he looked around. His daydreams had to be over. For a year he had worked alone. Now he would have his Mama back. He wouldn't need his girls anymore.

SAVE THE LAST DANCE FOR ME

JUDI MILLER

PUBLISHED BY POCKET BOOKS NEW YORK

"Save the Last Dance for Me" by Doc Pomus & Mort Shuman, copyright © 1960 by Rumbalero Music, Inc. All rights controlled by Unichappell Music, Inc. (Rightsong Music, Publisher) and Trio Music Co., Inc. International Copyright Secured. All Rights Reserved. Used by permission.

Another *Original* publication of POCKET BOOKS

POCKET BOOKS, a Simon & Schuster division of
GULF & WESTERN CORPORATION
1230 Avenue of the Americas, New York, N Y 10020

Copyright © 1981 by Judi Miller

ISBN: 0-671-83650-1

First Pocket Books printing May, 1981

10 9 8 7 6 5 4 3 2 1

POCKET and colophon are trademarks of Simon & Schuster.

Printed in the U.S.A.

To my agent,
Barbara Lowenstein

Acknowledgments

I would like to thank Bill Miller of the New York City Ballet Company for donating his time during the research of this book. Most especially, I want to thank Sergeant Walter Spalinski of the New York City Police Department for his expert technical advice.

Prologue

HE WAITED, STARING hungrily.

Then he took a deep breath and said, "Hi, guys, can I play?" A vein in his right hand kept throbbing. No one said anything. They acted like he wasn't even there.

"I said . . . can I play stickball with you guys?"

His stomach juices rumbled painfully but he stood perfectly straight, almost rooted. Then he heard the mocking, singsong voice with a sarcastic lisp.

"Can I play with you guysssss?"

The other boys laughed at the playful imitation. He shut his eyes and clapped his hands over his ears to block out the loud mocking laughter. Tears of rage burned in his eyes, but he wouldn't let them out. Instead he ran, stumbling, hoping they wouldn't follow and beat him up. He hated it when he got beat up by a gang of boys.

"Queer!"

"Pansy!"

"Fairy!"

"Cock-sucker!"

He ran and ran and ran, not daring to look back. Two blocks down one street. Three blocks to the right, falling up the porch steps, tripping until he stood on the fourth-floor landing. His breath was coming in short gasps. He wanted to be alone to cry. He was going to be nine and a half and he cried almost every day.

He never made it to his bedroom, his one refuge from a world that seemed to hate and ignore him. She was standing at the door. Her arms were folded under her breasts. Her mouth was slashed with bright, red lipstick and it was smudged all over her teeth. Her long blonde hair was falling down piece by piece from her sloppy ballerina bun.

"Where the hell were you?" she screamed. "You have better things to do than play."

His lower lip was trembling and his face felt hot. He looked at his mother carefully through the eyes of an adult. Her breath smelled. He wondered how much she had had to drink already. How soon would it be before she hit him? He knew he had to be careful to be a good boy now, but did he care?

"Put this on!" she ordered.

He stared at it in horror.

"Take off your pants and put this on!"

Obediently he unzipped his trousers and stripped down to his cotton underpants. He shut his eyes while she fastened it on. Then he watched her, puzzled, as she stepped back to admire him.

"Mama . . . it's for a girl," he said, pleading, now close to tears.

"Wear it. I wore that when I was your age."

He stood in first position wearing a sweaty brown T-shirt and a filmy pink tutu over his bare legs, his white briefs showing through the net. His mother tossed him his ballet slippers. He felt the urge to rip the tutu off and just scream and scream. But he didn't.

The record player was scratching out "Waltz of the of the Flowers." Again. The wall was their barre. His mother began to conduct her class. He followed obediently. Why was life so boring? Boring, boring. Ballet was boring. The same old dumb exercises. He hated it. His mouth opened before his mind had a chance to stop it.

"I took class after school. Why do we have to go over the same stuff again? I already did *pliés*."

"Do them again. You can't practice enough. If you want to be a star, you have to work harder than everyone else."

"But, I don't want to be a star. I hate ballet. I never want to go to class again. I told you that!" He almost started to cry. If she saw him cry, she would hit him.

"Concentrate!" she screeched.

Her dress was hiked up over her knees to her thighs. When she went down in a *plié,* he could see the rim of her panties. Usually he liked that. But today . . . today he could only think about those boys ignoring him. Treating him like a thing. How did they know he took ballet lessons? Who told them? He stole a quick look at his mother's crotch despite himself. Maybe it was her. Maybe she had been bragging. He could just see it. Sitting in some bar and bragging about how her son was going to be a great ballet star.

I hate you! he screamed inside. He felt a little dizzy. This time he saw some blondish fuzz creeping out of the sides of her panties. And then she stood up again. Well it was all her fault he had no friends. All her fault he wasn't like the other kids. He was the only boy he ever knew who had to go to ballet school. And everyone knew it now.

"Concentrate!" his mother yelled, her voice shrill with anger and impatience. But he couldn't hear her. The voices inside his head were louder.

The boys who made fun of him. The kids in his class who ignored him. The long, sweaty ballet classes he hated. The lump of rage boiling like a hot bubble in his throat. He opened his mouth and out came a blood-curdling scream. Was it coming from him? He couldn't stop it. His mouth was frozen until his mother came over and slammed him across the jaw and he stood there exhausted, sobbing.

Furiously, she tugged his ears, dragging him across the floor while his pink tutu was slipping to his knees. "Don't cry! No crying! Dancers have to have discipline, and you're going to learn it. Why, you good-for-nothing lazy little fool! Look at all the money I'm laying out for your ballet lessons! All for you! My whole life has been for you!"

The boy couldn't stop crying and shaking. His ears were numb from pain. "No, no," he sobbed when she got him into the kitchen and roughly forced him toward the stove. "Noooooo!" he yelled, terrified.

She laughed a crazy laugh. "Oh, you're going to learn who's boss around here. Who's the only person in the world who cares about you? Your fucking mother—that's who, you little bastard!"

With that she plunged his head into a full pot on the stove and kept it there. When she let him up his face was lobster-pink. He moved his tongue upward and caught a piece of carrot that was sliding down his stinging cheek.

The boy stood in the middle of the floor, sobbing and sniffling, stew sliding down his pretty ballet tutu, his head hung low.

She ignored him. She had taken the pot of stew and was busily mopping up what was left of it with a piece of folded white bread. There was a bottle of whiskey on the table.

"Get out of here!" she finally screamed. "You're a messy little boy. Go clean yourself up. Then go to your room. No supper for bad boys who don't practice their ballet. Shame. Get out of my sight. I don't want to look at you."

The boy turned from the kitchen and ran blindly to the bathroom. He switched on the shower and got in with all his clothes on, crying even louder, knowing the water rushing down would drown out the noise of his pitiful sobbing. Then he took off all his wet clothes and threw them in the hamper, wrapped himself in a towel, and padded into his small bedroom. It was still daylight when he jumped into bed. But he couldn't cry anymore.

He slept and when he woke up his head was facing the window. It was very dark out. He heard a scratching sound at the door. His whole body tensed.

"Punkin pie?" his mother called, her voice friendly.

He concentrated on the tree outside his window. There was a violet aura around it.

"Bunny rabbit?" came the whisper.

He pursed his lips together. He wasn't going to answer. Why should he? After the way she had treated him? He would pretend he was sleeping.

"Pussy pants?"

He squeezed his eyes shut. How drunk was she? Would she make him get up to play Doctor? Then he heard the creak of the door and smelled the musky perfume of her body. Her voice, when she spoke, was slurred.

"I know you're awake," she said. "Mama came in to apologize. You don't have to take ballet."

A smile popped up on his buried face. She continued. "I just want you to give it one more month. That's all I ask. After that if you still want to quit, I won't force you to go. Fair enough?"

She waited. There was silence, except for a little boy's nervous hiccup. He heard the door close.

The woman staggered back into the kitchen, pleased with herself. In another month she'd bribe him with something else. But she'd make him into the ballet star she wanted him to be. One day there would be no turning back.

In the moonlit bedroom the boy chuckled happily and hugged his knees to his chest. No more ballet. He slid out of bed and reached into the bottom drawer of his battered old dresser. It was still there. A melty Clark bar. He could break his diet if he didn't have to take ballet anymore. Sitting and staring out the window, munching, while the branches of the tree striped his naked body, he thought with awe how 1960 might be his lucky year. Someday he was going to be somebody. He was going to show everyone. But he wasn't going to be any dopey ballet star. He giggled. Then he hopped back into bed, licking the sweetness from underneath his fingernails. Someday all those kids would be sorry they never played with him. Someday he was going to be very important.

He remembered once how he had watched some boys playing with their slingshots, knocking sparrows and robins out of trees and then crushing them until all the guts squished out of them. He laughed and choked on some peanut butter that had stuck in his throat. He was thinking of those pink and white little girls in his ballet class. They all looked alike with their black short-sleeved leotards and their hair done up in stupid little buns. They always laughed at him. He was the only boy. They were cruel. Wouldn't it be fun to take the little girls and step on them and crush them and squish them until there was nothing left?

Chapter One

A year ago she said he could stop ballet. But it
never came true. Now he was in his first class
with Madame. The old witch. He stood at the
barre and bent over, his right knee in a plié, his
left foot pointed in front of him. Then he bent
from the waist, brushing his hand against the
floor. He jerked up his head. He could see everything on the little girl in front of him. The crack
in her rear end and almost some of her front. He
chuckled to himself. He had a great idea. Why not
take a giant razor or a saw and slit all the little
girls in half starting with their cracks? Like the
magician he saw on TV. Only he didn't do it
right. When he was finished sawing the girl in half,
she came out whole. Then Madame saw him and
whacked him on the back of the knee with her
pointer. "Black!" she roared. "What is this? Pants
and a T-shirt! You must come to class every day
in black tights, a black leotard, and black slippers!"

THE HEAVY GOLDEN curtain of the New York State Theatre fell to the floor and the audience began applauding, politely at first, then with more gusto and a smattering of soft bravos. Backstage the dancers dropped their poses, massaged sore muscles, took deep breaths, and joked playfully with each other. *Square Dance,* a ballet in one act with the simple, stark costumes Zolinsky preferred his dancers to wear, was over for the evening. The audience out front was warmed up and primed for the colorful *Harlequinade,* a ballet in two acts, a lovely, romantic story ballet with lush costumes and fairy-tale scenery. The audience had drawn a lucky evening and, judging from the commotion when programs were opened, they appreciated it. The part of *Harlequin* would be played by Yurek Ivanov, known as Yuri to his fans, and the darling of the American ballet world.

The curtain rose once more and the dancers took a

11

step forward, their bodies straight and aligned, their smiles gracious, their dance clothes sticking to their bodies. They bowed in ensemble. Then two soloists pranced forward holding hands. More applause. A bouquet for the ballerina. The curtain unfolded once more to the floor and the house lights came on in the Jewel Box Theatre as the audience stood and drifted out the exits to have a drink or one of the world's most expensive candy bars and fill the lobbies with clouds of smoke while they discussed whether Sidney would be accepted to Harvard or Julia would get a divorce.

Backstage, dancers ran straight offstage and into the halls like horses running through a field. Some stopped in the warm-up room to pick up leg-warmers they had tossed to the floor. One or two were cupping their hands to their mouths, breathing their own air slowly in and out until they got their wind. A few raced past. They would be dancing in *Harlequinade*. Others took their time. They could leave. They were through for the evening. But some were afraid to leave the warmth of the building.

Heather Cooper strolled down the hall, enjoying the after-performance euphoria. It got better and better as her parts did. She was almost a soloist. Twisting her nose as if to sneeze, she smiled at a private joke that had just crossed her mind. One of the girls in rehearsal had quipped that dancing was almost as good as sex. There were times she thought it was better. But, of course, she would never say so. Not to anyone in this catty company. Except Jennifer. Who had laughed and knew exactly what she meant.

She waited by one of the backstage elevators. Dancers were rushing by, voices hushed but shrill and excited, and everywhere was the combined scent of perfumes and sweat which was so dearly familiar to her. She rode up one floor alone and came out, walking toward the little dressing room she shared with Jennifer North. It was used as a principal's dressing room, but this season it was theirs because they both had important solo roles in the upcoming Christmas gala just two nights away. Apart from their little room, decorated with a vase and homemade paper flowers and stuffed animals and scented soap, there was no one else on the floor. Jennifer hated the thought of being in that dressing room all alone, but Heather thought she was being silly. There was a security guard with a gun on every floor, always watching.

Jennifer was rushing out as Heather strolled into the tiny room. A pair of baggy, moth-eaten legwarmers were hanging out under her filmy ballerina costume and she wore a cardigan sweater around her shoulders. She spoke quickly. "What about coming over to watch the show with us tonight?" All the while she was prancing up and down, warming up her feet.

"Thanks, but I think I'll take a bath early and watch it from bed. I'm really bushed. Do you have any Vitamin C's?"

"In the candy dish over there. Are you sure you don't want to come? Richard and I thought we'd order a pizza or something."

The dark-haired girl scrunched her face and laughed. "I have to lose two pounds and you want me to eat pizza? Thanks, but no, thanks, really. The only reason I'm even watching is because Daddy's going to be on it."

Jennifer wished she could be more like Heather. She wouldn't dare even dream of missing Mr. Zolinsky and the members of the company who would be on the "Dick Cavett Show."

"Okay. Do you want to wait so we can walk you home?"

"No. You know, Jennifer, I can't live in fear this way. Really. Millions of girls walk around this time of night. I'll make it."

"Yeah, but millions of girls are not ballerinas!"

"So something else happens to them."

"You're in a bad mood, Heather. Go home and sleep it off. See you in class tomorrow." She kissed the other girl on the cheek as Heather whispered *"merde,"* the typical ballet good-luck wish, because one couldn't say "break a leg" to a dancer. Then Jennifer ran like a duck in her pointed shoes down the hall to the elevator.

Heather turned and went into the little dressing room, closing the door behind her. Taking off her makeup, she was so lost in thought she barely heard the knock on the door a few minutes later.

The applause rippled out in waves of adoration as Yuri Ivanov took his ballerina by the hand and slipped out of the closed curtain for their final bow. He stood aside, letting her bow first alone, watching her wince a little as the flowers that rained from the balcony pelted her soft, smiling face. Then he stepped forward, bowing from the waist, and the crowd rose to their feet in a standing ovation, applauding, shouting, screeching, "Bravo! Bravo!"

Backstage, Jennifer North had already slipped out of her pointe shoes and was padding down the hall. Even standing near the elevator she could hear the applause for Yuri. She watched the crowd of giggling *corps de ballet* girls pass her and head to the main dressing room she usually used. They didn't even glance her way.

By the time she got out of the elevator on the upper

level, she had cautiously checked the hall and un-zipped her costume. In the dressing room she closed the door, but only halfway, shrugged out of her costume, hung it up, and slipped into the flannel bathrobe folded over her chair. Then she sat in front of the mirror and began to take off her eyes.

She was thinking about her solo. She wouldn't be a corps girl two nights from now. The stage would belong to her. The audience would be hers alone. She looked at the little clock on the dressing table. She had twenty-five minutes to get ready and be downstairs to meet Richard at 11:00.

As she was reaching for more cold cream, she thought she heard a sound. She rubbed off some of her makeup. Probably her imagination. She sat perfectly still, holding her breath. No, there was a sound. And another and another. Footsteps. Very soft footsteps. Jennifer felt frozen in her chair. Then, without think-ing, she sprang like a cat and threw herself against the door, trying to lock it. She was too late. At the same time the door was being pushed in from the outside and she fell back. Eyes shut, Jennifer screamed.

"Hey, take it easy. It's only me!"

"Richard? Richard!" She fell against him, hugging him, touching him and, looking down, saw the reason he had sneaked up on her was because he was wear-ing sneakers. With a suit.

"I didn't mean to scare you. But it was just as easy to come up here as wait downstairs."

She went back to her chair. "Why can't I be more like Heather? She walks home alone and everything."

He sat down in Heather's chair and pulled a candy bar from his coat pocket. "That's not so smart, honey."

Jennifer spotted him through her mirror. "Hey, you! What are you eating? Candy? Get away from me.

Don't let me have a bite. That's all I need is a choco-holic binge."

Richard stuffed the whole candy bar in his mouth and licked his fingers, never taking his adoring gaze off Jennifer.

"What's a doctor doing eating candy, anyway? Hmm?"

He smiled sheepishly, his mouth full. "I didn't have time for supper. Had to take two of Dad's patients. One woman I saw, Jennifer, she had been in a terrible automobile accident. She's been on crutches for three years. Dad usually sees her. She said to me, 'Do you think I'll ever walk normally again?' God, she's got such a terrific attitude. Just counts her blessings she's alive. Dad did two of her operations. Now she'll prob-ably be my patient. I had to tell her I didn't know the answer to her question, but, damn it, she's going to walk without those crutches! She is!" He banged his fist against the table. Jennifer waited for him to calm down. She was used to Richard's dedication to his work and the lines of fatigue that sometimes crossed his forehead.

"Catch the performance?" she asked, still working on her face.

"Yeah, some of it." He yawned. "Watch your ex-tension in your *arabesques*. You're tilting your hip a little, cheating for height. It's going to add up, Jenni-fer. You'll get hurt one day, believe me."

Jennifer shrugged.

"Now you shrug. When you can't dance because of an injury you won't be shrugging."

Jennifer nodded. He was right of course.

"I'll be ready in *uno momento*." She quickly slipped into her jeans, inched a tight turtleneck past her neck, and stepped into her boots. She scooped up her dirty tights and leotards and threw them into her practice

bag. Then she put on her jacket, popped a knitted cap
over her loose, long hair, picked up her case, slung it
around her shoulder, and said "I'm ready" to Richard,
who had dozed off sitting up.

"Huh? We going for pizza, or what?"

"Heather's not coming over. She's tired. I don't
want any unless you do."

"A slice? Broadway?"

She smiled up at him, nodding her agreement, and
he kissed her. But when he looked into her eyes, he
saw her face had darkened like a stormy sky. "How
did you get past the security guard?" she asked him.
"No one is ever allowed on this floor after a performance, except Heather and myself."

"The security guard wasn't there."

"What!"

"Well, maybe he had to go to the bathroom or something. Jennifer, look, nothing's going to happen in the
theater. I mean there're detectives and cops all over
Lincoln Center."

Jennifer frowned. "I still don't like it."

They were walking down the hall now and getting
into one of the elevators. Richard was whistling, hands
in his pockets. Jennifer almost wanted to walk across
the hall to where the security guard sat and say something, but she was thinking about her problem. She
had to tell Richard about it sooner or later. But, no,
she couldn't tell him now. Later would be better. Later
was always better.

They left by the stage entrance, where Jennifer deposited her dressing-room key with the rest that were
put in the little box near the switchboard operator.
Jennifer noticed Richard was right. There were a lot
more officers in the theater. More than usual. She had
to show her card and vouch for Richard, who had to
present identification. They were waiting. It had

been a long time . . . over a month. She shuddered and stuffed her hand into Richard's jacket pocket.

"Cold?"

"No. Let's go to that place on Broadway."

"Want to cut through near the Reflecting Pool?"

"Ugh. Too dreary."

They both knew she was afraid to walk in certain places in the dark. Even with Richard. Jennifer quickly changed the subject. "I think Yuri and Stephanie are the new item. She was sewing *his* shoes." Jennifer laughed.

Richard frowned. "Is she still learning your part? I mean, does he rehearse with her?"

"Richard, Mr. Z. gave that part to me. If Yuri is working with her, he's working on getting her to bed."

Richard snickered. "Doesn't seem like he'd have to try too hard."

They walked, arms linked, up Broadway. Neighborhood shops were just closing up, covering glittery, decorated windows with ugly iron gates. Jennifer, who loved to watch people, stared into faces. The faces she saw were tense and angry. They weren't the happy Christmas faces of her Midwest childhood. She looked in the window of one of the brightly lit record shops still open and made a worried face. Then she relaxed it but saw in the window's reflection that her face still looked worried.

Richard, lost in his own thoughts, was like the other end of a choo-choo train and suddenly found himself staring into a window full of records, Santa Claus displays, and Styrofoam snowflakes.

"Is this a hint?" he teased. "Do you want a record for Christmas?" They had both decided to exchange only small gifts this year because they felt Christmas was becoming so commercial.

She lifted her knee in a high *passé* and gave him a

bump on his rear. "No, I want a snowflake," she laughed.

Richard headed for the shop's door, leaving Jennifer stomping her feet on the sidewalk. "C'mon, Richard, I was only joking. Don't buy me a snowflake."

He came back with a ready-to-please expression on his face. "Vell, den, maybe da lady vould lake a Santy Claus. Very fine stock. For everybody what's else, twenty-five dollars. But for you, pretty lady, seventy-five cents."

She snuggled up to him and dragged him down the street. "C'mon. We'll miss the show. Honestly, for a young Jewish doctor, you fail on accents. Yours is the pits."

"Did I ever tell you the story about the mother who told her daughter to marry a rich doctor? And she comes back from Africa with a witch doctor . . ."

"Yee-eesss," Jennifer groaned. "It's getting *un*-funny."

He looked down into her smiling face. "Ah, but you're not *un*-happy anymore."

She stood very still. He was right. She had forgotten the dread that was like a constant death sentence. That familiar fear that held her in a prison, made her constantly alert to sights and sounds and strange-looking people. And now it was with her again.

Fifteen minutes later, after Jennifer had indulged in one slice of pizza and jealously watched Richard wolf down two more and another Coke, they were at the front door of her apartment on Seventy-fourth Street, off Columbus Avenue. Cautiously, they walked into the lobby, looked all around, and stood by the elevator.

"You know, honey, you'll feel much better when we get a new apartment. We'll get one with a doorman." He pressed the elevator button but they could see it had gone to six, their floor. "We should start looking right after the first of the year. We should move before the wedding. Way before."

Jennifer swallowed hard and hoped her face didn't give away anything. She took off her gloves and started stabbing the elevator button, impatiently. Richard gave her an odd look.

Finally, the elevator came and took them up. Richard opened the door and Jennifer followed him in. She noticed she had only one glove.

"I must have dropped my glove in the elevator."

Richard was warming up the television set. He looked up sharply. "Can you go alone?"

Jennifer's ears turned pink. "Of course!"

She started out the door and immediately spotted her glove in the hallway about two doors down. She bent down to pick it up. When she stood up she saw two people walking into the elevator. She could only see them from the back, but she could hear laughter. One was Heather. The other was a tallish man who limped. He was wearing a black overcoat and a checkered cap. She grabbed her glove and ran back to her apartment, unnoticed. How weird, she thought. But maybe Heather had a last-minute date. Or was she hiding someone from her? But the limp? Who would Heather know who limped?

The "Dick Cavett Show" had already started, so she didn't have a chance to say anything to Richard. On the show with Dick Cavett were Grischa Zolinsky, the Artistic Director and God of New York Center Ballet, Judge Martin Cooper, Heather's father, who was trading in his judgeship to take over the business management of the company, and Nora Hanson and Yuri, who would perform a short variation from Zolinsky's new ballet.

Suddenly Jennifer realized her stupidity. What if someone said something about it on the show? She looked slyly over at Richard. She was in luck. He was sitting lopsided on the big chair hugging a throw pillow, asleep. Quietly, she moved on the floor until she was practically on top of the television. Then she turned the sound down to a barely audible hum. She was only interested in the dancing segment, anyway.

When the phone rang, Jennifer almost jumped. She saw out of the corner of her eye, running to answer it, that Richard had waken up. Now he sat there rubbing his eyes, his hand out for the phone. Sometimes his father and partner, Dr. Richard Kupperman, Sr., called him late at night on some emergency in their orthopedic practice. But as soon as Jennifer recognized the voice, she motioned to Richard that it was for her and to turn the television off.

"Sorry to call so late, Jennifer," the voice said. "Can I speak to Heather?" Jennifer smiled, but it was more of a grimace. That was just like Judge Cooper to assume if Heather wasn't home, she was down the hall in her apartment. One would think he would want to watch himself on the screen, a balletomane's desire come true.

"Uh, she's not here," Jennifer said, her lips pursing together. She hoped she wouldn't have to lie for her best friend. She didn't like being put in that position.

She felt relieved when all Judge Cooper said was, "Listen, Jennifer, could you do me a favor? Just slip a note under Heather's door and tell her to call me as soon as she can. I want to see what she thought of me on the show. It doesn't matter how late."

"Okay," Jennifer said quickly, all the while seeing his face on the taped talk show. "See you at the gala," she said and hung up.

She and Heather had often joked about having cards made up at a printer which would read, "Call your father," and have a place for time and date. Jennifer sometimes felt like Heather's answering service. Then she would feel guilty for thinking that way. After all, Heather's dad had been both mother and father to Heather since she was a baby and her mother had died.

"Richard? Are you really up?"

Richard yawned loudly. "Heard the whole conversation."

She went over to the arm of the chair and put her arms around him, burying her face in his dark brown curly hair. She tickled his mustache and said softly, "I need you."

Richard bent down and felt for his sneakers. Jennifer got a long, yellow ruled pad and scribbled a note. Her long, silky blonde hair tumbled forward and covered her face while she wrote.

Richard glanced over and watched her thoughtfully. "Pretty soon this will all be past history," he said.

Jennifer snapped her head up. The panic that she had learned to live with came out in her voice. Her whole body felt tense. "Oh, Richard, it's been going on like this for a year. Sometimes I think it will never stop. There's always someone out there, watching, waiting. Oh, Richard, I hate it! I want to go away from it. To someplace . . . far. How do you think I feel having to ask you to walk me just five doors down like a goddamned bodyguard!" Tears were glistening on her cheeks.

Richard went over and lifted her out of the chair, carrying her to the bedroom alcove and their big, brass bed. "It's okay. I'll always be there for you. Always. You know that. You'll be free again. I promise."

They lay sprawled on the bed, holding each other tightly. She looked up into his face. "You know I love you, don't you?"

"Uh-huh." He was unzipping her jeans and reaching under her top.

Jennifer giggled. "Richard, we'll never get Heather's note delivered if we don't do it now."

Richard smiled, shrugging up and off Jennifer's turtleneck top. "Yes, my love, that's just what I had in mind. Let's do it now."

She watched as Richard unzipped his pants. She was a nineteen-and-three-quarters-year-old voyeur. She loved looking at his body.

"Hey!" She let her jeans fall to the floor. "Let's make a run for it."

"Naked?"

"Yes! We run down the hall and stick the note under her door. And then we run back."

"That's all?" he laughed.

Jennifer rolled over laughing. "No, I'm going to lock us out."

Richard laughed, too, and then rolled on top of her. "Little Ms. Ohio. You always keep your virginal underpants on, don't you?"

"I like to be undressed by a man," Jennifer said huskily. He fumbled with her panties and then they were nose to nose.

"Love me?" Richard asked.

Jennifer was suddenly serious. "More than anything else in the world, and you know it. Don't ever forget that, Richard, no matter what."

Tears glistened in Jennifer's eyes. Richard didn't see. His cheek was pressed close to her heart and his lips had turned to her nipples. Jennifer held on to his strong back and kissed his neck, his ears, his lips. And then she heard Richard moan and she gave her usual little gasp.

"It's good, isn't it, baby?" she heard him whisper.

"Always." He heard her reply and shut his eyes,

smiling. He would never tell Jennifer how much he loved her. He was afraid he might lose her if she knew.

Minutes later, Jennifer, dressed, ran down the hall, and shoved the note halfway under Heather's door. Richard had on only his pants and was holding their door open, playing bodyguard in the dim hallway. She turned and ran back and he couldn't help but smile. Even when she ran she looked as if she were dancing, a graceful gazelle, her long hair flying. A trapped gazelle, he thought sadly. But then no young ballerina in any of the three major ballet companies was a gazelle. None of them was free. It was a nightmare that constantly filled him with rage. But he could do nothing to help. Neither, it seemed to him, could the police.

She smiled at his smile and he grabbed her around her waist as, like a child, she touched base in a relay race.

"She's there," Jennifer said. "I heard noise. I think she had a date tonight."

Richard closed the door carefully and latched the two new locks and one old chain lock. "Yeah? I thought she was tired. She told you she was going home to go to bed early."

Jennifer laughed. "Well, you know Heather. She probably is in bed. But not alone. Someone must have changed her mind. I didn't tell you but I saw her before. She was leaving with a man. I don't know who, but . . ."

She knew Richard wasn't listening. He had slipped out of his pants and crawled into bed. Jennifer popped out her contact lenses and put them in their case. "Richard?" she whispered cautiously. She got no answer except a snore. She was satisfied. If he had been awake before, he would have heard the announcement of the tour on television and he would have definitely said something by now.

She went into the bathroom and shut the door softly, cutting off the flood of light to the bedroom alcove. Shrugging out of her clothes she put them in the hamper and hung her jeans on a hook. Naked, she placed her hands firmly on the edge of the sink. Then she rode her pointed, arched right toe up to the inside of her left leg, bending it at the knee into *passé* and skillfully aligned her hip to let her leg flow backward into a long, toe-above-head *arabesque*. She rose on *relevé* on her left half-toe, her weaker side, testing herself. Finally, she came down through her feet and *pliéd* in *demi*. She felt she could have stayed, arms out, forever.

Reaching for a piece of dental floss, she caught her image in the medicine cabinet mirror as one would see a stranger. For some reason, she thought of that television commercial for color TV. She came closer to the mirror and winked. "Hi, I'm Jennifer North," she said in a pseudo-sultry voice. She smiled brightly at her imaginary audience. "My eyes are green, my hair is yellow, my teeth are white, my skin is pink, and I'm a dancer." She flashed another Cheshire cat smile. Then she striped her toothbrush with Colgate, scrubbed her teeth vigorously, turned out all the lights, and dove into her side of the bed.

She ran through her solo quickly, in her mind, closing her eyes and picturing a little dancing figure doing the steps. It was one of her favorite ways to practice. This would be her first solo role and it was a big, important part in Grischa Zolinsky's new ballet, *Artemis Visions*. It would finish with a *pas de deux*. Her partner was Yuri Ivanov. The gala was just two nights away. The most exciting Christmas Eve of her life. Still visualizing, she took her bow, plucked Yuri a flower from her huge, imaginary bouquet, and waited for sleep. It didn't come quickly. She found herself rehearsing the best way to tell Richard.

"Richard," she whispered, feather-soft, "I can't marry you. The day of our wedding I'll be in Russia." Richard rolled over on his back again and smiled in his sleep.

He selected a black turtleneck sweater from a drawer. It would be cold out tonight. Snow was in the air. His black duffel bag was packed and he was ready to go. The zipper was locked in place in the huge duffel bag and he had pasted stickers on it that said TWA and Rome. Not that anyone would be able to see. It was still dark out and about two hours until dawn.

He went to his closet, tripping over a pile of clothes on the floor. He put on a heavy, black jacket, pulled a black cap over his ears, wound a black scarf around his neck, and put on black gloves. It was a good disguise. He would be hard to spot. Not like so many years ago.

There were two rows of little girls, all in identical short-sleeved leotards. Pinkish-white girls with pink ballet slippers and white tights. Each little girl had a sprig of artificial flowers or a pastel ribbon in her perfectly groomed hair. He was dressed all in black, the only boy. They laughed at him. He hated them.

The man looked up sharply, blinking his eyes, and picked up the duffel bag. Locking the door, he walked silently, carefully, down the carpeted steps. The first car he saw when he got outside was a patrol car cruising. He would have to be very cautious. And if anyone stopped him, he would say he had a plane to catch at La Guardia.

He walked slowly, keeping to the dark shadows, hugging alleyways, avoiding streetlights that would reflect a moving figure. His steps were straight and measured. He pretended the outsized duffel bag wasn't heavy and resisted the urge to stop every once in a while to rest. He couldn't afford that. He had work to do. The contents of the duffel bag must be disposed of.

He chuckled to himself and a small stream of saliva slipped down his chin and froze there. A Christmas present for New York's finest. Gift-wrapped and long overdue. He gripped the handle of the duffel bag tighter. Good bag. The only bag he'd ever found that was large enough to carry a dead body in.

Chapter Two

He had never known his father when he was little.
His mama had said he died. Then one day she
was drunk. So drunk the bottle tipped over the
table and dripped onto the floor. She smiled at
him and called him a bastard. Then she screamed
it as if it were his fault. After that he always
knew. He had a father who didn't want him. Only
his mother wanted him. She was all he had in the
whole world.

PERRY JENKINS WAS on the job every morning at 7:30. If he wasn't, his parole officer would hear about it. This morning he was wearing his galoshes. It was going to snow. His cap was pulled down around his ears, a cigarette dangled from the side of his mouth, and his mind was one million miles away as he picked up bits of paper and debris from the grounds of Lincoln Center.

He could feel the cold wind blowing right through his heavy sweater, which he had worn under his uniform under a storm jacket. Maintenance man. A job for squares. But Perry Jenkins was determined to go straight and stay out of prison for good. He had done time, this last visit, on a bum rap. He stamped out his cigarette and put it in the garbage.

Yawning, he watched a cloud of vapor spill out in front of him. Then he looked up sharply and squinted.

Something was out of order. Under the big statue in the Reflecting Pool was a wire wastebasket.

The wind rocked the wastebasket only slightly as it lay wedged between the beefy legs of the huge sculpture, Henry Moore's *Reclining Figure,* that sat all year round in eight inches of water. On warm nights lovers and lonelies sat on the benches around the pool and watched the water reflect up from the black bottom, aided by strategically placed spotlights. Reflections shimmered on the walls of some of the buildings around the pool. The overweight statue took on a graceful, elongated shape as it stretched endlessly at its base, mirrored as if in a clear lake. But when the trees were shaved and benches around the pool were cold, no one bothered with it. The rectangular pool sat unnoticed and slightly dreary, circled by the Public Library, Vivian Beaumont Theater, Juilliard School of Music, Avery Fisher Hall, and, to the extreme side, the Metropolitan Opera.

Perry Jenkins grunted and bent over. He stuffed his trousers inside his galoshes and then fastened the buckles tightly. Then he walked over to the edge of the Reflecting Pool and carefully stepped in. The dirty water came to the edge of his stuffed trousers. With his legs apart, he glided slowly over to the wastebasket still sitting under the big statue in the pool. He reached in his right pocket and pulled out a cigarette. With the other gloved hand he found his lighter. Cigarette in mouth, he inched around the statue's legs.

Reaching the basket, he gripped with both strong hands and dislodged it from underneath the statue's legs. There was a big, black plastic bag stuffed inside. He couldn't get it out. It felt like it was frozen solid. Dragging the basket behind him, he pulled it to the edge of the pool. The bag stayed snug inside. When he got to the edge, he put both arms around the basket and tried to hoist it up, but it was too heavy to lift. He let out a long sigh punctured by vapor clouds. He would just have to see what was in that bag.

The twist tie opened easily. He took off a glove and stuck his hand in, feeling around. There was something airy and damp. And something smooth and soft, but cold, like . . . He pulled his hand back and stumbled backward, horrified. He tripped, fell on his back, and fought his way back up, getting completely wet. Then he watched, mesmerized, his eyes popping.

The basket had turned and tilted to the side. Out of the bag floated a head matted with long, dark brown hair. Then came bare shoulders. He reached for his cigarette, but it was sopping wet, as was all the rest of him.

Standing there, he hugged his body with both arms to keep himself from shaking uncontrollably. His teeth were chattering like castanets. But he wasn't aware of the cold. In his throat he tasted this morning's black coffee and greasy doughnut.

Toward the center of the pool floated a dead girl. She was naked. A white girl, thin, small. She looked like a grotesque Buddha, with her knees pulled to her chest and her arms frozen around her legs. He gaped. A few days ago, or hours ago, she must have been a looker. There was a toe shoe around her neck tied with its own pink satin ribbons.

Perry Jenkins wasn't stupid. He read the papers. What was he supposed to do? Call the police? They would take him in. This was one bum rap he would never come back from. He had to run! Stumbling, he retrieved his sopping glove and leaped out of the pool, ripping his trousers and scraping his knee. He looked up. Someone had seen him! There was a man. He looked away sharply and ran. Two at a time, he dashed up the steps that led out of the closed-in area of buildings, skidded across to Amsterdam Avenue and Sixty-fifth Street, and kept running.

All was quiet in the small oasis in Lincoln Center. The body in the pool floated and circled in peace. From somewhere farther down Broadway, a horn honked loudly and persistently, cutting the silence.

Behind the tall column that stands between the Public Library and the Vivian Beaumont Theatre was the man Perry Jenkins had glimpsed. He stepped out and walked to the edge of the pool, studying the dead body. Then he did a clumsy, twisted jig and laughed. He seemed to come to his senses after a moment and, jerkily, he turned away.

His shoulders were hunched and his collar was turned up against the chill wind as he walked across the grounds of Lincoln Center, blending in with the winter backdrop. Just an ordinary passerby, unlikely to attract much attention. No one had seen him.

Or so he thought. A thin, white curtain trembled in David Funke's hand on the second floor of the Juilliard School of Music. He could see the Reflecting Pool and almost all of the Lincoln Center grounds even on an overcast day like this one. His mouth hung slack from his jaw and he kept shaking his head, trying to convince himself he hadn't really seen it. Everything had happened so fast. All he had done was to go to the window to see if it had started to snow.

"Oh, Jeez!" he said, finally finding words. "I don't believe it . . . I don't believe it! Come here, you're not going to believe this! Oh, Jeez . . . she has to be a dancer!"

His companion was fixing her pantyhose and straightening her pleated skirt. She slipped her feet into her low-heeled shoes then finger-combed loose strands of her hair into a tight bun. She walked across her office and laid a hand on the young man's shoulder. Then she gasped, her large horn-rimmed glasses slipping to the tip of her nose.

"It all happened so fast. This man opened the bag . . . and it . . . spilled out. Then he ran away! Then from behind that column comes this other man, Olive. He was really strange. He got all excited and kind of danced around. You know, I've seen him around here before. Yeah, he hangs around a lot. . . . Oh, God, it's making me sick to look at her like that in the pool. I'm going to call the police!"

Olive Pennington took his hand as he reached for the phone. "Davey, dear, no, don't. The police will come soon enough. But, for us to . . . you see, they'll have to ask us questions. Like: What were we doing here in my office before school started? You could lose your scholarship. I could lose my job. My husband would find out about us." She pulled him close in an embrace, but David Funke resisted.

"But what about that man behind the column and the way he was acting? The police should know!"

"Know what? An odd man? They're all over the city."

"You don't think he could be the killer?"

"Oh, Davey!" she laughed. "Your imagination!"

"Olive! She's got a toe shoe around her neck, just like the others!"

"All right! But he wouldn't stroll around the grounds of Lincoln Center after he killed someone, would he?"

She had him there. He let himself be sucked back into her embrace, felt her long, tapered fingers running through his bushy hair. She was right, of course, and he didn't want to lose her, no matter what. She was fifteen years older than he, but he loved her.

A woman stood by the Reflecting Pool and screamed. No one heard her. The only other person nearby couldn't hear anything. The woman had an urge to take off her coat and cover the girl's nakedness. In the eerie morning light, peering at the frozen girl hugging her knees, she knew what must be done. It was that black man she had just bumped into as she came down the steps from Amsterdam Avenue, taking her usual route to work. That madman! That murderer! That rapist! Screaming, she ran up the opposite set of steps toward Broadway.

"Police! Police!" she yelled.

All the while she rehearsed her story. She had seen a man. He was running, stumbling up the steps when she came down. And he was soaking wet all over. A crazy man. He had scared her half to death. Why, he had almost knocked her over. Then she had come down the steps, crossed in front of the pool, her usual morning shortcut, and seen that poor girl. That man did it! And she was the only person who knew.

"Police! Police!" she screeched.

She was up on Broadway now. A patrol car pulled up. An officer rolled down his window. The woman pointed toward the Reflecting Pool. "The Ballet Killer!" she cried. "I saw him run away!"

Jennifer was sitting knees to chin in the big wicker chair in the living room, smoking a cigarette. Her mouth tasted vile and she wanted some tea. She was wrapped in a faded purplish-rose terry robe. Richard was pacing back and forth on the flowered area rug. He was furious with her. That he was entirely naked seemed not to phase him. She had finally told him the truth.

His alarm had gone off at 7:30 A.M. and he had reached over for her. But she was gone. He got out of bed and found her sitting, alone, just thinking. As he now realized, she had staged it. At first he thought she was thinking about her big solo debut. But, no, that wasn't it. Then he asked her if it was something else. There was silence. She told him flat out, no prefacing, no softening of the blow.

"We voted to go on tour, after all. Under the circumstances, the season will close in April. I leave with the company for Denmark first, and then Russia."

She studied her toes and heard the sharp intake of Richard's breath. On the exhale he snorted, indignantly, "You what?"

Jennifer was angry. Now she felt herself sinking into another Jennifer, not the Jennifer who was Richard's. The ballerina Jennifer. She felt cold, distant, private. Her career was still her area, no matter what he thought.

"I said we took another vote a week ago. It turned out 'yes.' We're touring and leaving early because of the murders. Too much stress on the company."

Richard scratched his head in bewilderment. "I thought the company voted 'no' on the tour. Not enough pay. Poor sleeping arrangements. The 'no's' had it."

"Management asked for a re-vote. And it came out 'yes.'" Was he going to force her to ask her how she voted?

"Management!" Richard exploded. "Zolinsky, you mean. In a democracy, when the 'no' is 'no,' it stays! You don't go back and give the peasants another chance to redeem themselves. Now the vote is 'yes'?"

"Richard, stop shouting. It's a ballet company, not a country. We discussed it. Besides, Zolinsky would have gone and hired other dancers in Europe. No one wanted to lose their jobs." She was aware of the iciness in her voice. But she did nothing to soften it. Why was he always trying to interfere with her career? She had to go. She hated to leave him. Couldn't he figure that out?

"You say Zolinsky is worried about stress? You know, as an orthopedic surgeon, I find that amusing. A company that drives it dancers so hard they continually get injuries and then have to hire a psychiatrist to observe the strain and tell them what to do about it—that's laughable. He's a hold-over, Jennifer, from tsarist Russia. He'll ruin your body, I swear. And when you tour, just remember, you'll be dancing corps and soloist roles on a corps salary and sleeping on the floor in the other kids' rooms' to save money. I don't like it. You're not going!"

Jennifer stood up, her face flushed with anger. "I *am* going. I'm a member of the company. Everyone goes."

He backed off a little, seeing her anger. "You could be in National if you would just accept their offer. They want to make you a full soloist, pay you what you're worth. You'd have more freedom."

"Well, I want Zolinsky, and we've been over this again and again. Why won't you give up? Zolinsky made a part for me, and there will be others. In a few years there won't be a Zolinsky. Then I'll go to National. When I'm ready."

Richard studied the carpet, temporarily at a loss. When he looked straight into Jennifer's green eyes he felt a great sense of loss. She looked at him and felt he was again trying to manipulate her.

"What about the wedding in June? You won't leave the tour?"

"Of course not. I'll be gone almost all summer."

"What if they find this Ballet Killer?"

"It makes no difference."

He sat down on the small couch and for some reason covered himself with pillows, remembering he was naked. "So, we have to call it off," he said more to himself. *Odd,* he was thinking, *you wake up one seemingly ordinary morning and find your world upside down with no center. No Jennifer.* Well, what could he expect? She could have anyone. She was beautiful, almost twenty, destined for stardom. He was close to thirty and his hairline was just beginning to recede. He sighed the sigh of an old man and shook his head. It was over.

Jennifer studied him carefully. Her anger started to melt. She walked toward him. He looked so sad just sitting there. She wanted to take his curly head in her arms and just hold him, tell him it would all work out. She hadn't meant to hurt him. She was just doing what she had to do. She was a dancer. She had been one for over half her life.

But there was a crack in her voice and the pitch was high and whiny as she asked, "We could get married in September, couldn't we? What's the difference?"

Suddenly Richard looked up and, pillows falling to the floor, resumed his angry pacing. "September? September's impossible! I have a career, too, you know."

She looked at him, puzzled.

"September's when Dad takes his teaching post and I take over most of his practice. That's a lot of responsibility, Jennifer. The operations, the patients, the whole office. Hardly the time for a wedding and a honeymoon. I mean, have a heart. The whole world doesn't revolve around little Miss Jennifer, the ballerina."

Gone were her warm, maternal feelings as a rocket of anger exploded inside her. "I told you it would be like this when you insisted we get married. I told you my career would always come first for me. You said we could work something out. And we could; you know that." She walked away from him, about to open the refrigerator, then changed her mind and came back. "And another thing, Richard, who *are* you marrying, me or your mother, who doesn't like me, my profession, or my age? *We* have to get married in her lovely Long Island gardens. So of course we can't get married now or in the fall. It has to be spring or summer. Of course, I could borrow one of her mink coats to wear over my gorgeous bridal gown, which I'm sure she will help me pick out at Bergdorf's and insist on paying for "

Jennifer turned away, satisfied. It wasn't easy for her to show anger. She heard Richard say, in a low voice, "My mother has nothing to do with us," as he stamped off into the bedroom alcove. Jennifer shrugged, went over to the kitchen counter, and poured some orange juice, a lump of granola and a raw egg into the blender. It was her own high-protein, instant-drink invention. From the corner of her eye she could see Richard was getting dressed. She stirred some Sweet 'N Low into her concoction and then put it down. Something suddenly occurred to her.

She went into the bathroom, where Richard was attacking his face with an electric razor. "What do you mean you take over your dad's practice in September? You told me not for a year or two. Why didn't you tell me? And don't say it's because I didn't ask you."

"I didn't think you'd be interested."

"You didn't think I'd be interested? Do you think I'm some sort of child or something?"

He didn't answer. Jennifer turned sharply. Tears were rolling down her cheeks. She stomped around blindly looking for her half-empty pack of cigarettes. He *did* think of her as a child.

Richard was dressed in a suit and tie, and she gulped. All she could think of was how good he looked dressed up.

"You don't want to change your mind? Call National. Tell them you've decided to accept."

Her back stiffened. There he was again, pushing her, trying to control. "No," she said firmly. "I want to get out of town with the rest of the kids. In April. I can't live with this Ballet Killer business anymore. I'm totally unprotected." As soon as she said the last three words, she regretted it.

Richard's mouth opened and he said disgustedly, "You're not *totally* unprotected. I do pick you up every night at the theater, escort you home, do this, do that." His face twisted then, as if he realized the truth. "You know, I'm being used. And now that you don't need me anymore, I'll be kicked out, is that it? When you asked me to move in here, Jennifer, it was right after this Ballet Killer thing became a real threat. I had to give up my apartment so we could squeeze into yours so you would be close to the theater."

"Oh, Richard, c'mon," Jennifer tried to protest. "You know that's not true." But Richard was at the front closet getting his coat.

As he reached the door, he turned. "Do you still want to meet at the restaurant at eight? Am I still going with you to pick up your parents at the airport?"

Speechless, knowing if she opened her mouth she'd start sobbing and make a fool out of herself, she just nodded vigorously and managed to whisper hoarsely, "Please, I'd appreciate it."

Richard slammed the door behind him, unintentionally, and Jennifer stared at it for a few seconds before she ran to the bed and buried her head in a pillow and cried. How dare he accuse her of using him! She had asked him to move in because she loved him, and they both agreed it would be more convenient at her place. What was really happening was he just didn't love her anymore. Everything had to be his way. Well, who needed him? There were other men in the world.

Richard stood waiting for the elevator and stared at their door down the hall. Maybe he should go back. It was a terrible way to start the morning. They had had fights before, but this seemed so . . . so final . . . somehow. What was he supposed to say—"I'm sorry"? For what? Because she didn't want to marry him enough to compromise a little and dance with a company that was better for her? Oh, no, not him. He looked at his watch. He was going to be late. But for a fraction of a second he had the urge to give in, go back and apologize. Then the elevator came and he stepped in automatically.

The task force set up for the Ballet Killer case was on the sixth floor of the Twentieth Precinct. It was a large floor given over, originally, to the first task force headed by Frank Fazio, Lieutenant Squad Commander of the Sixth Homicide Zone. He was used to functioning alone, answering to no one but the deputy inspector. Now he had a desk, just like everyone else on the task force, though his was off to the side. In the middle of the floor toward the wall was a cubicle office with a door. It used to be Lieutenant Fazio's office. Now it belonged to Captain Bill Hogan, troubleshooter from Manhattan South and new head of the task force. Fazio had been replaced as head of the task force over eight months ago.

Captain William Hogan knew his job was on the line. If they didn't find the Ballet Killer soon, he would be replaced. That wouldn't look good. He thought when he was called in to head the task force it would be an easy jump to promotion. Commissioner was what he was shooting for. After that the sky was the limit. But he hadn't figured on a bastard like the Ballet Killer. Damn this case. At least Fazio wouldn't replace him. That would really make him look bad.

Lieutenant Frank Fazio sat at the other end of the table facing Hogan. The deputy mayor sat in the middle, facing the wall on which were pasted glossy publicity shots of the ten victims from the three major ballet companies in New York City. Next to that was a map of the city dotted with colored push-pins where each of the dead girls had been found. There was no distinctive pattern, but Hogan thought there should be. Four or five detectives, whom Fazio thought should be in the field, decorated either side of the table, cluttered with ashtrays and containers of coffee.

Hogan cleared his throat, lit a cigar, and made the introductions that needed to be made. He was a tall man with thick, wavy, yellow-orange hair and mustache to match. His six-foot massive build had never gone to flab. Everything about him spelled authority with a touch of rough charisma. People liked him instantly but didn't really know why. Fazio had never liked him.

"Okay, the last murder was November 3." He

pointed to the black-and-white photograph of a lovely blonde with flowered earrings. "Deborah Strong of the National Ballet Company—raped and strangled like all the other young ballerinas. *Victim number ten,* he thought to himself; *a nice round number to stop at.* Then he turned around to face the group full front. "It is now December 23. Over a month. I think that's a damned good sign we've got him trapped, cornered. Dubro, read the reports the shrinks gave us . . ."

He was interrupted by the deputy mayor, a thin man with black hair, a beak nose, and a nasal voice. "If I remember . . ." he said, opening his briefcase and pulling out some papers. "Oh, yes, here it is—the first and second week of last April everyone thought the Ballet Killer had stopped or would be caught soon—until the Sanitation Department discovered what was left of the fourth victim, Nicole Peters. It was then found that her body had been deposited in a garbage bag and originally left to be found in front of O'Neals' Baloon. She became ground garbage." He looked down at the cold slime forming on the top of his coffee and wished someone else had been sent to write a report on this morning's meeting.

Fazio glanced up at Hogan, thoroughly enjoying the man's predicament. Hogan's face turned a shade ruddier. He leaned over the table edge, as if to maintain control. "No bodies have been found this time. There have been no killings in over a month . . ."

Again the man interrupted him. "Are you hoping for a Jack the Ripper conclusion, Captain Hogan? I really don't think the mayor is going to like this particular killer not being found."

Fazio kept doodling on the yellow pad in front of him. Oh, yes, he was enjoying this. In big, box letters, he drew JACK THE SLIPPER. That was his original name for the killer. It had pizzazz. The papers would have had fun with it. They could have played with the killer, teased him. But, no. Hogan had named him the Ballet Killer. Not because it was a better name, but because it was Hogan's name. No wonder some of the papers had taken to renaming him the Ballet Thriller Killer.

Hogan started to speak, but there was a sharp tapping on the door. He looked up. Someone was gesturing for him to step out. He was only too happy to be interrupted. Fazio reached for a sip of lukewarm coffee and then discovered Hogan had used the container as an ashtray for his cigar.

Within seconds there was another sharp knock on the door. Fazio could see Hogan indicated through the glass door for him to come out immediately. He excused himself and left.

Hogan walked him out into the hall and paced around, slapping his fist into his palm.

Fazio knew. All he said was, "Where?"

"Damn it! The Reflecting Pool. You know, the pool in the middle of the Lincoln Center grounds. Wouldn't you fuckin' know it? The bastard did it to me again!"

Fazio felt the familiar churnings in his stomach. It was the beginning of an ulcer, some doc had told him. But he hadn't felt like he was swimming in a pool of acid for a while. Since the beginning of November.

"But this time we have *something!*" Hogan stopped his pacing. "A man was seen running from the pool, away from the dead body. The woman who saw him is on her way over. We'll get an artist's sketch and put it on the air, immediately. I don't care if I have to borrow half the force to get him!"

Not five minutes later, Fazio was in one of the squad cars racing to Lincoln Center. He was thinking of Hogan, who, right now, was explaining, uncomfortably, to the deputy mayor that the Ballet Killer had struck again.

In a half-filled coffee shop near Lincoln Center, there was a heated discussion going on by the counter right in front of the display of doughnuts and Danishes. Even the short-order cook had stopped to listen.

A regular customer was talking excitedly to the owner, who was also the waiter. "Saw it. The whole Reflecting Pool is roped off. Wait. It'll be on the news soon. They covered the body. But this is it. The goddamned Ballet Thriller Killer again. Sick. If you ask me, I think some dancer dumped on him." He took a sip of his coffee and pointed to a blueberry muffin in the case. "With a little butter."

The owner buttered the muffin, shaking his head. "If you ask me, it's bad for business in this area. Real bad. Those ballet companies are going to close up. People will stay away. It's going to affect Lincoln Center. Who needs it? I could have opened up on Thirty-fourth Street."

Two other people were sitting at the counter. One, a young woman, her hair up in a bun, a large case at her feet, almost choked on her coffee. "That's disgusting. You make me sick. There's a maniac going around murdering dancers and all you care about is your lousy business." She plunked her coins down on the counter and stomped out, near tears. At the door she turned and shouted, "I'm not a ballerina! But I've danced in the chorus in two Broadway shows, and, believe me, these killings affect all of us! No one is safe!" She dashed out.

The owner looked after her and turned to the man at the counter. "Crazies. We get 'em all here." He shrugged. "It is a terrible thing, though. I'd like to see them catch the killer."

The man at the counter nodded, his mouth full. "They will. This one's a crazie, too. Watch. Next coupla weeks, days, they'll get him and he'll be blubbering like pussycat. Then they'll zonk him in the booby hatch. And the taxpayers will pay for that, too."

The owner moved to the end of the counter. "There be anything else?" The man in the dark jacket shook his head and took out a dollar. He put it on the counter, smiled, and left. It was cold out and his cheeks were ruddy. He walked toward Lincoln Center. The man in the coffee shop was right. There was quite a commotion. He always enjoyed this part the best.

Listlessly, he dragged himself to the corner of the room for the end-of-the-class ritual called révérence. The little adagio, the salute to the piano player, the salute to Madame's tiny dog, Mishka, and the applause for Madame. That day he never applauded. He walked defiantly to the water fountain. He was so thirsty he couldn't swallow. He pressed the button. But there was no water. No water. And then he looked up into the scowling face of Madame. No wonder he couldn't get any water. Her finger was on the button, stopping him. "You're too fat already," she had said. "Water after class, no good."

He walked a little faster. There was plenty of water in the pool. He chuckled. In his pocket was a soft, pink satin toe shoe. A little remembrance. His private secret. He stroked his souvenir and then mingled unobtrusively with the rest of the crowd, drawn to the noise around Lincoln Center.

Jennifer was slightly out of breath when she reached the rehearsal studio on the top floor. She had dozed off crying and had waken up feeling miserable. She barely had time to eat, stuff her practice bag, and take a yogurt for lunch. She had splurged on a cab that had taken the long way around because traffic was congested for some reason. That had made her even angrier.

Everyone dressed at home these days. If things weren't bad enough, there had been a lot of thefts in the building, especially of dance clothes and cases. Didn't say much for security, she thought. She looked at the clock on the wall. It said 9:50. Company class was at 10:00 now instead of at 11:00 because Zolinsky thought everyone slept too much. Besides, they needed more rehearsal time with dancers either dead or leaving. After class she would talk to Heather. All she had to do was make it through class. When she had rung Heather's doorbell, she saw that the note was gone and Heather had left.

The damp smell of sweat was heavy already. She heard feet pounding on the floor. Everyone was warming up. Tying her pointe shoes, she zipped her bag and threw it in the pile with all the rest lined up against the wall. Gucci luggage, canvas cases, plastic bags from the supermarket, and a pile of coats ranging from army jackets to raccoon coats.

She headed for a barre, still lost in her own world, the thoughts spinning restlessly in her head. It wasn't until she finished the pliés in her own warm-up that she noticed something was wrong. No one else was warming up. They had stopped.

Everyone was gathered around Karin, who had just come in. Some kids were shaking their heads in disbelief. Monica went off into a corner, crying. Jennifer felt chilly suddenly. She stayed rooted to the barre, not wanting to find out what the terrible news was. Three-quarters of the class were there. The rest were in rehearsals. An emergency corps rehearsal. Heather must be with them, learning "Stars and Stripes."

Jennifer finally ran toward the cluster of dancers and asked, "What is it? What's happened?" She was met with the huge, watery eyes of a young corps girl who was so horrified she couldn't speak. From the corner of the room came a cry: "Let's go on strike!"

And another yell: "What good will that do?"

And still another: "Save someone's life, you asshole! We can all leave town!"

Then Jennifer knew another dancer had been killed. The Ballet Killer. She ran over to Yuri, who was standing on his head, his muscular legs resting against the wall. She put her head level with his. "Ours?"

He nodded. "Yes."

Jennifer's voice quivered. "Who?"

Yuri managed an upside-down shrug.

Just then Roger Torry walked into the room. He was the other ballet master. That meant Mr. Z. wouldn't be giving company class as usual. The tension was so thick it hung in the air.

A few of the men and Max, the pianist, rolled the piano out toward the center. Others carried the portable barres and still others got out chairs to hold onto. Roger Torry made no announcement. Nothing was said. All the dancers could do was to surrender to the familiar combinations and try to forget for a while.

Max tried to help them along. *Battement tendus* were done to a rousing rendition of "Rudolph, the Red-Nosed Reindeer." There were a few giggles in spite of the tension and Max smiled, a little joke between dancers and musician. The door opened then and the rest of the corps came swarming in, frantically trying to find space and catch up to the rest of the class.

Jennifer scanned the room. She began to feel dizzy and nauseous. The whole class was in *relevé*, right leg raised in *attitude*. Torry commanded, "Stay . . . and stay . . . and stay." Not an ankle wobbled. Jennifer's eyes searched the room. "And stay . . ." intoned Roger Torry. Jennifer lost her balance and tripped, letting out a little cry of pain. A few dancers looked over. She ran out of the room holding one hand over her mouth.

When she reached the hall, she rested her forehead against the cool wall. She was breathing in short gasps and she couldn't stop. She wanted to cry but no tears would come. The late group. That was Heather's group and there was no Heather. No Heather at home either. Jennifer knew. It was Heather. But it just seemed impossible. Things like that just didn't happen to people you loved. She closed her eyes and prayed, "Please, please, let me be wrong."

Downstairs in the Lincoln Center compound, the Reflecting Pool had been roped off and forensic experts were combing the icy pool, cursing their luck under their breath. The medical examiner had put in an appearance and the body was on its way to the Bellevue morgue for tests. The sketch of the man who ran away was now on the air.

Fazio stood, hands in pockets, hand shading his dark eyes, staring at the dirty pool water. He had been a cop for over twenty years and there were still some sights that sickened him even more than department politics. A young, beautiful girl floating naked in a garbage-littered pool was one of them. What the hell was her crime? That she was beautiful and talented? That she put a little brightness into other people's lives for an evening? And the girl. Of all the girls, it had to be this one.

Out of the corner of his eye, beyond the crowds that were being dispersed, he spotted a lone fur-coated figure. Eyes down, white hair lifting with the chilly breeze, he stood straight as a statue. Fazio sighed and went over.

"Mr. Zolinsky, has anyone contacted Judge Cooper?" Fazio pointed to indicate the television vans and other media flooding the area. "We don't reveal names until the family knows, but with this case and all those monkeys I don't know if I can promise too much, you understand."

Zolinsky nodded, sadly. "Martin is in court today, finishing up. I'll try to reach him immediately." Fazio thought he saw tears in the ballet master's electric-blue eyes when he said, "Lieutenant, we are in rehearsal for one of the most important ballets of my life. But, I open my theater to you. As before. We will all cooperate. Just please try to find this maniac. He has gone too far this time. Too far." He turned and said softly, "Why does he do this to me?"

Fazio's thoughts were interrupted by a man walking toward him. "We got into her apartment," he said. "We found this note brushed under the door to the side, near a closet." The detective unfolded a handkerchief and Fazio put his gloves on and read the note. It was on lined yellow paper. "Call your father anytime. The sooner the better." It was signed "Jennifer," and on the bottom was a picture of a toe shoe.

"We checked," the detective said. "It's the girl down the hall. A friend. Name's Jennifer North. She's a dancer."

"Same company?"

The detective looked blank.

"Find out! And when you find this Jennifer North, I want a complete statement."

Detective Joe Turk nodded and started toward the State Theatre. Fazio walked toward his car. There was something bothering him. It was something Zolinsky had said. *"Why does he do this to me?"* That was it.

An odd statement considering the Ballet Killer struck all three companies. Maybe they should talk.

David Funke sat in the lounge room at Juilliard and stared at the television. There was a sketch of the man whom he had seen run away. They were looking for an innocent man. That was the one who found the body. They wanted the man behind the column, he was sure. He, David Funke, was the only person who had seen it all.

He had never been faced with such a nerve-racking problem in his whole life. Olive was right, of course. Even Juilliard couldn't take that kind of scandal. He shuddered involuntarily when he thought of the consequences. Her husband was in charge of the scholarship admissions. Her husband had hand-picked Olive to be his piano teacher. Shit! What if he got kicked out of Juilliard? He didn't want to play gigs or have to work to pay for lessons. He needed the scholarship. He wanted a concert career.

David squirmed in his chair. The only trouble was he had long ago figured that the majority of the people in this world were crazy. They would be very happy to catch an innocent guy just to get their rocks off. Meanwhile, the real killer would go free. And kill again. He jumped up. Maybe there was a way to do it. He got up and reached for his checkered cap, then remembered it was gone. He must have lost it somewhere. He'd have to buy another one soon.

At the Twentieth Precinct, the four separate lines for the Ballet Killer were ringing so much it sounded like one continuous buzz. WINS radio had been the first to announce the eleventh murder and a rough description of the man seen running from the crime. The television stations were running a special bulletin with the artist's sketch. The floor set aside for the task force had begun to resemble the floor of the stock exchange on a record-breaking day.

Hogan had gone to the mayor's office for in-depth meetings. Fazio hadn't returned yet. Manning one of the phones was Sergeant Moskowitz, who was hoping, soon, to pass his third-grade detective exam. Right now he was turning a bottle of aspirin over and over in his hand. The only thing standing between relief and pain was a glass of water to swallow two of them with. He didn't even have time to go to the can.

The phone rang again.

"Nine-two-one-four, Moskowitz."

"Listen, the Ballet Killer?"

"Yeah?"

"I think it's my husband."

"Oh, yeah? Can I have your name?"

"He's been acting pretty strange lately."

"Name and address?"

The woman hung up on him. Moskowitz noted in the log: crank, hang-up. In the second's breather he had, it occurred to him, though not for the first time, what a waste of manpower all this was. Hogan had turned them into psychologists and clerks because he didn't want to be accused of a foul-up in forgetting an important lead. Since they were dealing with a loony, every lead was supposed to be important and recorded. He hadn't heard a real lead yet.

He picked up the phone again.

"Nine-two-one-four, Moskowitz."

"This is Mrs. Emelia Kurtz. I have a tenant in my building I think you should check out right away. I think he's your man."

Moskowitz's pen was ready. "Oh, yeah?"

"See, there was a leak in the pipes. He was out. The

man is always out. So we had to use a master key. What I saw! Such things you wouldn't believe!"

"What did you see? What kinds of things?"

"Stuff. All over the wall there were markings. Clippings of the killings, and in the corner there was a . . . You better send someone!"

"Could you tell me exactly what kind of stuff you saw?"

"Oh, please! I can't talk about it! You'll see! I don't want this man in my building anymore. I'm a widow. This is the man you want, believe me!"

The woman's voice had hit a shrill note of hysteria and Moskowitz knew it would be useless talking to her further. He marked down her name and address in the log and drew a big star next to it. He wrote the word "paraphernalia." But who could he send? No one. Not for a while. The phones were jangling.

He picked up for the next call and then put the receiver down, letting the call jump. There *was* something he could do. This was a lead Hogan would want followed up right away, any way. Someone had to go to Queens and talk to this Mrs. Kurtz. His head throbbed. Why not do it the easy way? On his desk was a big black book. He thumbed through it. He found the number of the One-hundred-eighth Precinct and dialed.

Trying to be inconspicuous, Jerry Turner bent down slowly and pretended to tie his shoelaces though he was wearing boots. The cop across the street was staring at him. Damn. He straightened and walked away. He couldn't wait for the dancers where he usually did. The stage entrance was flooded with cops. He kept walking around the block, not knowing what else to do.

Just one of them. That's all he wanted. Just one young ballerina. The delicate fine-lined faces, the small, thin bodies, the bright eyes. God, he loved them all. He crossed Sixty-second Street and hid behind a few parked cars. He was freezing. It had started to snow. But when he wanted something, he got it. He had to be clever, careful. He had to eventually get as many of them as he could.

Chapter Three

She remembered how she had finished the last little drop of wine in her glass, letting it linger. He had told her to stay as long as she wished. But he had left before dawn. It was a beautiful hotel. Not some cheap roach-infested flophouse with the neon lights from Times Square lighting up their lovemaking. And what a lover he had been. Her first. She loved everything about him. His hair, his eyelashes, the ripples on his muscles, the way he treated her like a lady. It was beautiful while it lasted. But it ended too soon. He refused to see her. He never knew it was his child. Wouldn't even listen. But someday he would. He'd listen good. The kid would do it for her. And then he'd be sorry. Real sorry.

GRISCHA ZOLINSKY PUT the phone down and stared sadly out the window. Judge Cooper had adjourned the court. He called the town house. He wasn't there. Messages were left in both places for Martin to call him back immediately.

He shook his head. Where would it all end? Heather. She had been one of his favorites. He had watched her for years as she moved up in the school. Such promise. One of his special children. Soon she would have been made a full soloist.

While he was thinking, he went through the mail his assistant had dropped on his desk. His hand started to tremble. There it was. But he had expected it. Usually it came right after the murder was known. Just a plain white envelope with his name and the theater's address typewritten. Inside there was a photograph of the now-dead girl. Disgusted, he unlocked the first drawer of his oak desk and threw the envelope inside. He had opened the first. Lisa. Then the second, Elizabeth. All girls from his company. But the third picture was of a dancer from National, and that was when the police decided it was a city-wide manhunt.

He would study it later. No, he wouldn't give these to the police. He didn't think it was the killer. It was someone out to get him. Oh, yes, he had made many enemies. They often tried to unnerve him and failed. He would take care of it somehow in his own way. He would let no one know it upset him. He would ignore it.

Sighing deeply, he changed into his soft ballet slippers. Someone would have to be chosen to replace Heather in the gala performance. He'd have to pick some new corps girls from the school. But it was not the same. Not the way he wanted his company run. He stood up, determined. Right now he couldn't think about it. He had an important rehearsal to attend for *Artemis Visions*. Nothing mattered but his new ballet, the first full three-act ballet in years. There was still one ballerina he had high hopes for. The only young ballerina left whom he truly cared about. Jennifer North.

Jennifer could feel the sweat hang close like a cloud in the windowless rehearsal room. Yuri was practicing lifts with her and her timing was off. Close by, Max sat improvising with part of the Stravinsky score for the ballet.

Jennifer gave up and went over to her bag and lit a cigarette. Yuri, his tawny hair hanging down over his seductive little-boy eyes, came over and took the cigarette out of her hands. "Don't smoke. No good for you." Then he sat on the floor finishing her cigarette.

Jennifer lifted her leg from behind in attitude and leaned over as far as she could with her torso for a stretch. She stretched the other leg. "Are we supposed to start or what?" she asked listlessly.

"Of course. Max is here. We'll just keep practicing the lifts."

"Nothing makes sense to me, Yuri. She was such a good person. She was my best friend. My only friend in the company."

"I'll be your friend. We'll get rid of your boyfriend." He flipped ashes into Christina's little portable ashtray.

She narrowed her eyes and glared at the Russian defector. The one man who did more for ballet with sheer animal magnetism and unequaled, flawless technique than any public relations expert could have ever dreamed up. He more than proved all male dancers weren't gay. And he was popular with the kids. Right now, she felt like throwing something at him.

"I don't see how you can joke around at a time like this, Yuri."

"I am not joking. I am trying to stay sane. Dancing is how I stay sane. Is terrible what has happened. I liked Heather. I liked Lisa and Elizabeth and Sheryl and Olivia. I like my family I leave behind in Russia. But I am a dancer and so are you. For this moment, we just rehearse. Next moment we get drunk, cry, laugh, have sex. People will come to see you in this ballet, Jennifer."

"They're coming to see you, Yuri. They know you're dancing the part of Achilles."

Yuri gripped her by the shoulders so hard she felt her teeth rattling. "They will discover you. Believe me."

Jennifer looked into his deep amber eyes. Then she held out her hand for the intricate finger-folding which made up their turns. The audience saw only effortless spinning. They had to synchronize every move as partners.

Jennifer spun into her cavalier and he looked at her

as he looked at all women, onstage, offstage, even in rehearsal. They were breathtaking creatures, goddesses who demanded all his attention. She whispered in a low voice, still moving, "I saw Heather leave last night with someone. From the apartment. I told the detective the whole thing."

"Oh, yes?" Yuri released her and they promenaded.

"Yes. Only I saw him from the back. Dark overcoat, checkered cap, and he limped. What do you think?"

"I think Mr. Z. is coming."

Jennifer's heart sank. She had hoped one of the other ballet masters would do the rehearsal, hoped he'd be too busy. She turned. Zolinsky was coming into the room, looking cool and crisp in his usual plaid shirt. He took a folding chair from the corner and placed it in what would be downstage. Then he sat down on it, backward, spine erect, unsmiling, with his arms resting on the top of the back of the chair. Out of the corner of her eye she could see other dancers drifting quietly in to sit on the floor near the wall, killing time between their rehearsals or talks with detectives, bringing their cans of soda and containers of orange juice, towels flung around their necks and shoulders.

Zolinsky gestured for Max to begin. Jennifer felt like a wind-up doll. Yuri whispered helpfully, "And-a-one . . ." But she missed her cue and had to start again. She noticed her understudy, Stephanie, had walked in.

Max gave her a very unballetic "shave and a haircut" intro to help her on and she glided across the floor with the little, mincing *bourrées* that were the first four measures of the long, dramatic solo Mr. Z. had made especially for her. There wasn't a sound but the beat of her pointes and Max's inspired playing . . . until Zolinsky clapped his hands for her to stop.

"No." He stood up and walked toward her. She stepped imperceptibly away. He got up on half-toe.

"Watch. *Bourrées*." Jennifer observed how crisp and clean his foot movements were, how his knees parted just so slightly. She had never looked at that simple step and seen it quite that clearly.

He finished. "Not clop-clop." He pranced around like a horse, punctuating his words with pantomime, as he so often did.

"You do it dead," he went on. "Put life in each little movement. Be like Fred Astaire."

More dancers were drifting in to watch her rehearsal, taking a minute or two of a break. She took a breath and *bourréed* across the floor, exactly the way he had. "That's *right*," he announced and went back to his seat. "Now go on with Yuri." Zolinsky looked at his watch. He wasn't worried about her solo as a young maiden seeing her young man before the wedding. She could do that. But this must be perfect. She must be perfect. They would be good partners eventually.

Jennifer was lifted, came down, and flowed into arabesque away from Yuri. Again Mr. Z. clapped his hands. He got up. "You!" His eyes bore into Jennifer's and she stood still, rooted. "You do not listen to the music. He plays it perfectly." He pointed toward Max. "But you are not following. You are not in the corps here. You must dance joy, then shock, then sadness, and then fear. You are going to get married and some crazy goddess has decreed that you must be sacrificed so ships can sail to Troy. You have been tricked. You find out from him." Mr. Z. pointed this time to Yuri, who had faded into the barre and was wiping his face with a towel.

Jennifer felt like her head was buzzing. She knew her face was pink. Her eye found Stephanie, her understudy, biting her knuckle in nervous anticipation, unaware that she was smiling. The anger that Richard had ignited began to flame.

"Mr. Zolinsky, I don't feel well. I . . . my best friend is dead . . . I can't dance full out." When she opened her mouth, she had no idea that would come out.

There was an audible gasp along the wall. No one ever talked back to Mr. Z., unless you were in the company long enough to trade cooking secrets with him and it was a good day.

"My dear young lady! You *will* dance full out for this ballet! In every rehearsal!" He turned toward his chair. The dancers on the sidelines fiddled nervously with their leg-warmers or shoes, too fascinated to leave. Another first. Mr. Z. never showed anger.

Jennifer had felt near tears before, but now she was furious. Why was he picking on her? It wasn't fair. Maybe she should have accepted National. Standing there, unconsciously prancing in place at the barre, she decided she hated everyone. Richard. Mr. Z. Richard's stupid mother. Even poor Yuri, who hadn't done anything. She heard her music cue. She stood on pointe and flew into Yuri's arms.

But he wasn't Yuri. He was Richard. And he had tricked her. And Artemis wasn't a goddess. She was Richard's mother. Jennifer leaned back from her waist and could almost feel the danger of the sacrificial fire. She spun, she leaped, she let her movements go on forever until, finally, he lifted her to his shoulders and raised her high. She pointed her toes and stretched her arms against the sky. It was like magic. She wasn't Jennifer anymore. She was a body dancing a Greek maiden's agony.

When she opened her eyes she scared herself. She was Jennifer again and standing on the floor of the rehearsal room. She had run not into a fire, but almost into the mirror that covered the wall. She heard applause and knew that it was for her. The kids in the company were applauding. She smiled self-consciously.

Their approval meant more to her than the applause of a full house. Yuri was applauding, too. Not Mr. Z. But he was smiling.

Then rehearsal was over and the kids filed out. Mr. Z. was walking toward her. "So you like wheat germ? You eat yogurt?" Jennifer nodded dumbly. He had put his arm around her. "I want you to go home now, Jennifer, and just rest."

"But, Mr. Zolinsky . . . I have a rehearsal."

"Well, you'll do it better rested. You have the night off, yes?"

Jennifer nodded. It had seemed an odd scheduling when she first saw it tacked up. All her performances at the beginning of the week and then a night off, when the one thing the company couldn't spare was dancers.

"This ballet is very important to me." He was walking her down the hall. Jennifer was very aware of eyes following them. Jealous eyes, she was sure. "You are important. You are upset and we must make allowances for our future ballerinas. We can't let the young Ivanovs upstage our budding Pavlovas, now, can we?" He winked and left her standing there.

Jennifer watched him disappear down the long corridor. Her mouth had fallen open. She stood very still, trying to savor the moment. He had practically told her her future with the company. A future ballerina. Deep down, she should probably hate herself. Heather was gone, forever. Richard would probably leave her. But she had to suppress a cry of pure joy as she practically skipped down the hall to shower and change. Zolinsky thought she was good. And that meant she was very good.

In Long Island City, Queens, two detectives from the One-hundred-eighth Precinct sat in an unmarked blue Plymouth conducting a half-assed stakeout. In the driver's seat was Harrison, a black second-grade dick who was chewing on his well-manicured nails. Next to him was his partner, Detective Rizzoli, who was reading the paper.

"See anything, yet?" Rizzoli asked, not looking up.

"Nah, just some kids came out to play," Harrison answered.

Rizzoli yawned and folded the newspaper in half. "So, whaddya think?"

"Nothing, really. He's a Nam veteran. Translation: crazy."

"Yeah. You think it could be the . . ."

Harrison shrugged. "Without tossing the apartment, who knows? That old lady? I can't understand a word she says. A weirdo has some clippings. A lot of terrible stuff. She didn't make much sense to me." Then he laughed. "Listen, if this were the Ballet Killer, you think Hogan would let us get the collar?"

Rizzoli laughed, too, his belly bouncing up and down. "You kidding?"

Rizzoli was just about to top that and get another laugh that would break the tedium of waiting, but suddenly the words disappeared. A man was walking down the street toward them. He was tall, thinnish. No hat, short hair, wearing a black jacket. He walked with some difficulty. He fit the landlady's description.

Both men leaned forward, their bodies tense. Rizzoli coughed. "Looks like him, huh?"

"Yeah, that's Ivan Roman," Harrison said softly.

The tall man was walking down the street, hands in his pockets, eyes unfocused. He was forty feet away from their car. Harrison fingered his gun but didn't take it out. Rizzoli put a hand on the door handle. They waited. Then in a split-second they were out of the car. Roman was now three and a half feet from the car, across the street, starting up the steps that led to his apartment.

Rizzoli, maneuvering his bulk gracefully, was easing quickly across the street. Harrison crossed in front of him. Ivan Roman didn't see either of them. He had just turned to go up the steps of his apartment building. Rizzoli grabbed his hands from the back and Harrison flashed his shield. "Police! Don't move!"

Roman seemed to slump as he looked around. His narrow bird-like eyes studied the black detective. His mouth drooped and he whimpered a little. Harrison and Rizzoli tossed a quick glance of relief at each other.

"We just want to take you in for some questioning," Rizzoli said, his grip relaxing.

Roman continued to stare at both men, his eyes clouded. He looked as if he were going to break down and cry. Then quickly, so quickly, it happened faster than the blink of an eye, he reached for the inside of his jacket.

"He's got a gun!" Harrison shouted. Rizzoli leaped at him before he had a chance to fire and with his weight knocked him to the ground. Harrison reached just as fast under the tangled bodies for his weapon. It was still in Ivan Roman's hand.

"Shit! Will you look at this . . . ?" he said, standing.

Harrison held in his big, black hand the weapon that Roman was carrying. It was a pink satin toe shoe. Pretty ribbons dangled from between his fingers as Harrison stared in disbelief. Rizzoli yanked Roman to his feet and frisked him. A leotard and a pair of dance tights were pulled from his pockets.

Harrison took out his handkerchief and wrapped the dance slipper in it. "Son-of-a-bitch," he muttered. Rizzoli shoved Ivan Roman out into the street, chanting, "Okay, you have the right to remain silent. . . .

Anything you say can and will be used in a court of law
. . . . Uh, you have the right to talk to a lawyer. . . ."

They all walked toward the unmarked Plymouth.

Lieutenant Fazio was just opening the doors to the
Twentieth Precinct when he felt a sharp tap on his
shoulder. He turned his head, his hand on his gun, a
reflex action he had acquired with over twenty-odd
years on the force. He had sent a lot of people to jail.

The sun had come out again and was blessing West
Eighty-second Street. Fazio squinted. There was a kid
standing in front of him. He had a halo of curly, light
brown hair with an unusual checkered cap sitting on top
of the friz. He wore granny glasses.

"Hi. Lieutenant Fazio? That's your name, isn't it? I
saw you on the news one time."

Fazio didn't take his hand off the door. It remained
half-opened, half-closed. "Yeah, that's me."

"Listen, I have to talk to you. In private. It's really
important!"

Fazio cocked his head in the direction of the vestibule inside the Twentieth. The boy shook his head
violently. "No, you don't understand! This is important
and private! I *saw* the man you're looking for. The man
who ran away from the body. He's not the one you
want. You see, you're making a big mistake. I'll tell
you what happened. I saw the whole thing. But you
didn't hear it from me, is that understood?"

Fazio closed the door to the Twentieth, never taking
his eyes off the boy's earnest face. Finally, he nodded.
"Okay, tell me what you know. You can trust me. Cup
of coffee?"

"No. I have to get back. I'm on my lunch hour. Let's
just walk up the street and talk."

Fazio put his hands in his coat pockets and the two
of them gave the appearance of being leisurely strollers

on a bitter, cold wintry day. "Work near here?" Fazio asked amiably.

"I'm a student."

"Columbia?"

"Juilliard," he said, reluctantly. "That's how I saw what I saw early this morning. The building faces the Reflecting Pool."

"What time? How early?"

"Look!" The boy's face got very red and he stopped walking. "Hey, man, are you trying to test me or something? Listen, I hitched all the way to Washington to protest the nukes, you know. Marched in a heavy rain to legalize pot. And I'm taking a big risk by telling you this, Lieutenant, because I could be out of Juilliard on my ass, and I have a scholarship. A big one. At around seven-thirty in the morning I saw everything from a window. You guys are looking for the wrong man!"

Fazio listened to the kid's story from beginning to end, his face remaining impassive. But his stomach was jumping, first because he was hungry, and second because he knew the hottest lead they had had in a long time was all wet. Just like he originally suspected. He had never been terribly excited about a soaking-wet man seen running up the steps. They were back to Square One. Worse. Now they had to find another man he wasn't terribly excited about.

"You say the man who found the body is really a maintenance man? Are you sure?"

"Sure I'm sure. Listen, I'm at Juilliard each morning the same time. That's his shift. I've seen him cleaning up."

"You go to school at seven-thirty? Isn't that a little early? I didn't know the building was even open . . ."

The boy got angry and cut him off. "Hey, you said I

could keep out of this! Are you going back on your word?"

Fazio looked down and spoke in a low voice. "No, I'm not. But you do understand . . . What's your name? Can I know your name?"

"David Funke."

"F-u-n-k. Right?"

"With an 'e' at the end."

"Okay, Mr. Funke, now you see, I happen to believe you. But no one is going to believe me. You have to make some sort of a statement. We've got bulletins on the air for this man you say is innocent. We can't just . . ."

David Funke turned and walked away. "Forget it. We had a deal. Just . . . forget it. It's off my conscience, man. I did my bit. What do I care for your asinine bureaucracy? I'm telling the truth."

Fazio grabbed him by the arm. "Okay, okay. We'll do it your way. But can you at least give me a description of the guy you saw stepping out from behind the column? And if we find him and we promise not to use your name, will you at least take a look at him, so we know we've got the right guy? Can we just call you at Juilliard, say you're a witness, a passerby, saw him on the grounds and reported someone suspicious? Huh? Can we do that, Mr. Funke?"

David Funke grinned in spite of himself. Fazio had a way about him. He decided he liked him. "Okay," he began. "You're looking for a tall, thin man with very short hair. Almost a crewcut. He wears a black jacket, long, not new looking or anything. And no hat or gloves. Even this morning when it was so cold. And he hangs around Lincoln Center a lot. I remember seeing him up close once and it was the eyes that struck me. They're weird. Like he's staring straight ahead at nothing. Oh, yeah, he has a kind of a limp."

Fazio thanked David Funke and then walked back to the Twentieth. He believed the kid. Probably he should have dragged him in to go through some pictures. Maybe he could do that later. Right now, he'd have to persuade Hogan that David Funke's story should be taken seriously, though David Funke wouldn't give a statement. Hogan wasn't going to like this. Not that it wasn't a good tip; it was a find. But this complication wasn't going to make him look good.

A tall man with salt-and-pepper hair walked up to the door of the apartment building on Seventy-fourth Street. A police officer stopped him.

"Do you live here, sir?"

"No, I don't. I'm Judge Martin Cooper and I'm visiting my daughter. She's at work, but I have a key to her apartment."

"What apartment is that?"

"Apartment 6M. Say, what's all this about?"

The officer cleared his throat and when he spoke again his voice had a nervous falsetto quality. "Well, Judge, I have orders not to let anyone in—that is, look . . ." Awkwardly, he gestured to a group of men just getting into a squad car. "That man near the car. Detective Turk. He's in charge here. You better talk to him."

The officer watched the man walk up to the car. He saw Turk's head look down as he shook it. Then it snapped up again. It happened fast. One of the men put a restraining arm on the tall man. But it didn't help. Judge Cooper slumped to the ground. Less than five minutes later, an ambulance pulled up.

Fazio closed the door carefully behind him. Almost one minute later the men working nearest to Hogan's office looked up, startled, and watched as a heavy glass paperweight he had hurtled at the wall fell and splintered.

Fazio gestured for two men to come over. "Go back to Lincoln Center and check to see if any maintenance men are missing," he instructed the detectives, "especially from the early morning shift."

"Maintenance men, Lieutenant?" one of the detectives asked.

"Yeah, that's right. One of them should fit the sketch of the guy we're looking for."

"You're kidding! You mean this is the suspect?"

Fazio sighed. "Let's just call him a witness for right now, okay?"

The men's faces fell in unison and he could hear their mumbled curse words as they got ready to leave. Fazio kept his mouth shut. He knew Hogan was trying to weigh the possibilities. It would look funny if he took that sketch off the air and admitted New York's finest had made a mistake. Very bad. On the other hand, Hogan had bought the story the kid had given him. And if it meant catching the killer, he would just have to look bad for a little while.

Fazio wasn't waiting. He radioed all his men. They were to start looking for a supposedly unarmed man who was tall and thin. He was a suspect. He was last seen wearing a black jacket and was often seen around the grounds of Lincoln Center. He had short hair, an odd focus to his eyes, and a minor limp.

Jennifer tried for the third time to reach Richard. To say she felt badly. To say she would miss their friend. Maybe even to say she was sorry about this morning and suggest they try to work something out. But the line was busy. Damn!

She slammed down the receiver in the pay phone and felt a stab of hunger. She realized she had forgotten to eat her yogurt. It was probably ruined by now. She'd go home and have lunch, but meanwhile she headed toward the sub-basement. There was a small cafeteria down there with a fruit machine.

Odd. The floor seemed practically empty. She put some change in the vending machine and listened to the sound of the coins as they traveled through the machine. An apple plopped out of the bottom. Even that sounded loud. She felt frightened. Where the hell was everyone?

She started walking fast, trying to calm herself. Stupid. She was being stupid. Probably everyone was busy somewhere. But she was aware of the sound of her boots clicking on the cold, shiny floor. She took a bite of the apple. It echoed like a clap of thunder.

She walked faster as she passed the tall, wooden crates used to ship costumes. She thought of the tour. That's how they packed. She and Heather would have been together. Now there was no Heather. She would be all alone. She chomped into the apple and it stuck in her throat so that she choked and coughed when she tried to swallow. Where was Heather now? Was she at the morgue? She couldn't imagine Heather dead. Jennifer was almost running now. She wondered what death was like. The nothingness of it. How did Heather feel when she knew she was going to die? There was no other sound in the hall except the clicking of her heels. Jennifer could no longer control the thoughts that kept crowding into her mind. She was almost running when she saw it and, clapping her hands over her ears, she screamed.

Loud and terrifying, the scream shattered the quiet solitude of the sub-basement, but no one came to help. She heard only the hollow echo. She stood frozen. There was the shadow with long arms and a small head. It was coming closer, getting larger. Whimpering, she crouched down between two large, white laundry hampers along the side of the wall. The shadow turned into a man. He called out her name and she closed her eyes and let out another piercing scream.

Then she opened them in disbelief and ran. She flung her arms around the man's waist and cried, "Max! Max! It's you!" Tension splintered off into breathless giggles as she sputtered, "Oh, I'm so happy it's you!"

Max smiled down at her awkwardly, surprised. "Listen, I'm sorry I frightened you. Hey, are you okay?"

Jennifer untangled herself, suddenly embarrassed. "No, no, I understand. It's not your fault, really. It's mine. I get stupid sometimes." She blinked back the tears. "It's just that Heather . . . I was thinking about her. I still can't believe it. And nobody seems to even care. Not even Mr. Z."

Max brushed a wave of sandy hair away from his forehead and his vivid blue eyes searched hers. "Oh, yes, he cares, all right. It's just that his ballet comes first. But I know he feels it, Jennifer. God, all of us do. She was lovely."

Jennifer stood silently, reverently, thinking of Heather.

"Hey, what are you doing down here with your coat on? Are you leaving? Don't you have a rehearsal?"

"Oh, no. Mr. Z. excused me from rehearsal. Wants me to get some rest." She smiled self-consciously.

Max smiled at her. Jennifer had observed that when he smiled, it was from the inside out. His whole face seemed to light up. She knew from the dressing-room gossip that many were the corps girls who were trying to figure out the easiest way to get shy Max into the sack.

"You were really terrific as *Artemis* today, Jennifer. I mean fantastic! I could hardly keep my mind on the music."

"Oh, c'mon."

"No. I think you're going to do it with your solo, really. Too bad, though, he didn't rehearse the whole thing. I know how important it must be to you."

Jennifer had been thinking much the same thing this morning. He was right. The last thing she wanted to do was rest. She really wanted to practice her dance over and over again. She looked longingly back up the corridor. "I wish I could find a room and rehearse." Then she thought better of it. "Nah, he'd find out. You off?"

"Yep. I have a crazy schedule. I play other places, as well."

"I'll walk out with you." They walked down the last segment of the corridor together, each wrapped up in their own thoughts.

Max interrupted the silence first. "Would you like to come over for lunch?"

"Oh, no, I can't really. Thanks," Jennifer said almost instinctively, though she dreaded going back to her apartment alone, passing Heather's door. "I'm going to practice in my living room, eat yogurt and wheat germ while I'm rehearsing, and not follow Mr. Z.'s orders at all."

"Do you have a tape recorder?"

"Sure. Why?"

Max smiled. "How about if I play the music for your solo and we tape it? You can take the cassette home and practice."

"Now that's a good idea. Sure I'm no trouble?"

"I was the one who invited you to lunch, remember?"

They linked arms and walked the last steps of the long hall in friendly silence. When they got to the exit, they saw it was snowing but the sun was out. Then they turned in the direction of Broadway, not realizing that they were being followed.

Chapter Four

Her parents had disowned her. Up until she was very pregnant, she worked days and nights to save for the baby. She wondered what it was like to be rich and elegant and have everyone wait on her. She waited tables at night and worked in a dime-store during the day, always careful to keep her pregnancy hidden. She kept writing him but got no answer. The letters were returned. She prayed the baby would be born dead. But it wasn't. The ugly, scrawny, wailing little bird-brat didn't even have the decency to be born right. It was a boy.

THE SCREAM CUT through the steady cadence of noises on the floor where Hogan's task force had intruded on the Twentieth Precinct.

"Moskowitz!"

Moskowitz looked up to find Hogan signaling, across the room, for him to come into his office.

Moskowitz looked around, his right eye twitching as he scratched his crotch. He was too tired to think as he doggedly crossed the room. Since the sketch went on the air, calls had tripled. And the slob wasn't even a suspect anymore. Several men looked up, curiously, when Hogan slammed the door shut behind them.

"Sit down," Hogan directed the pudgy, red-haired man who had already sat down. "Tell me, Moskowitz, what is Ivan Roman doing in Queens?"

"Who the hell's Ivan Roman?" Moskowitz said without thinking.

"Well, you ought to know, Moskowitz. You gave the

orders. I had a call from the One-hundred-eighth. Seems you sent them to check out a lead?"

"Oooo-ooohhh, yeah. Now I remember. Call from a landlady, Mrs. Kurtz. Came in at nine-thirty. I called the One-hundred-eighth."

Hogan tapped his big fingers impatiently on his desk. "I know that's what you did, Moskowitz." He was clearly enunciating every syllable. "I want to know *why* you did it!" The last line finished with a loud crescendo and Moskowitz pulled his collar away from his neck nervously, his eyes on the wall.

Hogan never gave him a chance to reply. "Do you know what kind of trouble this has caused, Moskowitz? What I had to do to get Roman out of Queens and sent speeding over here?" He looked down at his watch, which said 1:30. "Do you have *any* idea?"

Moskowitz was feeling weary. "No, sir, I don't."

"You know I could make life very difficult for you, Moskowitz. But I won't. Not this time. Forget about it now. But don't make this mistake again. You can go back."

Moskowitz stood, his eye twitching. He wasn't a brilliant man, but he wasn't stupid, either. There was something he was missing. Hogan had turned to his phone. Moskowitz did not leave.

"Sir," he said, carefully, "I can't remember not to repeat a mistake if I'm not sure exactly what the mistake is."

Hogan ran his hands through his hair, a gesture of extreme patience. "Ivan Roman could be our man. He's a prime suspect. And he *confessed,* Moskowitz. He should be here in about fifteen minutes."

"But, sir," Moskowitz said, "then I jumped right on a lead that was good. I mean that's great about the Kurtz phone call and this Ivan Roman. You told us to follow up on everything and . . ."

Hogan cut him off and leaned forward in his chair, making Moskowitz, who was standing, feel like a dwarf. "Moskowitz, we know all about this Ivan Roman through a lead that just came in to us. If this is our man, Moskowitz, and I think he is, after a year . . . you're going to let Queens get the collar? Because that's what the people will read about. We did all the work and they got him. Damn it, we deserve the credit! My task force!"

"But I couldn't send anyone." Moskowitz straightened up and threw back his shoulders. "You don't understand. There was no one around to send."

"Then you should have waited."

"But . . ."

"Moskowitz, I said forget it. I can fix it. Go back to your phones and tell the guys to send out for booze." He reached into his pocket and took out a large money roll, peeling off three $100 bills. "Here, take it. If this is our man, and I have a feeling it is"—he winked—"the party's on me."

Moskowitz left the office. Hogan picked up the phone and finally got through to the mayor. He doodled nervously as he talked.

"No, Your Honor, we won't know for a while if this man is legit . . . but I do want you to look good . . . no, I can't give you a press conference until after we interrogate him. . . . Yes, I'll call you. . . . Well, Your Honor, he might be an ordinary crank. . . . Yes, he's coming right over and I'll let you know immediately. Good-bye, sir."

In the mayor's office at City Hall, the mayor's chief aide and campaign manager had listened to the whole conversation on a conference phone. He was smiling. It was getting closer to election time.

Hogan hung up and lit a cigar. There was nothing to do now but sit and wait.

In City Hall, the mayor protested.

"He said to wait. You heard Captain Hogan. So what's a few hours?"

"And not capitalize on tonight's news! Did you see the polls lately? You're even lower than last month. You think having some maniac running around loose killing and raping young girls helps the Big Apple? You need all the help you can get!"

"But listen here, I don't think . . ."

"What difference does it make? I heard the whole conversation. There's a nut. He's caught with a ballet slipper and he has stuff in his apartment. What's more, he confesses. Look, he's crazy, right? He won't even go to trial. They'll lock him up. You'll look good. You'll look fantastic if the timing's just right. You'll get re-elected."

He turned around and picked up a phone, getting in touch with CBS, NBC, and ABC. He then contacted all local television and radio stations in the city and notified the city rooms of the three major New York City dailies. When he finished, he looked up and realized two things. His cigar was out and the mayor had left.

Richard clicked off the walnut dial on the clock radio that sat on his desk. He couldn't listen anymore to the news about the Ballet Killer. Heather . . . dead. He still couldn't believe it. A man who got away. Then another one. The newscasters were having a field day. He turned off WINS. Why the hell didn't Jennifer call? He had to talk to her, and it was more than usually impossible to reach her.

There was a soft tap on Richard's half-opened door and his dad walked in. Richard was always reminded of Santa Claus when his father wore his white doctor's coat. It made his hair look whiter, his face look pinker, and did justice to the thin-wired glasses perched on his nose. Dr. Kupperman sat down in one of the chairs in front of Richard's desk. "Lunch?"

Richard shook his head. "I'm not hungry, Dad, really."

"Well, you have to eat. . . ." Then he saw Richard's gray face and dropped the subject. "Has Jennifer called?"

"No."

"She probably can't get through. That place must be a madhouse."

They both stared at the carpeting for a while.

Dr. Kupperman said, "Nasty business. Sick. She was such a pretty little thing. Never hurt anyone."

Richard shook his head. "I still can't believe it. You can imagine how Jennifer feels. All these things keep running through my mind. How? When? Where? It could've been Jennifer. She lives only five doors down! God, why don't the police do something?"

"Now, now, Richie, I know how you feel, but those questions will all be answered. Jennifer will call. And speaking of someone who called, guess who called?"

"Mother."

"She heard the news on the radio. She wants to know if she should go ahead with the plans for the engagement party after the gala."

Richard's face flushed with anger. Leave it to his mother . . . but that wasn't fair. She had caterers, florists, and arrangements to make.

"Sure," he said. "Tell her to go ahead with the plans," Richard said. Why not? Why miss the fun? Besides, no one had to know there probably wouldn't be a wedding.

Richard knew his dad had caught the bitter intonation in his voice, but he also knew, from experience, that his father wouldn't pry. When he left, Richard twirled restlessly in his black leather swivel chair and twanged a pencil through a rubber-band slingshot. He looked out the window and, for a minute, it looked like one of those glass balls that when turned over produce a snowstorm. It would be a white Christmas. Christmas was the last thing on his mind.

He stood up, almost knocking his chair over. Christmas! They had promised each other no big gifts, just little gag gifts, some of which were already assembled under their puny little Christmas tree.

In the back of his mind ran the thought: *what have you got to lose? It may be your last chance to win her back. Why not?* He shuffled through his credit cards. He knew just what to get her. Something she wanted for opening night. They had joked about the price before. Well, what the hell! Oh, no, he wasn't giving up so easily.

Going out through the reception room, he stopped at the desk. "If there are any calls, take a message. I'll be at Tiffany's. If Jennifer calls, don't tell her where I am."

Fazio stood in the foyer of the elegant East Fifties town house, holding his hat in his hands. A woman, the housekeeper, emerged from a room and said in hushed tones, "It's okay to go in now, Lieutenant, but please don't stay too long." Her lower lip trembled and he knew she was on the verge of tears as she rushed down the hallway.

Fazio entered the library and saw Judge Cooper sitting in an armchair wearing just a bathrobe and staring straight ahead. When Fazio had seen him last he looked a dignified but still youthful man in his fifties. He looked like seventy now.

It was almost 2:00. They had radioed him on the

maintenance man, Perry Jenkins. The kid's story checked out. He was clean. Out on parole, he had run scared, gone home to mama and been picked up there. Hogan had sent him to talk to Judge Cooper, who had found out about his daughter in the worst way possible, passed out, and then refused the ambulance and insisted an officer drive him home. It looked to Fazio like he was still in deep shock.

Fazio took out his notebook and placed his hat on a mahogany end table. He remained standing. "I hate to bother you, sir. I mean, look, I know how you feel, but . . . Judge Cooper, we need your help in catching this killer."

Judge Cooper blinked and said in a thin monotone, "You can't bring her back. What good will it do to catch the killer?"

Fazio gulped. Damn Hogan. The man was in shock. No, he did not feel like making his usual speech—you can save the life of someone else's daugher. He gave it one more try. "You were trying to get in touch with your daughter last night. Do you have any idea where she might have been? Who she might have been with?"

There was a long, awkward pause. Fazio felt like he was at a wake. Finally Judge Cooper said, simply, "No." Fazio waited for more. There was nothing. Still, he waited a few moments longer. Then he picked up his hat.

"Well, maybe we'll talk again soon at the theater?" he said.

"I won't be going back to the theater," Judge Cooper replied.

Fazio nodded. The man was in shock. He let himself out of the town house. Walking to his car, he imagined finding the Ballet Killer, torturing him, electrocuting him, banging his head against a steel wall repeatedly.

Fantasies sometimes helped him cool down. Especially on a frustrating case. And this one took the cake.

Jennifer was moving in a small circle across the carpeting in Max's apartment. She was in her stockinged feet, making her solo as Max played it for her. His eyes were on her arched and pointed nimble feet as they sketched out the steps.

Suddenly he stopped and switched off the tape recorder. His voice was cutting. "Your counting's off there. I'm surprised Mr. Z. didn't notice."

Jennifer stopped, shocked. "Where? Show me?"

Max played a phrase. "Listen. . . . Ta-da-a-ta-de-dum," he said, in the nonsense language common to musicians and dancers. "Didn't you hear it? It's really a question of the right phrasing and just the right accent." He played the tricky bars of music again. "You do it." She did it.

"That's *right!*" Max burst forth, giving a near-perfect imitation of Mr. Zolinsky. Jennifer couldn't help but snicker. "Hey, thanks. You know, you're right. I'm surprised Mr. Z. didn't call me on that."

Max fiddled playfully with a G-flat chord. "Oh, well, your dancing was so . . . so . . . it didn't matter." Jennifer noticed a sexy lilt in his voice. She knew she must be blushing.

"Oh, Max, now stop! It's going to go right to my head!"

"Then let it." His beautiful blue eyes were wide with adoration. "You're the greatest thing I've ever seen. Especially this morning. I never saw you like that. You've got it. And believe me, Jennifer, I know."

"I know you do, and I'm flattered. I really am."

He was almost pleading now. "Did you ever see me with the sports page on top of the piano reading and playing at the same time like some accompanists?

No. I keep my eyes on what the dancers are doing. I know all the steps." He laughed, but it was soft, private. "Though I don't think Mr. Z. will throw anything my way." He was still laughing and Jennifer joined him.

She sat down cross-legged on the carpet while Max played the music through and it taped on to her cassette. Outside it was cold and snowy. Here she felt warm. It was like they were two kids coloring on a rainy day, safe and snuggly. Time was standing still for her with Max. And she needed this welcome escape for just a little while before she had to face reality again. Funny, she had always taken him to be shy. He really wasn't, she realized. He was adorable.

She looked up at him in his navy-blue, V-neck sweater with the checkered shirt collar sticking out, noticing him as if for the first time. In class her world was the one in the mirror. She saw only her reflection. She had never paid much attention to Max or any other piano player. Now she saw more than the sandy-colored hair and the boyish complexion. She saw his eyes, really saw them. They were blue, but they were flecked with gold, making them bright and friendly. And there were creases around them that crinkled when he laughed or smiled. She knew she should get up and go home, but she just couldn't bring herself to do it yet. It was so lovely.

Max was glancing over at her slyly while he was playing. He was thinking how nice it would be to run his hands down her smooth neck and never stop. Their gaze met and both looked away, but it all happened in less than a second. When he finished playing he got up from the piano and said, "Hey, how about a drink? After the morning you've had, you need one."

"That's for sure," she said, smiling.

He handed her the cassette and she put it in her bag. "What can I fix you?"

Looking at a clock in the room, she noticed it was almost 2:00. She thought about Richard. She felt funny calling him from Max's apartment. Richard would never stand for small-talk conversation today. Later, at home, when she had privacy she'd call. She felt slightly guilty and then angry with herself. Why couldn't she relax and enjoy herself? It was innocent enough. She'd call Richard when she was damned ready.

She looked up at Max and caught him staring at her in the oddest way. "Okay," she said. "Why not? A vodka with something in it. Orange juice, if you have it."

When he drove up to the Twentieth Precinct, Fazio noticed a crowd had collected. As he fought his way though the TV crews and tossed out "no comments," ignoring the questions, he went into the main room on the first floor and told the sergeant to maintain some order.

"Say, what's going on out there, anyway?" Fazio asked.

"They just brought in the suspect," the sergeant answered.

"Oh, the suspect's here," Fazio mumbled. Then he dashed for the elevator. Suspect? Who? The man the kid saw who stepped from behind the column? Nice of them to tell him about it. He checked his radio and it coughed up a noise. It was working.

When he stepped onto the floor, he could still hear the phones ringing, but he noticed immediately that most were going unanswered. Clusters of men were grouped together, some with coffee cups, talking. Two men he didn't recognize. A tall, well-dressed black, and a short, squat white man were standing apart from the rest. Moskowitz indicated the Squad Room. The door was closed. Fazio opened it and walked in.

He saw a tallish, but almost frail-looking, man, with lawn-mowered hair and pink-tinged ears. His pale eyes gripped the room with a vacant, spooky stare. A black jacket was draped over a chair near him and he wore a brown shirt. He kept licking his lips. Probably in his early thirties. Hogan had a look of pure joy on his face. When he saw Fazio, he got up immediately and went over to him.

"Frank!" Hogan put his hand on the door. "Step outside and I'll fill you in. Someone radioed you but got no answer." Fazio felt the last was added as an afterthought but made no comment.

As the door closed behind them, Hogan clapped his big arm around Fazio's shoulder so that they resembled Mutt and Jeff. Then he walked out into the hall while he explained what had happened.

Fazio shook his head over and over. It was incredible. He couldn't believe it. To have cracked this case, just like this, right before Christmas. But that was the way things sometimes happened. "If this is the guy, Bill," he said, genuinely excited, "this is fantastic!"

"He's the guy. Trust me. You know that maintenance man we brought in for questioning? He saw this guy behind the column when he was running out of the pool. And that kid? David Funke. We got him over right away and he gave a positive I.D. This is our man. We had a lead over in Queens. A landlady called in about her tenant this morning. We got him back to Queens. Same man. So, tell me, what do you think of him?" It almost sounded as if Hogan wanted Fazio to approve a future son-in-law.

"Well, that's hard to say. From what I saw, I'd say he was, well, a crazy, you know?"

There was a self-congratulatory note in Hogan's

voice. "I know. Go on in now, Frankie, my boy, and you interrogate him. No one does it like you . . . I hear."

They walked back in together and Hogan said, politely, but as if he were addressing a mentally retarded foreigner, "Ivan? This is Lieutenant Fazio. He's going to ask you some questions now."

The man peered at Fazio through squirrelly eyes, as if to size him up, and nodded. He sneezed and someone handed him a fresh white linen handkerchief.

Fazio sat calmly across the table from Roman and smiled. He smiled back at Fazio.

"Who was the fourth dancer you killed, Ivan? From what company?"

"Nicole Peters, Michael Bodney Company. I killed her on April 7."

"And the eighth?"

"Melissa Stone, National."

Fazio watched him very closely. His answers were mechanical. There was no play of emotion on his face.

"Why did you take the lives of these young ballerinas, Ivan?"

"I didn't mean to," he replied hesitantly.

"Did you know them, each of them, personally?"

Ivan shook his head from side to side, vigorously. "No, I didn't know them before. But I had to do it . . . had to."

"Who told you to?"

Ivan pondered that one a moment. "I'm not allowed to say." Before Fazio could fire his next question, Ivan Roman blurted, "Will you guys get me a Big Mac? I love Big Mac's."

Hogan opened the door and shouted for someone to go to McDonald's.

Annoyed by this interruption in the flow, Fazio said quickly, "Ivan, why did you leave the girls with only

one toe shoe? What did you do with the other one?"
There was no response. Ivan Roman looked at the ceiling as if it held a movie screen. His eyes seemed to cross.

One of the detectives leaned into Fazio, whispering, "He's spacing out again. He did that twice before."

Everyone waited.

Suddenly Roman looked straight at Fazio, his eyes clear, his attention alert, and said, "I kept it for myself."

"Okay, which shoe did you keep?"

"The left one."

"Why?"

Ivan Roman paused and consulted the ceiling again. His forehead was bunched up in deep concentration. He worked his mouth before he spoke, then said, "Because I'm righthanded."

"Wait a second. You just said you kept the left ones. Which one? Right or left?"

"Right. I'm righthanded."

They stared at each other, their eyes locking. Fazio was just about to shoot another question when Hogan's booming voice cut him off. "Okay, that's enough. Put him in the lock-up now. Get him ready for the Department of Corrections."

Fazio protested but was outranked. He trailed Hogan through crowds of noisy men, making ready to celebrate, to his office.

"C'mon in, Frank," Hogan said magnanimously.

"Now, listen here, Bill, I don't think . . ."

The phone rang and Hogan made his hand into a stop sign while he took the call. Imperceptibly, he straightened when he recognized the voice. "Yes, Your Honor . . . everything did check out, after all. . . . Come right over. . . . Press conference in an hour is fine with me. See you then." He fished in his top drawer and pulled out a navy tie.

"That was the mayor," he informed Fazio. "We'll have Roman fingerprinted up here and book him downstairs for the press."

"Yeah," Fazio said, a note of bitterness creeping into his voice. "Real convenient. Especially since the press is already jamming the vestibule downstairs. Bill, this guy will never make it. They'll throw the case out."

Hogan began to get angry. "Look, if the press is downstairs, it's not my doing. As far as it getting to court, well, that's not my problem, is it? This guy's got no record, never even been fingerprinted. He's nuttier than a fruitcake. You know that and I know that. C'mon, Frank, you know he'll never stand trial. He'll see a battery of shrinks and be declared legally insane. The taxpayers will support him for the rest of his days while he chirps away to all his imaginary friends in some zoo."

"You really think *that's* the Ballet Killer?"

"You don't?" Hogan had stopped midway in knotting his tie and was studying Fazio curiously."

"I'm not saying he is or isn't," Fazio said stubbornly. "I'm saying he hasn't been interrogated properly."

"What do you think we've been doing while you were gone?" Hogan shot back.

Fazio ignored the insult. "None of the questions I asked were answered to my satisfaction. I didn't have enough time. Look, why doesn't he know which toe shoe he tied around the girls' necks? We do."

"We found the toe shoes in his apartment, for Chrissakes! Even the dancers have to mark them right and left to put them on in a hurry. They're shapeless."

"Not really. Not after they've been worn. I'll tell you something. If it were one minute to Christmas, I'd keep him in that room until I got the right answers to those questions or I could break him."

"Forget it. Not with this one. He's crazy. How can

you get the *right* answers? Look, Frank, he confessed. He was identified by witnesses. He's got paraphernalia in his apartment. He has no alibi for any of the killings, which he knows all about. He even knows what we kept from the press. Like the fact that all the girls were raped, not just the first one. He knew that. We have to call in the shrinks to find out more. Frankly, Lieutenant, I think you're jealous."

Fazio stood rigidly still. The anger he had suppressed for so many months filled his body like a balloon pumped full with air. "Of what?" he said.

Hogan smiled smugly. Fazio thought, then, he was grateful to drop the polite facade. "Because I got your office, I got your case, and now I'm gonna get all the credit. While you'll be stuck in the interrogation room for years, Frank, because that's your mentality."

"I'm a cop. I don't know public relations. I'm not gunning for Commish or Mayor. I might be only a cop, but at least I don't have to kiss anyone's ass."

Hogan stared at him coldly. Each knew the charade was over. They didn't have to pretend to be nice to each other anymore.

Hogan's complexion was just starting to return to its normal color when Fazio turned and walked out of the office and down the hall.

"Hey, excuse me," someone said.

Fazio turned to encounter the slim, good-looking black he had seen before. "I'm Harrison, One-hundred-eighth. Hey, we got to get back to Queens. What's the story? We're the ones who brought in Ivan Roman."

Fazio smiled knowingly. "It's your collar, isn't it?"

"Well, we answered the call and brought the guy in, me and my partner."

"You could try, Harrison, to get your face on TV in the downstairs vestibule. But since you'll probably find

Hogan's hand in front of it, I would say go back to Queens and save yourself some time."

As he found his hat and coat, he heard Moskowitz yell, "Hey, Lieutenant! You staying for the party? Hogan's picking up the tab." He pretended not to hear and kept walking, past the elevator, down the steps to an entrance where he could slip away from the three-ring circus on the first floor.

Jerry Turner had walked slowly, careful to keep his distance. He didn't want to be seen. He had walked up and down Sixty-second Street, across the street from the stage entrance of the State Theatre, waiting. But all the young ballerinas were behind closed doors today, like a cloister of nuns.

Just when he had decided to try his luck elsewhere, he spotted one. He recognized her immediately. Raising his camera, he focused, snapped, and snapped again. It seemed like a perfect shot, but with the damned snow, he just couldn't be sure. And now she was too far away.

He followed. She seemed to be with someone, but then a crowd of people swooping into the street camouflaged her. When he got to the corner, he realized he had lost her. Cursing his luck, he looked to the right and then to the left. He wanted to cross the street, but there was a traffic tie-up and he couldn't move quickly. Finally, he came to a stop in a pile of slushy snow, out of breath.

He had to be patient. It was the secret of his success. He continued, confidently, walking very fast up Columbus Avenue. He knew just where to wait for her. He smiled. The next one would be lovely Jennifer North.

Richard sat back against the seat in the silent, rickety cab that was trundling its way through the Christmas traffic to his Park Avenue office. There was a smile of satisfaction on his face. He patted his pocket where the little package sat. Two thousand dollars, but who cared? Oh, no, he was not giving up without a fight.

The cab careened around a corner, but he hardly noticed. When he talked to her, he would have to be careful not to give away the surprise. That would spoil it. He'd give it to her in the restaurant right before they went to the airport to pick up her parents. And he had another surprise, too. He had called National and spoken to the artistic director. He told him that Jennifer would be willing to change her mind, in light of the recent killing, the fifth from the company she was in now. They had said, of course, they were still interested and for her to call them. Chuckling softly, he remembered his final touch. Jennifer would probably be furious with him. To make sure it sounded good, he had told National he was her agent.

Through an open door, Grischa Zolinsky saw a young dancer reflected in the mirror. Her legs were in a scissors split in midair. She was nervous. He could tell. She was trying to learn Heather Cooper's solo in a hurry, plus attend her other rehearsals and be ready for performance. Well, it was a minor role, but a good one. Heather had been perfect for it. She would have graduated to better parts soon after that. But, now . . .

Zolinsky gritted his teeth and continued his brisk walk down the backstage area on his way to the stage. At his right an assistant walked with a clipboard, taking notes.

"Flyers," he dictated, "to insert in the programs for the gala. *Artemis Visions* is dedicated to the loving memory of ballerinas Heather Cooper, Lisa Harmon, Sheryl Martine, Olivia Orgstrom, and Elizabeth Winters. A light mauve shade. Something very subdued but feminine."

The woman nodded and kept scribbling.

"Now, the shoes. This is no time to lecture on pointe shoes. But there is that bill from Capezio's for over $250,000. . . ." He muttered something to himself, then added, "Xerox the bill and post it backstage next to the casting list. Type a note to the ladies that we will go broke soon if they do not take care of the pointe shoes they have. There should be a pair for class, a pair for rehearsal, a better pair for performance. We should conserve."

The woman nodded. This was a familiar speech to her.

"And keep trying to get Judge Cooper, will you?"

"Mr. Zolinsky, he's just not taking calls. I tried several times, even said it was you."

Zolinsky waved his hand, dismissing it. "I'll call myself, then. Don't bother." Who knew more about grief than he? He had had four wives, all ballerinas; all made him suffer. Time healed everything. And he had decided long ago never to marry again.

A young woman came flying out of a Roger Torry rehearsal, her face in her hands, weeping. "I can't take it! I just can't take it!" Instinctively, a young detective hanging around in the hall moved forward, but then grinned sheepishly and thought better of it.

Another young dancer sat sewing a man's pair of ballet slippers on a chair in the hall. She smiled widely but her teeth were clenched. "I know how you feel Gina, dear, but this is no time to have one of your tantrums. Mr. Z. is right down the hall."

"I can't take it!" the young soloist screeched dramatically. "My Achilles' tendon is just killing me!" Then she said in a low voice, "Thanks, Steph." The girl sewing the slippers laughed softly and Gina entered the room, smiling, graceful, just as she had left it.

Zolinsky frowned. He would have to talk to Roger. This was no time to be too rough on the dancers. Everyone was overworked, scared, and that's when injuries happened. He couldn't afford that.

As they entered the stage from the side, he could hear the drift of another conversation.

"That's my fourth can of soda today, but I haven't eaten a thing."

"Dieting?" said a male voice.

"Should I?"

"When's the funeral?"

"She's being cremated."

"Oh, God, I'm going to cry."

"Honestly, Larry, you didn't even like Heather Cooper. You thought she was a bitch riding on her daddy's influence."

The man's voice was angry. "Keep your opinions to yourself. The poor girl's dead. And by the way, sweetie, yes, your thighs are getting a bit too much."

Zolinsky always heard everything. He kept walking past the scenery, stepping gingerly over cables, noting the onstage rehearsal of Yuri and Nora Hanson. His head followed the lifts, the bends, the *arabesques*. He should be attending, he knew it, but there wasn't enough time for him to be everywhere. Not now. He stopped to chat with the stage manager about a change in the cue sheet for the lighting on *Artemis*. His assistant scurried back to her office.

Zolinsky took an elevator up. He would have a little herbal tea and perhaps half of a croissant when he got back to his office. Then he would have to go back to rehearsals. As he reached his office he heard the phone ringing. He was waiting to hear from Martin Cooper.

He was disappointed. It was Captain William Hogan. Zolinsky listened carefully and made the appropriate remarks. He said only one thing: "Why did he do it?"

Hogan, who wanted to be the first to deliver the good news to all the ballet masters and artistic luminaries, said only, "Mr. Zolinsky, we don't know why. The doctors might tell us."

Zolinsky hung up and crossed the room to his stereo. Beethoven's *Seventh*. He needed to relax. He stretched out on his velvet couch, resting his feet on the Persian rug. So they caught him. He should feel happy, yet he suddenly felt depressed. Ten young ballerinas plus Heather. All dead, and for what? Because the man was crazy. The world was getting harder to figure out. No discipline, no order, no respect for tradition. No wonder everyone was going mad. They took what they pleased, did as they wished. It was freer in tsarist Russia before he got out. At least there one knew who to watch out for.

A voice was yelling outside the door. He got up and turned down the stereo. "Mr. Zolinsky! An accident! There's been a bad injury!"

He rushed to the door. Outside stood his assistant.

"Who?"

"Eric."

Zolinsky didn't even stop to ask how bad. All he could think of was, thank God, it was a man. At least they still had some male dancers to go around. He got out a pencil and paper and began diagramming while he walked. Eric was to dance in *Fancy Free*. Who could replace him on the spur of the moment? Yuri, of course. But he was saving Yuri for the gala. Armond would do. Yes, he could put Armond in Eric's part. But then who would he put in Armond's part in the ballet in front of it? He sighed. Some things never changed in a ballet company.

Jennifer leaned back on the couch. Max sat on the other end. When she lit a cigarette, he scurried across the room to dig out an ashtray from underneath a pile of music.

"So . . ." Max lifted his drink in a toast. "Here's to you and your star, which is rising." He was staring into her eyes so directly Jennifer found herself unable to meet his gaze.

"Thank you, Max. You're sweet. Really."

"But how does it feel to know that one day you're going to be an internationally famous ballerina?" he persisted.

"Maaax!" Jennifer laughed. She found herself drinking her screwdriver like it was straight orange juice. She was thirsty. She was always thirsty. She was also getting a little high.

"You know, Max," she said, staring into her glass, "I have come a long, long way. I mean, a girl from Cleveland Heights, Ohio, dancing with New York Center. Nora found me, you know . . . when she was on tour. I came to New York all alone to dance with the company when I was just turning eighteen. Now here it is a little over a year later and I'm given this fantastic solo and *pas de deux*. I guess I'm a pretty lucky girl, huh?"

"It's just a little more than luck, Jennifer. You have it. Zolinsky will make you a principal soon. I'd be willing to bet on that."

"Principal? I'm not even a real soloist yet." She looked at Max hungrily. "What makes you so sure?"

She waited, holding her breath, wondering if he knew something she didn't. Max shrugged. Then he broke into a wide grin. Jennifer felt a flurry of excitement. He did know something, but he wasn't telling. She wouldn't say anything more about it.

"All my life since I was eight years old," she went on, "I've dreamed of being a ballerina. Not just a member of the corps, but a star. Nothing else mattered. Nothing. Not the last dances at school, not having boyfriends or dates, not even school itself. Only class. I would run to the ballet school as soon as school was over, and be there all day Saturday." She sighed and stopped, looking into space at nothing. "But after what's happened, oh, I don't know, Max. This is the chance of a lifetime, but if I just get through that solo and *pas de deux,* it will be a miracle."

There was a pause. "You mean Heather?" he finally asked.

"Yes! She was my best friend. Why did she have to die? And all the others? Why? Because they were all good dancers, destined to be ballerinas someday. Why was I spared?" Jennifer lit another cigarette. Max was silent. "I shouldn't be bothering you like this. I'm sorry. I guess I'm just drunk."

Max reached over and picked up her empty glass. "That's ridiculous. Talk all you want. That's what I'm here for, to listen." He smiled at her warmly. "All you need right now is a refill."

Jennifer shook her head. "Oh, no! Really, I should be going." But even as she said it, she realized she wasn't very convincing.

Max ignored her and disappeared into the kitchen, coming out with another full glass. "All that stuff is not the only thing that's bothering you, I bet."

Jennifer looked at him, startled. "No, you're right, it isn't. But how did you know?"

Max smiled, sat back down on the couch, and

folded his arms behind his head. "Oh, maybe I just guessed. Or maybe because I watched you when you came into class this morning. You were in some fog."

"You're very observant. I had another fight with Richard. A mean one. Maybe the final one. Which reminds me, I have to call him." She hiccuped.

"Richard?" Max said vaguely. "Oh, the guy you're living with," he said, dismissing him as nobody really significant. He pointed to the phone underneath the coffee table and Jennifer shrugged lazily. "I'm in no hurry."

"Ever hear Mr. Z's speech on ballerinas and men and how when you mix it with marriage it doesn't mix?" he said gently.

"Oh, yes, the one about when she gets married she's no longer a she but part of a he? A real ballerina can't afford that?"

Max nodded.

"But several of the principals are married, even to each other, and he doesn't mind."

"Ah, yes. Some get married and with his blessings. It depends on which ones he decides can handle it. Or which ones he reserves for himself. Or his fantasies. I mean, he is seventy-five." A dark cloud seemed to pass over Max's face and then lifted just as quickly. "But it's worth considering, Jennifer. You are a ballerina. You need the right man. Not someone who upsets you or . . . doesn't understand you. You're not an ordinary woman." He broke into one of his sunny smiles, satisfied that he had said everything he wanted to say.

Jennifer realized he was sitting closer than before— In fact, very, very near. Somehow he had inched closer. Instinctively, she moved back. Then she jumped up.

Looking down at him, she asked, "Do you know how to play jazz?"

"Sure. Love it. What do you want to hear?"

"Oh, I don't know. Something old, something mellow, something I can improvise to. I took a few jazz classes a long time ago."

Max moved to the piano and played what Jennifer thought was gorgeous stuff, an old swing melody that was sad and yet hopeful at the same time. She moved her body slowly at first, her hair spilling around her rotating shoulders. She felt totally free, not at all inhibited.

"Hey, you know, you're really good at that," Max said, his voice husky, but Jennifer never heard Max. She was lost in the movement. She kicked her leg high and then swiftly recoiled it to her knee. She did a stomach contraction, falling dramatically to the floor. Max continued to play, swaying to his own music. Then he saw Jennifer had never gotten up from the floor. He took his hands off the piano keys and waited. Then he heard loud, racking sobbing.

Quickly he got up and awkwardly sat down beside her on the floor. He took her in his arms and stroked her hair. "Poor Jennifer," he murmured softly, rocking her. "Life is so unfair."

Jennifer made no effort to move out of his arms. She didn't see the smile of satisfaction on his face.

Across the street from Jennifer's apartment house near Columbus Avenue, a man hid behind the trash cans, waiting. A cab came close to the building and a young woman wearing sunglasses got out. Jennifer! He aimed his camera and shot. Click! Perfect. He just needed one good really close shot. He looked up. Then he kicked the trash can over angrily. That wasn't Jennifer. Looked like her, though. That wasn't even a dancer, and he ought to know, because he knew them all by sight. His hands were freezing. Maybe it was too soon after Heather.

Jerry Turner decided to give up his vigil in front of Jennifer's apartment building. For the time being.

In a small cell in the Tombs, a temporary prison belonging to the Department of Corrections, Ivan Roman sat on the edge of his bottom bunk humming. There were strange voices cutting through his usual voices. He stared at the light bulb hanging from the ceiling. Then he snapped his head around. The voices were coming from the other cells. There were people in the other cells.

"Hey, Rapo!" a man's voice, loud and ugly, yelled. "You! The Ballet Killer! Think you're so big, huh? You're a turd! A common rapo!"

"Shut up!" another voice yelled, as Ivan Roman spun around in his lonely cell. "He'll get his when they send him up. Oh, yeah, did ya get a peek at his cute, little ass?"

"Whaddya, crazy?" The first voice again. "He's a weirdo. A nut job. Nothing's going to happen to him. He'll go to a nice booby hatch and no one will lay a finger on him."

Ivan Roman heard their raucous laughter and trembled. What would become of him? Oh, he had no regrets. He would do it all over again if he had the chance. It had been fun. But he was guilty. In the eyes of almighty Zeus and his dear, departed mother, he was guilty and must be punished. Would they not punish him? He got down on his knees and started praying but ended up banging his head against the hard wall. There was so much vibration and noise in his head. He had to stop it. It was unbearable. It was this room and the bars.

"Guard!" he screamed. "Let me out of here! Please!" No one came. There were no sounds except loud laughter from the other prisoners. He looked up and saw the swinging bulb. He studied it. Maybe the light would tell him the answer. Tell him how to escape.

Chapter Five

He was about eight or nine, something like that, when it first happened. He was taking a bath. His mother was there with him. She soaped him up first and then she lifted herself out of the tub and scrubbed herself down there with the soapy washcloth. All of her fur was glistening white. He looked down at himself then. His dingle was floating on top of the water and it felt hard. He grabbed the washcloth and tried to cover it up. Mama kissed him on the forehead, ripped the washcloth away, and giggled.

IT WAS CLOSE to 3:00 when Richard picked up the phone, impatiently. Jennifer hadn't called. That was so like her. What did it take to stop for one minute and go down the hall to a pay phone? He tried the State Theatre again.

To his surprise, he got through.

"New York State Theatre," the switchboard operator droned.

"This is Dr. Richard Kupperman and I've been trying to reach Jennifer North, a dancer. Please, it's an emergency."

"Wait a second, please."

Richard tapped a pencil against the desk, beating out the seconds of his wait. If they wouldn't let him speak to her or if she had left, then what?

The operator came back. "Yes, Jennifer North. She's scheduled for a rehearsal at two-thirty for *La Bayadère*. We never give this information out, but considering you said it was an emergency and the kind of day we're having . . ."

Richard took a big breath. It was worth a try. "Please call her to the phone."

The operator sucked in a gasp. "I'm sorry. I just cannot do that."

Richard could hear the phones ringing and knew he'd lose her. "Okay, listen, just leave this message for her, okay? Tell her Dr. Kupperman called. It's an emergency."

Richard hung up, satisfied. His next patient would be coming through the door any minute. If Jennifer's rehearsal was for *Bayadère,* it could last for hours. One never knew with that ballet. He decided to try to stop worrying about her until the end of the afternoon.

Jennifer sat in a heap, still sobbing on Max's chest. Max sat, rather stiffly, holding her close, trying his best to comfort her. He groped in his pocket and found a hanky, then fumbled trying to find her face, handing it to her. He accidentally punched her in the nose and apologized three times. Finally, Jennifer looked up, half-laughing, half-sobbing, and blew her nose.

"I'm sorry," she said in a shaky voice. "Really, you've been too nice. I don't know what came over me. I guess I'm not a good drinker. I'd better go. . . ."

Max continued to stroke her hair. "Jenny, Jenny, I understand. I want to help you."

Jennifer wiped her wet face with the back of her hand. "Jenny," she whispered softly. "No one calls me that anymore. My father used to call me that when I was a little girl."

She started to cry again and Max held her close. He moved over on his side and she didn't resist when he pulled her down with him, firmly but gently, to the floor. She clung to him, allowing herself to be cuddled, finishing out the last of her tears. She felt his hand on her back, rubbing in circles, massaging. Up and down and around. She knew she should tell him to stop. No man except Richard had ever touched her with such intimacy since she came to New York.

His hand just kept rubbing her back, going higher, going lower. She seemed unable to find the words to tell him to stop. She knew she was attracted to Max. His hand was like a feather giving off sparks of electricity. She would stop it, though, if he tried to go any further.

Then gently she felt him lower them both onto the carpet so they were locked in an embrace. She could feel herself pressed into his body, her chin resting on his shoulder. She heard a moan and thought how odd it was that it had come from her. And still Max kept massaging her back, drawing big circles with his magical hands, but not really relaxing her. Now every part of her body wanted him and it was too late to stop. The thought of Richard was becoming vague and suddenly unimportant.

Slowly, at first, she put her arms around his neck. He whispered, "Jennifer," and pulled her even closer. Jennifer adjusted her body so she could feel his hardness pressing against her. Then his hands stopped and she opened her eyes only to look directly into his as his face came closer and he kissed her.

A gasp escaped her throat as she felt her lips on the top of his wavy head of hair and she knew his hands were inching her top up. Those marvelous, sensitive hands. She had fallen over on her back now and with her top coiled around her neck felt the delicious sensation of his mouth on her breasts as his hands moved softly over her body.

She made an attempt to lift off his sweater, but he forced her hands down. "Not yet," he murmured, opening her jeans. For a second Jennifer clamped her legs together, but he parted them gently. She waited. She felt powerless to stop him and powerless to make a move of her own.

She was aware of observing herself from afar as he shrugged off her jeans and bit the inside of her thighs. Shutting her eyes, she wondered why the room was spinning. God, she must be so drunk. But who cared? Richard's face flew in front of her mind and she dismissed it as she felt her body free of the damp, silky panties. He massaged her there with his fingers until she heard herself cry out. And then he stopped.

Then he was on top of her. She felt the fuzziness of his sweater and heard him loosen his belt. But her bare legs felt his clothes. "I can't wait," he whispered and it didn't matter that he was dressed. When she felt him in her, her excitement was almost explosive. She turned her head to the side and let the delicious feeling of release carry her. Jennifer never made much noise when she came. So Max didn't know. He hardly heard her little gasp of surprise before he moaned something and seemed to sag on top of her just seconds after. The room was going around and around for Jennifer. She shut her eyes and imagined Richard's face as a balloon bouncing up and down. Then she thought of something. What was the word Max had seemed to almost grind out through his teeth? It sounded like "Maaaa." But that was absurd.

"I'm sorry," Max said suddenly, keeping his head on her breast.

"For what?" She felt strange now that it was over. Was she feeling guilty? She tried to put it out of her mind.

"You didn't come," Max said.

"Oh, but I did, really I did." Somehow she felt unsatisfied now.

"I'd like to make it up to you, Jennifer. I'm always nervous the first time."

She started to protest, but he had stood up and was zipping up his pants. He seemed to tower over her. Then he bent down and picked her up.

"You're so light. What do you weigh?"

Jennifer couldn't answer. She knew now this shouldn't be happening, but somehow it was. She felt dizzy and nauseous. Too much to drink on an empty stomach. Way too much.

Max was carrying her toward the little bedroom. "Why don't we rest for a while and then try again?"

She knew she should put on her clothes and get in a cab. But it felt so nice putting her head on the pillow when he placed her gently on the bed. Her eyes were closing. The last thing she saw was Max sitting on the bed, taking his sweater off, looking down at her and smiling.

At the Twentieth Precinct the guys in the task force were celebrating Ivan Roman, Christmas, and free booze. As liquor and beer rained into plastic cups, more was carried in. Everyone knew Hogan had picked up the tab. He had come to the party, briefly, shook hands all around, and then left for the mayor's office and a private Christmas party.

The press conference had gone as if it had been choreographed. And, indeed, it had been. Nothing much was said, directly, about the suspect, Ivan Roman, but much had been implied. He was not allowed to speak. But no one could force the cameras to stay off the slightly befuddled man who waved and smiled irrepressibly at the lights as he was booked in the vestibule. He was then scurried off under heavy protection to the Tombs as a ward of the Department of Corrections. Everyone knew the judge would emphatically deny bail. She was an old friend of Judge Martin Cooper.

In the corner, a makeshift barbershop quartet was singing Christmas carols. All the phones for the special line assigned to the Ballet Killer case had been taken off the hook and the disconnect buzzing was indistinguishable from the rest of the hum. A giant order of egg rolls from a nearby Chinese restaurant was being dished out on a table constructed from three desks moved together.

A reporter from the *Daily News* circulated in the crowd.

"Hey, you guys, Merry Christmas," he said, coming up to a circle of detectives he was fairly friendly with. "Some party. Where's Lieutenant Fazio? Didn't he come?"

"Yeah, he's around somewhere, ain't he?" someone said.

"No. He wasn't at the press conference, either. Say, is it true what they say about Fazio and Hogan? That they don't exactly have kind words for each other? That Fazio's nose is a little out of joint and has been since Hogan kind of pushed him to the side?" The reporter had in mind an in-depth story about cops, something with human interest.

The detectives exchanged glances. Just then, Moskowitz stepped into the circle from the outer rim. Like a tugboat in a sea of big ships, he steered the reporter away.

"Hey, you're not drinking. Let me get you something. Look, have an egg roll. Listen, I read you all the time. I like your stuff, but believe me, you ain't got no story with Fazio."

"Oh, c'mon. He's not here. I hang around a lot."

"Forget it. Believe me. Fazio's got a wife and two kids. A boy, and his daughter's expecting a baby any minute. He's real happy this thing's settled. But he's a family man—you know what I mean? Lots of guys ain't here. Look around. See for yourself."

Moskowitz hurriedly introduced him to a detective from the Sixth Precinct who had wandered in for a free drink. "Now, there's a story. Get him to tell you about those crazy movies being shot in the Village. Real human-interest stuff there, huh?"

Moskowitz walked away. He was thinking. It had been pretty well known, but left unsaid, that Fazio's ego had taken a beating along with his prestige ever since Hogan took over. Most of the men there in and out of the task force were yukking it up, eating Hogan's food, drinking Hogan's booze. If they didn't like him, they did respect him. They thought he was a tough but good captain. Moskowitz had once thought so, too. But ever since this morning, Moskowitz had come to the conclusion that Hogan was a horse's ass. And that Fazio had gotten dumped on.

Just a few blocks from the Twentieth, tucked away on a sidestreet off newly chic Columbus Avenue, sat the unchic Titanic. Uncorrupted by noise and interruption sat Lieutenant Fazio. He was trying to get drunk.

He was undisturbed, except when he looked up suddenly and found someone staring at him. It was a face with a beard and a winning smile. He was a new bartender in his early twenties.

"Hey, you're Lieutenant Fazio, aren't you?" he said. "I've seen you around."

Fazio grunted, not much in the mood for conversation.

"Say, I heard on the radio that you got the Ballet Killer. That's really terrific what you guys did right before Christmas, huh?"

"Yeah, guess so."

"So, it's all over then, isn't it?"

Fazio looked at him sharply. "Not until he's convicted. I'll have a plate of lasagna. Got that today?"

The young man nodded eagerly. He turned and gave the order to the hot table closed off behind a steamy window. Then he swung back to Fazio. "Boy, it's a relief," he continued. "I couldn't stand to see those girls being murdered that way. A lot of them live in the neighborhood, you know?"

"I can see you don't like dancers, huh, kid?"

"What, are you kidding? They're like goddesses. Ever study their cheekbones? Every one of them is beautiful. Not like the girls you usually meet."

A balding man with a potbelly came over and seized the barstool next to Fazio. "Little tits, though," he said. The bartender moved away quickly to take someone else's order.

Vinnie, the owner of the Titanic, slapped Fazio on the back. "Merry Christmas, Lieutenant. Have a drink on the house." He waved to the bartender to get Fazio another drink. "Say, I hear you cracked that Ballet Killer case."

Fazio took a long swallow and his voice was muffled. "Oh, yeah, we cracked it."

"Where are all the guys? I thought they'd be in here celebrating. They found a new dump?"

"No, no, nothing like that. There's a big bash over at the Twentieth. Booze is free."

"But *you* came back here. I like that. Another drink on the house." The bartender passed Fazio his drink and went to pour another Scotch and soda.

"Hey, whaddya think of him?" Vinnie said as he walked away.

"The new bartender? He seems pretty good."

"I just hired him. Said he needed the job real bad.

He'll work out okay, I guess, but he's a little strange, you know? You're a detective. You think he's a queer? I don't want him bothering none of the customers."

"You mean homosexual?"

"Yeah. He's always talking about ballet and ballerinas."

Fazio took a closer look at the bearded bartender at the other end of the bar. "Nah, I don't think so. Maybe he's an artist or musician or something. Needs a bread job. He seems okay."

"I don't know. Say, I wonder if it wouldn't be too much trouble . . . I mean, he probably doesn't have a record or anything . . ."

"You want me to check him out?"

"Yeah, if it wouldn't be too much trouble. His name's Turner. Jerry Turner. He lives around here."

Fazio got out his notebook and scratched himself a reminder with the ballpoint Vinnie shoved in front of his face. "Okay, sure. No problem."

"Thanks, Lieutenant. I appreciate it." He moved away to talk to another customer and Fazio's lasagna arrived. Not anything compared to Connie's, but he was starved. While he ate, he thought. Hogan would move out. He would go back to where he was before. But he knew it was all over for him in the Department. Hogan had replaced him. Hogan had solved the case. Bullshit. He just couldn't believe that twirp Roman had committed all those murders. Call it a hunch, but he had learned over the years to trust his hunches.

Fazio put his fork down. He had a wild idea. What if . . . ? He dismissed it. That would be impossible. To go against the whole Department and prove Hogan was wrong? No orders, men, back-up? Just a one-man investigation for law and order on his off-duty hours. It was crazier than Ivan Roman was. Maybe he *was* just jealous of Hogan. Sure, maybe that was it.

On the other hand, there was something about Ivan Roman that was bothering him . . . something he couldn't put his finger on . . . a thread no one had bothered to tie. He finished eating and still couldn't think of it. Fazio shrugged to himself. What wasn't important, you didn't remember. He might as well go home and spend Christmas with his family.

He left a tip, paid his bill, and got his coat and hat. As he opened the door to leave, he happened to glance around and saw the young bartender, Jerry Turner, waving good-bye to him. Come to think of it, he reflected, there was something just a little strange about him.

A loud scream, almost not human, cut through the hallway. Chairs were shoved aside, playing cards dropped, and keys jangled as the attendants rushed into the ward. But it was still. Then a frightened student nurse pointed down the hall and they all turned around and dashed down the long corridor. Another scream. This one choked, agonized, a plea for help.

The patients in the closed ward of Manhattan State Hospital began to seep into the hall, timidly at first. Many were drugged, docile, but all were curious, yearning for some excitement. Each attendant took a side and jammed a key into every door, looking. Then a patient drifted forward and indicated the observation bedroom on the other side of the hall.

They ran. The noises got louder. Loud cackling and soft, defensive whimpering. "Who left this room open?" the head nurse screamed. No one answered. Inside they could see a big rear, covered by a flowered housedress. Behind this shape, peaking out, was a white-haired old gentleman. He was crying. She was trying to bang his head against a hard wall.

Patrick, the muscular male nurse, rushed in first. But even his two-hundred-pound bulk couldn't control the wild woman in his arms as she tried to attack back. Miss Kleinert, the head day nurse, rushed over to the poor little old man. She searched first for physical damage. The student nurse stood in the hall frozen with fear.

There was a loud crash. The woman managed to strike out, knocking over a nightstand. "Goddamn it!" roared Patrick. "Hypo! Quick!" Miss Kleinert rushed to the nurse's station. Patrick ordered the petrified student nurse to clear the crumpled old man out and put him in his own room.

Patrick lurched around then, propelled by the wild woman who was tinier than him but possessed with almost demonic energy. Together they knocked over a chair.

"I'll kill him . . . !" the woman screamed, her face distorted with rage, her hair flying in her eyes. The patients watched the show from a distance, wide-eyed, fearful, but totally absorbed.

"Oh, no, you won't, Mama," Patrick said as Miss Kleinert moved fast from behind with the needle. Deftly, while Patrick got a good grip, she raised the woman's soiled dress and jabbed her with the needle. Patrick loosened his grip but was sorry he let go. She reached up and with a raspy, terrifying scream that sent some patients running back to the ward room, she scratched his face with her jagged nails. Then, her features contorted, she spat in his face.

"Get the doctor on the floor!" Patrick screamed, reaching to restrain her once more. Miss Kleinert dashed to the phone. It was a crisis. And then in the shifting of just a minute or two, it wasn't. The woman's violence subsided. She blinked and looked around her. She seemed ashamed of her dirty dress and messy hair.

Confused, starting to become drowsy, she let the exhausted Patrick lead her to the bed. When she heard the click as the door locked behind her, she was already giving in to a fidgety drowsiness. Holding a handkerchief to his face, he peeked into the circular porthole for one last check. Then he shook his head and muttered something to himself.

Back inside the nurses' station, he poured himself a cup of coffee and it a cigarette. Miss Kleinert noticed his hands were shaking. "Want me to get something for your face?" she asked. "You have a pretty bad scratch there."

"No, thanks, Carol, I'm okay." Then the tension welled up and he exploded. "Jesus H. Christ, though! This is the third time this month! Are they still giving her shock?"

Miss Kleinert nodded.

"I don't believe it. Sometimes I think the doctors are crazier than the patients. Do you know she almost killed him? Another time, the television in the ward blasting, and she's going to succeed. But when she doesn't have shock, she doesn't give us any trouble."

Miss Kleinert thought about that for a moment. Then she went to check the big black book on the desk. "Patrick?"

The male nurse was shuffling his cards.

"Do you want to hear something odd? Listen. She doesn't have her attacks after shock. Here, look at the pattern."

Patrick took the big book in which all the patient reports were kept.

Miss Kleinert pointed to the dates. "It only looks that way." They heard footsteps down the hall. That would be one of the doctors. "But I think she acts up before her son comes to visit. Each time. Then she's fine when he gets here. Did you ever meet her son?"

Patrick shook his head blankly. "I'm too busy watching the patients to meet the visitors. They all look alike to me."

"Oh, I think you would recognize this one. Such a nice boy."

No one was more surprised than Lieutenant Frank Fazio when he showed up at the Twentieth Precinct for the celebration. He had been driving toward Brooklyn and home and then turned around, having remembered something. Joe Turk. Just a few hours ago, which seemed like a few years ago, he had reported in, briefly, quickly. He *had* talked to the girl who left the note under Heather Cooper's door. She said she had seen Heather leave her apartment the night before with a man. And she had given a description. That's all Joe had had time to tell him before things got out of hand.

Had anyone checked that out? Where was Turk? Had this girl been called in to identify Roman? What was her name, anyway? That was why he had turned the car around. If he could just satisfy himself on that, he would feel better about this case. Besides, it was a good idea to show up and have a drink with the men. After all, Hogan would leave soon and he'd have to work with most of them again. It would look like he was sour grapes if he didn't put in an appearance. So, he parked his car in front of the precinct house and walked in.

But he knew in his heart that he was lying to himself. He was there for one reason only. It was the simple revelation that if he was right in his hunch, then Ivan Roman wasn't the Ballet Killer. That would mean the real killer was still walking the streets. And the only way he would know if his hunch was right was to sit back and wait for the body of another dead dancer to be found. Frank Fazio couldn't live with that.

He heard the noise before the elevator doors opened on the sixth floor. It sounded like a bar mitzvah or wedding. All those people having a drink on Bill Hogan, Fazio chuckled. Good old boy, Bill. He would be willing to bet Hogan wasn't even at the party. When he walked in and quickly counted tall heads, he could see that he was right. But officers, men and women, detectives from every precinct had turned up, as soon as the word got out, and were enjoying a Christmas freebie. Fazio didn't know half the people in the room. Locating a bar, made out of two desks and a thin paper tablecloth, he poured a little Scotch and a lot of water into a plastic cup. Then he searched the room for Detective Turk. The one thing he didn't want to do was let anyone know what he was up to. He heard a familiar voice calling him.

"Hey, Lieutenant, you showed up! Great party, huh?"

"Yeah, Moskowitz, terrific. Merry Christmas. Say, you seen Joe Turk?"

Moskowitz's red face scrunched up in concentration. "Turk, Turk. Oh, yeah, didn't come. I think he's off for a few days. Must have gone home. Excuse me, Lieutenant—I'm real glad to see you, but my back teeth are floating."

Fazio wended his way through the crowd. It was like trying to have a drink in a subway at rush hour. Then he spotted just the person he wanted: Detective Shipley. He knew Shipley had been with Turk earlier.

The man was close to passing out. He was in the middle of a raucous group singing bawdy Christmas carols. His knees were beginning to buckle and he looked like his head had been held underwater too long. Fazio calculated he had about fifteen minutes before the man either got ugly or passed out.

"Hey, Merry Christmas, you old son-of-a-bitch!" Fazio said, slapping him on the back to wake him up. Shipley whirled around, his face menacing. Then he saw Fazio and smiled.

"Oh, Looootenant . . . !" Shipley roared drunkenly. "Ho, ho, ho!"

"Exactly my sentiments, Shipley. Listen, I'm looking for Joe Turk—got a little Christmas present for him. Did he tell you where he was going when he got off? Did he go home? Where the hell does he live, anyway?"

Shipley belched and swayed backward. "Wait a second . . . . Lessee, too many questions. Joe Turk. Yeah, yeah. He's off."

"Do you know where he went?"

"Said he was going to spend Christmas with his in-laws."

Fazio kept his voice natural, nonchalant. "What borough do his in-laws live in?"

Shipley thought about it for a second then said, "Phoenix. Yeah, that's right. They live in Phoenix. But I wouldn't bet on that." Fazio watched as the man's eyelids closed and he passed out on the floor. He shrugged, stepped over him, and moved through the crowd. He knew he could bust into Turk's locker and look for his notebook, but that was risky . . . if it was in there. He had to be careful not to be stupid. Suddenly he felt sad. And very lonely.

He poured himself another drink for something to do. Phoenix? He looked at his watch. Almost six. Connie had a big family dinner planned. Connie. Then it hit him. He ran to the hall and got his coat, came back and said his good-byes, beaming, smiling, wishing everyone a merry Christmas and congratulations all around and then dashed down the steps, not bothering to wait for the elevator.

As he left, a few of the men on the task force were standing in a huddle. "Hey, do you really think Fazio's nose is out of joint like that reporter says?" one man asked.

"Looks happier than a pig in shit to me."

"Damned rumors."

"Good man, Lieutenant Fazio."

Fazio was outside now. He was looking for a dime in the handful of change he pulled out of his pocket. He'd call Connie from a pay phone nearby. She was the one person in the world who would know where Turk's in-laws lived. His wife had worked on every volunteer committee the policemen's wives had and she was the biggest gossip in the world.

When Jennifer woke up her mouth tasted sour, her tongue was fuzzy, and she was thirsty. It took a few moments to connect and then she remembered. She was in Max's apartment, in Max's bed. But where was Max?

"Max?" she called out. There was no answer. All the lights in the apartment were out. She must have slept too long and he didn't want to wake her. He had covered her. Maybe he had to go out. It was dark out. Richard! She had to meet Richard at the restaurant at 8:00.

She jumped out of bed and saw that he had put her clothes on the chair. How thoughtful. Jennifer couldn't remember when she had had a worse headache. On the dresser were her contact lenses. She must have gotten up and taken them out. There was an alarm clock on the dresser. Thank heaven. It was only 6:30. She would have time to grab a cab, go home, take a shower, and change. She dabbed a lens on each forefinger and rushed into the bathroom. It felt creepy being in someone else's apartment all alone. It was so quiet.

She thought of Max. He had been so different, but so sweet. It was the first time she had cheated on Richard. She bent toward the mirror in the medicine cabinet and opened her right eye wide. At the same time she ran the right lens briefly under the tap water and placed it in the middle of her pupil, blinking a little. "Positively wicked" was the phrase that popped into her mind. She had actually had sex with another man. It felt very grown-up, and she liked the feeling.

She wet her left contact lens and placed it in her eye, then jumped. It stung. She popped it out and waited a second. She wondered if it was written all over her face. Richard read her too well, sometimes. Would he know the minute he saw her? Well, she certainly wouldn't tell him. Not after the way he acted this morning. Slowly, expertly, she aimed her left lens toward her left eye. She stopped to adjust the medicine-cabinet mirror by pulling it out a few inches. Then she put her lens in. Just at that moment she spotted something pink and shiny in the mirror.

She turned and her first reaction was curiosity. Then amusement. She parted the shower curtain a little. How odd. A pink pointe shoe. She yanked the shower curtain all the way back across the tub. There were more. All were hanging from a little rope which ran from the tiled wall to the little bathroom window. Like a little clothesline. Dusty pink, soiled white, a once-pretty soft blue and a crinkled black. She caught the blue one in her hand and held it. It was autographed.

Melissa Stone. Was she that famous that they would sell her autographed slipper in the theater's lobby? Jennifer couldn't recall ever having heard of her. Must be someone new. She felt a pang of jealousy. Her head was throbbing so it was hard to think. But how cute of Max to string his collection across the tub. They looked like baby shoes just hanging there. Someday she'd ask him about it. She headed for the foyer, where her jacket was hanging in the closet. There was hardly any time, and she couldn't remember where she had left her practice bag.

As she was putting on her jacket in the dim apartment and just about to leave, she was aware of a light clicking on. In the kitchen. Her knees felt weak, as in a second a rush of panic immobilized her. Someone was in Max's apartment. She had to move. Her fingers were trembling as she tried to pick at the chain lock. It didn't matter about her case. She had to open the door and get out. From a distance she heard a thump-thump, like a slapping of someone's foot on the hard floor. And then she had a sickening thought: Why was she fumbling with locks unless someone had tried to lock her in?

Even before she turned, she knew. Melissa Stone. A soloist with National. Murdered by the Ballet Killer sometime early in September. Her pointe shoe was almost at the end of the little rope. Jennifer squeezed her eyes shut. There must have been about eleven shoes on the tape. Eleven murders. She opened her mouth to scream, but no sound came out. She never got a chance to finish it.

Chapter Six

They had sat in the cramped waiting room for three hours. Max's foot was limp; his crutches rested against the wall. "He's a great doctor, Punkin. Everything will be okay. You'll dance for sure. So you lost a few months, that's all." Max sat silent, blowing bubbles with his gum. Finally they were ushered in. The other patients waiting their turn heard the screams and shouts. Charlotte ran out, dragging the boy, who was stumbling on his crutches. "You're supposed to be a great doctor! Where did you get your medical degree? In a Crackerjacks box?"

All of the faces in the waiting room were turned to the woman who was sobbing. The nurse was trying to comfort her.

Even the boy was whispering, white-faced, "Mama, it's okay, I don't mind."

Then the people in the waiting room were stunned. The nurse said, "But, he'll be able to walk again. The doctor assured you there's a way."

"Who cares!" the woman screamed, now hysterical. "He's finished, don't you understand!" He'll never be able to dance again! Never be a ballet star, you bitch!"

CAPTAIN WILLIAM HOGAN stood in line for first-class boarding at Kennedy Airport when he felt a tap on his shoulder. He turned around sharply and heard his wife whisper, "Smile. More reporters."

"Captain Hogan!"

When Hogan turned around to face them, he was flashing a smile that showed a full set of perfect teeth. "Just a few questions," said the reporter who had trailed Hogan all the way out to the airport and considered himself lucky. Hogan saw the photographer's camera out of the corner of his eye just before the picture was taken and made a mental note to buy up all the New York papers just as soon as they arrived in Bermuda.

"Is it true," the reporter asked, "that the solving of this Ballet Killer case was the toughest case to crack in New York City?"

Hogan gave the impression of being in deep

thought. "Well," he said finally, "I wouldn't feel free to say that. But it was certainly the toughest case I ever solved."

"Captain Hogan," the reporter pressed on though the loudspeaker was instructing boarding time. "Are you planning to run for mayor?"

The question surprised Hogan. His eyebrows raced up to his forehead and then came back down in an instant. "I'm just running to catch this plane to Bermuda for a well-deserved vacation with my wife," he said casually.

"Get a shot of Captain Hogan with his wife," the reporter directed his photographer.

Hogan put his big, burly arm around his petite streaked-blonde wife of one year and smiled. People in and around the boarding gate were staring. People in line who hadn't recognized a celebrity on board were literally gaping. Hogan and his wife held the pose until the line started moving and they had to move with it. The two members of the press walked away satisfied.

"How'd you like to live in Gracie Square Mansion?" Hogan whispered to his wife as they waited to show their boarding passes.

She pressed against him, pulling her new raccoon coat up around her chin and crinkling her button nose. Her tongue rolled around her lips, making her glossy lipstick look even wetter. "Sure," she giggled. "Might   well live somewhere like that before the White House."

He pinched her fur-padded behind and she giggled softly. "You think big," he whispered.

She stared him straight in the eye and said, "And you think bigger."

They both laughed.

When they were settled in, seat belts fastened, Hogan looked out at the light, swirling snow rushing against the side of the plane and then flying back into the blackness. He thought pleasantly of long, luxurious hours relaxing in the sun. He envisioned long, sensuous nights with his new wife, sheer curtains flapping in the warm breeze while perfumed breezes washed over their naked bodies. But the only time he really smiled was when he thought of Lieutenant Frank Fazio. And how he was going to fix his ass.

Fazio whipped through a wind pocket as he rounded the corner and entered the steamy warmth of a little diner near the precinct. He scanned the coffee shop first to see if it was a safe place to make a phone call. Satisfied that it was practically empty except for neighborhood regulars who ate dinner there every night and a few stragglers warming their hands over a cup of hot coffee, he put a dime in the phone.

In Brooklyn, Connie Fazio was peeling potatoes. The aroma of a roast cooking in the oven was filling the kitchen and her pregnant daughter, Theresa, was sitting on a high-backed kitchen stool trying to learn to knit. When the phone rang and she picked it up in the kitchen, she knew it was her husband. With the sixth sense that a policeman's wife develops, she also knew that the family would sit down to dinner without him.

Fazio was speaking low when she answered and she had to concentrate to hear him. "Hi, babe. Listen, do you remember Ava Turk?"

"Ava Turk? Of course I remember her. We organized the picnic together last summer."

"Did she ever mention her parents? Did she say where they live in Phoenix?"

"Are you talking about Ava Turk?"

"Yeah. Who are you talking about?"

"Frank, her parents live in Staten Island. Not Phoenix. What's all this about?" Her voice cracked slightly: "Why do you want to know about her parents? Is that who she's with? Nothing happened to Joe—did it?"

"No, no, c'mon, Connie, nothing like that. I just need to ask him a question, and I know he's at his in-laws. Next question. Do you know the name?"

"Now, let's see. What would be the word association?" Fazio smiled and tapped his finger against the pay phone impatiently. Connie was always reading self-improvement books. Her latest kick was this memory stuff. "Let's see," she went on. "It's the name of a dog. Now, which dog . . . ?"

"Spaniel, collie, mutt . . ." Fazio said quickly.

"No. No . . . wait, I have it! Great Dane!"

"Connie, Ava Turk's maiden name was Ava Great Dane?" Fazio said, exasperated.

"No. Dana! That's it. That's her parents' name. Dana on Staten Island. Don't know the first name. Frank? What's going on? I can tell by the tone in your voice something's going on. And when are you coming home? All the kids are here."

"I'll tell you what's going on when I get there, which should be in a few hours. Give my love to the kids."-

"Frank, I saw it on the news. I guess it's all over now, huh? But he looks like such a creep, that killer. How do you feel, Frank? Angry? You're not even talking about it. Well, I guess Hogan hogged the show again. Makes me mad. You worked on the case!"

"Don't worry about it, babe. That's his way. He needs the publicity and I don't."

"Now, Frank, you know you can't stand the way he's always . . ."

Just then the operator cut in and they were both forced to listen to the cracked tape recording that told them their time was up. "Gotta run, babe. See ya later," Fazio raced to say, then hung up. He put down the receiver and stared into space. He and Connie had been married almost twenty-five years. They had no secrets from each other. She told him he was jealous of the younger, flamboyant Hogan and, in a way, he supposed she had been right. But this time he had a secret that he was keeping from Connie—his hunch that Hogan had gotten the wrong man, that Ivan Roman couldn't kill a cockroach. Yet, was it a hunch, or just his jealousy? He didn't like the feelings he had now. He didn't even like himself. What was it that males go through in their forties? He wasn't sure it wasn't just his age. He wasn't sure of anything at the moment.

He dialed Staten Island information for a Dana. He was in luck. Of the five names he got, the first one was right. And Joe Turk was there. It sounded like a bad connection. He could hardly hear Joe Turk.

"Could you speak a little louder?" Fazio said.

"Sorry, Lieutenant. Big family party. Like this every year. Can you hear me now?" he shouted.

"Yeah, fine. Listen, Turk, I need some information."

"Shoot."

"That girl who left the note under Heather Cooper's door this morning—did you talk to her?"

"Of course. Why?"

"Got your notebook?"

"Yeah, in my jacket. Hold on a second. I'll get it."

Fazio could hear the delighted squeals of children and the loud babbling of the family get-together as he waited for Detective Turk.

"Hey, what's going on?" he asked when he returned. "Something I should know about? I saw the news. I heard it on the radio. Hogan brought him in. What's going on?"

"Take it easy, Turk. Hogan's sunning himself in Bermuda and I have the shit-work end of the case to pack it up. What about the girl?"

"Name's Jennifer North."

"Yeah, that's the one."

"Saw victim leave apartment approximately eleven-twenty-five in the company of Caucasian male, rather tall, wearing dark overcoat and a black-and-white-checkered cap," he read. "The man had a limp. . . . Yeah, well, that figures; this guy Roman has a bum leg; you could see it even on TV. Okay, she saw them for only a few seconds getting on the elevator . . . victim showed no signs of stress . . . couple laughing . . ." Turk was skimming now. "Jennifer North is a dancer in the New York Center Ballet Company, so forth and so forth. Not much else, Lieutenant. She lives five doors down from the deceased, and the rest of it is what she knew about Heather Cooper, habits, boyfriends, patterns, etc. Oh, yeah, she only saw them going into the elevator, so she saw the man from the back."

"That's it? Nothing more about that man?" Fazio made a mental note to question Jennifer North about those habits of her friend. He couldn't go into detail with Turk.

"Nope. That's it. Basic description she gave was tallish, black overcoat, and that limp. She did describe the hat as being kind of funky or unusual. She thought it had the shape of a police officer's hat and it was black-and-white-checked."

Fazio got Jennifer North's phone number, verified her address, and then said, keeping his voice casual, "Thanks a lot, Turk. Sorry to bother you. But with all this celebration, the parts are missing for the follow-up. You know the guys. Hey, Merry Christmas to you and your family."

"Lieutenant? Is there something I'm being left out of? It was my case, too. Any doubt about this Roman guy? I mean, I got home and I found out they found him. I mean, after the splash it got, you know, it would be real messy."

"Yeah, Turk, I agree. Real messy. But like I said, I'm on a routine check. Sorry I can't make it more dramatic for you. Also, it's a mess. You were the only one with this information. You're missing out on a great party. Hogan's footing the bill."

"Oh, yeah?"

On that note he hung up and dialed New York Center, going right through to the executive offices and reaching Mr. Zolinsky's exhausted assistant. He was told that Jennifer North left the theater after morning rehearsal, did not attend afternoon rehearsal, and was not performing that night. Fazio then dialed Jennifer North's apartment. He let it ring ten times. No answer. He hung up.

Fazio slid into a counter stool and ordered a cup of coffee. All he could think of was what a monumental fuck-up and con artist Hogan was. Why didn't anyone call Turk? Then they would have known there was a girl who saw a man, and this Jennifer North could have been brought in for an I.D., too. He held his hand over his mouth and stifled a belch.

Fazio sipped his coffee but his mind was elsewhere. It was on an image. He could see a black-and-white checkered cap. The one Turk was telling him about. Where had he seen it? Then he remembered. The kid. David Funke. He was wearing a cap just like the one Turk described. Interesting. David Funke had turned them on to Ivan Roman. That was very interesting. He plunked down some coins on the counter and started out of the diner.

Jennifer felt like she was swimming in a black sea and bobbing to the surface. She tried desperately to open her eyes but they were heavy, so heavy. They were glued together. When she did force them open, the bright, white light was so painful that she had to squeeze them shut again. She had to get the brick off of her head. It weighed a ton. She opened her eyes wide this time. There was no brick on her head. It only felt like that because she had been hit on the head. Hard. She looked around. Everything seemed white, shiny white. She tried to focus more clearly through the blurriness.

She was sitting straight up, leaning against a cold backrest. Her knees touched and felt stiff because her legs were extended straight out. She looked at her feet. They were tied together. Her hands and wrists were tied tightly, too. Something tight was around her mouth. She stretched her aching neck to get a better view. It was familiar. Then panic mounted in waves as she woke up, really woke up. She was sitting, tied up and gagged in an empty, cold bathtub. It was Max's bathtub.

Her eyes floated up to the thin rope of pointe shoes sagging in the middle under the weight and she re-membered. A quick chill made her shiver. Her own shoes were in her practice case. Would one of them go up there with her autograph on it and her body be found like . . . ?

She began to cry. Deep, racking sobs at first, until she found she couldn't breathe. Gasping, she tried to catch her breath. The gag was choking her. She shook her head frantically from side to side, trying to shake it off. But she had to stop because of the pounding in her head. She gave a grunt of frustration. Then she thought about the reality of it. It was unbelievable. Max . . . the Ballet Killer . . . Max . . . it was like a bad joke. But it was no joke.

Oh, God, how long had he left her like this? She twisted from her waist a little to ease the stiffness in her joints. What time was it? Why didn't she wear a watch? The apartment was quiet, very quiet. She was almost positive he had gone out. There were no sounds at all. Richard! He would be waiting at the restaurant and think she had ditched him. And her parents. They would be wondering where she was. She had to escape, fight, get out, do something.

The first thing that had to come off was the gag. She saw the bathtub spigot. If she could just bend over enough to put her mouth under it, she could at least loosen the gag. She rolled over on her side, grunted, and then flipped over onto her stomach. She inched up so that her head was under the large faucet and then she picked away, stabbing at one side and jabbing at the other until the gag slipped off and fell around her neck.

She exercised her jaw for a few seconds and then sat back up concentrating on her hands. He had tied them in intricate little knots. She would just have to be calm and patient and undo all those little knots one by one. It couldn't be too much worse than unraveling a knotted gold chain. Then she let out a sob of exasperation. How could she untie the knots if she couldn't reach her hands? Max had tied her hands together so that she couldn't get her right hand far enough over to pick at the knots on her left hand. Her left hand wouldn't reach over to her right hand. It wasn't a lot, but just enough to make it impossible. It was no use. Damn! He was crazy, but he was clever. A fresh spurt of tears trickled down to her chin.

She looked down at her ankles. They weren't as bad. She could at least try. It would have to be feet first, and she'd figure out what to do about her hands later. She smiled a crooked smile more like an angry grimace. Did he think she couldn't figure out a way to do it? Max had forgotten about her jazz dancing. She had this terrific stretch in her back. Groaning a little because she felt so stiff, she kept reaching, reaching until her chest touched her thighs, stretching, stretching until her awkwardly bound hands reached her feet. Fumbling at first, but going as fast as she could, she unscrambled, one hand at a time, the knots on her right leg. It was slow but she let out a victorious squeal each time one of the knots gave. Maybe her skill came from years of having to unknot the ties on her pointe shoes very quickly. After she had most of the knots loosened on her right leg, she began to feel a sense of hope. All she had to do was keep up the pace and she would free her legs. Then she would free herself.

When Richard arrived at the stage entrance of the State Theatre, he had no trouble getting in. He explained that he was a doctor and he had to talk to one of the dancers backstage because of an emergency. He was allowed to pass. He breathed a sigh of relief. They had let him through easily. A little too easily, he thought as he walked to the elevator.

When he got to Jennifer's dressing room, it was empty. The security guard was dozing. Maybe she was dressing downstairs. Sure, that was logical. She wouldn't want to come into this dressing room after Heather . . .

When he arrived on the floor below, he stopped two giggling girls from the corps. They were dressed in bathrobes, hair pushed up in buns, eyes already slanted like does.

"Have you seen Jennifer North?" he asked both of them.

They looked at each other and thought for a moment. Finally, one said, "She doesn't use our dressing room anymore. I wouldn't know." They both turned and walked away.

He turned the corner and saw the dressing room of two male soloists. The door was half-open. One dancer was singing his off-key version of an aria from Pagliacci and the other was laughing at his amateur attempt. Hesitantly, Richard knocked on the door. Both men turned around and saw him.

"Excuse me. I'm looking for Jennifer North."

One dancer smiled, looking Richard up and down. "Sorry, we have segregated dressing rooms. Girls don't dress with boys."

"I know that," he sighed, beginning to feel like Alice in Wonderland. "I already checked her dressing room. The thing is it's an emergency and I can't find her. I know she's not dancing tonight, but I thought perhaps, at the last minute, she might be covering for someone—you know? She must be."

The two dancers looked sympathetic. "But the truth is, she's not dancing tonight. Or covering. There was one injury, but it wasn't a girl dancer."

"Please, don't talk about it," said the dancer nearest the door. "I'll be lucky if I survive what I have to do tonight without an injury. Such shifting, like you've never seen."

The dancer who was continuing to apply his makeup was still trying to help Richard. "I saw her at the *Artemis* rehearsal, but she wasn't at *Bayadère*. Someone covered for her."

"Wasn't at *Bayadère*?" Richard asked incredulously.

"But the switchboard operator said she was. She was supposed to give her a message."

The dancer stopped applying his makeup. "Listen, we never get messages around here at the right time. And I wouldn't worry. The schedules are so screwed up lately, she was probably not in *Bayadère* because she was at a rehearsal for *Stars and Stripes*."

Richard turned to walk away. "Oh, well, thank you. I appreciate it."

One of the dancers shouted after him, "Listen, look at it this way; you'd be in a sorrier state if they hadn't found the Ballet Killer."

Richard came running back to the dressing room. "What? When? They found the Ballet Killer?"

"Didn't you know?" the dancer near the door said. "My, God, it's been on the news all day."

"I guess I've been in a fog," Richard said feebly.

The soloist who was now putting the finishing touches on his makeup smiled. "I'll say. Here." He handed Richard the *Daily News*. Richard's eyes almost popped out. The headline, covering almost one-third of the front page, screamed: BALLET KILLER FOUND!

Richard stood trance-like, clutching the paper, trying to get every word until the dancer who gave it to him grabbed it away from him, laughing. "Sorry to be stingy. But you can go get your own. I'm framing this under glass."

Richard nodded and thanked both dancers again. As he walked down the hall he was aware that they were watching the movement of his buttocks and legs as he walked. Richard was used to Jennifer's world, was even used to homosexual dancers, but he would be willing to bet his face was crimson-red as he walked that long hall. Still, he felt less uneasy than he did about a dancer by the name of Yuri Ivanov. Now, he was something to worry about. And he was dancing with Jennifer. partnering her. Funny, he could never understand what women saw in the man. Still, it must be something. Yuri Ivanov used women like other men used a box of Kleenex during a cold.

Richard then saw what he had overlooked or couldn't see before. The tension was gone backstage. There were celebrations going on in the dressing rooms. Everywhere there was an atmosphere of gaiety and relief. He noticed now that as dancers came out of their dressing rooms there were no quiet taps of *"merde"* for luck, but big bear hugs and kisses. He smiled at it all. Then he stopped walking.

Coming toward him was Yuri Ivanov, strutting down the hall in tall boots, a fur cap, and skin-tight, silver-studded Levi's. On his arm, brushing her breasts against his suede vest, was a much taller brunette in a red gown. Richard was savvy enough to realize it wasn't one of Yuri's girls. He was squiring her around, giving her the grand tour, because she had enough money to be a patron.

"Yuri!" he yelled.

"Oh, yes." He smiled. "The boyfriend."

Richard gritted his teeth but forced a smile. "Listen, I'm looking for Jennifer. I haven't talked to her all day. Have you seen her?"

"Yeeeees. At *Artemis* rehcarsal. And then not for rest of day. Sorry." He smiled at Richad, his amber eyes sparkling. "But is terrific what happened, no? Not so much worry, then, huh?" And then just as suddenly Richard didn't exist for him and he turned his charm back to the brunette hanging on his arm.

Richard walked down the hall, avoided the stage entrance, and cut across to the passageway that led to the buildings that the audience entered and left by. For a year he had worried so much about Jennifer and this Ballet-Killer threat that dominated their lives that he had gotten used to it. Okay, she was upset about Heather. So was he. But the fact that the killer was found colored everything. And maybe it was just a question of unfortunate coincidences. She might have called him when all the lines in the office were tied up or she might have run out of dimes. Or maybe she went shopping to celebrate. It was getting close to Christmas. He began to walk with a brisker, more confident pace. He'd stop and get a newspaper and read about the whole glorious thing over a drink while he was waiting for Jennifer at Ming Joy's.

The woman sat in a bright, red plastic chair. The tables in the drab ward cafeteria were lined with the small, almost childlike chairs done in all the colors of a box of crayons. She sat quietly, slowly twisting and turning the hem of her cotton dress through her fist. It was a hospital dress. They had given it to her. They could have it back. She wanted out of this place.

Soon two men entered the room. One was a doctor in a white coat who nodded hello to her and sat down opposite her. The other was her son, who kissed her on her softly wrinkled cheeks. "Mama, how nice you look. Here, I got you two candy bars. Just what you asked for." Eagerly, the woman started to unpeel the wrapping, first on one, then on the other. Her dress was clean and ironed, her fingernails had been filed, and her hair was combed. She even wore a touch of makeup, very faint, just right. Max Forrest prayed she wouldn't jam both candy bars into her mouth at once and ruin everything.

"Mama," he said carefully, sending a message, "the doctor wants to talk to you about our little visit over Christmas."

The doctor looked at his watch. He didn't have

very much time. "Yes," he said, looking carefully at the woman. "Your son has requested that you be allowed to take your first home pass for Christmas. It would be considered a weekend. Do you want to do that, Mrs. Forrest?"

The woman nodded and said "yes," but her voice was flat, expressionless.

"Well, we're going to give it a try. But if you find yourself in a bar or anyone else finds you there, I can assure you there will be no more visits for a long, long time."

The woman nodded solemnly in agreement.

She was a social drinker. Why couldn't anyone understand that? Just a little belt now and then. To ease the pain. Because the pain got deeper when Max took all her dreams and crushed them. No one could make her believe he did it by accident. She had a right to drink. But it wasn't her fault. She wasn't an alcoholic. She didn't need a drink or anything like that.

The doctor stole another quick look at his watch. "At any sign of trouble, your son has promised to bring you back." He creased his forehead. "You were very, very sick today but we've decided it was due to the shock treatments. You don't have to have any more shock, Mrs. Forrest. We want to see, instead, how you will improve with your holiday." He smiled benevolently, a skill he had perfected.

The woman nodded again, fingering the unwrapped candy bars. "When can I get out of here?" she asked in the same hollow monotone.

The doctor, who was just getting up to leave, sighed. "It's very complicated, Mrs. Forrest. You were sent here by a judge for creating continuous public disturbances in bars and for repeated shoplifting charges. You will go before a hospital review board shortly." He looked her directly in the eye. "That doesn't mean you'll pass. But as the doctor in charge, I do have the authority to prescribe occasional short visits the other patients are allowed. Your son, however, is wholly responsible. You don't want to get your son in any kind of difficulty, do you, Mrs. Forrest?"

She shook her head violently.

"Good, because he seems a good son and a very responsible person. Have a nice holiday and I wish you both a Merry Christmas."

He stood up, shook hands with Max, and walked briskly out of the room. Max looked at his watch. They still had a few minutes together for a visit. They could hear the doctor outside talking to the nurses.

"Nice doctor," Max said amiably.

His mother smiled and nodded.

They were both quiet, listening for receding footsteps. Finally, they heard them. There was silence. They looked at each other and Charlotte Forrest let out a laugh. It was more like a snort.

Then abruptly she stopped laughing and said in a voice no one in the hospital had ever heard her use, "Why did you kill that girl? I saw it on television!"

"Now, Mama, shh!" Max bowed his head, obviously agitated. "I knew what I was doing. Trust me."

"Trust you," she said spitefully. "We had agreed that it would be Judge Cooper's daughter. It was perfect. You could have killed her afterward." Now her voice was vibrant, animated.

"Now, now, Mama, she really wasn't right."

"Don't touch me, you pervert. You don't know what to do with a woman. You come one step closer and I'll kick you in the . . . balls! You

*tricked me. Had me come over here. Don't tell me
I don't understand . . . goddamned Gimp!"*

He stared straight ahead, remembering it. His
mother punched him in the arm.

"Why not?"

"She fought back. Would have been trouble. It's
better this way."

"How better? She's dead."

"Mama," he pleaded, whining, "I'm only doing this
for you." He smiled inwardly. He loved it. Killing
them. Playing with their bodies first and then watching the life ebb out of them. Taking them by surprise.
Of course, Mama didn't know about the other. He
would never tell her. She definitely wouldn't approve.

"Max!" she said sharply.

"Yes, Mama!" He sat up straighter in the ridiculous
plastic chair, obedient again. Then he broke into a
toothy grin. "I've found someone better. She's star ma-
terial. Better than the other one. This time it's right."

"Tell me about her," she said. "Do you have her?
Can you keep from killing her? Can we do it or not?"

Max raised his hands for her to stop, and she did.

"Everything will be done exactly as I promised,"
he said. His mother smiled and relaxed. Then, happily, she started to jam the now-melty chocolate bars
into her mouth. She took first one bite from one and
then from the other. He noticed the chocolate smudges
on her fingertips and quickly wiped them off with his
handkerchief.

"Good behavior, Mama, promise? Or it's not going to work. They said you attacked some old man."

"Don't remember. Oh, him? I didn't like his looks.
For a moment I thought it was . . . oh, forget it. This
damned medication they give me. I just crave candy."

"Listen, Mama, for the plan to work we need *that* medicine!"

"Pills?"

"No. The doctor said you were given an injection of it."

"Oh, that. No problem." She cackled. "Haven't I lifted bigger things than that?" Her voice drifted off on the last words. Those days were over. All those new security measures in the department stores today. She started to hum, licking the rest of the sweet brown splotches from the candy wrappers.

Max didn't have time to wait until his mother remembered their plan and returned to her normal self. He shook her by the shoulders. Suddenly she looked at him alertly.

"Can you get some?" he asked.

His mother nodded.

"Okay. Here's the paper."

"The what?"

"The newspaper, Mama. On page ten there are instructions. They'll tell you exactly what to do. Don't show the paper to anyone, and rip it up as soon as you read it. Don't let anyone see that message. It will tell you what you must do before I pick you up tomorrow afternoon. Mama, this is very important!"

His mother was gaping at the newspaper with its huge headline that covered three-quarters of the page: BALLET THRILLER KILLER'S CAREER OVER!

She looked admiringly at her son. "I thought you knew," he said.

She laughed. "Who, me? I've been half-zonked all day." She put her hand on her son's wrist and rubbed it. "Ah, Maximillian, I underestimated you."

Max blushed and looked at the floor. "Thanks, Mama."

"Please, Mama, tell me I'm a good boy. Don't hit me. I like it when you tell me I'm a good boy. Ow! I'll be good for you. I promise. Don't hit me, Mama. I love you."

It was getting late. He helped her out of the chair and said, "We both have a lot to do before tomorrow, don't we?"

But when they left, Max's spirits sank because he saw that his mother had left the newspaper on the table. He rushed back and planted it firmly under her arm. When they walked out the door a student nurse was waiting at the big doors that locked the ward to let Max out. Max kissed his mother good-bye.

The student nurse stifled a yawn. "Say good-bye to your son, Mrs. Forrest. It's getting late." But her eyes were devouring Max. He was one of the best-looking men she'd seen in a long time. There was just something so charming about him. She explored his hands for any sign of a small gold band but found nothing. Maybe next time she would find a clever way of approaching him. It didn't matter if his mother was crazy. He was adorable.

"Good-bye, Max, dear." Frantically, Max raised ten fingers to remind his mother to look at page ten in the paper. She smiled and said, "I'll look for you around ten o'clock." The last was said loudly and Max breathed a sigh of relief. She had gotten his message. She knew he would pick her up in the afternoon. There was too much to do to come any earlier.

Jennifer's hands were still shaking as she successfully untied the last of the knots around her left leg. In the process, both of her feet had fallen asleep and her legs were almost numb. Perspiration was forming on her forehead in tiny little drops. Her beautifully long, tapered nails were chipped and stubby. She shook her legs out first and then very quickly did pointe and flex exercises to get her feet, calves, and thighs working all at once. When she was fairly sure of her control, she folded her legs under her, cross-legged, because she couldn't really grasp onto anything, and stood up in almost one fluid motion. She slipped a little, scaring herself, but quickly balanced against the tiled wall with her shoulder until she was firmly upright.

She stood for just a second to catch her breath. Everything was quiet. Then she stepped out of the empty tub and quickly ran to the bathroom door. She could open it with just one hand, even though they were both tied together. And then what? What if Max was still in the apartment? She pressed her ear to the door for several minutes. Then she yelled, "Max! Max!" No answer. That didn't mean he wasn't there. But she was positive he wasn't. She would hear him walking around. The floor creaked. And there was no light coming in from the cracks around the door. The apartment was silent and safe. All she had to do was run out quickly.

Her heart felt like she could hear it pumping in her chest. She turned the door handle. It was stuck. She tried her left hand and twisted it around so hard she hurt her wrist. Then she kicked the door and stomped her feet up and down, crying angrily like a little child. The goddamned door was locked from the outside.

She looked around her, her breathing all out of control. She was trapped. In a little box with a toilet and a tub and those hideous toe shoes. She mustn't look at them. She was liable to lose her sanity. She focused her gaze straight ahead. And then she saw it. Behind the shower curtain was that small window. She had forgotten. A window. An opening to the outside. She rushed over and shoved the shower curtain aside. Awkwardly, she tried to open it. She placed both hands, still separated by ropes, on the top and tried to pull the window up. With all the effort she had, she kept trying until her palms burned. It just wouldn't budge. She studied the bottom of the sill, where the problem had to be. Sure enough. Max had had his bathroom painted recently because there were strips of hardened paint around the bottom. He probably never opened the window. She thought for a moment. All she really needed was something to scrape off that paint and then maybe it would budge.

Walking across the tub, she opened the medicine cabinet over the sink. He had everything you would find in a normal man's medicine cabinet, including a shaver, and it wasn't electric. If there was a shaver, there had to be a razor blade. And there it was, on the second shelf. She almost sobbed in relief. Gingerly, she lifted one out, hoping she could cut the binds around her aching hands first. But again the gap was too wide. She could try manipulating her wrist, but even then the razor was about a half-inch away. It would take hours and hours of little stabbing attempts, and she didn't even have minutes. If she was right, and she knew she was, Max was out of the apartment. But he could come back any minute!

She went quickly to the window. Working fast but cautiously, she was able to slice and lift off some of the major chunks of paint around the rim of the sill. Again she tried to force the window open from the top, but it still wouldn't lift. It did seem looser, though, but maybe it was her imagination. Trying not to give in to the panic of claustrophobia, she jabbed, stabbed, slashed, and hacked every which way with the razor. When she nicked her finger, she sucked the oozing blood until it stopped. Then she put the razor down again and with all her might put her separated hands on the bottom of the window and pushed. When the window went flying up and the first cold blast of air hit her face, she never noticed the pain in her hands as they slammed against the top sides of the window with the force. Tears were streaming down her sweaty face as she stuck her head out of the little window. It was so dark out. A light snow was falling, almost a rain now. She leaned out as far as she could and looked around, up and down. She stared blankly. No ledge, no fire escape, no nothing. The only way out would be down, four stories down, and she'd have to jump. She might live, but she'd never be able to dance again. The courtyard below was cement and was only covered with a thin, icy blanket of snow.

But if she didn't jump, Max would kill her just like all the others. She thought of her funeral. Richard crying, her parents crying, the whole company paying her homage . . . well, some of the company. It would be just like the funeral they would have for Heather tomorrow morning. She didn't think she had any more tears left, but she cried again for the sadness of it all. And Richard. He would grieve and then, eventually, marry another girl. Someone who was less trouble than she was. A nice, normal girl his mother approved of. College-educated. Not a ballerina. She gave up then and put her face in her hands. It was too much. Too much to ask anyone to have to go through. If she had to die, why couldn't she have been run over by a car instead of this? Then she saw the thin rope quivering with the outside breeze. Her constant reminder that eleven other girls went through probably much the same thing. She would make an even dozen.

She shuddered. It was cold out. She was still trying to decide whether to risk the jump or not when she saw clearly that there were three buildings facing the courtyard in a crooked semicircle. There were other buildings behind them. All of the buildings had people in them. She could see because drapes were drawn and curtains were pulled aside and shades were up. People were moving about. Some were more clear than others. Here and there she saw the glow of a television set or the on-off sparkle of the lights on Christmas trees. It looked to her like campfires in the wilderness. But it was the people she was most intrigued about. They moved about like characters in a silent movie. Beautiful, blessed people.

Her decision was made for her. She took a deep breath and filled her lungs with air. Then she screamed at the top of her voice, "Heeeelp! Murrrrrder! Heeeeellp Meeeeeee!"

Chapter Seven

There was a man once. A widower. He lived in the neighborhood. He tuned pianos. Charlotte thought he was a nice man. But Max used to sit in the living room every time he came to call. Max didn't like the piano tuner, whatever his name was. The man told her there was something wrong with her son. That he needed to have friends. Get out and play. One night the man touched her breast and tried to pull her dress up over her thighs. Then she knew why he had said what he had about Max. He wanted to get rid of her little boy so he could try dirty things. She threw him out and told him never to come back.

WHEN FAZIO LEFT the diner, his head was down and his mind was trying to weave together impossible threads. Until it actually happened, he had no idea that he was going to slam right into someone trying to come through the door as he was trying to go out.

"Excuse me," he muttered.

"Lieutenant!" came a booming voice. Fazio stood in the doorway with Sergeant Moskowitz with enough light to see his carrot-colored hair and light blue eyes. Moskowitz was the only Jew on the force who was automatically assumed to be an Irishman until he introduced himself.

They walked out together. "Lieutenant, what a coincidence! You're just the person I wanted to see. Looked all over for you, but you had left."

"Moskowitz, maybe another time. I'm kind of in a hurry. Listen, let me buy you a drink real soon."

"Aw, c'mon, Lieutenant. It's Christmas, it's a celebration. Let *me* buy you a drink, huh?"

"Weren't you going in there for coffee?"

"Nah, I just remembered I forgot to call my wife. But she can wait."

Fazio smiled for the first time. "Guess they always do. But, really, Bernie, not tonight."

Moskowitz colored slightly when he heard his first name from Fazio. Okay, he lost. But he was damned if he would leave it that way. Not the way he felt.

"Okay, Lieutenant, then let me walk you to your car. I assume you're parked close by. You see, I really have something to tell you and I hate saying it this way, but . . . what the hell?"

Fazio was surprised by Sergeant Moskowitz's sudden outburst but didn't show it. They walked up Broadway in silence for a while. Finally Moskowitz blurted out, "Look, Lieutenant, maybe I'm way out of line, but I think all the talk about you happens to be bullshit."

"Talk? What talk?" Fazio said, though he had been aware something like that was going on.

"Oh, c'mon, Lieutenant, you don't have to kid me. I'm your friend. You know what the gossip is. You're jealous of Hogan and all that. Hogan made you look like a jerk. Listen, Lieutenant, I happen to think Hogan is a horse's ass and you got dumped on royally. You're a damned good homocide detective. The best in my book."

"Moskowitz, how much did you have to drink?" Fazio's voice was gruff and hoarse, but Moskowitz could see he was touched.

"Not that much, Lieutenant," the sergeant said laconically. They had stopped to wait for a light before crossing the street. The two men stared at each other for a second. Then Fazio said, "Say, Moskowitz, how much do you want to pass that detective's exam?"

"You know how much, Lieutenant. It's not my first time. I don't know. Maybe I get nervous."

"Now, let me ask you another question. Do you think Ivan Roman is the Ballet Killer?"

Moskowitz looked surprised. He chewed on his lip, thinking. "I don't know. It checks out. I mean, I never thought to question it. Captain Hogan definitely thinks it's him."

"Exactly. And what did you just say you thought of Hogan?"

"That he's a horse's ass. The man is interested in promoting himself and . . ." Moskowitz stopped in mid-sentence. "I think I see what you're getting at. But I don't think he would go that far just to . . ."

Fazio clapped him on the back. "Moskowitz, believe me, I'm not saying that, either. I don't think Hogan would go that far . . ."

"Then what are you saying?" Moskowitz interrupted him.

"I'm not saying anything. Say, are you curious enough to come somewhere with me and help answer this question? Because if you are, you're welcome."

Moskowitz was out of uniform and he had his days off. But he knew if he didn't go with Fazio he wouldn't be able to keep his mind off it. "Remind me to call my wife," he said.

They walked the short way to where Fazio's car was parked and passed a pay phone. Moskowitz made his phone call and Fazio made one afterward. He called Jennifer's North's number. Again he got no answer. Fazio stopped to double-check an address in the beat-up old phone book and they were ready to go.

Their drive wasn't very far. In about ten minutes they were ringing the doorbell of an apartment on One-hundred-tenth Street, close to Columbia University. Fazio breathed a silent sigh of relief when the voice of David Funke yelled down three flights. There was no intercom system.

"Hey, remember me, Mr. Funke? It's Lieutenant Frank Fazio."

There was no answer at first. Then David Funke yelled down, "Any law says I have to let you up?"

"Nope. But we just have some routine questions. Take a minute. No statement."

"Okay," the voice drifted down.

Fazio and Moskowitz hiked up three long flights until they got to David Funke's apartment. The door was open in the small studio apartment and they just walked in. David Funke was sitting at the piano making marks on music paper.

"Theory," he explained when they walked in. Fazio closed the door behind them. David Funke indicated the studio bed in the apartment. The piano took up most of the space. Fazio could see it was a Steinway baby grand. The studio bed was nothing more than a roll-away bed with a cover and some small pillows piled on it. There were a few books on the floor, piles and stacks of music, a stereo, and a stack of records, mostly classical. There were orange crates and some shaggy pieces of small furniture most likely found on the street after someone had discarded them. A typical struggling student's digs, except for the magnificent piano.

Fazio sat on the studio bed with Moskowitz and kept his eye on one of the orange crates. On top of it sat David Funke's black-and-white-checkered cap. It was just as he remembered it and just what Turk had described.

"Mr. Funke, we just want to double-check your I.D. of the man we brought you in to see."

"Ivan Roman?" he said, somewhat arrogantly.

"Without me, you would have gotten the wrong guy, huh?"

Fazio smiled. Moskowitz, sitting right next to him, recognized it as one of his fake smiles. He had seen him use it once before he got very nasty.

"Oh, yes, Ivan Roman. But I need to clarify something, Mr. Funke. You said you had seen him hanging around Lincoln Center several times. Is that right?"

"Yeah, that's right. I never forget a face." He now had the funniest feeling he should be on the defensive. It was the tone of Lieutenant Fazio's voice.

"Did he ever wear a hat?" Fazio's eyes were squarely on the checkered cap resting on the orange crate. "Say, oh, like that one." David Funke glanced over at his hat and then back to Fazio.

He shook his frizzy head of hair vehemently. "Nope. I never saw it. Not once did he wear a hat. No matter how cold. I told you that's one of the things I thought was weird about him."

Fazio lowered his voice. Moskowitz waited. *Here it comes,* he thought.

"How long have you known Heather Cooper?" Fazio said gruffly, locking his eyes into David Funke's.

Funke, sitting on the piano stool, almost reeled off. "Who?"

"You heard me. Heather Cooper. The last victim of the Ballet Killer."

David Funke's face went pale and he started pacing the small room. Then he got his color back and turned angrily on Fazio. "Are *you* crazy? Boy, try to be of some help and this is what I get. What is this, the C.I.A.?" He jabbed a finger in the air. "You know how long I've known Heather Cooper. Never when she was alive. And for a few minutes when I saw her floating around, a frozen stiff with a toe shoe hanging from her neck."

Fazio studied the young man carefully. He saw the neck muscles vibrate in his anger and the sick look of nausea that passed over his face when he remembered the scene he had witnessed.

Fazio raised his hand. "Okay, okay," he said, softening his voice to a soothing lull. "I had to ask. Part of the routine questioning. Say, where did you get that hat?"

David Funke flipped his head around to the cap resting on the orange crate. Something weird was happening, but he couldn't keep up. The sudden switch in mood had him in a mild state of shock. "That?" he answered dully. "At a men's shop on Times Square. Right in the middle of Times Square near all those porno flicks. They have the kind of hats I like. Why?"

Fazio shrugged. "Just wondered."

Moskowitz watched the whole exchange as if he were at a tennis match. But the only thing that moved were his eyes.

Finally, David Funke exploded. "Hey, wait just a second, here! This isn't a routine investigation, is it? I have the strangest feeling you think *I'm* the killer!" He sat down on a flimsy chair and wiped his brow. "But that's crazy. They have Ivan Roman. I helped."

Fazio looked down at his hands. He had to be very careful. He wasn't Lieutenant Frank Fazio of the task force anymore. He was a cop going against the whole department. One slip and he would prove nothing. He changed his tactics to honesty.

"Look, kid, no one thinks you're the killer. It's just that last night when Heather Cooper left her apartment she was seen with someone wearing a black-and-white-checkered cap exactly like yours."

Moskowitz's eyes opened wide but he said nothing.

David Funke was still on the defensive. "Well, believe me, I wasn't with her. I didn't even have the cap then. I just bought it this morning before I came to see you. I mean, I had one just like it, but I lost it two days ago. Then it got cold so I bought another one just like it." He looked at both men intensely. "Just because I never saw Ivan Roman in a hat doesn't mean Ivan Roman never wore a hat, does it?"

Fazio smiled and stood up. Moskowitz followed. "No, you're right," he said, though he couldn't picture Roman in a funky hat like that. "Say, do they sell a lot of those hats at that store? Where is it?"

"Middle of Forty-second Street. You can't miss it. I don't remember the name. Yeah, they always have the hats."

"But maybe they carry them all around."

"Nah, I've never seen them. They're kind of different, you know?"

Fazio reached over to shake the stunned young man's hand. "Again, you've been a great help, Mr. Funke."

David Funke stared at the two detectives. "Oh, I get it. You guys really don't think it's this guy, do you? You're still looking. Hey, this is real interesting. If I can be of any help . . ."

Fazio laughed and slapped Funke on the back. "C'mon, kid, this isn't television. Nope. Just a routine check, like I said."

Moskowitz laughed, too. Up until this time David Funke hadn't heard him say anything. "Just drudgery—that's all detective work is. For excitement, even we got to go to the movies." He laughed again.

It wasn't until both men left the tiny studio apartment and walked down the steps and were outside that either of them allowed themselves to speak. Moskowitz let out a whoosh of air and a contained, "Well, I'll be damned!"

Fazio lit a cigarette and inhaled deeply. But he said nothing.

"I was on that floor all afternoon, all morning, the night before, and no one said anything about a witness. Someone saw Heather Cooper leave the building with a man?"

"It was her neighbor, a young ballerina in her company, good friend. Dancer by the name of Jennifer North."

Moskowitz shook his head from side to side in sheer disbelief. Finally, he said, "Then why didn't Hogan call *her* in for an I.D. Even if the guy she saw wasn't the killer, she was a witness. And this thing about Roman always hatless and the man with Heather Cooper before the murder in this checkered hat. That should have been checked out, Lieutenant."

"Moskowitz, you're going to make a good detective. Jennifer North wasn't called in because Turk went off duty and Hogan didn't get or read his report on time. Or maybe he did and didn't bother with it. Because the way he saw it, the case was solved."

Moskowitz scratched his head. "That's really a little sloppy, you know what I mean?"

"Hogan doesn't think so. He's winging his way to Bermuda, thinking he's got the killer."

"I wonder who Heather Cooper was with last night."

Fazio chose his words very carefully. It was hard to be a department of one. "That's what I'm wondering. That's what I'd like to try to find out, Moskowitz."

"But, Lieutenant, you have no orders. You're going against the department. Alone."

Fazio nodded. "But, you see, I think whoever she was with, in the time span we have, had to be the murderer. And I just can't see Heather Cooper going out with Ivan Roman without force. Turk, who interviewed Jennifer North, says there was no pressure. So she was presumably out for an evening of fun. On the other hand, the man she was with limped. So the evidence still points toward Roman. And I just have this hunch, Moskowitz, that he is not the killer."

"I get the picture, Lieutenant."

"I don't think you do, Moskowitz. There are risks involved." Fazio knew he was taking a risk even now, but he trusted his instincts. He knew what was coming next.

"Lieutenant, I'd like to help you. You can't do it alone."

"But, Moskowitz, there are risks involved for you, too. I could be wrong, and if anyone got wind of this . . ."

"I'm on, Lieutenant. Tell me what to do." Fazio made a vow that Bernie Moskowitz would pass that detective's exam no matter what.

"Okay. The first thing to do is go to that little store on Forty-second Street and check out those hats. See if they keep any records . . . if they take Visa or Master Charge. It's not much to go on. But it's a beginning."

"Right, Lieutenant. What about you?"

"Me, I'm going to the Titanic. But we'll meet at the two-oh. Wait for me."

Moskowitz stared at him.

"I'm not going there for a drink. There's a certain bartender I'd like to know more about." Fazio pulled out his notebook and flipped through the pages. "Ah, yes, Jerry Turner. A young man who acts a little strange and has a fetish for ballerinas."

Fazio dropped Moskowitz off at the subway and then continued to the Titanic. His acid stomach was burbling again. Poor Moskowitz. Well, if he wanted to be a detective he might as well learn what it was like.

It was worth a try, anyway. Never could tell when luck would be on your side.

Jennifer kept screaming for help. She had no idea how many minutes had passed, but her throat burned so much she could hardly swallow. No one answered back.

Exhausted, she stepped back into the tub, walked across it, took both tied hands, and turned on the sink water. She bent under the faucet and took deep gulps. Then she turned the faucet off and walked back to look out the window and think clearly for a minute. The snow had stopped entirely. The night was clear. She realized her teeth were chattering. But, of course, it was freezing out. Not one neighbor had a window open. No wonder no one heard her.

A tear trickled down her cheek and she knew water was dribbling down her chin, but she didn't care. She couldn't give up. She would just have to yell even louder and longer. It was her only chance now Somewhere out there was just one fresh-air fiend who had a window opened, even if it was just a crack. She would make that person hear her.

If Jennifer could have crossed her fingers, she would have. She took a deep, deep breath, praying. *This is for you, fresh-air person out there. Please hear me. Please?* The eerie sound that peeled from her wide-open mouth panicked her. It was so terrifying, so hysterical it didn't seem as if it came from her.

"Heeelllp! Murrrder! Hey! Somebody! Heeeelp!" Finally, she choked on her saliva and had to stop for a second. In that silence she realized something. Someone was screaming back. Someone had heard her.

Jennifer leaned hungrily out of the window, looking up and down, trying to discern where the voice was coming from. Her own voice was hoarse now. But she needed just enough power to shout the address and apartment number for the police. She never got the chance.

She watched in horror as a gray-haired woman slammed her window shut. Before she did, Jennifer heard what she was yelling loud and clear. "Turn down that goddamned TV! I got a sick husband!"

Jennifer stared in disbelief. She screamed one more time, "I'm not a TV! I'm a person and somebody's trying to murder me!" But no one heard her enraged, sore voice. It was too late. She stumbled out of the tub and slumped to the cold tile floor. She curled up in the fetal position contemplating the existence of God. If there was a God, why was this happening to her? Had she been such a terrible person? These things happened to people you didn't know about, people you turned off the television for so you didn't have to hear about them on the news. And then she caught herself. This thing had happened to Heather.

She sat up. Was that a noise? Yes, it was a door slamming. And more noises. Footsteps. Coming closer. Jennifer stuffed her knuckle into her mouth to stop from screaming. Max was back.

Across the courtyard the woman with the gray hair who had screamed at Jennifer sat on the edge of her husband's bed. "That TV woke you up, didn't it? There's no consideration anymore. Everything has to be loud. Must be that music they listen to. Makes them deaf."

The man in bed shook his head. "No, I'm not so sure it was a TV. I heard the screaming. I'll tell you, it sounded like someone in trouble."

"Yeah, trouble. Who wants to know about trouble? Trouble invites more trouble. You know the way the neighborhood's changed over the years."

"I think we should call the police."

"Yeah?"

The man nodded his head, his eyelids starting to close as his head sank back on the pillow. The woman laid her hand across his warm forehead. "Okay, maybe you're right. But first let me get you some more soup. The doctor said plenty of liquids."

When the woman returned with the plate of soup, she smiled maternally. Her husband had fallen asleep. His mouth was open and his head had rolled to one side of the pillow. He had a sweet, peaceful smile on his face. Better not to disturb him. She switched off the light on the night table and tucked the comforter up under his chin, though the apartment got so steamy she had to keep some windows open. She tiptoed out of the bedroom, humming, their conversation completely forgotten.

The doorbell rang at the Cooper town house in the East Fifties. The housekeeper shuffled up and peered out the big bay windows. No more reporters, she hoped. She saw a dignified gentleman with a fur coat and hat and recognized him immediately. "Mr. Zolinsky!" she cried, opening the door. "Oh, I'm so glad you're here. I . . . I still can't believe it. I've taken care of Heather since she was eight. Like a daughter to me." She was dabbing her eyes with a sopping-wet Kleenex.

Mr. Zolinsky touched her arm. "I know, Alice. Where is he?"

She pointed down the hall to the library, where Martin Cooper had not moved since he first sat down in the chair earlier today. She said, sadly, "He's not himself. Don't be shocked." Then she walked quickly down the long hallway back to the kitchen.

Zolinsky hung up his hat and coat and started to-

ward the library. The house was dear and familiar to
him. He had spent much time there and was probably
the reason Martin had allowed Heather to move into
her own apartment in the first place. He didn't want
his daughter to bask in any favoritism. Zolinsky
sighed. She didn't need it. He had lost a potentially
brilliant ballerina. But the man in the library had lost
a beloved daughter.

It had gotten dark out but Martin Cooper hadn't
bothered to turn on any lights. Zolinsky turned on
a small lamp that would not disturb Martin but would
let him see his way into the room. There, slumped in a
big chair, was the large shape of Martin Cooper. Yet
somehow he appeared shrunken. His shoulders were
hunched, his chest sunken. He sat there staring into
space. Zolinsky wondered what was running through
his mind or what he could possibly hope to find in
the shadows, poor man.

He crept softly in and touched him gently from behind on his shoulder. "My dear Martin, what can I
say? What can anyone possibly say?"

"Grischa," Cooper said in a ghostly voice.

Zolinsky pulled up a needlepoint-covered stool and
sat literally at the man's feet. He placed his hands on
Cooper's knees for just a second.

"Have you eaten?" The rigid figure shook his head.

"Some tea, perhaps? A brandy?" Again Martin
Cooper shook his head.

There was a long silence in the room. Neither said
anything. A clock somewhere in the old town house
chimed the quarter-hour. Almost eight. Zolinsky had
much to do. But his place, he knew, was right where
he was.

"Listen, Martin," Zolinsky began in a careful voice,
"very few people call me Grischa. You are my very
good friend. The others, they call me Mr. Zolinsky or

Mr. Z., but you . . ." He leaned forward and looked intensely into those vacant, staring eyes. "Martin, I know the grief you feel. . . ."

For the first time there was a hint of life in Martin Cooper's voice as he interrupted him. "You? What do you know about grief? You've never lost a wife you loved more than life itself in a plane crash. You've never had a daughter murdered by a maniac for no reason at all."

Zolinsky cleared his throat. He debated the wisdom of telling Martin they had found the killer. Obviously the news hadn't broken through his prison of mourning. He finally decided this wouldn't be the best time. The agony of knowing that if they had only caught the man yesterday Heather would be alive today would be too much for him to take.

"Martin, Martin," he continued, "there are all kinds of grief. To each it means something different. I do not show mine. You do. Maybe that's better, but in time it will pass. All the girls I lost were like children to me. And wives? Martin, I had four wives. All ballerinas. I made them stars. I served them. And they all left me. But always I returned to my work. Believe me, you must, too. Your work is with us now, and we need you at the theater. Take a few more days, rest, but then you must come back. For your own good."

Martin Cooper looked straight at Zolinsky. "I am never setting foot in that theater again. I'm through. You can rip up my contract; you can sue me. I want nothing to do with ballet ever again." Zolinsky felt numb. That voice, so lifeless, so chilling. He stood up. For just a second, he lingered, wanting to say something more, be more comforting, more persuasive. But he understood. What could he say to the man? What did he have a right to say? He walked out of the room, silently, collected his hat and coat, and left his friend's house.

The snow had stopped but it was bitterly cold as Fazio walked into Jennifer North's apartment building. His car was double-parked out front. He rang the outside doorbell several times. No answer. He had no time to wait for Jennifer North to magically appear. He would have to find her.

It was a short drive from her apartment to the Titanic. He walked in whistling nonchalantly. Someone had strung balloons and a string of little Christmas lights over the bar. The place was crowded. He recognized a few familiar faces from the two-oh and he waved. Then he zeroed in on Vinnie, holding court on the opposite side of the room.

He strolled up to the portly man and tapped him lightly on the shoulder. Without looking, he knew Jerry Turner was standing behind the bar wiping a glass.

"Lieutenant!" Vinnie boomed, showing a broad smile and revealing nicotine-stained teeth. Fazio motioned for him to step off to the corner.

"Can you spare the kid?" Fazio indicated Jerry Turner, who immediately recognized him, smiled, and waved.

Vinnie's smile folded into a scowl. "I knew it. I always call 'em, don't I? What kind of trouble is he in?"

Fazio clapped Vinnie on the back. "Listen, don't worry about it. Just have to talk to him for a little while. Is that okay?"

"Okay? What am I supposed to say? Just don't take too long, huh? I got a Christmas rush here, Lieutenant." Vinnie walked over to the bar, leaned over, said something quietly to Jerry Turner and soon he came out from behind the bar and went with Fazio to the farthermost table in the back.

"What's up?" Jerry Turner asked. "Vinnie said you wanted to ask me some questions or something."

Fazio leaned across the booth. "Tell me, Mr. Turner, what is it that you really do?"

Jerry Turner laughed self-consciously and threw his hands up in the air. "Me? I'm a bartender. What does it look like I'm doing?"

Fazio's eyes were hard and direct. "C'mon, you don't expect me to believe that. You're a novice. You can't even mix a drink right."

Turner's face flushed. He looked down. His hands were resting on the table and he turned them over almost in a gesture of confession. "Okay, you're right. I'm a photographer. But I need this job. It's a bread job. I didn't want to tell Vinnie. He wouldn't understand."

Fazio's unchanged expression told Jerry Turner he wasn't buying his story even before he opened his mouth. "Listen kid, I know that photographers have studios, equipment, clients. Anyone in New York can say he's a photographer. Buy a camera, shoot some pretty girls. Zap! You're a photographer. What's the real story?"

"I told you! I need the money from this job. Equipment and film cost money, especially when no one will give you a chance. Zolinsky kicked me out of the inside of the theater three weeks ago."

Fazio's eyes narrowed. "Mr. Zolinsky of New York Center Ballet?"

Jerry Turner suddenly got belligerent. "Yeah, that's right. I'm a ballet photographer, or trying to be one. But it's a sewed-up field. One or two have a monopoly. You have to break through somehow. I used to be able to at least hang around inside the theater. Now I have to stand out in the cold. So I have no shots to sell unless one of them comes out and I can catch her."

"Why bother with ballerinas? There's more money in, say, pornography. If you were smart . . ."

At that, Jerry Turner got up to leave. Fazio pulled him back down. "Take it easy. You made your point. I believe you." He smiled at the confused bartender. "By the way, you don't own a black-and-white-checkered hat, do you?"

"What is this, some kind of crazy nightmare? I don't even have a pot to pee in."

"Okay, okay, just asking."

Now Turner's voice was getting high and nasal. "Look, if you want to take me in and book me for something just for the hell of it, go ahead! I've got two days to cough up the rent or I'll be evicted. Then I lose my darkroom, probably my equipment, my pictures. Fine. Satisfy your cop's ego." He lowered his voice then. "Lieutenant, have you ever considered a head-shrinker? They caught the Ballet Killer today. It was all over the news. You knew that."

Fazio laughed. "Okay, okay. I apologize." He shrugged. "It's my style, I guess. I come on too strong. We're just making a routine check on the man because we've got to make sure no parts are missing. Nothing's going to happen to you, Mr. Turner." Jerry Turner looked puzzled but relieved. "What I need to know, though, is those pictures of dancers—you do have them for proof?"

"Sure, I've got them plastered all over my apartment like wallpaper. I just need a break."

"I understand. Say, did you ever take a picture of Jennifer North, with New York Center. Do you know who she is?"

Jerry Turner laughed as if they had discovered a

mutual friend. "Are you kidding? Of course I know who she is. I took a few shots of her just this afternoon. Followed her through the slush after she came out of the theater just this afternoon and then lost her in traffic somehow. She left with someone. As usual, just my luck. It's not so easy to have to work like this, you know. I'm not exactly making a fortune. I like to shoot them in action, preferably dancing. Flat studio shots are not for me."

"Did you take a picture of the person she left with? Was it around one o'clock?"

"I'm not sure what I got. I have to develop it. But it was around one o'clock." He smiled out of the corner of his mouth as he said, somewhat cynically, "Someone want to buy it?"

Fazio looked directly at him. "Yeah, me. I'll buy whatever you shot. How long does it take to develop pictures?"

"Not too long. My bathroom's my darkroom."

"Sit there. Don't move." Fazio got up and located Vinnie, who was yukking it up with a crowd of customers, and pulled him aside.

"Say, can you spare him for a few hours?" Fazio indicated Jerry Turner, who stared back from the booth.

"Spare him? Look around. This is my busy season. All the office parties along Broadway come here to finish it off and get sicker. Plus my regulars." He spoke low. "He's in some kind of trouble, the kid, huh?" One of Vinnie's steel-gray eyebrows sneaked up.

"No, Vinnie, really. He's clean. I checked him out. But I need his help on another case. As a witness. Listen, though, I don't want him to lose his job or anything like that."

Fazio looked around. The place was full and another crowd of half-drunk, tottering people poured in the door, warming themselves and looking for a table. He could feel Turner slipping right through his fingers. He had to be careful. Every minute was important, and the Titanic wasn't just the favorite hangout of the two-oh; it was the center of precinct and department gossip. Very subtly, he reached in his pocket, obviously a gesture to get out his wallet.

Vinnie stopped his hand. To the observer on the outside, it looked as if Fazio wanted to pay for his own drink and Vinnie wanted to treat. "Oh, c'mon, Lieutenant, forget it. Half my business comes from you guys. Take him. But bring the creep back as soon as you can."

As Jerry Turner and Lieutenant Fazio left, a man turned around. He was sitting at the bar. He finished his drink, paid, and left inconspicuously. As inconspicuously as when he came in, which was right about the same time Fazio did.

The wooden floor in the foyer outside the bathroom creaked and Jennifer held her breath as she heard the footsteps get louder. He was coming closer. She shut her eyes. She heard a key turn in the door. Not even thinking, she scrambled up and hid in the bathtub, pulling the shower curtain around her, hitting herself cruelly in the head with one of the dangling toe shoes.

She felt a breeze. The door had opened. She backed up against the bathroom wall, almost doubled in half pressing against the tiles. She couldn't see out. Yet she could feel he was there. Her teeth were chattering. She hoped he couldn't hear her. But what was the difference? He knew she was there. The silence. It was like torture. She tried to count the seconds. Her mind was going blank from panic. She almost wanted to get it over with so the horrible nothingness would stop.

Then her mouth opened into a scream, but she was so frightened nothing came out. A sandy-colored wavy head of hair was tipping through the small opening in the shower curtain. He looked just like a ventriloquist's dummy. His eyes were huge and wooden. And something she had never seen in Max. His eyes were the eyes of a crazy person. Slowly, he put one foot in the bathtub. Then the other, and then . . she couldn't stand it! She screamed. The scream exploded out of her. She couldn't stop it.

Max stopped it. He clamped a hand over her mouth until she couldn't breathe. The other hand sneaked around her throat. Desperately, she fumbled for the words to the Lord's Prayer. Wasn't that what you were supposed to say? She couldn't remember them. She couldn't remember anything except that the razor was still on the windowsill, and why hadn't she thought to get it? Why? Now it was too late. She felt his body pressing against hers. His hands gripped tighter around her throat and she pumped courageously for air. But it was getting harder and harder to breathe.

Across the courtyard the man pulled his aching body out of bed and wrapped a terry bathrobe around his pajamas. He shuffled slowly into the kitchen, where his wife was, and picked up the phone.

"What are you doing out of bed?"

"Couldn't sleep. Another scream. Someone's in trouble." He dialed 911.

"This is Operator 430," the voice on the other end of the line answered. "Where is the emergency?"

The man stopped and thought. He put his hand over the receiver. "Where do you think the screams came from? What building?"

"You think I know?"

He went back to the operator on 911. "Look, I don't know what building. I live on Eightieth and Amsterdam. It's either on Columbus or maybe Eighty-first Street. There's courtyards separating these buildings."

"What is the nature of the emergency?"

"Someone screaming. Someone in trouble. Hey, what is this? Are you coming or not? I'm trying to do a good thing and I'm talking to a computer."

"I am not a computer," Operator 430 said, rising to his own anger. "And we can't send anyone if we don't know where the trouble is or even if there *is* any trouble, *sir!*"

The "sir" sounded like an insult to the man's ears, and it was. He held the receiver at arm's length, made a face, and then slammed it down. His face was flushed with anger, not fever. He began to pace around. "Years ago, it wouldn't have been like this. Try to be of help . . ."

His wife went over and physically placed him in a kitchen chair by the table. She put a plate of soup in front of him. "Relax. It was probably the TV or someone just having a fight. I'll keep the windows shut if you can't sleep."

The man dipped a spoon into the homemade broth. "Yeah, you're right. The hell with it."

Chapter Eight

One day when he was in the eighth grade he was lying in his room, pants off, underpants rolled around his ankles just holding it in his hands. But it wouldn't do anything. He was thinking about his mother. She was always drunk. It was all his fault. Just because he wasn't a dancer. Everytime he thought about that nothing happened. He tried again. Then he heard his door open. He froze, eyes plastered to the ceiling. She came into the room but she didn't say anything. Oh, God, she put her hand on the inside of his thigh. It got hard. He took his hands away. Eyes shut he let it happen because it just felt so good, so good. He knew in his mind that it was wrong. But he couldn't stop it. If he kept his eyes shut, he could pretend she wasn't there.

IVAN ROMAN LAY on the floor of his cell still staring at the hanging lightbulb. He was whispering to someone. No one was there.

"You made me do it. I didn't have to."

There was a silence.

"That's not what you said. You said I had to be punished."

Another silence and then he sprang to his feet. The light bulb was on, though the lights in the jail had gone off. He went over and caressed it, oblivious to the heat on his hand. He had his answer. The voices were coming from the light. They told him what he had to do.

He dragged himself across the floor to the sink. He put his good leg on the rim and then swung his bad leg up. He was now perched on the edge of the sink. He waited for more orders. Then he turned on the water. Rusty cold water trickled out of the spigot. He waited.

"My shirt?" he asked. Then he ripped off his shirt, tore it into bits, and stuffed some of it down the drain, plugging it up. The sink began to fill up. Then he giggled and unzipped his fly. He looked around to see if anyone might be watching. No one was around. He pee-peed in the sink. It felt good.

Leaning over as far as he could, still in a crouch, he brought the light bulb slowly but surely to him. He held it close to his chest, stroking the long wire, listening intently. He nodded, understanding. Quickly, he unscrewed the bulb and placed it carefully on the top of the old sink. Plunging his right hand fully in the water, he held his breath and jammed three fingers of his left hand directly into the live socket. His body jerked and writhed and he fell off the sink, stiff as a board, onto the floor. No one in the other cells paid any attention to the noise because they were tired of the strange sounds he was making. Ivan Roman was free of his controlling voices at last. His face was free of tension and he was smiling sweetly. He had gotten out of his prison. Crazy Ivan Roman had successfully managed to electrocute himself.

"Unusual place you have here," Fazio commented as Jerry Turner located the camera he had used that morning. It was on his waterbed under a pile of clothes. His bedroom contained the bed and a stereo. Everything else in it, covering every inch of space, was either a camera, a tripod, stacks of pictures he had taken, or boxes of film. In the corner was a tiny bookcase made of bricks containing only books on photography. Beyond the bedroom was a narrow hallway you had to walk sideways to get through because more photography equipment was stacked high on either side.

At the end of the hall, right outside the bathroom,

was a series of shelves with timers and developing devices. A black curtain separated this area and the bathroom, which doubled as a darkroom, from the small kitchen at the front of the strange apartment. Photographs of dancers captured in various movements and spontaneous expressions lined the walls wherever there was space. Fazio studied them. Very artistic was Fazio's impression. Although he didn't know that much about photography, he knew the kid had talent to spare. As far as his apartment was concerned, there wasn't an inch to spare.

"Just close the curtain and wait in the kitchen," Jerry Turner instructed him. He heard the bathroom door close, a timer go off, the door open, the door close, and waited. It must have been fifteen minutes before Turner called him in. The lights were on now. In the bathroom on top of the toilet tank were four vats of fluid with four pairs of tongs. Jerry Turner explained that the picture was agitated lightly in each vat of developing fluid. It finally came to rest in a huge vat on the bottom of the bathtub, which had a hose affixed to it. The pictures now rested and floated in the water, bobbing in and out with the stream. Both Fazio and Turner stared into the water like kids at Marineland. One picture surfaced to the top. Jerry Turner fished it out and they both stared at it.

"Not what you're looking for," Turner said, showing it to Fazio, and he put it on the rack hanging on the wall to dry.

"Not quite what I'd hoped. Are most of them like that?"

The picture was a shot of Jennifer North swinging her head so that her hair swung gracefully about her face.

"Most of these were shot right at the stage entrance as they came up. I focused only on Jennifer and no one saw me. The man's back was to me and stayed that way as they walked away, though I think I have him in several shots. Jennifer, though, is very expressive, so I know I have her in profile. But even if I just got her back it would be worth it. I'm interested in the body movements of dancers. I used a medium-speed film."

"That means you can shoot even though they're far away and still get it."

"Sure. You just keep shooting. But the figures do get smaller. Half the shots I take are useless."

About five more pictures washed up. In one they saw the shoulder and part of the torso of a man. Fazio was starting to feel disappointment.

Carefully, Jerry Turner pulled out the last picture and studied it. Fazio was looking at the other pictures on the rack.

"This might be a little better."

Fazio quickly turned. Both figures were far away, but the man had turned around in a three-quarter angle for some reason. Maybe he heard something. Or maybe they were looking for a taxi.

Fazio studied the picture. "Looks kind of small."

Jerry handed him a loupe, the small magnifying glass photographers use, and showed him what to do with it. Fazio squinted and turned the picture slightly to the right and then the left. Finally, he gave up.

"Nope. Too small. Say, do you think it would make it clearer if it was blown up? That way we might be able to tell who it is. Could you do that now?"

Jerry Turner looked at him oddly.

"I mean, it might make the features clearer. Could you do that now?"

"Do you want glossy or matte finish?" Turner asked, purposely sarcastic.

"Mr Turner, this is not a favor. I'll pay you and you won't lose your bread job."

"Sorry, Lieutenant Fazio, it's just that I'm not used to following orders. I like to understand what I'm doing and why I'm doing it. Why *am* I doing this, by the way?"

Fazio sighed. It was the sigh of a tired cop. "Just routine. Believe me. Part of the non-glory that goes with being a cop, which is all I am. We have to check out every aspect of this case because it will eventualy go to court."

Turner shrugged. "Okay, you're the boss. Out!"

This time Fazio tried walking down the narrow passageway in the dark apartment. He made it without injury and sat down on the waterbed at the end of the apartment. He closed his eyes for just a second, not realizing how tired he was, and allowed himself to be rocked into a relaxing state of half-sleep. But his eyes snapped wide open and he was alert when he heard Turner's scream.

"Heeeeey! Now we've got something!"

Fazio rushed down the hallway so fast he almost knocked over half of Jerry Turner's equipment.

Dr. Richard Kupperman sat at a table for two in the back of Ming Joy's, watching customers come in. A half-finished drink sat in front of him, and a plate of ice-cold egg rolls he hadn't even touched. He checked his watch again. He couldn't believe it. It was 8:45. But it was only a minute later than the last time he checked. Amazing how time never moved when you were waiting. He had gone past impatience, past anger, and kept coming back to one thing. It was so unlike Jennifer, especially with her parents coming. She would have called the restaurant. He couldn't shake the feeling, like the feeling you knew when you were coming down with a chill and a cold, that something was wrong. Very wrong.

He had called the apartment at least fifteen times. Though it was more like twenty-five if he really wanted to be truthful with himself. The same dime sat by his drink. He was ready to call again, except it was getting embarrassing. People were beginning to stare. The restaurant was filling up and though they needed the table, none of the waiters disturbed him. He and Jennifer were regulars. Occasionally, one would shoot him an Oriental glance of support and encouragement. He knew what they thought. That his girl had stood him up.

And they were probably right. He might as well face facts and stop trying to read between the lines. For whatever reason, she had stood him up. He fingered the little box in his suit pocket. He was pretty sure Tiffany's would take it back. It then occurred to him that Jennifer might be on her way to the airport now, somehow, or with someone else to pick up her parents. He felt hurt. But on the other hand, why did she tell him to be sure and meet him here?

He drummed on the table, unconsciously, with his fingers. A week ago he would have been going out of his mind with worry if she was missing. He stared down at the newspaper on the table. But they had found the Ballet Killer. He shoved the newspaper across the table. He had read it twice. Funny, he had wanted to share it with her, celebrate together. Now, maybe, maybe she wouldn't be so insistent about doing the tour.

Richard didn't realize how angry at Jennifer he still was until he accidentally kicked the small table all the way over when he decided to get up and leave. A waiter rushed over and righted it, bowed, and smiled. Richard, blushing with embarrassment, apologized, put down a hefty tip, and left the restaurant. As he walked back, in the cold, to their, her, apartment, he realized she could always try to reach him there. And if he had nothing to do, he could start packing his things.

Jennifer thought she was going to pass out. It wasn't that she was dizzy. She was light-headed. The fear was gone. She didn't feel like she was dying. She read about people who lose their minds before they are going to be murdered or executed. She hoped it would happen to her. She felt so light-headed, so floaty. She tried to stay detached on this plane, where she wouldn't feel it. But she couldn't breathe through her mouth or her nose. His hands squeezed tighter on her throat.

Shit! He was kissing her. No wonder she couldn't breathe. She sagged against him because she had no strength and then he pushed her away and she fell.

He stared at her with those crazy eyes. She was rubbing her throat and gasping for breath, sitting on the tub. But she was alive. She looked up at Max through sad eyes that were clouded with tears of relief. Maybe it was all a joke: the pointe shoes, everything—maybe he just had an odd sense of humor. He had extended his hand and was helping her out of the tub.

Then she looked into those eyes again. No, it wasn't a joke. He didn't even look like the real Max. The Max of before or the Max who played piano for class. His eyes looked like marbles.

Max glanced around. Bathrooms. He remembered the bathroom in that apartment in Queens. It didn't have a lock.

"Mama! I'm taking a shower. Now, come on. Don't come in. No, I don't want you to help. My

*God, Mama I'm thirteen now! I can stand okay."
And then he had looked down. It stood out. He
held it in his hands as it stuck straight out. He
knew where it should go, too. Oh, God, he wanted
her to come in. But she had laughed and walked
away.*

Max took a step toward Jennifer. She shrank back,
cringing, as he took a pocketknife from his pants.
Then she held her breath as he cut the ties on her
hands. She flapped them around, trying to shake the
stiffness out of them. Max said, in a flat voice, "You
must be hungry. I'll make us something to eat."

Jennifer stared, her mouth falling open. She didn't
know what to do. She was like a prisoner on death
row, condemned to die, and she knew it. She wasn't
sure how much more of this she could take without
cracking up. She didn't know how strong she was.
Jennifer remembered how prisoners of war kept their
sanity. They did math problems in their minds, but
math was never her best subject.

She climbed back in the bathtub and sat there cross-
legged, folding her arms across her chest. Then she
sang, in a feeble, little voice, a song she had learned
in kindergarten: "Cookaberra sits in the old gum tree,
Cookaberra sits in the old gum tree. . . ." She couldn't
remember all the words, so she kept singing what she
knew over and over.

Fazio ran into the bathroom and, now experienced,
looked right into the tub. There was nothing there.
Jerry had pinned the picture up and was clearly
pleased with himself. It couldn't have been better if it
had been re-touched. The picture showed Jennifer
talking to the man and looking up at him. His features

were fairly visible, if not his whole face. He was in three-quarter view and smiling down at her.

Jerry Turner snapped his fingers. "Damn! I know I know who that is."

"Who?" Fazio asked eagerly.

"Give me a sec. I just can't remember. One of those people you know their faces but always forget the name. He's in the company—that much I can tell you."

"Dancer?"

"No. I don't think so."

"Hey," Fazio said, "my wife's into this memory thing. Here's how it works. You associate. Like 'dog' equals 'Collie' equals 'Collier.' Get it? Does that work for you?"

"No, because you have to start out that way."

"Oh." Fazio was losing his patience. How long had they been here? Was it worth it? Who was this guy in the picture? She might not be with him now. And if he was in the company, that meant another trip back, more questioning, after the killer was caught and during a performance. It was too damned close for comfort.

He was so lost in thought he almost didn't hear Jerry Turner's outburst when it came. "Max!"

"What?"

"Max Forrest! That's who the guy is! He's one of the piano players in the company. You know how I remember? All the girls seem to like him."

"Thanks, Mr. Turner. Let me give you a lift back." Fazio reached in his pocket, took out his wallet, and handed Jerry a folded bill. Jerry looked down and his face lit up. It was a fifty-dollar bill.

"Hey, listen, if there's any other way I can be of help, just let me know."

"You already have been of help, Mr. Turner. I

would help you get a photographer's job in the Department, but it would be a real waste of talent. Keep plugging."

Jerry Turner smiled. "You know, they caught the killer but I say you're still looking."

Fazio smiled back. "Yes, I am looking—for Jennifer North. To talk to her and ask her some very important questions so I can clean up the loose ends and spend Christmas with my family."

They said nothing much to each other on the drive back to the Titanic. Each was lost in his own thoughts. Jerry was thinking. Maybe he should hang around and keep his eyes open. Something might be up. And if he got just the right picture at the right time, that could be his ticket. Fazio was thinking that as soon as he dropped Jerry Turner off he would find the address of this Max Forrest and pay him a surprise visit.

When Max yelled, "Come into the kitchen!" Jennifer stopped singing and began to shake uncontrollably. She had to have a cigarette. Where was her bag? In the living room, where she had left it just that afternoon. Just that afternoon. She turned the phrase over in her mind. It seemed like years ago.

She walked into the kitchen, still trembling, and said in a quaky, thin voice, "I . . . I want a cigarette. I'm going into the other room."

Max didn't reply. She didn't know what to do. He was taking food out of the refrigerator and cooking, concentrating on every little motion. Again, those eyes. Fixed, glassy. He seemed to know what he was doing, yet the eyes were far away. She waited for an answer.

Max moved from refrigerator to stove, slapping pre-packaged hamburgers into a heavily greased pan.

He was aware Jennifer was there. If they had more money, they could eat better.

"Why can't I see my daddy, Mama? I'm sure once he sees me he'll give us money. You could stop being a waitress and I could have real piano lessons. Don't hit me, Mama! Maybe I don't have a daddy." And to himself, he thought—I hate you.

Jennifer still wanted an answer. He was oblivious to her. She waited a minute more, shrugged, and went into the other room.

She spotted her bag near the couch. The ashtray was there. It had been cleaned and the glasses had been removed. She played the scene over in her mind, painfully. Just having a drink with a good friend. And making love to that good friend. Only he turned out to be the Ballet Killer, and it wasn't her imagination; the lovemaking had been strange. If he tried anything else, she would be physically ill. She lit a cigarette and sat on the couch, flicking her ashes into the ashtray, trying to relax. She looked around. *Not an apartment anymore,* she thought bitterly. *A goddamned prison.*

Then she noticed it. Quickly, she crushed out her cigarette in the ashtray. Out of the corner of her eye she glanced over at Max. He wasn't looking. Her hand was flapping like a fish out of water. She was so nervous she didn't think she could pull it off. If he saw her he'd probably kill her on the spot. Rather than bring it up to her, she sat on the floor. She took a magazine lying nearby and pretended to read it. But her hand traveled across the floor, closer and closer to the telephone sitting under the coffee table. The push-button phone.

She kept an eye on Max. He didn't seem to be in

this world. She shut her eyes and prayed. Then she punched out the number very quickly. Hearing a pick-up, she blurted, "Richard?" She was talking very rapidly. "Max Forrest. He's the killer. He's got me. Call the . . ." And then she heard the phone ring again.

Terrified, she looked up, over shoes, past pants, up into the enraged and distorted face of Max. He was in the foyer. She whimpered. He pointed to the kitchen. She remembered. There was a wall phone in the kitchen. So she had underestimated Max. He had marble eyes in the back of his head. It was Max all the time. Richard had never even answered. It had all gone so fast.

She closed her eyes, clenched her fists, and tensed her whole body for what she knew was to come. She winced when he came over, lifted the coffee table up, and yanked her to her feet. Her eyes were wide open now and she tried to avoid his face, the veins popping in his forehead, the bulging, furious eyes. She cried as he put his hand on her neck and ripped. He tore her top in two, throwing the pieces anywhere they fell. Instinctively, her hands flew around her body, hugging herself, covering her breasts. She was sobbing now, whispering, "No, no, please."

Max had gone beyond his wooden insanity into un-controllable fury. He slapped her across the face so hard she could barely see, and then he pushed her. She landed on the floor, just able to break her fall so she didn't injure her back. Then he bent over and pulled her legs apart. Jennifer lay spreadeagled on the floor, hands cupping her breasts, eyes wide, body rigid with fear.

Max's hands were shaking with fury. He went over to her practice bag.

*None of them had fought back. Only Heather,
and he had to kill her. She wouldn't dance.
There was no last dance. He had loved her and
killed her, but he hadn't enjoyed it. It wasn't
enough.*

His thoughts made him angrier. Rummaging
around in the bag, he pulled out a pair of pink tights.
Then he came over and stood on top of her, strad-
dling her body with his legs. She looked up at him,
cowering.

"You know what these are for, don't you?" he
said, a new evilness in his voice.

Jennifer nodded, though she hadn't the vaguest
idea of what she was supposed to say. He kicked her
and she cried out in pain. "That's not good enough!"
he growled and kicked her again.

Jennifer tried to keep her sobbing soft. "Yes," she
choked. She knew he was going to strangle her now.
Tears were falling in puddles onto the carpet and her
stomach was contracting furiously in and out. "Please,
Max. Please, I'm sorry," she pleaded with him, trying
to cut through his madness. "I'll be good. I'll do whatever you say."

But Max wasn't listening. He ripped off her jeans,
not even bothering to unzip them first. Then he pulled
her panties down to her thighs. He started to take his
belt off. But he stopped, standing frozen, stiff, as if
he were listening for something. Jennifer sucked in
her breath, not daring to distract him in any way. She
could sense the wheels spinning inside his head like a
piece of defective machinery.

*Lovely Lisa. She had danced for him. Then they
had kissed and gone to bed. She was his first. So
sweet, so natural. In the dark he had strangled*

*her with a pair of pink tights just like the ones
he was holding now. And the others had been
so nice. No one had caught him. He had been
too smart. But it couldn't, didn't, work anymore.
Mama was right. It was time to move on to
something better.*

He looked down at Jennifer as if he were disgusted
to see her there. Jennifer gulped, one hand trying to
slide her panties back up. But he was too fast. He
pulled them off and took them. "Here," he commanded. "Get dressed." From her bag he threw her
her leotards and, oddly, a pair of leg-warmers. The
tights were in a crumpled ball. Jennifer clutched
them, trying to cover herself, as she watched him
walk back to the kitchen.

Jennifer rolled over on her stomach and pounded
the carpet with her fists. She did that until her knuckles burned. Then she tried to get into her tights, her
jagged nails starting a runner. She was trembling so
much she put them on backward, getting them all
twisted up, and had to start all over again. Then she
slipped into her black, long-sleeved leotard and
pushed up the sleeves. She rolled on the leg-warmers.
That part was odd. Did that mean she was going to
warm up for something?

"Come in here!" called Max. Jennifer crept in
shyly like a dutiful little girl being called by Mother.
She had no shoes on. Max pointed to a chair. She sat
down opposite him at the table. She eyed him cautiously, carefully. His rage had cooled down. She noticed the plate he put before her and she looked up
into his eyes. She didn't know which made her feel
more squeamish, the food or him. She swallowed
hard and tried to adjust to the change.

The other Max had somehow returned. He was

smiling his usual shy smile. His bright blue eyes were leveled on her. She forced herself to smile, though it was confusing dealing with his brand of loony-tunes. Weakly, she picked up her fork and looked down. That was a big mistake. Floating in a pool of grease was a hamburger bleeding with ketchup and leaking all over two pieces of white bread. Soggy potato chips were lodged in the drooly puddle—and all on a paper plate. She almost gagged. Then she put her fork down and did what he was doing, but a little more mechanically. She picked up the whole mess and took a bite. If she just didn't think about it or look at it, she might be okay. That wasn't as hard to do as she thought. Because she was obsessed with only one thing. As soon as she got a chance, any kind of a break, she would be at that phone again. Only this time she would be smart.

Two guards walked down the corridor of the almost-empty Tombs making the rounds. Every once in a while they would shine a flashlight into a cell and somebody would groan and go back to sleep, throw a paperback novel at the bars, or look up, squinting, from a game of solitaire. The hall lights were now out. But the cell light bulbs were on. All except one.

"Hey, his light's out. It's dark in there," one guard said.

They opened the cell and went in, both of their flashlights working like searchlights. They saw it all—the sloppy sink, the unscrewed light bulb, and Ivan Roman, fly unzipped, lying on the floor face up to the ceiling, staring.

"Oh, Jesus!" whispered the guard who rushed over to Ivan Roman first. He bent down and put his ear on the man's chest. "Son-of-a-bitch!"

The other guard stared, unable to move.

"Dead. The crazy bastard killed himself," he whispered.

"How could he hang himself? He's on the floor."

"He toasted himself. Shut up. I'll explain later. Help me get him back on the bed."

"I ain't touching no stiff." The frightened guard backed away.

"Keep your voice down, for Chrissakes. You want your name in the paper? You want to lose your job? Help me get him on that bed. We'll cover him, clean up, and leave the blame on the next shift. And screw the light bulb back in so we can see."

The other guard still stood transfixed in horror. "Shut his eyes first, will ya?"

The other guard wasn't listening. He was quietly dragging Ivan Roman's rigid body across the floor to the cot. The guard in a trance finally came to his senses and picked up the dead man's feet. They got Roman on the bed and then rolled him over to his side, putting his hand under his head so it looked like he was sleeping. They covered him and the guard taking charge finally closed his eyes. Then he said in a voice, louder than a whisper, just in case any other prisoners were even half-listening, "Stay there, Roman, and go to sleep. We don't want no one sleeping on the floor."

They quickly cleaned up, fixed the light, and locked the cell. Then they flashed their lights from side to side walking down the hall. They were lucky. No one had heard. All the cells around Roman's were quiet.

Jennifer stopped and put her sandwich down. She just couldn't eat anymore. She was unable to swallow. Max shoved a cardboard carton of orange juice in front of her and a glass and, with a full mouth, said helpfully, "Here." Jennifer poured herself a glass and drank it down in one gulp just to make sure she would be full. Then she poured another glass to sip slowly so Max wouldn't notice she wasn't really eating.

He was calm now. Friendly, even. She opened her mouth to say something, then lost her courage. "You were going to say something?" he asked. Actually, he liked Jennifer. Always had. She was one of the nice ones. He had always wanted to kill her. But she was too useful. He must try to keep her happy.

Jennifer kept her head down and eyes lowered. "You," she whispered. "It was you I saw with Heather."

She looked up, half-frightened. But he wasn't angry. He smiled cordially and nodded.

"But you were limping then. I saw it. And before I heard the sound of . . . it was like a foot slapping against the floor . . . and I saw you; I'm sure I saw you limping. It was just before I . . ."

Max wasn't listening. He seemed to be looking over her shoulder.

"Mama, I hate taking ballet. I'll do anything . . . anything. . . . I'm no good at it; really, I'm not. Ma . . . Mama . . . I'm so thirsty. I want a milkshake! I want a milkshake! Ow! Don't hit me! The doctor said not to hit me on my ears!" Then the rage. He had to take ballet always, she said. He slapped her fist away and ran and ran. He heard her calling but he kept running. Near the train station he heard a train in the distance. He could get on it and find his daddy. His eyes were blinded by tears. She didn't love him. Nobody loved him. The train . . . it must

*be coming from the front . . . he couldn't see . . .
no the back . . . His mother . . . screaming his
name from afar . . . then more screams . . . a
screech of metal and iron. And the pain. He saw
a face looking down at him from the window
. . . horrified . . . and before he passed out, the
realization. It was coming from the front.*

Jennifer stared at Max, holding her breath. He
seemed silent.

"You're not eating, Jennifer," he said abruptly. She
forced herself to take another repulsive bite. She
wasn't going to get an answer to her question, but she
couldn't stop now. She had to know. "But, you . . .
you . . ." She tried to swallow. "You killed all the
others. . . ."

Max giggled happily, nodding, as if accepting a
compliment.

Something caught in Jennifer's throat. She gulped
down some orange juice, but it was stuck in her wind-
pipe so she was sputtering, tears streaming down her
face. Max rushed over and banged her on the back,
making it even worse. Now she was coughing and
gasping at the same time. She thought she would suf-
focate when, with no warning, he clamped a hand
tightly over her mouth. She kept swallowing to get
control and then she understood. Max's downstairs
doorbell was ringing.

It rang again. Max never moved a muscle. Jennifer's whole body was tense, expectant. Who was it?
Someone wanted to see Max? Did they figure out
where she was? If it was the police, they would just
come up. It rang again. And again. Jennifer was
squeezing her face so hard, hoping, hoping that it
made Max press his hand tighter against her mouth.

He was wondering who it could be. No one ever rang his doorbell. Unless someone was looking for Jennifer and knew she was here. But that was impossible. It was probably someone trying to sell something or a charity asking for a handout. It was right before Christmas. And then it stopped. The apartment was silent.

Max took his greasy hand away from Jennifer's mouth and she breathed semi-fresh air again. But he still held her clamped down in the chair with his hands. A few more seconds went by. Jennifer's spirits plunged right through her body down to her almost-bare feet. It had really stopped. Whoever was there had given up.

Finally, he released her and went over to the cupboard. He opened a can of cling peaches and then tossed the empty can into the wastebasket. When he saw he missed, he stomped over and crushed the can over and over with his shoe as if he wanted to wipe it off the face of the earth. Jennifer studied him very carefully. He had changed again. The doorbell. He was angry. It wasn't normal for his doorbell to ring. She was right. He looked at her and sneered.

"Oreo cookies," he said, making a statement. She looked puzzled. He tossed her a package. "See," he said, "I know how you dancers like your sweets."

"Thanks, Max. I'd really like a cigarette, though. Gee, I guess they're in my bag." This time she'd try and see if she could punch 911 with her toes and let them discover her with Max. She'd lift the receiver off the hook so they could trace the call. She got up and fed herself mental doses of determination as she started to cross into the other room. She never made it.

When she pitched forward, she muffed an "oomph" because Max had tackled her and she lay under him,

his hand circling her mouth, her body pinned painfully to the floor. It wasn't long before she knew why.
Someone was knocking at the door.

The wind blew through the bars in the window,
sweeping in drops of moisture. The woman in bed
shivered. But she would wait until her teeth were
chattering before she went in to see Miss Johnson,
the night nurse. She wrapped her arms around her
and rocked from side to side. Mustn't get too much of
a chill. She didn't want to miss anything in the next
few days. She had waited for them for too long.

*"I don't want cereal for supper! I don't! We
had it last night! I want a hamburger!" Max
started to pound the table and cry. Her hand
went up and before she could stop it she
smacked the kid across the face. He looked at
her, stunned, tears rolling down his face. It's just
that she was nervous. Larry had fired her two
days ago. He said he expected more of her than
just to wait on tables. That if she played her
cards right . . . if she was nice to the customers
. . . dirty old man! Sickening, disgusting. She
wouldn't flirt and wiggle her body. She was too
good for that. And she told him.*

*Then he let her go. "You're fired, Miss Hoity-
Toity. See how the tips are at Nedick's."*

*And the cereal. She didn't even have any
money in her purse for food. She had taken the
cereal off the shelf in the supermarket. An old
woman with a cane had eyed her suspiciously.
She kicked her, left her sprawling on the floor.
Then she ran out of the store with the cereal under her coat.*

She couldn't wait any longer. She got up, threw a hospital robe over her paper-thin flannel nightgown, slipped into her dusty scuffs, and started to leave her bare bedroom. She turned around, reached out the window through the bars, dabbed her fingers with soot, and put them under her eyes. So it looked like she had deep smudges of fatigue.

Leaving the solitary room she had gotten because of her silly attacks, she scuffed slowly, sadly, down the hall, teeth chattering, body sagging, until she reached the nurses' office and just stood in the doorway watching Miss Johnson sort the next morning's meds in little paper cups. She did it the same way at the same time every night. Charlotte Forrest knew it. And she knew that the medications were kept in the supply cabinet, and to take them out she had to open the door.

"Nurse Johnson," she said in a little-baby voice, "I'm just so freezing. Could you get the pole and close my window from the top?"

"You have your window open in this weather, Charlotte?" She made clucking sounds with her teeth. Nurse Johnson weighed over two hundred pounds, was widowed so long ago she forgot what her husband looked like, and had worked in Manhattan State, same ward, as the night nurse, for almost forty years. She was well past the retirement age, but no one did anything about it. She loved all the mentally ill patients as if they were her own children.

She eyed the poor, shivering woman in front of her and thought, just a child, a sick child. Her heart melted. The day staff had probably opened her window. She got these reports of how bad Charlotte Forrest was during the day, but it was beyond her. Charlotte was sweet. She just needed love and attention. The day staffers were animals. She took down the pole. "Come with me, Charlotte."

"I have to use the rest room," Charlotte cooed back, the innocence still oozing from her voice. She watched the lovable nurse waddle down the hall singing her song, her favorite song, which they would probably play at her funeral. As soon as the last strains of "When Johnny Comes Marching Home Again" faded, Charlotte rushed into the nurses' quarters. Just as she had suspected. Nurse Johnson had closed the door, but it wasn't locked. She found what she needed right away. Max had told her what to do on that page which she had ripped up and flushed down the toilet.

Now she rushed back into the communal bathroom and flushed the toilet again because she heard Nurse Johnson coming down the hall, singing her song softly, dragging her extra poundage. Charlotte Forrest stopped her and looked into her eyes adoringly. "Thank you, Nurse Johnson." Like the rest of the love-starved patients, Charlotte gave Nurse Johnson a big hug and kiss.

The elderly nurse beamed. They were all her children, poor souls. "I see you're getting a pass to go out for Christmas," she said.

"Oh, yes. I'll be visiting my son."

"You have a good time, then, Charlotte." She went back to the nurses' office, finished counting out the pills, locked the medicine cabinet, and settled down to half of a banana cake she had taken from the kitchen during her supper hour. The other half she had cut in little bits and given to her girls as a treat.

In her high, lumpy hospital bed, Charlotte Forrest turned over on her side and smiled. It was like having a tooth under her pillow for the Good Fairy to find.

"Sweet dreams, Charlotte," Daddy had said. "The Good Fairy will leave something. Just put your tooth under the pillow." Then he had kissed her. She had rubbed her tongue under the space where the tooth was missing. Daddy would have to leave something nice. Daddy had knocked her tooth out.

But no one would leave anything under her pillow. Because the Good Fairy wouldn't come tonight. So no one would find the shiny hypodermic needle or know what was in it.

Chapter Nine

His music teacher at school first noticed he could play the piano. He told him to come by for piano lessons. The teacher said it didn't matter if he had no money. He would teach Max for free. Because a talent like his came by once in a lifetime. But he lied to his teacher and he lied to his Mama. He would practice a piece, stumbling, until he knew how it should be in his mind. Then he would play it perfectly somehow. The teacher didn't know he never bothered to read the notes. He just knew the music. He would have been angry. Mama didn't even know he was taking piano lessons. She would have beat him.

RICHARD PACED UP and down their apartment waiting for Jennifer to call. He felt like he was in a prison. He didn't dare use the phone or leave the apartment in case she might be trying to reach him. Anger and rejection were replaced by worry. He couldn't help it. Damn it! He loved her! And he had worried about her from the time she first came into his office as a patient and he had treated her Achilles' tendon for strain.

Passing the oval mirror, he studied his face. Not a bad face. If Jennifer only knew how many women had made more than subtle approaches. He had no interest in them. Only Jennifer mattered. Suddenly he wondered why he was staring at himself in the mirror. He had an eerie sense of aloneness. It spooked him.

Everywhere he could feel her presence. The ashtray full of cigarette butts he despised because he wished she wouldn't smoke. Her powder-blue hairbrush on the kitchen counter. He smiled in spite of himself and put it in the bathroom. The bathroom, where you might get slapped in the face with wet tights or leotards hanging everywhere.

When the phone rang he scrambled to answer it so fast he all but knocked over a chair. It was her; he knew it. His hands were shaking as he answered. If he had to use words to describe how he must have looked then, he figured it would be the old cliché—his face fell. Because it did both in shock and disappointment.

"Richard? You must be Richard," a woman's voice said.

Richard nodded dumbly.

The woman didn't wait for an answer. She just kept rambling on in a Midwestern accent. "This is Jennifer's mother. Where are you two kids? We've been waiting over forty-five minutes."

All Richard could think of was, *Oh, my God, I forgot all about them.* But he had figured, angrily before, that Jennifer had picked them up without him.

Richard ummed and errrred and realized the woman must be thinking that for a doctor he was a cretin. Great debut as a son-in-law, if he ever made it that far. "Oh, Mrs. North, you haven't answered our pages . . ." He was thinking as he lied. *Clever, Dr. Kupperman; now figure out why you were paging.*

"No, we didn't hear them. Is anything wrong?"

"Wrong? No. Nothing's wrong." He knew his voice was too high. "It was just that we realized we were going to be late . . ."—he was speaking slowly, enunciating every word as it came, and by some sort of grace finding the next one—". . . because Jennifer had a late rehearsal and we wanted to go together so we kept trying to page you and . . ." He didn't know what else to say. So he said, "I'll pick you up as soon as I can, Mrs. North. I'm five-foot-ten, have a tan overcoat, and brown, curly hair. I'll pick you up by the TWA ticket counter."

He hung up, grabbed his coat, checked for his car keys, and ran out. Two seconds later he ran back in, scribbled a note for Jennifer, and left it on the table. Then he dashed out again. Only he had no intention of picking up his car and heading for the airport. Her parents would have to wait a little longer. He was going to the police.

Jennifer struggled against Max's grip as he forced her silently away from the door. She wanted to bite his arm so hard he would cry out, but it was impossible. He had her pinned to the floor, dragging her quietly, his hand over her mouth, his arms wrapped tightly around her.

"Who is it?" Max shouted cordially in a neighborly singsong voice that made Jennifer want to lose that putrid dinner all over his arm.

"Lieutenant Frank Fazio, Mr. Forrest. I'd like to ask you some questions if I can," a man standing outside the door said. Max felt a mixture of fury and fear. But just for a half-second, during which Jennifer tried to take advantage of her opportunity and kick him between the legs.

A cop, he thought in agony. *They know. But why now? They found the killer. And what could they prove?* He was too smart for them. All he had to do was keep calm.

Jennifer was thinking, *Richard's found me and called the police. Soon they would rush in and take Max by force. It's all over, it's going to be okay,* she told herself. There was a smile on Jennifer's face when Max stood her up, grinding her arm behind her. Keeping his big hand clamped over her mouth, he kicked her farther away from the door.

"Be right with you, Lieutenant!" he shouted. "Can you give me a moment? I was just getting out of the shower. Let me get dressed."

Jennifer knew he was going to hide her somewhere. But it didn't matter. She almost felt like laughing in spite. Let him shove her around. Not for long. Because no matter what he did, she was going to let this lieutenant know where she was within seconds flat.

In the hall Fazio paced quietly back and forth, double-checking his watch. He would have walked away and gone home, but for the little old lady downstairs who had let him in after he had flashed his badge. So here he was at 10:30 waiting for this Max Forrest, who had been taking a shower and was getting dressed. He leaned against the winding banister and reached in his pocket for a cigarette. He shook his head in disbelief. He was actually going against the whole department. Of course, if it backfired, that was it. But better to go out this way than walk in Hogan's shadow, which he knew would follow him for too long a time. He tapped his foot and lit his cigarette. What the hell was Max Forrest doing? Dressing for a recital? All he had to do was throw on a robe. Nothing inside a door would surprise Fazio. He had seen it all.

A chain latch unlocked and he saw a pair of blue eyes peek through the crack in the door. Wordlessly, Fazio flashed his badge. The chain clinked to the side and the door opened. A good-looking, tallish man with light brown, wavy hair and friendly blue eyes stood in the doorway. Fazio was surprised somehow. He imagined piano players to have long hair, dress a little more individualistically, and look

somehow different, more intense. Here he was face
to face with an All-American type. A man in a shirt,
V-necked sweater, and jeans, and a towel thrown
over his shoulders because his hair was still wet from
his shower. Max smiled at him. He was thinking that
the short, greasy-looking man in front of him was
no challenge. A dumb cop, no matter what his rank.

"Mind if I come in? Fazio asked. "It will only take
a minute."

Max kept the pleasant smile on his face, but Fazio
noticed that he stepped aside just a little so that
Fazio had to edge his way in and even then was only
about a fourth of the way into the foyer. Still, it
gave him a pretty complete picture of Max Forrest's
apartment. It was a large studio; the bathroom door
was open. He could view part of a kitchen in the
rear, and next to that a bedroom, bedroom door
open, main room, lots of plants, a piano, of course.
But beyond that he saw nothing irregular. One of
those old rent-control finds. A very old building.
Fazio's practiced eye was able to absorb all this in
about two seconds without giving anything away to
Max Forrest.

Now he addressed himself to the cleancut young
man in front of him. He took a drag out of his cigarette which he had lit when he came in. "Mr. Forrest,
I'm looking for Jennifer North. I understand she's a
dancer with your company."

Max nodded. "And?" he asked, confused. "Why
did you come to me?"

"Well, you were seen leaving the theater with her
this afternoon at around one o'clock. Did she go anywhere with you? Do you know where she is? I have to
ask her some questions."

Max wiped his damp head with the towel. "No,
as a matter of fact, we did walk out together, but

then she went her way and I went mine." He smiled apologetically at Fazio, as if he were sorry that he couldn't help produce her. Then he thought of something. "I do know she had the afternoon off and she wasn't performing tonight." He paused, thinking. "Gee, I hope she's not in some kind of trouble or anything like that." he said, his brow creased with worry.

Then he looked down at Fazio, who was holding an erect cigarette with about one-half inch of ash. "Oh," Fazio said. Max walked quickly into the living room and brought out an ashtray that was sitting on the coffee table. Fazio stubbed out his Kool and he was very aware of something. He could always tell non-smokers. The smell of smoke physically repulsed them, but in this case Max Forrest was too polite to say anything.

"Can you tell me anything else about Jennifer North?" he continued. "Did she say where she might be going when she left you?"

Max Forrest shook his head. "I really wish I could help you. But she didn't say anything. Oh, she wouldn't tell me. I'm only the piano player." He smiled shyly. "Actually, I don't know her that well. But I wish I did." Again the grin, all charm.

Fazio shook his hand and thanked him. He was now nowhere and ready to pack it in for the night. As he was opening the door to leave, Max asked, "Say, Jennifer's not in any kind of trouble, is she?" He sounded very concerned.

"No, nothing like that. We just have to ask her some questions."

Fazio noticed that Max was talking a shade faster. "About the Ballet Killer thing. Terrible. I heard it on the news. But they did catch the killer, didn't they?"

Fazio weighed his words. All he said was, "We

have to tie up the case, the loose ends. Routine
check. Talk to everybody."

Max nodded vigorously.

Fazio added, "Detective work is boring. Over and
over the same thing. Much like practicing the piano,
I imagine, Mr. Forrest."

Max smiled, but oddly enough Fazio didn't think
he comprehended. Actually, Max was thinking of the
little conversation he had overheard between Jennifer
and Yuri during rehearsal. Jennifer had seen too
much. That was one of the reasons she was such a
natural choice.

Max smiled at Fazio quickly. "I'd really love to
help you, Lieutenant, but I came right home from the
theater. I have a few days off for the holidays. Actually, I've been here all alone this afternoon."

As the door closed behind him, Fazio stood for a
moment in the hall with his back pressed against the
door and listened for sounds. Max's footsteps got
farther from the door. A buzzing sound came after
that. Probably a hair dryer or styler or an electric
razor, Fazio figured. He went softly down the steps.

Sergeant Moskowitz walked up Forty-second Street,
passing through the tarnished glitter of the Times
Square area. He turned his problem over and over in
his mind. The owner of the hat store did have receipts,
boxes and boxes of them overflowing, spilling out of
a dusty back room where he kept a hot plate. Moskowitz had started to go through some of them. The
receipts went all the way back to 1972. He had found
one that said black-and-white-checkered cap and was
Master Charge, so he marked it down. But he knew
what that would be like. Then you got the address,
went over, found out from a neighbor the guy moved

three years ago, and then eventually tracked down the guy who checked out clean as a whistle.

Moskowitz had left after over an hour of going through the boxes. It was useless. The owner had stuck his head in and said, "You know, that hat only cost ten dollars and ninety-five cents. I don't take checks. Not in this area. Most people pay cash for it."

Moskowitz knew it was a stupid, amateur question, but he couldn't help himself: "But you keep records on cash transactions, don't you? Mailing lists, things like that . . ."

"No, I don't bother," the man had said. "Should. But, like I said, in this area it doesn't pay. I'm going to send them a brochure in jail?"

It would take many men from the task force to go through those boxes and check out anyone who had charged a black-and-white funky checkered cap. And even then the one person they were looking for might have paid in cash. Two men couldn't do it. One man? Impossible. He strode angrily toward the sub-way which would take him back to the two-oh. He was angry because Hogan should have used his men to check out this hat thing. Most of all, they should have brought in the girl who saw the man who was wearing it. And this *couldn't* be the only store in this city that carried this crazy hat. Oh, no, the city would have to be combed. Of course, there was still no reason to do any of this. Hogan was dead positive Roman was the killer. That troubled Moskowitz. He wasn't yet sure Ivan Roman wasn't the killer. But he was sure Fazio was a good man. And he'd stand by him.

After Fazio had left, Max waited just a few more minutes. Then, laughing softly to himself, he walked across the room. He went to the space between the two windows in the living room and took down the reproduction of the tulips and windmill scene he had gotten at Woolworth's. As a double-check, he went back to the door to listen for sounds in the hall. Nothing. The stupid cop had left. Back at the wall, he lifted the latch the painting had hid. Then he gave a tug and pulled the Murphy bed out from the wall. Jennifer, bound loosely and sloppily, but tightly gagged, came flying through the air, landing with a bounce and a groan.

Max sat her in an upright position, then stood her up, enjoying the huge eyes and dilated pupils that told him she was his. Vulnerable. He put the Murphy bed back up, covered the latch, and brushed his hands as if to indicate a job well performed. And he thought it had been.

Untying Jennifer's gag, he pulled her lower lip down, held his hand out under her chin, and waited for her mouthful of wet pebbles to come spilling out. He tossed them back into one of the potted plants on the window ledge. Then he lowered his voice and said mildly, "If you scream now, I'll kill you." Jennifer nodded. She was incapable of screaming.

Downstairs Lieutenant Fazio stood on the front steps of Max Forrest's apartment building. He was thinking. It was just one of his hunches, but he couldn't throw it. Something was wrong with this Max Forrest. He started walking toward his car, got in, turned on the ignition, but just sat there. He lit a cigarette. Suddenly he knew. Max Forrest was a non-smoker. He purposely let his ashes dangle on his cigarette so Forrest would rush for an ashtray. But that was just to watch him walk. No limp. It was something Jerry Turner had said—that the girls liked him. And something else. Non-smokers usually clean out dirty ashtrays, if they even own one, immediately. When he crushed out his cigarette in Max Forrest's ashtray, there was a cigarette stub and ashes still in the ashtray. But Forrest had made a point of saying he had been home all afternoon. Alone.

Fazio rolled down his window and looked up at the building across the street. Forrest's apartment was four flights up. Maybe he should go back upstairs, say he lost his lighter, pretend to ask one more question he forgot. In other words, see what might happen if he took him by surprise. Maybe that wouldn't be a bad idea. He sat staring ahead, finishing his cigarette.

Upstairs in that fourth-floor apartment, Jennifer North was sitting on the couch. Her hands and feet had been untied, but she sat stiffly as if she were still tied up. A policeman had come to the door and left and she had never screamed. She had been buried alive in the wall. Trapped in dark space, nowhere, with pebbles in her mouth. When she tried to scream, it came out a gurgle. Her last chance and it was over. Everything was over. She stared into space thinking of everything she had had to live for. She was going to die.

Fazio rolled up the window. The only answer was that this wasn't an ordinary case. He had to watch his step. Going back upstairs might be too risky. He had better check out this Max Forrest first.

When he came into the Twentieth Precinct about ten minutes later, Bernie Moskowitz was sitting at a desk on the sixth floor reading a newspaper. He looked up when Fazio entered but looked down just as quickly and pretended to keep reading. There were still a few hanger-oners. The party was over but men were still talking, and Shipley, the detective who had passed out, was still sleeping on the floor.

They sat close and kept their voices low so it looked like they could have been talking about anything.

"What did you find?" Fazio asked Moskowitz.

"*Bubkes.* Most of their sales are cash. No receipts unless acceptable credit card. I tried to go through . . ."

Fazio cut him off. "Don't worry about it. Thanks for trying."

"Anything?"

"Zilch. Can't find this girl anywhere. Well, she's a dancer; she's bound to turn up to perform. Found a photographer, this Jerry Turner. He had a picture of her leaving the theater with this guy, one of the piano players, Max Forrest. So I went to see him. He says they went separate ways. Funniest thing, though, I have this hunch about him."

Moskowitz's eyes grew wider. He wondered how many people knew how great a detective Fazio was. He called that "zilch" nothing? Moskowitz's mouth was in the shape of a worshipful "Ah!" "So now what?"

"You go home to your wife and I go home to my wife before they divorce us."

"But Lieutenant, what about . . . I mean, do you want me to check on this Max Forrest for you? I could check the files, ask some questions."

Fazio studied the man. "You know, you're crazy, you know that? You're almost as crazy as I am. You're going to make a good detective someday, Bernie. I don't want to mess it up."

Moskowitz opened his mouth and the words that came out were a surprise even to him. "Lieutenant, I think you're right. I don't why, but all of the sudden I think you're right. The real killer is still out there. I can't go back now."

Fazio looked around, surprised, but pleased that Moskowitz was with him.

"Tell you what. Why don't you pay a call on Mr. Zolinsky and check out Max Forrest, maybe get a feel for where this Jennifer North would be? The main thing is to try to get in touch with her." He smiled apologetically. "I'm too visible here, if the gossip is what you say. I'll head for home." He wrote down his phone number on a piece of paper and handed it to Moskowitz. "Call me for anything, anytime. And, Moskowitz . . . thank you." Fazio walked out of the task force offices and thought they looked almost like a ghost town.

As he was on his way back to Brooklyn, he remembered a piece of the puzzle he had been trying to fit in for hours. It was one of the questions he wanted to ask Roman but didn't get a chance. About the time of the murders, there were those weird thefts in dance studios, especially the major ballet companies. The cases were never connected; one was petty theft, the other homicide. But he had found out about it. Could it have been that Roman merely stole the dance clothes? And someone else did the killing? That would mean that Roman was a crank of the first order, and a good thief. If so, the killer was still loose. He could feel his foot press the gas pedal. Or it could mean that Roman was the killer and because of that had been able to steal all those dance clothes.

A sixth sense made Fazio look in his rearview mirror just then. The same car had been behind him for too long. He continued to keep his eyes straight ahead and then turned on an exit. The other car followed him as Fazio made a screeching U-turn and continued to Brooklyn. Two minutes later he checked the rearview mirror. The same car was behind him again. A purple Impala. He wondered why he was being tailed and who had set it up.

Jennifer sat on the couch, hunched over, holding her arms around her waist. Max sat on the piano bench facing her. His eyes had the unblinking glare of a cat's. He just sat there staring, saying nothing. How long they had been sitting like this she didn't know. But she knew there was a wet circle underneath her on the couch. She knew also that she had wet her pants, but there was nothing she could do about it.

Max was slapping his right hand against his left palm. In his right hand he had one of her pointe shoes. Between his second and third fingers was a marking pen. Just perfect for autographing a pointe shoe. He loved to play little jokes on people.

Chapter Ten

He had seen her after school. She was beautiful. Tall and graceful, with long blond hair. He was in love with her. He followed her home every day but hid behind trees so she wouldn't notice him. He dreamed about her every night. She was a goddess. She was the girl he was going to marry when he grew up. Then one day he caught up with her and got up the nerve to ask her if he could walk her home from school. She said "okay." They talked a little. Then he asked her to stop somewhere and have a Coke. She looked at him sweetly and smiled. Her voice sounded like music to him. Until she said, "I don't go out with boys who, um, limp."

RICHARD SAT ACROSS from the detective who had been assigned to his case. He kept glancing nervously at his watch. He still had to pick up his car at the garage. Tapping his foot, he watched impatiently as the man filled in the blanks on the Missing Persons form on a decrepit old typewriter.

While the detective was typing with two fingers, Richard looked around. He was on the first floor in a back room with a Detective Noonan, choking on the smoke curling up from the cigar which sat on an ashtray on the desk. He looked back at the middle-aged detective with the potbelly. Somehow they were different in the movies.

The man was finishing his report. For the third time Richard interrupted the detective, appealing to the man. "Listen, this isn't like her. She hasn't called all afternoon. Her parents are waiting at the airport for her."

The detective nodded understandingly. Richard felt

he was doing it mechanically. Damn it! Jennifer wasn't a statistic. A missing person. Something was wrong. He had this chilling feeling that something was very wrong. And he was getting impatient.

"Okay, let's see if I have this straight," Detective Noonan droned. "She left the house after you and probably arrived at the theater before ten to attend her dancing class."

"She's a professional dancer, Detective. She takes class every morning with her company."

The detective looked at the young man oddly and said merely, "Oh." Then he recapped his report. "Let's see, she called you at her office. She was last seen at a rehearsal. She probably left the theater at around one o'clock this afternoon. What time do you have?"

Richard looked at the man in disgust. There was a large clock on the wall. Was this man retarded? "I have," he said angrily, "ten-forty-five. You don't understand. I have to go to the airport now and face her parents and I don't know what to tell them. She's missing!"

"I understand perfectly, Mr. Kupperman."

"Dr. Kupperman."

"Excuse me. But I don't think you really understand. Your girl friend has been missing only a little over nine hours. You do know that the Ballet Killer has been found?"

Richard gave up. "I'm sorry. That doesn't help. See, I know her and you don't. This isn't like her. She's in some kind of trouble. There are plenty of other nuts in this city even if that killer has been found."

"True. But let's be logical. Let's suppose she went somewhere and can't get in touch with you. People do that, you know."

"What? She's dancing the most important solo of her career tomorrow night! The only way she could be dragged away from that is against her will!"

The detective nodded again and made a note, which infuriated Richard even more. He started to get up to leave. The detective motioned him to sit down. "Relax. I'm trying to help. What was her state of mind when you last saw her?"

Richard looked at the floor and mumbled. "We had a fight."

The detective uttered a loud "Aha!" which Richard tried to overlook. It was getting late. "Look, I know what you're thinking. She's angry. I'm a jealous lover. I've though* of all that."

"But that's a good reason for her to be missing, isn't it?"

Richard stood up, feeling it had been a mistake to come to the police. The good old community-minded Twentieth Precinct. That was a joke. "Look," he pleaded, "I also know she was upset because her best friend was the last victim of the killer. I've thought of that, too. But it all boils down to this—she told me she would meet me at that restaurant at eight, and she wasn't there. Her parents have come all the way from Ohio and she didn't show up. She has to be in some sort of trouble!"

The detective sat chewing on his pencil. In the files were reports on missing persons who had been missing for over a year. Finally, he wrote down a number on a piece of paper and handed it to Richard. "Go to the airport and pick up her parents. Then come back to your apartment. If she is still missing or you still feel she's in trouble, call me."

"That's it," Richard said sarcastically. "You're not going to call the hospitals, or"—his voice lowered—"check the morgue. I have to do all that myself."

Detective Noonan got up and stared at Richard. It was an icy stare. Richard took the piece of paper and jammed it into his pocket, then turned and walked out of the room and down the hall. Detective Noonan stared after him, then took the pencil he had been chewing and broke it in half.

Sergeant Moskowitz sat in a graceful, high-backed chair opposite Mr. Zolinsky, who sat with his legs crossed casually, feet in slippers, on a brocaded wing chair. His apartment was in the West Sixties and Moskowitz still couldn't believe that this legendary man would find time to talk to him. Of course, it helped when he changed his name to Detective Moskowitz. He liked Zolinsky's fractured Russian pronunciation that made his name come out "Muscovitz."

And Moskowitz couldn't take his eyes off the man or his apartment. He couldn't believe the vital, white-haired man in front of him with the electric-blue eyes was actually seventy-five. And the apartment! Like from another century. The ceilings were enormously high and everywhere were these chandeliers with little hanging parts that tinkled all at once. It sounded like distant music. On the walls were dozens of mirrors and they multiplied everything in the room over and over. Golds, blues, whites. Moskowitz had never seen anything like it.

He explained carefully to the ballet master that they had to backtrack and ask some more questions as a routine finishing of the case. Zolinsky seemed to believe him. Moskowitz felt a little sorry for the old gentleman, too. He probably was lonely. Sure, even famous people got lonely.

Zolinsky offered him tea, but he declined. He got out his notebook and looked up. He almost dropped it. A beautiful young woman in a lounging gown, her long auburn hair glowing under the lights, stood in the doorway leading to the bedroom.

"Will you be long, Grischa?" she asked in a velvety voice.

"No, no, my dear. I should be but a minute. Try to amuse yourself." The gorgeous young woman vanished like a mirage into the bedroom.

Moskowitz cleared his throat. He had a lot to learn about people. He got down to business. "We're looking for Jennifer North. We have to ask her some questions. I understand she had no performance tonight and no rehearsal this afternoon. So that would mean she left the theater at one o'clock. . . ."

"My dear Detective Muscovitz, wait a second. The Ballet Killer has been found. What do you want with Jennifer North?" Then Moskowitz detected a note of alarm in his voice. "Is there anything wrong with her? Is she okay?"

"Oh, no, we just have to ask her some questions about her friend, Heather Cooper, and she's not around. Do you have any idea of where she goes on her days off?"

Zolinsky frowned. "It wasn't a day off. I ordered her to rest at home." Moskowitz was sure, though, he saw a fleeting look of annoyance or anger pass over the old gentleman's face as he said, "She has a boyfriend, a lover. He comes to the theater often. I believe his name is Richard. Yes, Richard Kupperman. A doctor, orthopedic surgeon, treats some of our dancers." Again the scowl on his face. Moskowitz thought it odd. Maybe there was something wrong with this doctor. He made a note to check him out.

Moskowitz noticed Zolinsky was now impatient to finish the interview. He asked one more question. "What about Max Forrest?"

Zolinsky looked slightly surprised. "What about him? He's one of our piano players." Zolinsky's usually impassive face flashed with impatience. The sooner he got this little detective out, the sooner his evening could begin. God knows he needed his share of recreation.

"I don't know him as a person, mind you, because he seems merely part of the piano. I hired him about a year and a half ago. He's one of the best pianists for class or rehearsal I've ever seen—and I know music. My father was a conductor in Russia. But Max seems a quiet, shy sort. I don't think he'll be with us much longer."

"Why not?"

Zolinsky stood up, indicating the interview was over. "Oh, common sense. A man with that kind of musical genius—we couldn't hope to hold him. He's probably composing a symphony. Or at least a Broadway score. He probably could have been a fine concert pianist."

Moskowitz thanked him, took one last eyeful of the wonderland that was Zolinsky's apartment, and left. So Max Forrest was a musical genius. Or at least Zolinsky thought so. Not that he knew that much about musical talent, but he had taken the time to study Max Forrest's file before he came. Why would a musical genius who could have been a concert pianist have loaded boxes in a warehouse for five years before coming to New York Center Ballet? He wondered if Zolinsky knew. Or perhaps Max lied and was never asked for any references because Zolinsky liked him. Perhaps this Max Forrest was some kind of a liar.

Lieutenant Frank Fazio was standing in the kitchen of his home leaning over the sink eating a hot roll with butter waiting for his dinner to be re-heated when the phone rang. He knew by the expression on his wife's face when she passed him the phone that this was not somebody calling to wish him a merry Christmas.

All during the phone call, Fazio was aware of background noises. His young son, Michael, in the basement with a friend lifting weights. His son-in-law and daughter trimming the Christmas tree. A radio somewhere in the house playing nonstop Christmas carols. His only replies to the phone calls were a grunted "Yes, sir," "I see," and "Of course." When he hung up the phone he stared into space wordlessly.

"What is it, Frank?" Connie asked cautiously. "Something's happened."

Without batting an eyelash or looking at her, he said, "Ivan Roman's dead."

"What?"

Fazio came close to her and held her tightly, putting his finger on her lips and whispering, "Shh! Connie, don't breathe a word about this. Not a word. Not even if reporters call and beg."

"But how . . ."

"He killed himself in his cell," he said bluntly. Then he added, under his breath, "Son-of-a-bitch."

"Frank, no one will really know if he killed all those girls if he's dead. You don't think he did it, do you?"

He couldn't help but smile. She knew it all along. "I love you, babe. I'll call when I can. I have to check it out. That was the chief; called me personally."

Connie noted the hint of pride in his voice, in his stance.

He started to walk away. "Frank, can't I just make you some roast-beef sandwiches, at least?"

"No time. I'll grab something."

Fazio left from the back door. He didn't want to say anything to his daughter and her husband, who were in the living room. But going to the garage, he bumped into Michael, who was coming up from the basement.

"Hey, Dad, where are you going? You just got here."

"Back to work."

Fazio could see Michael's friend in the shadows. He was staring at him with awe in his eyes. Michael was a popular kid. He had a dad who was a famous cop, who sometimes got on television.

"Hey, Dad, how come you weren't on the news tonight? It was your case."

Fazio reached down and tousled his son's chestnut-brown hair. He laughed. Because he didn't know what in the hell to say to his son.

When Fazio pulled out of the driveway, he had an idea. He would stop at the precinct house and see if Moskowitz was there. He had a right to know about Roman. Then he would go to the Tombs from there. And then probably nowhere. He couldn't question Roman now, that son-of-a-bitch. He couldn't see him fall apart under questioning that would have nothing to do with what the shrinks thought.

Fazio slammed on his horn angrily. So much traffic this time of night. He couldn't believe it. He sat and waited furiously. And then he looked in his rearview mirror. The same car, a purple Impala. Almost bumper to bumper behind him. There was a man in the front seat: hat, sunglasses. He stared straight ahead patiently, waiting.

Jennifer couldn't take her eyes off the coffee table. There were the pointe shoe and the magic marker. But she hadn't autographed it. At the last moment he went mad again and grabbed everything out of her hand. She thought he had changed his mind, but she knew it was more of Max's brand of hideous torture.

She tried to breathe through her nose and keep her mouth shut. It was an old trick she had learned to calm panic. She used it for stage fright. But it didn't work for her anymore. Not with Max Forrest, the maniac. She kept her mouth closed, anyway, because if she dared to open it she was positive she'd scream and never stop. She would lose control. And then he would have to kill her. She wondered how long she had to go before her spirit or her mind broke. Before it got so unbearable, she simply didn't care whether he killed her or not. Only that it be over. She hoped with all her heart that would never happen. She was a dancer. She had strength and she was a fighter. Oh, God, she didn't want to give up. She wanted to live.

Max stood in the middle of the floor. He was thinking. Maybe this apartment wasn't the right place to work, as he had originally planned. Perhaps they should go someplace else. But there wasn't much time, and so much to do. He smiled. It could all work as smooth as clockwork. Just like his mind. Everything would fall into place. He felt better now since he had gotten rid of that dumb cop. He grinned happily. He just thought of the perfect place to take her to.

She never knew how much he always watched her. The way she had of sticking the tip of her tongue out of the right side of her beautiful mouth when she was concentrating. And those long, elegant legs. Sometimes he thought she had the highest extension of anyone in the company. Including the principals. Yet Jennifer had never

*looked at him, really noticed him. All those days
in that sweat-filled classroom. He was just the
piano player.*

Jennifer heard Max call her name. She stood up.
Tired. She was so very tired. If only she could sleep.
But she wouldn't trust herself to take a nap. He might
kill her.

Where was he now? At the door. He was pointing
to something. Oh, yes, the pointe shoe on the coffee
table. More games. He wanted her to pick it up and
bring it to him. She did so, and like a dog answering
a command from its master, she went over to where
he was standing, obeying his gesture. He took the
shoe. She turned away. She was sick of his moods.

Before she had been able to run through her solo in
her mind just to keep herself sane. But now what was
the use? She'd never get to do it. She had been thinking of Richard. But even that was painful. If only they
hadn't fought this morning. If only they had at least
kissed good-bye, as usual. What would he think when
he discovered her missing? That she didn't care?

And so she now made her world very narrow. If he
told her to eat, she would. If she was to sit, she sat. If
he wanted her to bring something to him, she did it.
She concentrated only on one thing at a time and did
only what she had to do to stay alive for as long as
possible.

Max reached into the front closet and pulled out a
pearl-gray, loose-fitting cloth coat. Mama used to look
so pretty in this, he remembered. He helped Jennifer
on with it. Then he got her boots. She tripped trying to
put them on. She had to steady herself against the
wall.

Were they going outside? She was afraid to ask.
And why couldn't she wear her own coat? Max

handed her a flowered scarf. She put it around her neck and he waited until she was done and then ripped it off angrily. He put it over her head, tying it like an old lady's babushka. He handed her a pair of round-rimmed sunglasses and made her put those on. Jennifer didn't even try to think where he got all that stuff.

"It will work," he pronounced gravely.

Max put on a jacket but Jennifer didn't see him stuff a tape recorder inside it. Then he stuck his head out the door. Satisfied no one was in the hallway, he shoved her out of the apartment ahead of him. Jennifer took a deep breath. Out of the apartment! They were getting out of that horrid box! When they got outside, there would be a chance.

The halls were dimly lit. Slowly, carefully, they walked down the steps. Max kept behind her, but she was aware he was holding something in his hand. She held her breath. The apartment house was quiet, too quiet. But when they reached the second landing, she heard the creak of a footstep. And then another. Someone was coming up the steps. Max's hand gripped hers so hard she gasped. He whispered huskily in her ear, "Don't try anything funny. I have a gun in my hand." Jennifer moaned. She could feel it sticking into her back. Her knees began to buckle under her and Max grabbed her under her armpit before she fell. With the sunglasses on she could barely see, but she could hear. The footsteps were coming up the steps.

She made out a man's shape coming up the steps, a fat man, coming closer and closer and standing to the side, sucking in his stomach to let them pass. Jennifer's mouth fell open dumbly. But no sound came out. The gun was pressing into her back. Max was actually talking to the man.

"Merry Christmas, Mr. Geberhardt," Max said, keeping his grip on Jennifer.

Jennifer flapped her lips like a puppet, but still no voice came out. And then she had a revelation. How could he shoot her in front of this man?

"Ah, yes, and a white one, too."

Jennifer found her voice. She croaked out, "Oh, God, please help me! He's trying to murder me! Please call the police! The man's a killer!"

Mr. Geberhardt, or what she could see of him looked at her, or through her, and smiled pleasantly. "Ah, yes, Mrs. Forrest. Well, good to have you back." He cleared his throat and stared back up the stairs.

Jennifer thought for a moment she had lost her mind.

Max pressed the gun even harder into her back. "Don't try anything like that again! I'm warning you!" He took one of her arms and bent it all the way behind her back until she yelped in pain. Then he pushed her fast down the rest of the steps until she landed at the bottom with her sunglasses slipping off one ear. But now she could really see clearly. There was a light in the hallway and a small foyer with tacky carpeting. She stood and stared at the door leading to the street and waited. Once they got outside she'd run, she'd scream. Let him kill her if he wanted. People would see. Anything was better than this hell.

Then she felt herself being shoved again and heard a soft laugh. Max was pushing her away from the door, away from the outside. He pointed down the hall to another door in the building. The disappointment struck Jennifer so hard her body sagged. The boots, the coat. He had tricked her again. There would be no chance at freedom outside.

But the front door . . . the door was so close. Jennifer grabbed hold of the wooden banister and refused to budge. She would hold on tightly until he had come closer and then she would raise her knee and kick him in the balls as hard as she could. While he was doubled over in pain she would dash out the door, screaming, and run for the first policeman. She could do it. Oh, yes, she could. Her strength was in her legs. Max was coming closer. She knew it, though he was behind her. She raised her knee. The next thing she knew she was flat on the floor.

Max had very quietly walloped her in the stomach. She could barely get her wind. Before she did, she felt herself being lifted from under her armpits and just about dragged down the hall. Until they got to the door at the end.

Max stood her up. He opened the door, shoved her in, and closed it tightly behind them. Jennifer squinted. It was dark. Then he flicked on a light switch and they walked down some steps. They were in the boiler room of the apartment.

Jennifer began to feel queasy. There were more steps leading down to another basement. There was a strange, dank smell. The stairs were rickety and uneven and one or two were missing. Slime hung down from the walls like dirt icicles. Max put his two hands on her shoulders, keeping in back of her, and they walked down the treacherous steps. There were some moldy cardboard boxes here and there. A sudden movement across the floor sent balls of soot and dust scattering. Jennifer gagged. Rats.

Behind her, Max guided her until they got to another door. He took out a key and unlocked it. It was a door to a room way in the back of the obviously deserted sub-basement. He pushed Jennifer into the room. She took one look and whispered, "Oh, my God, no!" Cobwebs laced the corners of the walls, complete with spiders. There was a part of an old

washing machine half-falling apart. Even a wet, mil·
dewed box of Fab rested on the floor. In the corner
was a wrecked dryer and all along the wall wires had
been pulled and electrical plugs stood naked and
covered with dirt. It was an old laundry room. Or it
had been once. Now it was deserted, as was the rest
of the sub-basement.

Again she felt the gun press against her back. She
stiffened, waiting. Then she heard ripples of hysterical laughter. Ugly laughter. The pressure was out of
her back. She spun around and saw immediately what
Max thought was so funny. The gun he pressed into
her back all this time. It wasn't a gun. It was the
hard, wooden tip of one of her pointe shoes. She
wished it was a gun that she could grab out of hi·
hand and use on him. But it was herself she was fu
rious at. All this time there was no gun. She could
have escaped anytime. Now she never would

Sergeant Moskowitz yawned. It was half-past mid·
night. He just wanted to make some more notes on
this Max Forrest and then he'd go home. Men on the
new shift had invaded the old task force floor. Tables
were cleared away. The coffee machine had been
turned on and men were coming up. The floor belonged to everyone now, and shortly it would be a normal floor in the Twentieth with file cabinets, detectives,
equipment. He had to be careful to look inconspicuous.
But nobody ever paid much attention to Bernie
Moskowitz, anyway.

"Any more coffee?" someone asked.

"Sure. Help yourself." Then he turned around.
"Lieutenant . . . what!"

Fazio stirred in some Coffee Mate and three lumps
of sugar and motioned for Moskowitz to button up
He came to the desk where Moskowitz was sitting and

took a piece of paper. On it he wrote in big, black letters: IVAN ROMAN KILLED HIMSELF.

Moskowitz stared at it, then watched Fazio rip it up into tiny bits and let them snow into the wastebasket underneath the desk. "Orders to keep this quiet. No press for as long as possible." Fazio was speaking in little more than a whisper.

"Oh, Jeez," Moskowitz said so softly Fazio couldn't hear. "That means . . ."

"It means we'll never know unless another ballerina is . . ."

They were interrupted by the loud, unmistakable voice of Detective Noonan, on duty downstairs. He was quite close to them. He had come up for a cup of coffee. And he was talking to another detective. "Shit, I get all the dirty work. Ordinary Missing Persons case. You know how long this girl's been missing? Not even a half of a day, and her damned boyfriend calls me every ten minutes. It's like I'm haunted. He keeps insisting something's wrong. She's probably screwing someone else. He's a doctor, and you know doctors. Won't let anyone forget it. Jennifer North, Jennifer North. If I hear that name one more time . . . Oh, well, the broad'll turn up. Missing persons. I got missing persons missing for months, maybe years. Nobody raises such a stink. Doctors, huh, privileged characters. . . ."

He walked out of the room, his last words trailing past. Moskowitz and Fazio had heard every word. They exchanged knowing glances, then pushed their chairs aside, getting up almost as if it was choreographed in unison. Without a word they followed Detective Noonan.

Chapter Eleven

It first started the night Mama was taken away to that hospital. He was lonely. In all his life he had never been separated from her. He had paced up and down the silent apartment; then he had gone for a walk. He met Lisa by accident on a corner. They had started talking. Then she suggested they have a drink. They stopped in this little bar. Did he know what he was going to do then? It was hard to tell. She came up to his apartment and he insisted she dance for him. It was a lovely dance. Just for him. Her last dance, though she didn't know it. Then they made love. She was his first. When he heard her cry out with pleasure, he laughed. Then he took her tights, which were near him on the bed, and he strangled her.

RICHARD'S HANDS FUMBLED as he turned the key in the door. He was still shaky from the ride back from La Guardia Airport. He never was much good at making small talk. He hoped as he felt the key turn in the lock—*prayed* was more like it—that Jennifer was in the apartment. He visualized her sitting there with a towel wrapped around her freshly washed hair, wearing her ragged bathrobe, apologizing, having a plausible excuse. The door opened. The apartment was dark and silent. He turned all the lights on. There was no Jennifer. Quickly, he turned the pad with his note to her face down.

At the airport he had managed to sneak in a phone call to that idiot, Detective Noonan. On the ride home he had pretended to stop for gas and then called again. He wanted to call the man again now, but how was he supposed to do it with her parents standing right over him? They stood now in the middle of the floor, look-

237

ing very awkward. He was certain they sensed something was wrong.

"Let me take your coats," he said, overly solicitous. He still felt uncomfortable with the idea of being alone with this Midwestern couple who knew he was living with their daughter and privately wanted to brain him for it. It wasn't exactly Ohio stuff, he figured. But, oh, the hell with it, he was going to marry her! Or he wanted to, he amended, and swallowed hard.

"Coffee! Can I get you some coffee or tea? We have herb teas or regular tea. Apple juice? Orange juice? A drink?" he said rapidly.

"I'll have a glass of water, thank you, Richard," Mrs. North said.

"Herb tea sounds interesting," Mr. North said, lighting his pipe.

"We have cinnamon, lemon, some sort of spice . . ."

Mr. North interrupted him, raising a hand calmly. "Oh, anything you suggest will do."

"And cookies," Richard went on, unable to stop. "I think we have some cookies. Yes, oatmeal. Or would you prefer a sandwich . . .?"

He stopped. He realized they weren't listening to him. Their eyes were wandering around the apartment. They sat stiffly in the small wicker loveseat, half-looking around, half-studying Richard as he bustled around the kitchen alcove. He could have said, "Have a look around the apartment," but in their apartment, once you stepped in the door you saw pretty much all there was to see, unless you had to go to the bathroom. It probably wasn't like the big house they had. He wanted desperately to say, "Listen, I love your daughter so much. One day I'm going to buy her a house, any kind she wants. I'll do anything to make her happy." But he had already made her unhappy. Pouring the tea, he spilled a drop of scalding water on his thumb and almost jumped. He could feel their eyes watching him, silently. Running his thumb under ice-cold tap water, he blurted out merrily, "I guess Jennifer should be here any minute!"

Mr. and Mrs. North exchanged glances. Mrs. North, a petite, still slim, grayish-blonde woman spoke first. "Richard, we should be getting to our hotel, but we'd like to see Jennifer first."

Then Mr. North said bluntly, "Is there something wrong?"

Richard came into the living room alcove balancing a plate of oatmeal cookies on his arm, a glass of ice water in his right hand, and a steaming cup of herbal tea in his left. "Wrong?" he asked, as he served them and sat down, holding the plate of cookies in his lap. "Why do you think anything's wrong?"

Then he bit on an oatmeal cookie absentmindedly; it got stuck in his throat and he choked and sputtered for about two minutes. He ran to get a glass of water, wiped his eyes, then came back. He stood in the middle of the floor and looked at them, just looked at them. In that one moment Jennifer's parents had the first glimpse of the fact that this bumbling, fumbling, hyper young man their daughter had chosen might actually be a doctor of medicine. He said solemnly, very much in control of his voice now, "Yes, there's something very wrong. I've been to see the police. All the calls I made on the way here—those weren't to Jennifer." He looked down at the floor. "They were to the detective I talked to." He looked up sadly. "Jennifer's missing."

Jennifer stood in the middle of the dingy old room feeling naked. Max had told her to take off her coat and she was wearing only her leotards, tights and leg-warmers, hugging herself to keep warm. He handed her her pointe shoes and told her to put them on. What did they call what he was doing to her? Chinese water torture—that was it. Any second he could kill her. But now he was just playing. In another second he might stop playing.

She stepped out of her boots and bent down to put on her shoes, mechanically knotting and tying the ribbons. Instinctively, she put her weight on first the right foot, rolling the toe forward, and then the left. She looked around. It was impossibly dirty. She couldn't dance here.

She soon saw she was wrong. Max was unrolling some sort of linoleum carpet. It was smooth and clean but didn't look slippery. He put it in the middle of the floor, waving her aside while he placed it properly. Then he pulled out a small tape recorder from his jacket. So, he had it all planned, she thought. She would dance to some recorded music on a large square of linoleum. And then what? Oh, why hadn't she made a run for it! Why didn't she know he didn't really have a gun? How could she figure out his craziness?

Max smiled, satisfied with himself. "I want you to dance for me, Jennifer."

Jennifer stood and stared at him. Max was glaring at her, leaning jauntily against a long old table that must have been been used for the laundry room. He reached over and pressed "play" on the recorder.

Jennifer got ready to do her solo. But the music was all wrong. It was Stravinsky. "That's not the music to my solo. I can't dance to that. That's from something else. I can't remember."

Max smiled again. "You can forget your solo, Jennifer. You'll never do it."

Jennifer's shoulders slumped and her waist caved in. She felt dizzy, light-headed. He was going to kill her in this basement, this filthy dungeon. Then she remembered the rope with the pointe shoes. They were used, dusty. Some were soiled. They had had to dance for him, too, and then they were murdered. As in the ballet *The Red Shoes*, they must have danced and danced until they died. Only no blood. Max strangled. She touched her neck, feeling a little nerve pulsating.

"You know where the music is from," Max teased.

Jennifer looked up, unable to hide the fear and anger on her face. She shook her head from side to side like a rebellious child. Now he had shifted to the role of ballet master.

"It's the music from *Petroushka*. Do you know the solo at the fair?"

"Which one, Max? There were two solos for girls."

Max smiled gleefully. "The one with all the turns, of course! She just keeps turning on one pointe until the crowd applauds her virtuosity."

"I . . . I don't know it. I've seen it once, maybe. But I heard Zolinsky does it a little differently . . ."

Max interrupted her with a ragged laugh. "I know!" he exploded. Again Jennifer was aware of the fact that the oddest things struck him funny. He would roar with laughter over nothing. Was he going to swing again into another mood? She backed away slightly. His eyes had that funny stare again. It was as if he were looking through her, looking past her, at something not in the sooty laundry room.

    She was trying to teach him the part. He protested. "No! Mama! Not a girl's part!" But she had insisted that a good dancer can do any part. He backed away, trying to run. "It's a girl's part. I'm not gonna do any girl's part . . . Maaaaa!" She raised her hand and slapped him so hard

across the face, he fell back. She raised it again,
but he put his hands over his face and nodded.
Then he began to learn the first few steps of the
solo. She made him wear pointe shoes.

"Max?" Jennifer whispered, not realizing she had
said anything.

But Max was instantly alert. "I was just thinking,"
he replied. "Where should we begin?"

Now Jennifer had the oddest sensation that they
were at a rehearsal for *Artemis Visions* and he was
acting as he always did. Like a piano player. Like a
professional musician. It was absurd. Insane.

She looked at her pink satin pointe shoes. They
wouldn't get dirty if she stayed on the square of linoleum. Well, she only intended to mark it, whatever
nonsense he would teach her. And how could a man
she had seen limp even begin to teach her that kind of
solo? Jennifer felt more confident somehow. She would
try to humor him. More time meant she would be res-
cued. Surely Richard knew she was missing. He was
probably with the police already. It must be close to
midnight. She had seen a clock as they left the apartment and it wasn't that long ago, though every minute
seemed like a year now.

She looked up at Max and smiled, confidently, almost cheerfully, trying to be the old Jennifer. "Max?
Why don't we begin at the beginning?"

Max snapped his fingers when she presented him
with the answer to his difficult problem. Then he
switched on the music and walked slowly toward Jennifer.

There were two straight-backed chairs in front of
Detective Noonan's desk on the first floor of the Twentieth. Fazio sat in one, smoking. Moskowitz sat in the

other, wondering how Fazio was going to handle this one.

Fazio offered Noonan a cigarette and the harassed detective declined, pointing to his ever-smoldering cigar in an ashtray on his desk.

"What are you hanging around for, Lieutenant? You should be out celebrating. The Ballet Killer is sewed up." Fazio stubbed out his cigarette and laughed. "Over. Yeah, over for Hogan. I get all the shit work. Interesting Missing Persons case you have."

Noonan looked confused. "Which one?"

"That girl, Jennifer North. Couldn't help but overhear you complain about it, Noonan."

"Oh, yeah—her pain-in-the-ass boyfriend. I told him to call me, but I didn't think . . . aw, hell, forget it. It's really no problem. What can I do you for? Obviously, you want something."

"Maybe I want to give you something. But you'll owe me."

"I owe everybody."

"This girl, Jennifer North—she's one of the people I have to double-check. You know, backup, statements on the Ballet Killer case. Do you know she lived almost next door to Heather Cooper?"

Noonan shrugged. "The killer's been found. Stress, a fight with her boyfriend, another boyfriend. She hasn't been missing that long, Lieutenant, but this Dr. Kupperman's driving me crazy." He relit his cigar.

Fazio lit another cigarette. His mouth felt like the army had marched through without socks. He smiled at Noonan. Inside he was very nervous. He wanted to twist some red tape and take the case. "The boyfriend." Fazio laughed. Moskowitz laughed to help him along but was sorry he did. Noonan was looking at him strangely, as if seeing him for the first time.

"Nothing, Noonan," Fazio said to dismiss his laugh. "I just thought of something funny. Here I've been busting my ass just to talk to this Jennifer North, get some information from her. I swear, one shitty little detail and I can't find her. And here you are bitching because her boyfriend's busting your ass to find her and it's a run-of-the-mill Missing Persons case to you."

Noonan frowned. He failed to see what was so funny. "You think her missing has got something to do with the Ballet Killer case? They're not sure that's the guy?" he said craftily.

"Oh, c'mon, Noonan, you're reading too many detective novels. I think what I know you think. She's shacking up with another guy and the boyfriend's jealous."

Noonan relaxed back in his chair. That was exactly what he thought, and it was why Kupperman pissed him off so much. "But," Fazio said, "I still need to talk to her. I mean, I'll take the whole case off your hands for you. You can pay me back anytime. It's okay."

"Gee, thanks, Lieutenant. This guy's a headache." Just then the phone rang. "Hey, you wanna bet that's him? How much you want to bet?"

Fazio shrugged. Noonan picked up the phone.

"Detective Noonan. . . . Yes, Dr. Kupperman . . . yes, I understand. . . . Whoa! Slow down." He smiled broadly and said, "Lieutenant Frank Fazio has just been given your case, Dr. Kupperman." He raised his other hand in a gesture that said "I give up" and handed the phone to Fazio.

Captain William Hogan and his wife, Barbara, were just coming back into their hotel room when the phone rang. "Did you order anything from room service?" she asked, confused. They knew no one there.

"Just champagne to seduce you with. They're probably calling to say they're all out." Then he was serious. "I'll get it."

There was a crackling and a heavily accented woman spoke. Her accent was unmistakably New Yorkese. His wife sat on the bed watching him. He held his hand over the receiver. "It's just a nothing call from the department. Go down to the lobby and get me some cigars, will ya, sweetie?"

His wife left the room and Hogan said to the operator, "Yes, I'll accept the charges."

"I've been following Fazio all night, Captain," said the familiar voice from New York. "Very odd. He's working with Moskowitz somehow. I tailed him all the way out to where he lives in Brooklyn. Then he comes out again and goes all the way back to Manhattan. This was less than two hours ago—our time."

"Did he recognize you?"

"Not a chance. I'm pretty good at disguising myself. But you're right, Captain; he's up to something, and something's up."

Captain Hogan sighed. He was thinking of putting everything out of his mind. Maybe a walk on the beach in the moonlight with his wife. A vacation at last after the long year he'd just been through. And now Fazio was going to ruin it for him. It made him damned angry.

Hogan sighed loudly. "Tell you what, call me first thing tomorrow. Let's leave it for tonight."

"Okay, Captain, anything you say."

"Oh, just one more thing. How did you get on to him?"

Shipley chuckled over the phone. "Oh, well, you know my drunk act. Fazio kept asking all these questions. Then I started following him and I decided the best place for me was on the task force floor pretending to have passed out, ya see? I overheard the whole conversation he had with Moskowitz. I knew they'd come back there. Well, I heard parts of it, anyway. Enough to guess they're up to something."

"Good work, Shipley."

Hogan lit a cigar and waited for his wife to come back. No, nothing would ruin his vacation. Actually, Fazio wasn't as smart as he had given him credit for. And that wasn't too much to begin with.

There was a steady drip somewhere in the pipes. Patches of green mold showed in the corner growing like a clump of moss in the dampness. Jennifer shivered, standing on her patch of linoleum waiting for Max's next move. He had come very close, walked around the linoleum, and then walked back to the table.

"Jennifer!"

She looked up sharply, squinting her eyes as if there were a spotlight aimed at her.

"Take hold of that barre!"

She looked around. What on earth was he talking about?

"The barre, the barre!" he screamed. Then she saw it. A rusty pipe about the same size as a ballet barre. Swallowing down a rising nausea, she touched it.

Max slipped another cassette into the tiny tape recorder and she could hear the exact music he played for company class. Almost the same sequence. *"Plié!"* he shouted.

She winced and began a *demi-plié*. Max was shouting, "Two *demis* in fifth, four *grande,* arms, bend from the waist, back-bend, arms in fifth, *relevé* and stay."

She followed the instructions, which were at about the level she was on when she was very little. She wondered if there was a name for his madness. "Schizy" was the best she could come up with. She did her back bend and realized he wasn't even looking at her. He was pacing and mumbling.

He hated to be singled out. Madame was looming on top of him. All he could see were her glittering eyes and that pointer. His teeth crunched into his lower lip. His thighs were quivering. "Boys are supposed to jump high!" she yelled. "Plié and jump!" Whack! The pointer hit him behind his knee so that he almost fell. "Plié! Plié! If you don't plié right, how will you jump? Plié! Plié!"

"Plié!" Max shouted, and Jennifer jumped down from half-toe, and began to *plié* once more. It was madness. She needed double leg-warmers and a sweater in here. She felt chilled. It was like she was playing a game with a demented child, except that Max was big and strong and his little games were deadly.

The panic didn't rise in her again until he came toward her, eyes bright, and tweaked her chin. "We'll skip the rest of the class, Deborah, and go on to *piqué* turns."

Jennifer stared at him, not comprehending. Her stomach felt like it was curdling. That was the first time he had ever called her by someone else's name. But who? Her frantic mind raced through the list. Yes, there was a Deborah on one of the toe shoes in his bathroom. Did that mean he was going to kill her now? Maybe that's what it meant.

She clutched on to the putrid pipe, more to steady

her wobbling knees than for use as a barre. She kept the pretend-class sequence going. He seemed to be staring at an old hole in the wall where a washing machine had probably once been.

He tried to swallow but his throat was so dry. He saw the line of little girls on the other side watching him, as it was his turn. "Piqué and piqué!" commanded Madame, her hands on her hips. Slowly, nervously, he bent his right knee and put his foot behind the ankle of his left leg. Then he made his arms like a basketball hoop, iutted his jaw way out, and leaned back. He did a piqué turn. The next thing he knew he was sitting on the floor. Whack! He felt the pointer come down painfully on the inside of his thigh. Then a perfectly formed pink-and-white little blonde girl came forward. Madame pointed to her proudly. "Deborah, you show him how to do it." He didn't watch Deborah. He was dreaming of putting ground glass in her ballet slippers.

Jennifer longed for a break. She went through the little pattern of practice steps five times before she dared steal a glance at Max. When she did she saw he was watching her, his hands on his hips.

"You must practice, Jennifer. Especially those *pliés.*"

She nodded. His voice sounded funny. Weird. This was a new voice. Deborah! Yes. Now she remembered. How could she have forgotten? Deborah Strong. Blonde. The last one in November before . . . Heather. There was some talk she would switch from National and come to New York Center. She never got the chance.

Max turned abruptly and went over to the tape recorder. He took out the cassette and put in another one. Soon she heard the Stravinsky music.

"Do you think you can turn on pointe?" Max said sarcastically.

Jennifer just wanted to lie face down somewhere, even on the filth-encrusted floor of the old laundry room. Smiling, her insides screaming, she took a perfect preparation for her turn. She looked up at Max and stopped. Her mouth fell open. Max was marking the solo from *Petroushka*. He actually knew all the steps and the arm and head movements!

It was almost two in the morning when Fazio jiggled the lock and opened the door to Ivan Roman's apartment in Long Island City. The first thing that hit his senses was the stench.

He turned on the light. There were cages, and in the cages were rabbits. Ivan Roman kept rabbits. He looked around. Much of it had been shown in photographs in the papers. The markings on the walls, the clippings with red arrows. Supposedly Roman's plans for the next murder. Everywhere clutter and disorder. But no guns or weapons had been found.

It was a long, oddly shaped apartment, much like Jerry Turner's. Except for the rabbits, it had a strange quality to Fazio. Life was missing from it somehow. There was some sort of bed, and everywhere piles of junk you might find on a street corner. Stray bits of decaying lumber, broken chairs with the stuffing falling out, a table with one leg missing. He walked over to the cages and stroked a rabbit. Much of what Hogan called evidence—the dancers' clothes and shoes—had been removed. But underneath a soiled newspaper, Fazio saw something that had been overlooked.

One pair of pink dancer's tights. He put on his gloves and fished them out. They were soiled.

Who was this man, Ivan Roman? he wondered. He had served in the Vietnam War, but he had enlisted. That was odd for those times. He was crazy. Everyone agreed on that. But he was smart enough to kill himself, in a damned ingenious way. Fazio had just seen how smart when he had investigated the death at the Tombs a short while ago. Now Ivan Roman, the enigma, was lying in the morgue and no one would really know who he was. Fazio sighed. The story would be splashed all over the newspapers in the morning. Some clever reporter, a bribe, an offer to tell the story for money by someone, whatever. All he had done for the chief was to let the story stay quiet a little while longer. Which would make it appear even more sensational when it broke.

God, he was tired. He couldn't even think clearly. After Moskowitz got through talking to Jennifer North's boyfriend, he had been given orders to go home and get some sleep. That's what he knew he should do, too, but he couldn't sleep when he had a puzzle that didn't fit. On the other hand, he wondered if it would ever fit.

Still holding the tights, he walked nervously around the apartment. As he got away from the rabbits he could swear he smelled a different kind of odor. He walked farther away. Then he sniffed the tights. Fazio leaned back on his heels and laughed. It was so simple.

The smell. The crusty, white substance all over the tights. Semen. It was obvious Roman had masturbated into these clothes. And the others? Probably. The laugh was on Hogan. Ivan Roman wasn't the Ballet Killer. Fazio was sure of it. He was the thief and a jealousy killer with a photographic memory. He needed to be punished for masturbating. A real head job. Sooner or later everyone would figure it out.

He was still chuckling when he realized he desperately needed to sleep. He'd drive back to the precinct and sleep in the car, park it in the back of the driveway where no one would see. He even had a blanket and pillow in there. There was no time to go home. He was on a case. Tomorrow he had to be alert. Jennifer North was a young ballerina and she was missing. He knew now the Ballet Killer was still out there. He also knew it wouldn't be wise to tell the chief what he had really found.

At 2:00 in the morning, Jennifer North was being made to do the first few steps of the *Petroushka* solo again. She stumbled, cried out, then fell to her knees exhausted, sobbing loudly.

"What's the matter? Are you tired?"

"Kill me now, please. I can't take any more of this!" Jennifer wailed, her head buried in her thighs.

"Do you want to go to sleep?" Max smiled at her. His voice was soft and understanding.

"Yes, in a nice bed, and could I please take a bath first?" Jennifer was aware that she was talking like a little girl.

Max laughed, enjoying that. "Of course not. But you must sleep. I'll get you something." Jennifer stood up wearily and pinned up a piece of hair that had fallen down from her bun.

"I need to take out my contact lenses. My case is in my purse."

"I'll get it."

"I have to . . . go," she said pleadingly.

"I said I was leaving."

"But there's no bathroom down here!"

Max pointed to an old drain that must have been used for the washing machines. Jennifer looked at him, astounded. He met her gaze. She was to use the drain like a dog raising its leg on a curb. She let out a sigh. No wonder Max killed women. He really hated them.

Without a word he opened the outside door and locked it again behind him. Let him drug her then, she thought. What difference did it make? She already felt a little loony. She inched down her black leotard and then took one leg out of her tights. Watching the steady stream as if from a distance, she tried to bring Richard back in her mind. She envisioned herself back in her own apartment. Right now she would be in their brass bed snuggled against him. He always fell asleep first. Then she liked to play with the hairs on his chest until she fell asleep.

She stepped back into her leotard, wanting to cry, but there were no tears left. A wave of hopelessness and depression settled over her. In just a few hours she had been through so much horror. She thought wistfully of the fight she had had with Richard this morning. The tour. It seemed so silly. It seemed so long ago. If only somehow, through some miracle, she could survive this, then she wouldn't even go on the tour. She would join National. It didn't matter anymore. Nothing mattered but staying alive.

She touched her hand to her face. It was wet with tears. She had been crying and she thought there was no more left. Her nerves were taut because she knew that any minute Max would come through the door. The thought of him made her stomach feel cramped. She had slept with him. He had touched her. Oh, God, part of this was her fault. If only she had left.

If anything happened to her, people would think she had been raped. Then Richard would never know. She had never wanted to hurt him. Being with him felt so safe and secure. Why hadn't she realized before how much she loved him? What if she never saw him again and he never really knew?

Chapter Twelve

*The little bastard's been good to me, after all,
she thought. She didn't feel so badly about not
having a daughter. Well, maybe not as badly as
she used to feel. Of course, she would never forgive Max for botching up his true calling, but
then, again, he was a good son to have around.
Faithful, loyal, devoted. Everyone in the hospital
said so. Hah! If they only knew why. But she
would never tell the doctors that part. She wasn't
crazy. But Max was. That nice-looking young
man was like an instrument for her to use. Charming and kind. What a joke! Oh, yes, he fooled
them all. Raising Max was like taming a wild beast.*

THERE WAS A tapping at the window. Fazio woke up with a start. It was still dark out, but the first rays of morning were creeping into the wintry sky. He looked out at the other side of the locked car and saw a cauliflower nose and triumphant smile pressing against the window. Damn it! he thought. Reporters. They didn't waste any time. Three of them ready to go. That would be some picture of him that hopefully wouldn't get in the paper.

He rolled down the window one-half inch and smiled gamely. "Can't you give a guy a chance to shower and shave? Huh?"

As if they never heard him, one fired away immediately: "How does Ivan Roman's suicide affect his credibility as the Ballet Killer?" Fazio stared back. "Where's Captain Hogan?" Fazio put his hands over his ears, then noticed one reporter had his forefinger in the little space in the window. Quickly, Fazio flicked it away and rolled up the window. Then he waved good-bye, smiled at them, and sank back into his homemade bed of rumpled blanket and pillow. He needed just a half-hour more of sleep, he decided. Plus the five minutes it would take those guys to stop pounding on the car and shouting and go somewhere else for their story.

Fazio didn't get his full half-hour. Ten minutes later there was a gentle tapping at the window. He looked up. This was a face he would stay awake for. Outside was the red, chapped-looking mug of Moskowitz, complete with bleary eyes and a stream of vapor coming out of his mouth as Fazio saw his lips form the words, "Lieutenant?"

No two ways about it, it was time to get up. He folded the blanket and put it with the pillow in the corner of the back seat. Then he leaned over and unlocked the glove compartment. He scooped up a case with toothbrush, toothpaste, soap and razor. Something Connie had taught him years ago. Connie. He would have to call her first.

Fazio climbed out of the car and stretched. He could see the pile of reporters now streaming into the vestibule. He grabbed Moskowitz and headed for a side entrance.

"When did it break?" he asked.

"Early this morning. It's the biggest story since Christmas, Lieutenant."

"And you're reporting for work on your off-duty?"

"Aw, c'mon, Lieutenant. It's not work for me. I think we're on to something."

"Or off something. We'll never know from Roman, that's for sure." They were inside now, safe, pressing the button for an elevator to take them up.

"And what about Dr. Kupperman and the parents?"

"I talked to them last night. Well, Lieutenant,

they're worried. Say it isn't like her. Tonight's a big night for her. Her big solo, you know. I don't know. The whole thing sounds funny to me. Why would a girl who wants to be a ballerina pull a disappearing act right before her big break? But I did like you said. I never let on. Just took a lot of notes." He tapped his pocket where his notebook was.

"Good."

Fazio and Moskowitz reached an almost-empty sixth floor. So far the floor was still abandoned, as the task force had been dismantled and the men had gone back to their usual duty. Fazio felt grubby. But the first thing he was going to do wasn't to head for the men's room or even call his wife. The first thing he was going to do was to go into the office he had always had as Lieutenant Squad Commander of the Sixth Homicide Division and with one hand sweep away all of Hogan's junk that was on top of his desk.

At 7:30 the line had already formed in front of the locked door to the cafeteria in the closed ward at Manhattan State. There was no reason to line up. The door would stay locked until the kitchen staff was ready. Still, they did it. Because there was nothing else to do. Bernice, a lifelong patient, was walking aimlessly about. She wore a clean hospital dress, her hair was shiny, shaped like a black helmet around her once almost attractive square face. Her finger was going even faster over her nose and she was emitting little squeaky sounds.

Charlotte Forrest smoothed her hands over her good navy-blue dress that Max had brought for her. Max really did so much for her. But she deserved it. She had raised the little bastard all alone. With no one to help her out. His father didn't even know he existed.

*That one day when she went to see him, her
belly stretching out a sweater, because she didn't
have money for real maternity clothes, she had
been turned away. He didn't care. People like
that are the enemy. People who don't care. Because they don't have to. They have everything.
She had taught Max long ago who to watch out
for, what might hurt him if he wasn't silent and
careful.*

Her forehead was damp. She had been perspiring
in her anger. But soon she wouldn't have to be angry
anymore.

She patted the space between her shoulder and her
bra. Inside the top of her good dress was a filled
hypodermic needle. The large part was cradled inside her bra. The needle was pierced like silver
stitches through the thick strap of her bra. And just
to make sure it wasn't noticeable, she had pinned a
big lipstick-tinted Kleenex flower she had made in
occupational therapy to her dress, hooking it onto the
hypodermic needle.

She looked around. Today would be her last day
in this lunatic asylum. She shuddered. Oh, my God.
What if she had to stay here like Bernice, who was
a walking vegetable. Charlotte tried not to stare at
what she thought of as the "female thing," but Bernice
stood in front of her, stopping like a car at a red light,
and stared right into Charlotte's eyes, flipping her
finger furiously over her nose. Charlotte moved away
from her. Just this one more morning and she'd be
free of the sights that assaulted her nerves and senses.
She was, after all, such a sensitive woman.

*That stupid Judge Martin Cooper, who had had
her thrown in Bellevue and then farmed over to*

this zoo. He was one of them. Sure, he could
go home to his manicured lawn and play tennis
in his backyard, probably, and just forget all
about the people he had pushed around. Forget
all about Charlotte Forrest, whom he had plunked
in the booby hatch, telling her she was lucky she
didn't go to jail. Luck, hah! Max had ended up
killing his daughter. Though it would have been
more fun if he hadn't.

The cafeteria door was opening. As they lined up
their trays for what Charlotte called "that slop,"
they could see through to the men's kitchen on the
other side. She went in, trying to keep her mind on
her sliding tray, but made the mistake of looking
up. There he was. The white-haired man they said
she had attacked. His large, mournful eyes searched
hers as if to say: What did I ever do to you? He had
a bandage over his head. Charlotte looked away. He
didn't exist. He never really did. She didn't hit him
purposely. It was just that she didn't like his fine
manners and elegant white hair.

She had met him at one of the dopey dances they
had every week so the two sides, drugged and salt-
petered, could have some physical contact. He had
asked her to dance at the one yesterday, almost
bowing. It was after her shock treatments and she
had trouble remembering things. Her mind wasn't
working yet. She accepted and they waltzed into the
hall and then she dragged him into that room. She
remembered now she couldn't control herself. She had
wanted to kill him. Because of his fineness and soft
voice. She told the doctors it was the shock treatments. Had to be. But now she smiled as she turned
and took her tray back to a table. It had felt so good
banging his head against the wall. When she shut

her eyes she could pretend it was someone else. But, of course, there were much better, much more subtle ways of disposing with phony high-and-mighties who moved people about as if they were on some sort of checkerboard.

"Boy, Mrs. Forrest, you look nice. What I wouldn't give to be in your shoes," a young girl at her table said suddenly. "I have to spend Christmas here." Charlotte smiled and nodded at Irma but said nothing. Sometimes the girl chattered happily and sometimes she sat cowering in a chair in a catatonic trance, looking like a hostile sphinx. Charlotte didn't like the girl. But she smiled again. The shoes she would be wearing tonight would be like the ruby slippers Dorothy wore in *The Wizard of Oz*.

Max was three when she took him to see that movie. She had called him Maxie then. He had screamed and cried, frightened by it all. But she had made him stay and made him shut up and mind his manners, too. A woman raising a little boy alone? She didn't want a sissy. She felt pleased he had turned out the way he had.

Jennifer was just waking up in the sub-basement of Max's building. She was lying flat on her back on the old laundry table, a pillow under her head. She didn't want to open her eyes. If she did, she would remember where she was. This might be her last day alive. Her head ached and she felt so stiff and grimy she wanted to crawl inside herself. She just lay there rigidly, hands at her sides, cover on top of her, eyes closed. She didn't think she could stand up without help.

It was when Fazio had first walked onto the sixth floor that he noticed something familiar. Something that had stopped the day Ivan Roman was declared the Ballet Killer by Hogan and the media. All the phones were ringing at once. When he got into his office he pressed a button and picked one up. "No, Captain Hogan is not here. Who is this? This is Lieutenant Frank Fazio. Well, if you want to talk to him, you'll have to call him in Bermuda." He slammed the phone down. Then he picked it up again. "Yes, Chief. Yes, I held it for as long as I could. No, no foul play. Strictly a suicide, like I said. I'm sure. I'll file a full report. Hogan? Oh, he'll take over from here? Cutting his vacation short, is that it? Well, good. Yeah, merry Christmas to you, too." He hung up.

"Son-of-a-bitch," Fazio muttered.

"What?" Moskowitz said, somewhat confused, wondering whether to answer all the calls or let them ring.

"Hogan's winging his way back."

"He'll fight for Roman."

"Probably resurrect him from the grave."

One phone kept ringing and didn't stop. Moskowitz picked it up. He listened, then put his hand over the receiver.

"Her boyfriend, Dr. Kupperman."

Fazio put out his hand for the phone.

"I'll take it."

All he got a chance to do was nod. Finally, he said, "No. His suicide does not mean there's a chance he's not the Ballet Killer. How could it?" Fazio was a good liar when he wanted to be, he thought to himself.

"Look, Dr. Kupperman, where's she due next? What's her routine? Company class at ten o'clock. Okay, we'll meet you there." That seemed to satisfy him, and Fazio finally put the phone down with a sigh. He said to Moskowitz, "Answer the phones or not, I don't care. But remember, we're not even supposed to be here. Frankly, there's no one in the world I want to talk to right now." He took his case and started to walk out of the office.

"Lieutenant!" Moskowitz shouted. Fazio turned wearily. Moskowitz was holding a receiver out. "Your wife." Fazio walked back into his office.

Max felt good. The sun was shining through the little bedroom. He had slept in Mama's bed last night. Now he bent down to the bottom of her dresser, opened the drawer, and lifted it out. It was wrapped in yellow flannel. No Saturday Night Special for him. He lifted it out and stroked it. Oh, no, he had driven all the way to North Carolina and bought this gun in a drugstore. Then he had gone, for a whole year, out to New Jersey and practiced with a target in the woods. He had taught himself to shoot. And he was a pretty damned good shot. Funny, he never used the gun with the girls. No, he liked to feel their softness first. Then he liked to feel them with his own hands as they died.

He remembered them all vividly. Delicious Lisa had happened by accident. But Elizabeth. She had stopped by for coffee. He had left her body in the fountain at Lincoln Center. He scratched his head. No, that was wrong. Elizabeth had been found in the middle of Washington Square Park in a lawn-leaf bag. Ah, there was Nicole. Nicki. With her jet-black hair and violet-tinged eyes. She had whispered she loved him right before he strangled her. He smiled. Then he frowned. There was that mix-up with her. She was mistaken for a bag of garbage, and it took them so long to get her back from the Sanitation Department. And then in parts. He giggled. It had all been wonderful. Only Heather Cooper had ruined it. She knew from the start and fought him. It wasn't any good with Jennifer, either, because he knew he had to be careful not to kill her.

Charlotte Greene in June had been the best. Even better than Lisa. Because she had the same name as Mama. It had been fun to fantasize Mama as a young girl. Mama under him, moving like that lively young dancer had. Mama. Suddenly he looked around. His daydreams had to be over. For a year he had worked alone. Now he would have Mama back. He wouldn't need his girls anymore.

Putting his gun back, he went into the kitchen. It was almost 8:30. He had already eaten and washed and dried the dishes. Bacon, scrambled eggs, hot buttered rolls, and hot coffee. She should be getting up now. She would enjoy the breakfast he had prepared for her. Of course, it wasn't as good as the breakfast he had had. He shrugged. He deserved a better one. He was doing all the work. As an afterthought he went into the living room and reached into her bag.

The hall was empty when he double-locked his door. Wearing a brown V-necked sweater over a checkered shirt and khaki pants, he walked quietly down the hall and started down the steps. If anybody was curious, it would look like he had to go to the basement. Nobody went to the sub-basement. It wasn't even used for storage. None of the new tenants had probably even seen it.

Jennifer had dozed into a drugged nightmare. She was half-awake and half-asleep when she heard the loud click. Max. Her rest was over. Her body felt like it was connected to a vibrating machine, she was trembling so all over.

When she finally did open her eyes, Max was standing over her looking at her like she was a patient. He looked well rested. Though it didn't seem like either had had that much time to sleep. Grinning broadly, he showed her he was hiding something behind his back.

"I brought you some breakfast," he said. He produced a Thermos from somewhere. "Coffee," he said triumphantly and unscrewed the lid, which was to be her cup.

"I don't drink coffee," she said, turning her head away. Max shut his eyes. Images, memories; they came back so quickly lately.

> "Drink this, Ma. Please. The man said to make you hot, black coffee."
> She had slapped his hand away and the hot coffee spilled on his pants. "You little brat. It's all your fault. Look at how ugly and deformed you are. If you had listened to me, you could be studying ballet. Now what good are you?"
> He turned away, tears burning his flushed cheeks. Now Mama was drinking more and more. The police brought her home from bars. And it was all his fault. Someday he would show them. Someday he would make it up to her.

He opened his eyes and realized they were wet. Now, he would make it all up to her. She would have a better life once they got away.

He reached into his pants pocket and took out a cluster of sugar packets. He had stolen them from coffee shops to save money, though he made enough now to buy real sugar. A habit from Mama, he guessed. He ripped apart three sugars and poured them into the little Thermos cup. Jennifer's stomach growled.

"Drink the coffee, Jennifer. You need it."

She took the cup in both hands, yelping because it was so hot and sat up. Immediately she felt dizzy and everything was blurry. Taking a sip, she made a sour face.

Then, like a child pulling presents from a Christmas stocking, Max pulled out of his pockets two hard-boiled eggs, salt folded into a tiny square of wax paper, a squashed roll, and an apple. Jennifer smiled with relief. Food. Un-greasy, edible food.

Greedily, she peeled the eggs and ate while Max watched her. "I'll save the apple," she said, in a small voice, as if it was a question.

He handed her her compact so she could put in her contact lenses. Jennifer rinsed them with saliva and put them in, blinking away the tears until they stopped burning.

"And now for the final surprise!"

Jennifer looked at him. This was the Max now who played the piano for class and rehearsal, who all the girls in the corps had a crush on.

In his hands was a cigarette. A precious cigarette. She grabbed for it. "I need a light," she snapped.

Max laughed and clicked his thumb and forefinger together. "I knew there was something I forgot."

She waited, not knowing what she was waiting for, wanting that cigarette more than anything in the world. She looked around the dirty laundry room hungrily, searching every corner for an old, stray book of matches.

Max watched her, obviously enjoying her fit. Cigarette-smoking. It sickened him. People only did it to make themselves look important. Maybe he wouldn't let her have that cigarette. After all, she'd have to give it up someday. He liked watching her squirm. She was a slave. His slave. Then he thought of Mama. He was supposed to keep Jennifer happy. Relenting, he pulled out a pack of matches and tossed it to her so fast she missed and had to stoop down to pick it up. She almost cried as, shakily, she lit her cigarette and took the first sweet drag.

"Disgusting habit, Jennifer," Max said, stepping away while she sat there smoking and drinking her sweetish, bitter black coffee. The cigarette made her feel even more dizzy, but she didn't mind. She had only smoked about three-quarters of the cigarette when Max came up to her and, impatiently, grabbed it from her hand, squashed it with his shoe, and tossed it down the drain.

Jennifer watched it disappear, sitting on the table, her legs dangling. "What did you give me?" she asked.

"Oh, nothing much. Just something I had around. To help you sleep and relax you. Forget it."

Jennifer bent back from her waist and then slid off the table. She put her feet on the floor, bent her knees, and slowly stood up. She skidded a little as she tried to stand alone.

"Pliés!" Max commanded.

Jennifer went obediently to her pipe barre, which seemed slimy in the morning light. Her head was throbbing, her body felt as if all the parts were attached with Scotch tape, and she felt nauseous. She didn't feel like doing pliés.

She went through the motions, not caring that her hips were too far back, her knees were turning in, her heels hit the floor too fast, or that her arm was flapping up and down.

Max felt a rush of red-hot anger. The little twit was

going to ruin everything. He had fed her and let her have her lousy cigarette and this was her gratitude. He turned off the tape and quickly went over to her. She was just rising out of another sloppy *plié*. He took her face in his hands and pinched her cheeks so hard her teeth bit into the sides of her mouth.

"You're fooling around!" he said accusingly. She grunted, trying to release her face from his grip. She looked into his eyes. They were huge again.

Then he took one hand off her cheek and slapped her hard across her face. She half-slumped from the pain. But he held her up with his other strong hand still under her jawbone. She tried to look away, tried to avoid those hypnotic, crazed blue eyes, but she couldn't turn her head.

"It's nine in the morning, Jennifer. If you want to live until noon, you'll do it right. Understand?" He smacked her again, hard, and Jennifer's head involuntarily lolled forward, as if on a pivot. A tear fell on to her dirty leotard. When Max took his hands away, she nodded.

Max went back to the tape recorder and flicked on the tape of class warm-ups. He wanted her to have a full class this morning. He watched Jennifer, back straight, knees turned out, chin high, doing perfect *pliés*. He grinned.

On the morning of the big gala at New York Center, the morning Heather Cooper was cremated in a very private service and the morning of Christmas Eve, nerves were crackling. Everywhere, throughout the theater, the tension was electric.

But at 10:00 in the morning temperament was tucked away and company class had to go on as usual. For the dancers it would have to be like any other morning. Principals, soloists, corps girls and boys concentrated on the same basic exercises they had been doing every day of their dancing life. Class gave them the corrections and adjustments they needed to keep perfecting their technique. Class was almost a religious ritual.

Outside the studio on the top floor, three men paced in circles like expectant fathers waiting for news. Fazio's hunch had grown, together with his fatigue, into a depressing certainty. Richard Kupperman was biting his nails, his face ashen. Sergeant Moskowitz kept tweaking on his mustache, tapping his foot. They were all hoping Jennifer would appear, flustered but alive and well with some excuse. Any excuse would be accepted. Jennifer did not troop in with the other dancers at the beginning of the class. They waited. She never showed up.

At 11:00 the door flew open, releasing a stream of sweaty dancers who would now go to rehearsal for other ballets in the season, big gala or not. When the room emptied out, Zolinsky appeared. He saw the men immediately.

Mr. Zolinsky shook his white head gravely from side to side. "I would like to have a talk with you." He looked at the other two men and then back to Fazio. "Alone."

Fazio glanced briefly into the empty room. A head was coming up from the top of the piano as the pianist collected music. It was a woman. Not Max Forrest.

He turned to the other two men. Richard Kupperman looked lost, helpless. To Moskowitz he said, "Go to his apartment and keep trying to see him. Ask him questions. Try to catch him off guard." Moskowitz nodded and walked toward the elevator. He knew without any translation that Fazio meant Max Forrest. Fazio turned to the nervous young man in front of him.

"Don't you have to go to your office, Dr. Kupperman?"

"My father will cover for me. We share an office. I . . . I wouldn't be much good today."

"What kind of doctor are you, anyway, Dr. Kupperman? I forgot to ask."

"Orthopedic surgeon. My father and I."

"Oh, bone, limbs, legs, stuff like that. . . ."

"Yes."

"That's good to know."

"Listen, Lieutenant, if there's anything I can do . . . anything to help . . ." His voice broke. "Can you just give me some little job?"

Fazio looked into the young man's bloodshot eyes. "Okay," he said. "Here's what I want you to do. Make a list of all her friends, all the people she knows or ever knew, friends in other companies or classes, childhood friends or sweethearts. Get in touch with as many of these as you can and ask them if they've seen her recently or if she's called. Then make another list of anything you can think of that she might have said lately that struck you as odd. Like she may have expressed a wish to jump on a plane and visit Bombay. In a Missing Persons case, nothing is too farfetched."

"Right. I'll do it. Her parents can help me."

"Good. I'll be in touch, or you can reach me at the precinct a little later."

Richard grabbed Fazio's hand and shook it, pumping up and down.

"I really appreciate the time you're spending on the case, Lieutenant. That other detective was the pits."

Fazio smiled. "Okay. Go to work." He wanted to say, "Don't worry" or "She'll show up," but the words didn't come.

Mr. Zolinsky had stood quietly waiting while all

this was going on. He was wearing his plaid rehearsal shirt, a towel was flung over his shoulders, and he had on ballet slippers. His forehead seemed creased, but other than that he looked to Fazio as he usually did, cool as a cucumber.

"If you'll follow me, Lieutenant," the old gentleman said somberly.

Fazio and Zolinsky took the elevator up to the executive offices without saying one word to each other. When Zolinsky opened the door to his private office, he indicated the royal-blue velvet couch and Fazio sat down. The winter sun showered in through the window and the white sparks flashed on silver photograph frames and antique vases.

Zolinsky stood. "Something is wrong," he announced to Fazio, his hands on his hips, feet astride.

"In what way?" Fazio asked, his face impassive.

"Jennifer North. She missed class today. Some of them, oh, I know, they don't take my class. They study somewhere else. I don't like it, but"—he made a gesture to match his words—"as long as they perform for me . . . But, Jennifer . . ."

"Do you think she took class with someone else this morning?"

"Jennifer? Never! And to miss class on the night of the most important . . . She has a big solo and a *pas de deux* with Yuri Ivanov."

"I understand."

"Your Detective Muscovitz came to visit me last night. I thought nothing of her disappearance. But then this morning, the Ballet Killer is dead. Something is wrong."

Fazio's stomach was jiggling in the old, acidy way again. "I think he also asked you about Max Forrest. I noticed he wasn't in class, either."

"Oh, Max has his own schedule. He took some vacation days for Christmas." Zolinsky seemed to dismiss the question and any possibility that Max could be anything more than a good, dependable pianist. He turned and walked resolutely over to his oak desk by the window. Unlocking the top drawer, he sighed the sigh of an old man.

"I didn't get a picture of Jennifer yet," he said almost hopefully. Then he added, "But it's Christmas. The mails are slow."

"I beg your pardon, sir," Fazio said from the couch.

Zolinsky took out eleven white envelopes. "These. They always came right after the murders. Heather's came the day she was found."

Fazio got up quickly and went over to the desk. "Oh, I suppose I should have shown these to the police," Zolinsky said sadly. "But I'm a stubborn old man. And I have many enemies. I never connected these with the killings. Now, I think you should see them."

Fazio stared at the envelopes in total disbelief. He would have whipped out a handkerchief, but it was too late. There were fingerprints all over them. It was too late for a lot of things. Zolinsky gave him the first snapshot from an already-opened envelope. "The first girl. Lisa Harmon. About a year ago. I got a picture. A snapshot."

Fazio took the picture and the envelope. The girl was posing in a leotard against a plain background. It looked like it was taken with a Polaroid camera. The envelope was standard size. The name and address were typed. The postmark said New York City.

He almost didn't hear what Zolinsky was saying. "The first three were from our company. But then I got pictures of all of them. None of the other ballet companies reported anything like this, so I thought it was someone's private prank with me."

Fazio couldn't help himself. He whistled. If only they had these even six months ago. But could a whole task force trace the make of a camera and where it was bought and who bought it? Impossible. He looked closer at the typewriting. Nothing unusual. Could have been typed by any office typewriter. No light letters, no filled-in "o's" or "e's" or "a's."

Zolinsky handed him the stack of envelopes. "Here, I give them to you now. Maybe it will help." Then he said in a small voice, "Do you think anything's wrong . . . ?" He seemed to be at a loss now for words. "Do you think Jennifer's disappeared like the others?" he finally blurted out.

Fazio looked into the old man's bright blue eyes. He knew enough about ballet to know she just had a solo and would be covered by another dancer.

"Is she special?" he asked softly.

"All of them are," Mr. Zolinsky replied. "But Jennifer is a ballerina. I can make her into a star. A superstar."

Fazio's voice was low. "Then she wouldn't want to miss tonight."

"No, Lieutenant, not Jennifer North, unless . . ."

Fazio knew there was more to Mr. Zolinsky's sentence, but it remained unfinished because it was unthinkable.

All he could see were Madame's angry eyes and, looking down, the sweep of her long dance skirt. Whack! The pointer hit him on the inside of his thigh. "Ouch!" he whispered. It hurt. Whack! He got hit again. Rivulets of sweat crawled down his forehead, but his mind was somewhere else. He was drinking a frosty, thick chocolate milkshake.

Jennifer was crying. Max had found a long piece of wood shaped like a stick and he was beating her. Yelling at her to do better. Then he suddenly stopped and seemed to be staring at or through the floor.

Max was working her hard. She didn't know why. A stupid solo from *Petroushka*. But she still couldn't get over it. He knew the whole solo by heart.

He walked over to the table and poured out some more coffee into the top of the Thermos. Only this time he drank it. She watched him, not knowing what to do or say. She looked down. The top of her leotard had slipped down somehow, revealing too much. She pulled it up quickly and thought, her stomach cramped from the coffee, her skin crawling with grime and her knees shaking again—what was next?

Upstairs in Max's apartment there was the steady ring of the doorbell. For five minutes, Moskowitz kept buzzing. Then he buzzed another apartment and surprisingly got buzzed back. He climbed up the four flights of steps to Max's apartment and knocked on the door until his knuckles were raw. After another five minutes he gave up. Max Forrest was definitely not home.

Chapter Thirteen

Mama hated it when he played the piano. But she had loved it when he used to be able to practice ballet. Everyone told him he was a musical genius, but Mama made fun of him. She said his music sounded tinny, amateurish. Once she broke her toe kicking the piano trying to make him stop playing. It wasn't until he was older and there were no longer any opportunities did he realize Mama had been right. He really wasn't a very talented pianist, after all.

IN BERMUDA, HOGAN and his wife had walked into their room and quickly peeled off their bathing suits. They undid the bed that had been carefully made. The cool whirring of the air conditioner had felt good on their hot, wet bodies. Then the ringing of the phone cut into the room like an unexpected thundershower.

As soon as Barbara Hogan had heard her husband's surprised "Yes, sir," she knew. She kept her eyes level and hadn't needed to study his face to tell if it was important. Just his erection. In the two seconds it took for it to wither, she knew their second honeymoon was going to be ruined. Hiding her head under the pillow, she waited for the call to be over.

Bill Hogan had put down the phone, for a few seconds unable to say anything. He had expected Shipley. He wished it had been Shipley. He climbed back into bed, reaching for his wife's soft body. "Honey, I don't know how to tell you . . ."

"You don't have to. I know. We have to go back."

He squeezed her. "How soon can you be packed? That was the deputy inspector."

The deputy inspector. Hogan's angel, or "rabbi," in the department. The one man who had such complete faith that Hogan was destined to go further and would see that he get promoted up through the ranks to prove it. He was responsible for Hogan's getting the Ballet Killer's case. He had suddenly felt a sour taste in his mouth.

Then he turned to his wife and said, "Last night, in the Tombs . . . Ivan Roman killed himself."

"What!" Barbara Hogan had sat up, her pert breasts bouncing.

"That's right. Crazy as a loon and he electrocuted himself. Honey, I'm sorry. We'll talk on the plane. We have to get ready fast. I'll make it up to you, I swear."

"It's okay, Billy Bear. But what can *you* do when we go back?"

Hogan's face became a study in hate. "It's what I have to do to stop Frank Fazio. I've had him followed. He's up to no good. He doesn't believe Roman did it."

"That little twirp! You make the arrangements, honey. I'll do the packing."

"You're sure you don't mind? We didn't even see a day's worth of sun."

"I only mind that that little greaseball is trying to stand in your way. You're going to be a big man someday. The idea of him messing up everything you've done makes me . . ." She couldn't locate the words to describe her anger, so she just stomped her bare foot.

Hogan gave her a little love slap on her rear end and reached for the phone while she turned to pack.

His sense of urgency had made him think he could just get on a plane right away.

Fazio calculated it would take him twenty minutes to get from Sixty-second and Columbus to Long Island City. He was about right, arriving at Ivan Roman's apartment a little before 12:15, managing to avoid some of the heavy lunch-hour traffic.

The streets were empty. The reporters had all gone. They had taken all the shots of the old red brick building they needed, he guessed. He passed the guard and let himself in, still using the keys he had gotten from Ivan Roman's personal effects, and went up the stairs softly. Once inside the apartment he could see immediately some changes had been made.

Fazio was about to look around when he stopped. He had the oddest feeling someone else was in the room with him. He felt for his gun and then slowly spun around. He was met by the steely gray eyes of an old woman.

"You got any right to be here, Mister?"

Fazio flashed his shield. "Lieutenant Frank Fazio, New York Police Department."

The old woman put her hand up as if to signal him to stop. "Okay, okay, Lieutenant Fazio. I believe you. I even seen your name in the papers. They came by earlier and took all them rabbits. The Department of Health, I guess."

Fazio studied the apartment. That was one of the changes, but you couldn't tell immediately because the stench still clung to the place.

"Usually I would raise the rent for an apartment when a tenant moves out, but this one? I'll probably have to lower it. Who would want the Ballet Killer's apartment?"

"Plenty of people looking for apartments, Mrs. Kurtz."

"Yeah, in Manhattan. Not in Queens. I cleaned up a little, if you notice."

Fazio had noticed that. Piles of junk had been packed into cardboard boxes and the place had been swept of rabbit pellets. The semen-soaked dance clothes he had found had disappeared, but it didn't matter. Others like it had been taken for evidence, he was sure.

"You won't find much if you're looking for something. Guess you people take all this stuff. He don't have no family, it turns out. Really something, huh? Him being the Ballet Killer. But I always knew there was something wrong with him."

"Why's that, Mrs. Kurtz?"

"He wasn't normal. Always sneaked around. Went out nights. Came back days. Had no job. And he didn't talk much. Had no friends who I ever saw. And I used to hear him talking to himself at any time of the day. Babbling in a kind of loud, excited voice. Strange boy. Of course, I told all this to the reporters when I was interviewed." She smiled and then sighed. "But he paid his rent. Had some kind of check from the government." She smiled again, showing the hint of a gold-capped tooth. "I guess I cracked this case for you people."

Fazio smiled back at her but said nothing.

"No reward or nothing," she went on. "Those people from the ballet company, you know, offered me a reward. I called them. Rotten deal." Her voice rose in anger. "They said they couldn't give me the reward until Ivan Roman was found guilty. And now he's dead." She shook her head at her misfortune.

Fazio shook his head in mock sympathy.

Almost as if she was reading the impatience in his

mind, she turned to leave. "Be downstairs if you need me. Anything you need to prove he did it, I'll be glad to help."

Fazio heard the landlady's mule house slippers clop down the steps. He could begin. Going into each room, he looked first for the typewriter. He found it in what must have been Roman's bedroom. A homemade plank of wood built into the wall with a foam-rubber mattress was the bed he had seen before. Piles of old pornographic magazines had been stacked neatly in the corner. Under the bed he found it. An old Underwood typewriter.

Fazio didn't touch it. He didn't have to. He could tell that typewriter never produced the imprints made on each envelope. They were clearly made by an electric typewriter, not this ancient relic. But that didn't mean anything. Roman could have had access to an office or had them typed all at once. If only the department had had these from the beginning. He grimaced. Hogan would still have found some way of making Ivan Roman the Ballet Killer.

The camera. That was the clue. He walked around the apartment still looking. Everywhere was the same scenery. Cardboard boxes packed high, piles of debris swept into the corner, stacks of junk on broken chairs and tables. No camera. There was nothing left of the man Ivan Roman had been, had he been much of a man. Fazio knew by instinct that Roman wasn't the Ballet Killer. His was the classic case of the jealousy killer, a cuckoo, a nut job. It wasn't unusual for someone to memorize all the facts of a case and confess. But Fazio was compulsive. He had to prove he was right. He knew he wouldn't leave that apartment until he went through every cardboard box and proved to himself that Ivan Roman owned a camera that could have taken the shots. Or to satisfy himself that

Roman did not own a camera that produced the eleven snapshots he had seen.

Max leaned against the wall, watching his ballerina. She had a certain quality. For a moment he took his mind off the steps she was doing and imagined her dancing onstage. She was lovely, wasn't she? Her hands were small and exquisite. They looked like birds fluttering around her. And her feet. They were delicate and perfectly shaped. The look on her face was pure rapture. Audiences would fall in love with her. But she was dancing only for him now. He looked at her sweet, heart-shaped face, the huge eyes that illuminated her face, the silky blond hair that was falling out of her ballerina bun. He was falling in love with Jennifer. Or had he always been in love with her?

He shut his eyes and then opened them, smiling. Then he blinked. Mama! It was Mama as she used to look dancing around the apartment. Her blond hair falling down, the small, nimble feet. Mama was dancing for him again. He reached out his arms. "Mama!" he whispered and barely heard his own voice. "Mama!" he growled desperately and staggered forward.

She looked up. "Max?"

He stood bewildered. It was Jennifer again and she had stopped dancing. His mind had been playing tricks on him. Though it had seemed so real, so . . . Max flicked off the tape recorder. It was time to get down to business and stop fooling around. Jennifer was slipping. She had lost that silvery perfection he had seen at the *Artemis Visions* rehearsal. It was too late to find a new girl. Plus he would have to kill Jennifer. No, he would just have to make her work harder. He knew how to do it.

Jennifer, sweat dripping from her forehead even in

the cold, damp room, throat scratchy with thirst, had to stop dancing. He had been working her too hard. Not even a one-minute break to catch her breath, which was unusually short. She had learned the complete solo he had taught her and she thought she had done it beautifully. Even Max was smiling. But it was a funny smile.

He started walking toward her. He was still smiling. But Jennifer moved back an inch. Then his smile changed. His eyes were almost oval. He was angry. Maybe she shouldn't have done it that well. In his hand was the stick or homemade cane he had found. Before she had time to think she might be wrong, he whacked her very fast first on her inner thighs, which still throbbed from before, and then on her back. She sucked her breath in, gasping, able to feel the pain, yet somewhere beyond it.

"No, stop, don't do that," she heard herself whisper. It made her angry to be hit that way for nothing.

"I thought you were a dancer," he said coldly.

Jennifer's bloodshot, mascara-smeared eyes opened wide with horror. That hurt. She had learned that solo very quickly and then had done it over and over until she had it perfectly. She knew it. She was a dancer and it didn't matter if she had seen it performed only once. He was crazy. She cried silently to herself. Of course, he was crazy. Max got an unreachable look in his brilliant blue eyes. Jennifer waited. He was spacey again.

"You will join a ballet school and work even harder!" All he could hear was the tune thumping from the jukebox. . . . *"You can dance every dance with the guy who gives you the eye . . . but save the last dance for me. . . ."* Then she hit again but missed because he ducked. No

thoughts went through his mind as he ran. He scrambled away from her, trying to reach the train station, wanting to go and find his father. He couldn't take it anymore. He hated the ballet lessons. His eyes were swimming with tears and he could hardly see. His throat choked compulsively. Then his brain exploded as loud as the grinding rush of the train he heard. Then nothingness. And his life changed. In later years she had accused him of doing it on purpose. Sometimes he believed her.

"Max, please," Jennifer pleaded as he seemed to come back from wherever he had been. "Please, I have to go to the bathroom and I'm so tired and thirsty. Can't we please take a break?"

"No! Not until you learn to dance. You're not a dancer! Whoever told you you could dance?"

The room was silent for a second. Jennifer stood up to her full height. In a very firm, sure voice, she said icily, "I'm a better dancer than you are a lover." And at the same time it slipped out, she clapped a hand over her mouth. But it was too late. There was just enough time to regret what she had said. Looking into those maddened eyes, she knew she had broken, lost her control, and she couldn't even guess what would happen now.

Max's face was red. His eyes flashed over her, but his eyes seemed far away again.

"You can dance every dance with the guy who gives you the eye . . . but save the last dance for me. . . ."

He always heard that tune in his head. And when he heard it, it was time to kill.

"That was the last dance you'll do, Jennifer," he said in a hollow monotone.

Jennifer gulped and it felt as if her insides would come tumbling out of her. He reached up to the neck of her leotard and yanked it down. Then he pinched and squeezed her breasts as she cried, "No, no, please! No more!" If she could have taken the words right out of the air and put them back in her mouth, she would have done so gladly. The panic was rising again as he yanked her leotard off and told her to step out of it. She stumbled, sobbing, wearing only her tights and thinking of how much she wanted to live. Thinking of how hurt Richard was going to be when he found out she was dead. He would feel dead, too. Max came closer and lassoed her neck with her leotard.

"Do you know what the girls look like when they're being strangled, Jennifer? They have these pretty pink faces that turn purple-red and their eyes sort of bug out like they're going to pop. They look like little fishes gasping for air. I like that part the best." He pulled the leotard closer to him and Jennifer gagged at the thought of what he had just said. She started to hiccup. Max pulled together the two long sleeves of the leotard. Tighter around her neck. Jennifer couldn't breathe. She felt like she was underwater, her chest heaving for air. Everything was becoming dim until she couldn't see at all. Just as she sagged to the ground, she heard Max making weird sounds. It seemed as if he was crying and laughing at the same time.

Jennifer was rubbing her neck, pumping air, trying to get her breath. She had dropped to the floor and lay there. Max was pacing around the room in jerky steps.

She had said to him, "Maximillian, I underestimated you." Those words stayed in his mind and

he could pull them out and savor them whenever
he wanted. Mama had called him by his real
name. Mama had been proud of him.

He couldn't do it. Couldn't do it because of Mama.
God, how he wanted to kill that girl! He could taste it,
feel it. One less ballerina in the world. But he couldn't.

Jennifer crawled over to the drain and puked up
whatever was left of her small breakfast. She saw Max
walking around the room holding his hand on his
head. Then he came toward her and picked her up almost gently. Like a wobbly colt she stood up, half-
terrified, half-thankful she was still alive.

"Water . . ." she said in a thin, shaky voice. From
now on she promised herself she wouldn't talk, would
only say what was necessary. She would be totally
obedient.

Max took the top of the Thermos and went to an old
sink. He turned on the faucet. It sputtered and shook,
but a little water did spurt forth. It was rusty, but
there were no bugs in it. Then he took a pill from his
pocket.

He came over to her with the cup of water. "You're
too high-strung. I want you to take this." He gave her
a shiny, little pill.

Jennifer was too weak to refuse and too petrified to
rebel. She swallowed the pill, throwing her head back
and gulping, and then choked on the bitter water.

Max switched off the tape recorder and went to the
door. Jennifer followed right behind him. At the door
he stopped, turned around, and shook his head. Jennifer took a step back. Then she heard the click of
the lock and knew she was alone. Alone in the sub-
basement.

She picked up the dirty leotard from where it had
fallen and put it back on. Her whole body was sud-

denly crawling with itchiness and she scratched herself all over, digging a drop of blood from a scab on her arm. She walked around the sub-basement avoiding the sloppy drain. She hummed. But she had nothing to think about. She hummed again. The hum seemed to stay in the air long after she had stopped. She was alone. In the sub-basement. A rat or big mouse scooted under one of the old machines and Jennifer sucked in a scream. She didn't have the energy to scream anymore. Then she went over to the table, sat on top of it, crossed her legs, and began to sing, rocking herself. Softly in a little girl's voice that she didn't recognize as her own, came *"Frère Jacques, Frère Jacques, dormez-vous, dormez-vous . . . ?"*

Fazio had just packed and re-packed the fourth box. He had already checked every loose space in the apartment. There were more boxes to go. He looked at his watch. It was close to 1:30. He wondered if Moskowitz had reached Forrest. He could just imagine how many times Dr. Richard Kupperman had tried to reach him. Then, when he wasn't even thinking about the camera, his hand touched something hard and smooth. He uncovered it, bringing it up from the bottom. It was a Polaroid camera.

Fazio reached in his inside jacket pocket and pulled out the stack of envelopes. The picture of Heather Cooper was on the top. Her eyes were wide but she looked alive, with a dancer's serious smile on her face. She was posing against a flat, blank wall. Ivan's walls were a drab beige-olive. It could have been taken here, though he didn't think it was. He looked at the camera more carefully. It was dusty and old, but did it work? There was no film in it. Then he looked at the picture of Heather Cooper and all the rest. They were almost all alike. Except there was something different in the

snapshot of Heather Cooper. A diamond-like flash of
light somewhere near her head. Overexposure? That
was a clue, though. Two months, even one month, ago,
a team of experts would have been put on this.

Fazio found some old newspaper and wrapped the
camera in it. Then he quickly put everything back the
way he had found it, dusting off any fingerprints. He
locked the apartment and started down the stairs. At
the bottom step he saw two eyes peeking out through a
tiny crack in the door. He juggled the newspaper bun-
dle to his other arm and went out the front door. The
whole neighborhood was bedecked with Christmas
decorations. Across the street was a Santa on a sleigh
with reindeer sitting on a rooftop. He wondered if
Connie had put out the window lights this year. Funny,
he had forgotten to look.

Driving toward Manhattan, Fazio noticed a purple
Impala following him in another lane. He squinted but
couldn't get a clear picture of who was driving. He
was positive it was the same car he had seen before.
Well, whoever it was, the person wouldn't find anything fishy about Fazio's next stop. In fact, it made a
lot of sense.

Max stood very still in the bedroom. He could hear
the clock ticking. Softly, he opened the bottom drawer
of the dresser again. He took the gun out of the warm
piece of flannel and stroked it.

Downstairs Moskowitz entered the building as he
had been doing at ten-minute intervals and rang Max
Forrest's doorbell. A couple of times someone in the
building had buzzed him up and he had knocked on
the door, but no one had answered. Moskowitz was
beginning to think Forrest might have left town for the
holidays. Maybe he should be checking out the train,
plane, and bus stations. Or maybe he had a car. That

would be almost impossible for him to check out alone.

He rang five more times and then he decided to call it quits and go back to the precinct. After all, he had kept close watch on the building and no one with Forrest's description had either left or entered. Fazio was probably back at the precinct, anyway.

Upstairs, Max's hands were shaking. He stood silently, listening for more. But there was no more. Was it that dumb cop again? Would he come knocking on the door like last time?

He couldn't think. He closed the bedroom door and went into the kitchen. It was time for lunch. It would be a long day. He wondered if she was hungry. Maybe he should fix her something to eat. Then he decided against it. Why should she be hungry? She was resting now. She didn't have to eat. And if she was hungry, well . . . too bad.

Taking out two pieces of plain white bread, he slapped some bologna on one and poured a blob of ketchup on the other. He washed it down with half a container of milk, using no glass. Who was it downstairs who had kept ringing and ringing? He looked at his watch. So far, so good. No knock at the door.

But he didn't feel like working. He felt like taking a little nap, resting. He went into the living room, sat down on the couch, and closed his eyes, shielding them with his hands.

"Max, don't go off and leave me. I wanted you to be a great dancer. Was that my crime? You're not a great pianist. They gave you the scholarship because they felt sorry for you. Look, Max, you don't want to go away from me. I know you better than you think." She had started to unbutton her blouse. *Mama had been*

*right. He had decided not to go away, even if it
meant losing the scholarship.*

Max sprung off the couch and marched resolutely
into the bedroom. He took out his mother's nightgown and buried his nose in it. He hadn't washed it
at all since the day that they had ordered her to go
to that place. It still smelled like her, too. He had
missed her so this past year. How he had loved to
stand in the doorway in the morning, drinking his
coffee, while she got dressed. Or sometimes at night
she would let him come into her little bedroom while
she got undressed.

This was her day. No more resting. It was time to
get everything in order.

When Fazio came in through the door, the first
person he saw made him breathe a sigh of relief.
Jerry Turner was tending bar at the Titanic. The
jukebox was blaring and he could see Christmas was
starting early.

Vinnie came over to him. "Lieutenant, let me buy
you a drink." You never could tell how much Vinnie
had to drink. Fazio guessed that if he were ever asked
to give blood, they would draw a pint of Johnny
Walker from him.

"No time, Vinnie. I'll take a raincheck. Say, you
know, the kid? Turner? Mind if I . . ."

He looked up into Vinnie's rheumy eyes as he was
being interrupted. "Uh-uh," Vinnie said. "I do mind.
He's on until tonight. Good kid, but not experienced
enough to handle the Christmas Eve rush. Get him
then."

"Could I just talk to him, Vinnie? I promise it will
just take five minutes."

"Something up, Lieutenant?" Vinnie asked, with a

spark of new interest. "I mean on the radio and TV, they say the Ballet Killer killed himself. Does this mean the case isn't closed?"

Fazio pulled Vinnie close, as if he were going to whisper something confidential. Vinnie was eager to hear the secret, as he was all department gossip. Fazio said very slowly, "The case, Vinnie, is never closed."

Vinnie nodded solemnly, understanding, and then indicated a very curious Jerry Turner, trying to tend bar but glancing over Fazio's way.

Fazio came up to him, making a little space for himself at the bar. "Hi, Lieutenant. Everything work out for you?" Fazio watched him. He was getting a little more expert or confident at mixing drinks and serving customers.

"Could you step away from the bar for just a minute, Mr. Turner?" Jerry Turner shot him a puzzled frown. "No, it's okay. Vinnie said it was all right. Just take a minute. I have a question."

Jerry Turner turned to the back part of the bar, lifted a section of it, and came out. The only other bartender on duty gave him a dirty look.

Fazio took out the parcel he had half-hidden under his coat. He spoke quietly.

"I have a camera in here. A Polaroid. It might work; it might not." He reached inside his coat pocket and pulled out the packet of envelopes. He took the picture of Heather Cooper out of one of them. "Here, don't lose this. One of a kind. What I want you to do is tell me if this picture came from this camera."

"Jeez, I don't work with Polaroids, Lieutenant."

"I know. But you know enough to tell, don't you?"

"And you can't get anybody else?"

Fazio ignored his question. "Just asking for a favor. I'll see that you're taken care of."

"Yeah, sure. Hey, I'll need some film." He turned around then and noticed the other bartender frantically motioning for him to come back.

Fazio gave him two rolls of film which he had stopped to get. "Anything else?"

"Yeah. I get off work tonight. You said you'd take care of me. How about letting me in to shoot some pictures at the gala?" Fazio smiled. He could see the tenseness in the young man's face as he waited the beat of a second before Fazio replied.

"Listen, you got it. Take all the pictures you want. If Zolinsky gives you trouble, tell him you're working for Lieutenant Fazio." He clapped Turner on the side of the arm and then walked out.

It was 2:30 in the afternoon when Max drove out of the huge drive. He was finally driving his mother away from Manhattan State Hospital.

He put his hand on his mother's knee, glad to have her back with him. "How do you feel, Mama?"

"Never felt better, Max, my dear. How's the girl? Hope you managed to keep your hands off her."

"Mama!"

There was an awkward silence. Charlotte thought there was something odd in the tone of Max's voice. As if he had . . . but that was impossible. Max had never shown any interest in girls. It made her feel hurt. Maybe he hadn't meant anything by it, she told herself.

Max bit his lip. He was afraid he had given himself away. He naturally thought she had meant you-know-what. But he was lucky. The papers had never mentioned rape or sexual assault. Except for Lisa.

And Mama had never said anything to him about that.

Finally Charlotte said, "She's still alive, isn't she?" Suddenly the air was cleared.

Charlotte reached inside her bosom and unfastened the hypodermic needle. Then she cackled, whooping loudly. "Good thing I didn't accidentally prick myself, or the whole thing would have ended up like *The Sleeping Beauty* ballet. This, my dear boy, will knock out an elephant. And for a long time."

Max grinned happily. You wait and you wait and then, if you have enough patience, your big day arrives. Max knew that this was his big day.

Stephanie pulled up and let Yuri lift her. She came down in *arabesque,* his arm around her waist, and let him lower her into a deep *penché,* touching her hand to the floor, her extension breathtaking. Then he raised her up and she rolled into his arms.

"Your timing is off," he said, stopping. There was no piano player. This was a special rehearsal.

"Here, like this." Yuri mimicked all her movements but did them slightly faster. Stephanie nodded. Then suddenly she started jumping up and down like a little girl. "Oh, Yuri, isn't it exciting? I'm actually going to do the solo. Just think, I could become a star!"

Yuri studied the brunette. She was beautiful. She was a reasonably good dancer. Potential. But she was beginning to become tiresome. Maybe it was time to move on.

"She could still show up," he said in a flat monotone, in spite of himself. Stephanie pursed her eyebrows together. "Or, she might be in some trouble." He was going to say, "Doesn't that bother you?" but he left it unsaid. Obviously, it didn't.

"Good," Stephanie reassured him. "Listen, I want this solo more than anything in the world." She hugged him. "Oh, Yuri! I want them to see us dancing together."

Yuri looked beyond their reflections in the mirrors. He was thinking about a lot of things: Jennifer's boyfriend looking for her; the radio announcement this morning that said the Ballet Killer killed himself; the fact that he knew Jennifer wanted this solo even more than Stephanie.

He was getting a strange feeling about Jennifer. A sick premonition. He knew he should be rooting for Stephanie to dance the role of Iphigenia, but he hoped that wherever lovely, sensitive Jennifer was, she could get herself back to the theater on time for the performance tonight.

"Yuriii!" Stephanie said, impatiently, interrupting his thoughts.

"Yes, lovely one, we do the lift over again." He smiled the smile that melted hundreds of thousands of feminine hearts. But he thought: *I hope I do this* pas de deux *with the right girl tonight.* Then he held out his hand to Stephanie, nodding, thinking again how wrong she was for the part.

Jennifer lay with her back flat on the laundry table in a drugged sleep. Before she fell into the deep sleep, she had imagined herself dancing her solo at the gala. She knew as the room began to turn around and midnight crept into her mind that she should be trying, yelling for help. "Help," she whispered as she fell asleep, wondering if she wasn't dead already.

Chapter Fourteen

Jobs? He had had all sorts of jobs. Sold shoes, worked as a clerk in a grocery store, lifted boxes in that warehouse. Until it was obvious to him. The one thing he could do that came naturally. Play piano. So he played piano for ballet classes. It amused him to see those straight-faced, serious bitchy little girls again. They never changed no matter what the year. Now he was with the company playing for grown-up little girls. How he loved to watch the young ballerinas. The ones who were just at the threshold of making it, really making it. Those were the ones he wanted.

CAPTAIN WILLIAM HOGAN paced the floor in the Bermuda airport. His wife sat, staring at the floor, tense. The other passengers waiting for the same delayed plane were wishing the tall, red-haired man would just sit down and be quiet. They were all in the same boat. No one knew when they would take off for New York.

"What time do you have now, honey?" Hogan asked his wife.

Barbara Hogan sighed. She knew her husband was wearing a watch. It was not even five minutes from the last time he asked. "It's almost two o'clock, honey."

"Which means it's almost three o'clock in New York."

Hogan continued his pacing, almost knocking over a potted plant. It took three and a half hours to get from Bermuda to New York. They would land at Ken-

nedy. He could rent a car. Screw it! He went to the
phone. Someone could damn well pick him up. He
gave the operator the number of the two-oh. She said
she couldn't put the call through because all the lines
were busy.

Hogan was angry at everyone and everything when
he came away from the phone. There was a baby
crawling on the carpet and he almost kicked it before
he checked himself.

"Let's go for a drink, honey," Barbara said, tugging
at his sleeve.

"Yeah, it looks like we have time for a few drinks,"
Hogan grumbled, grinding out his cigar into the royal-
blue carpeting.

Offstage, the friends of the ballet, volunteer ladies
who helped with the gala, were beginning to argue
among themselves. Mrs. Twyler, who was in charge of
bringing in the big names and celebrities, made all the
noise. But Mrs. O'Conner really did all the work. The
dancers liked her. She was close enough with them to
pop into the dressing room of the corps girls, even
when they were naked, and have a chat.

Downstairs in the Promenade of the State Theatre,
the tables were being set for the lavish buffet cocktail
party preceding the performance. Mrs. O'Conner had
purchased red and green candles. Mrs. Twyler was
miffed; she preferred silver candles. Mrs. O'Conner
claimed that the silver paint gave off a funny odor.
The ladies were no longer speaking. Another volunteer
was crying in the ladies' room because someone had
criticized her gown for the gala.

Upstairs in a small office of her own, Mrs. Twyler
was making sure the governor, a senator, Andy Warhol,
Liza Minnelli, Jacqueline Onassis, several top fashion
luminaries from Seventh Avenue, and all her society

friends were coming. The mayor had just canceled out. Her nerves were frazzled but her voice stayed carefree and light.

Onstage was a full dress rehearsal with the orchestra for *Artemis Visions*. No guests had been invited this time. Nora, the star, was standing stage center motionless.

"Change the tempo!" she yelled into the lights. "I simply cannot do that many pirouettes to *that* music!" There was a low buzz along the sidelines, where dancers sat watching and waiting. Some were resting in splits for a stretch. Some were sewing shoes. Most were drinking anything wet. The steady hum of whispering centered around the belief that Nora couldn't do anything correctly anymore no matter what the tempo was because she was getting too old. Nora would be the next gala, they decided. Her big retirement. One dancer suggested that by this time next year all of her roles would be given to a younger girl, and this was really her swan song.

The conductor tapped his baton. The musicians picked up their instruments once again. Mr. Zolinsky apparently had broken his rule that no one tamper with the music and slowed it down for his beloved Nora.

No one gossiped about the reality of Jennifer North's disappearance. To do so would be to admit that the man who killed himself wasn't really the Ballet Killer or that the nightmare was starting all over again. It was easier not to say anything.

When Fazio walked into his office, he saw he had a full house. Moskowitz was sitting behind his desk playing with a pencil and Richard Kupperman and a middle-aged couple were sitting, faces tense, in chairs in front of the desk. No one had to tell him who they were.

Moskowitz got up when Fazio came in and crossed over to another chair. "Lieutenant," he said, his voice somewhat higher than usual, "you know Dr. Kupperman, and here are Jennifer North's parents from Ohio, Mr. and Mrs. North. They've come for the ballet." He cleared his throat.

Fazio nodded to Richard and shook hands with Mr. North, a tall, slightly graying man, who was smoking a pipe. Mrs. North looked like an older version of the pictures he had seen of Jennifer. He thought of his own daughter, Theresa, safe at home with her family, and though his face said nothing, his heart tugged for this confused couple.

"Dr. Kupperman?" he began.

The young man seemed even more distraught than before. His hands had a slight tremor as he produced a large yellow ruled pad. "We checked everyone, called everybody. Must have made God knows how many long-distance calls. Old dance buddies, childhood friends, distant relatives."

"And?" Fazio asked, realizing it was a dumb question.

"And nothing. No one has seen or heard from Jennifer in years." He started a smile, then stopped it. "Jennifer's a notoriously bad letter-writer."

"That's right, she is," Mrs. North added.

"Now what?" said Richard.

Moskowitz spoke then. His face was red. "I checked and kept ringing the bell but he just wasn't home, Lieutenant. I looked at every car parked for two blocks around and took the license plate numbers. I'm going to check them out. See if he drives."

Fazio nodded reassuringly at Moskowitz, though the

fact was it didn't make a damn bit of difference if he drove. If he had a car and wasn't home, he was probably in it. And there was nothing much they could do about that.

Richard Kupperman looked from one to the other as if he were watching a play. Finally, he exploded. "Hey, wait a second! Who are you looking for, anyway?"

Fazio stared directly at him. "Did she ever speak of a Max Forrest? Ever go out with him?"

These were the kinds of questions Richard was secretly afraid of. That she had left him for someone else. His eyes avoided Fazio's stare. "No. Never. I don't even know who he is."

"He's a pianist with the company. Plays for class and rehearsal."

"Oh, that Max Forrest. Max? You think she ran away with him or something like that?" Fazio ignored the nasality in Richard's voice as it traveled up into a hurt whine.

"I don't think anything. We're checking everything out."

"Hey, wait a second. I get it. There could be two Ballet Killers, or . . . you think they got the wrong one!"

At that, Mrs. North looked like she would keel over, and Mr. North sputtered on his own pipe smoke. Fazio was silent for a moment, thinking. Finally, he said, his voice mellow and soothing, "You're overtired and worried, Dr. Kupperman, and I don't blame you."

Richard had gotten up and started to pace the floor. "Then where the hell could she be!" He turned to face Fazio. "Do you know how much this solo means to her?"

"Yes, I do know. We're going to check all the hospitals in the city."

"Oh, dear God!" Mrs. North gasped.

"Just a routine check," Fazio said. "You said she was under a lot of stress. She could have been daydreaming and accidentally been hit by a car. She could have fainted in the street or lost her memory. Someone might have found her."

"I don't think Jennifer would faint. She's always been very healthy," Mrs. North said.

"That's right, she has. Been dancing since she was eight. Very strong girl," Mr. North added.

"Just a routine check," Fazio said softly.

There was a glum silence, interrupted by Richard. "It's almost four. What can we do?"

"Nothing at this point. Rest. You all have tickets for the gala?"

Everyone nodded.

"Complimentary tickets," Mrs. North added.

"She may show up. She just may show up. If she wants to dance in that ballet badly enough, no matter what kind of trouble she's in, she'll find a way to get there. We'll all be waiting backstage."

There was a faint glimmer of hope in everyone's eyes but Richard's, although he tried hard to disguise his doubt.

"We'll check out the hospitals and we'll continue to interview everyone in the company," Fazio went on. "Think hard about Max Forrest, Dr. Kupperman. Did she ever say anything about him? She was last seen coming out of the theater with him."

Richard nodded but there was a blank look on his face. "She just never mentioned him. . . ." Then he looked at Fazio, light coming into his eyes. "So you have been working on this case all along. You've checked. You've . . ."

Fazio cut him off. "I think all three of you should get some rest and meet me backstage an hour before the curtain. At seven sharp. Is that okay with everyone?"

Richard's answer was a sad, stony silence. They each got up and seemed to Fazio to file out of the office.

After they left Moskowitz got up to leave Fazio and use one of the phones outside. As he was at the door, Fazio said, "Moskowitz?"

Moskowitz turned. "Yeah, Lieutenant?"

Fazio was chewing on a pencil. "Rent us some tuxedos for tonight."

"Okay, Lieutenant."

Fazio winked. "So we blend in with the crowd, you know? Not look like a pair of seedy dicks crashing a fancy party."

Moskowitz smiled but it wasn't genuine. He knew what Fazio was really saying. They were on to something, but they were forced to be very careful.

Max had stopped the car near a delicatessen on the West Side. His mother had been complaining about the food in the hospital. But she wanted to wait inside the car because it was so cold. Besides, Max knew what she liked.

It took him twenty minutes to weave through the lines that always crowded Zabar's. He got the potato salad, the cold cuts, the Greek olives, the rolls, and, as a special treat, chocolate cake. He was whistling happily as he walked to the car.

Then he saw the car was empty. Mama had disappeared. The best day of his life and she was going to ruin it. He was so angry at her he wanted to find a stick and smash every car window down the street.

He opened the car and got in, staring sullenly ahead, remembering.

The second time they gave him a chance at a scholarship, he was determined to go. "I want to go for that scholarship audition, Mama. It's in the city. It's Juilliard. Mama, are you all right . . . ? Say something, Mama. . . . Wish me good luck. . . . They told me I was really good . . . that I had talent." She had just stared at him. "Mama, don't look at me that way. I'll spend time with you." So he left with her eyes burning in his mind. But he never did take that piano scholarship audition. When it was his turn, he was handed a message. It was from a neighbor and it said to come right home. Mama had been taken to the hospital. But she promised she would never slash her wrists again. The next year he couldn't take the scholarship audition. It was too late. And he was too old. Then there was nothing.

He felt that old anger toward her coming back. Then he realized he was being cruel after all she had done for him. Her whole life had been devoted to him. He knew just where to look for his mother, too. Oh, yes, he had had years and years of practice. But they would lose precious hours today.

Less than three blocks away, Charlotte ordered her second gin-and-tonic. She only had money for the first, but she knew Max would find her. He always did. And then he'd pay the man.

She took another sip and jiggled the swizzle stick between her thumb and forefinger. She could have made him into the finest male ballet dancer in the world. Better than what's-his-name, Ivanov, and

American, too. Max thought he didn't want to, but he never really gave it a chance. She took a long swallow and let it linger in her mouth for a minute.

A man moved over to the empty barstool next to her and bellowed, "Merry Christmas, sweetheart!" Charlotte was always comfortable in bars, but she never tried to pick up a man. She never even let men buy her drinks. One thing always led to another. Men had dirty, ugly thoughts.

She could see herself reflected in the oval mirror behind the bar. True, her hair had turned to gray over the years, but she still had a good face. Bright, red lipstick didn't hurt, either. Her tummy stuck out a little and she wasn't as thin as she used to be, but she was still a looker. She always had been. Hadn't Max told her over and over, especially when he was little? He would say she was the most "beautifullest" Mommy in the world.

She smiled at the delicious memories a mother keeps tucked away. His first pubic hairs. His . . . she took another quick swallow. Through the mirror she saw him come in the door before she heard his voice.

"Mama, there you are!"

Everyone at the bar turned to stare at the handsome young man, standing straight and tall, wearing a topcoat. Charlotte took a quick sip. She knew it would be her last.

Max came over to her, frowning. "Mama, how could you? You know we have that Christmas party tonight."

She smiled sheepishly and bowed her head. They had played this game before.

Paying for her drink, Max left a generous tip on the counter. To Charlotte's surprise, when she tried to stand up, she found she was a little shaky. After not even two drinks? Impossible. But when was the last time she had had a drink? She couldn't even remember.

Max gripped her firmly under her elbow to steady her. "C'mon, Mama, we'll be late for the party."

"Yes, dear," she said docilely.

As they left the bar, a slobbering drunk said tearfully to the bartender, "Ain't it nice to see a son treat his mother so good?"

Outside, walking to the car, Max was silent.

"Maximillian?" his mother ventured in a soft voice. He said nothing.

"Maxie-Waxie?"

"I'll get you some black coffee."

"I'm not drunk!"

"Oh, Mama, you know I'm doing everything just for you. How could you?" He looked at his watch instead of at her.

She stopped in the street, the cold flapping open her unbuttoned cloth coat, thinking. "I don't know," she said at last, the frosty air sobering her. She and Max kept walking. "I'm sorry," she added.

They had reached the car. He unlocked her side and let her in. "That's okay, Mama, I understand," he lied. Then he came around to his side and got in. "Just a few more blocks and we can get started." It was close to five already. There wasn't much time.

At the same hour Stephanie was being pinned into Jennifer's costume so it could hurriedly be altered. She was shorter than Jennifer but a little bigger in the back. Richard was lying face down, his head buried in a pillow on their big brass bed, unable to rest, even with the Valium his father had insisted he take. Mr. and Mrs. North were in their hotel making small talk, afraid to discuss the reality of what was happening.

Zolinsky was still working with a small group of principals, holding them long after he usually would before a big performance. The Friends of the Ballet, all dressed, their smiles pinned on, were putting last-minute touches on the decorations and conferring with the caterers. Nora was in her dressing room practicing *pirouettes*. In three hours the curtain would rise on one of the most spectacular galas in the history of ballet. It was Zolinsky's first full-length ballet in forty years.

In the two-oh, Moskowitz had checked out Max as belonging to a yellow Volkswagen. He remembered seeing two on the street. He had also called all the airports and the train and bus stations and was still calling to see if they had a Max Forrest who had left New York or was leaving today. So far he had come up with nothing. Fazio was calling hospitals and also had no information. He would have liked to have gone over to State Theatre and interviewed each and every member of the company about Jennifer, but he had to be more subtle than that. Besides, he personally thought it was a waste of time.

As far as the department was concerned, the Ballet Killer had been found. Ivan Roman's suicide had changed nothing in the deputy inspector's mind. The chief had clearly indicated he only wanted to find out if there was foul play involved in Roman's death. Evidence had been found. The man had confessed and he had no alibis.

Fazio was tired of going through the certainties of Ivan Roman's guilt. He didn't buy any of it. And he was riding the tide of something. He knew it; he could smell it. The frustration of having his hands tied behind his back in a case that wasn't a case was starting to get to him. There he was, off duty, sitting in his office calling hospitals in the city, New Jersey, Connecticut, anywhere, and charging it all to his home phone. Because unless some dancer turned up dead, there was no one who would believe him.

Max turned the key in the front door.

"It's good to be home, Max," his mother said. Max continued down the hall. "Aren't we going upstairs? Where are we going?"

Max smiled and kept walking. "Trust me." His voice became softer. "I've been keeping her in the sub-basement."

"Oh? The old laundry room?"

"Yes. Shh!" He didn't have the heart to tell her about the cop who kept ringing his doorbell. Well, it didn't matter, anyway.

"Tell me, is she really good?"

"Zolinsky's next star."

Charlotte threw back her head and laughed from the throat as Max opened the door to the creaky stairs that led them down to the double basements.

Outside, Sergeant Moskowitz cruised past on his way to pick up the tuxedos he had rented. He noticed the yellow VW parked, but it was not in the same spot it had been before. That bothered him. He stopped the car, parked it, and went into Max's building again. He buzzed Apartment 4D hopefully. He waited. No answer. Then he buzzed all the doorbells just to get in. No one buzzed him back. After a few minutes he shook his head in disgust and left.

In the sub-basement, Jennifer was lying on the floor in a fetal position. Her leotard was smudged with dirt and her hair was matted and falling in her face. There was a bloody scratch showing through her tights where she had hit herself when she stumbled off the table trying once more to call for help. After that she had slumped to the filthy floor. She was sucking her thumb.

Max turned the key in the laundry room and they both walked in.

"She's the one?" his mother said, her voice rising in anger and disappointment.

"Now, Mama, she'll be okay. I gave her some medicine to quiet her."

"Medicine? Not my old pills! You've knocked her out."

"She'll be okay, Mama. She's good. I promise you. Besides, we'll have to keep her drugged after it's over and we leave."

"We'll have to clean her up." She walked over to the sleeping Jennifer and circled her. Max followed.

"Stand her up," she ordered.

Max yanked Jennifer up from the floor, both hands under her armpits. Jennifer, still in a drugged sleep, opened one puffy eye. Her mouth opened to say something, but nothing came out. She slumped against Max.

Charlotte came up close and slapped her face a few times. Jennifer stood up, eyes still closed, whelping. There was a ring around her leotard near the crotch and her face was streamed with lines where tears had cut through dirt.

"Pee-yoo! She needs a bath," Charlotte said.

"Yes, Mama."

"Plenty of good, strong black coffee first, though."

She took her coat off and arranged it around Jennifer, buttoning the buttons, though her arms were inside the coat. They both half-carried, half-dragged her out of the room and up the steps. Max looked to see if the halls were clear, propping Jennifer between the wall and his mother. He gave a low, all-clear whistle. Then he dashed back and they continued to lead the now-stumbling Jennifer through the halls and up the four flights of steps.

As she was being hoisted, Jennifer was beginning to be aware that she was going up the steps. Like a baby she tried to put one foot first and follow it with the other. It felt like she was walking in midair. Why couldn't they let her just go back to sleep? She was so tired. She had never felt more sleepy in her life. Her whole body ached for it. Who were these people, anyway?

"She needs some raw meat. That will put new blood in her. Give her some pep."

"Yes, Mama."

Jennifer made her first sound. It was a low, guttural, half-animal-like sob.

Chapter Fifteen

There had been one or two girls he had liked when he was younger, but he knew they would never like him. Nobody did. Then he grew up and found that women did like him. A lot. It wasn't that he didn't like them. It's just that he didn't care. They were okay. Sometimes he felt that part of him had been emptied and could never be replaced. He wanted to feel what he thought other people felt. But the only time he could feel was when he knew he would be the last man to make love to them.

THE PROMENADE IN the New York State Theatre was packed with the kind of people who could afford to pay two hundred fifty dollars a seat. The ladies wore couturier gowns; the men were in tuxedos. They were watched over by two twenty-foot-high marble statues, one on each side of the room, each weighing twelve hundred pounds. They were a favorite stopping place for reporters making notes and camera people and photographers changing film. *Women's Wear Daily* planned to feature the gala in a bitchy center spread. It probably would make the network evening news.

It was a glittering Christmas Eve. The tables were covered with gold tablecloths. The lights were dimmed to a soft, pink glow so that the Promenade was bathed almost entirely with the magical touch of candlelight. Butlers moved about in dinner jackets carrying trays of champagne, their arms raised high as they sailed through the crowd. Mingling with the crowd, also, were a few people who quietly conversed about general contribution pledges, very subtly soliciting donations. People were queuing up in line before the abundantly laden tables to nibble on roast beef, turkey, wild rice with mushrooms, salads of every kind, and little Christmas pastries. Every once in a while a pale, thin girl with her hair in a bun or a slim but muscular young man would float in, eating nothing, but giving the guests a chance to see real-live dancers.

Mrs. Twyler glided quickly and gracefully about in a mauve chiffon gown, kissing lightly on the cheek everyone she knew and cooing over those she would like to know. Mrs. O'Conner, dressed in a simple black dress with pearls, took her post at the tables and was fussing and constantly telling the waiters to replace trays even before they were half-empty. But the center of attention, wherever he stood, was always Mr. Zolinsky. Patrician, gracious, considered a legend in his lifetime, he had learned to play this game with patrons and would-be patrons masterfully. Sipping his champagne, he thought of Martin Cooper and then forced it out of his mind. When he thought of Jennifer North, though, his wrist shook so much he almost spilled some champagne on his jacket. No one noticed. All the while he smiled, chatted, and made charming compliments to the ladies.

Backstage, no one was smiling or charming. Dancers were nervously doing last-minute private rehearsals. Corps girls in full makeup and exquisitely designed costumes were warming up in threadbare leg-warmers. In her dressing room, Nora was mumbling. A set of dusty rosary beads was in her hands. In the dressing room that used to be Jennifer's and Heather's, Stephanie sat coolly, all made up and dressed, counting, with a traveling clock, the seconds until the curtain rose and she would dance the part instead of Jennifer.

At the same time that the gala was taking off, Hogan and his wife finally landed at Kennedy Airport. Hogan's face was ugly with anger. He had stopped to get the latest edition of the *Post*. He flashed the newspaper at his wife. They were waiting for the squad car to show up.

BALLERINA MISSING! read the headline in big letters. Hogan clenched his cigar in his teeth and began to read the paper very carefully. All he could get out of it was that the Ballet Killer had killed himself and some dumb dancer hadn't been seen by her boyfriend for about a day. What really made him burn was Lieutenant Frank Fazio was referred to as being in charge of the task force in Captain William Hogan's absence. They even said he was on vacation. Fazio had had the gall to call Ivan Roman *his* investigation. He was quoted as saying: "In my investigation I found no reason to believe there was any foul play in the case of Ivan Roman. It was a clear case of suicide." Dumb wop. Who was he to say, using just his own judgment, that Ivan Roman committed suicide? Maybe he wasn't capable of it. Maybe he was murdered.

His wife tapped him on the shoulder. The squad car had arrived. As they were scooping up their luggage, Hogan made up his mind that when the department got through with Frank Fazio, when they found out what he was really doing, he would end up as a security guard in a supermarket somewhere.

Richard Kupperman, Mr. and Mrs. North, Richard's father, Moskowitz and Fazio stood in a little group backstage. It was 7:35. The light was dim but they could see the dancers moving about, going through their last-minute rituals.

The conductor had not yet taken his place, though most of the orchestra members were seated in the pit. Over half of the audience was still in the Promenade munching and sipping and trying subtly to capture the eye of the photographers. Mr. Zolinsky had slipped backstage to be with his dancers and was quietly making the rounds, tapping them on the shoulders, whispering *"merde"* and calling them by name. Every once in a while he would tell someone to remember to pay special attention to a tricky step or watch their *port de bras*. When he got to Stephanie, he smiled but he never tapped her or said anything. Stephanie was then even more determined to be brilliant. The thought occurred to her that maybe that's why he ignored her, to make her try harder. Zolinsky handled everyone differently. Well, she would rise to the challenge.

The little group scanned the dancers over and over again, hoping, somehow, still not giving up, that any second they would find Jennifer among them. Fazio watched everything and everybody. When they heard a commotion behind them, they all turned at once.

Two security police were holding back a young man. "Lieutenant Fazio said I could come in," he snapped. He had three cameras. Two were slung across his shoulders.

"Oh, yeah? Didn't Zolinsky kick you out a few weeks ago for taking too many pictures?"

Fazio walked over and flashed his shield for effect. "It's okay. I gave him a pass. He's helping me." The security guards released him.

"Listen," Jerry Turner said to Fazio, "I tested this

camera and took some pictures in the bar. It works. But look."

Fazio looked at the picture of Heather Cooper and the picture Turner had taken of Vinnie. The size was noticeably different. Also, Heather's picture had a clear, sharp quality, while the one taken with Roman's camera was blurred. It was as if the camera had never really been good, even when it was new.

"I don't think this camera took that picture," Jerry Turner said. "But, like I said, Polaroids aren't my specialty. I can tell you where to go. A camera store that might be of more help. But you asked for my opinion. I don't think it's the camera that took this picture of Heather Cooper." Then he rolled his eyes upward. "God, I have some good shots of her at home, but they're worthless now, I guess."

Fazio watched the young man. His face was flushed with excitement. He was still clutching the snapshot of Heather Cooper.

"Look, though. Look closely at this picture. That whitish-yellow diamond splash in the right-hand upper corner. What did you say that was?"

Fazio studied it again. "Overexposed?"

"No. I don't think so. Not entirely. It's a light coming from a lamp or something hitting a polished surface, a high surface, maybe another lamp or a mirror or a high piece of furniture. So there's a clue as to where this picture may have been shot, if that's what you're looking for." Then Jerry Turner's face fell suddenly as something new came into his mind. "Come to think of it, though, it's not much of a clue, if all it is is a high piece of furniture."

Fazio stared at the snapshot. A high piece of furniture. Roman had had hardly any furniture at all. But a piano was a high piece of furniture. Max Forrest had a piano and light walls. He noticed it when he stood in his doorway. Damn it! His hands were tied. Max was missing and Fazio would need a search warrant to get in. What judge was going to give him a search warrant because someone had a high piece of furniture that produced a diamond-like light in a snapshot? It would take an hour to explain the whole thing to a judge. It would take less than an hour to be eased out of the department.

It was only Christmas Eve at the Titanic, but somehow it resembled New Year's Eve more. People were dancing in the center of the floor to music that wasn't playing. Some alone. Drinks were sloshed and tipped as people tried to move from the crowded bar to the equally crowded table and booth section.

At a big table near the center sat five detectives from the two-oh.

"Did ya hear Hogan is rushing back from his vacation?" one started, as the conversation naturally turned to department gossip.

"No kidding? I thought he was in Bermuda," another detective said.

"He was. But a squad car was sent to pick him up at Kennedy."

A detective, who had been quiet so far, said, "Does he think he can bring the Ballet Killer back from the grave?"

Someone else chuckled. "No. But Fazio's been put in charge, and Captain Bill don't like that."

No one said anything for a minute or two. Then one detective rubbed his chin and said quietly, "You know, I think Fazio's up to something."

The others said, "Whaddya mean?" almost simultaneously.

"Just this. He's off duty. I happen to know that. But

at the same time he's working on some sort of case, and it's not just Ivan Roman's suicide, I'd bet."

The detective at the end of the table leaned in. "I don't think the lieutenant thought it was Roman. I think he's still looking for the Ballet Killer."

"Alone?" someone else said.

"But he'd be going against the department," a detective said incredulously.

"He's a pretty stubborn guy, that Fazio. Personally, I don't think he really gives a damn," the one at the end of the table said.

Someone else said, impulsively, "Fazio's a good man."

"Good detective," another agreed.

"Hey, does anyone know where he is now?" someone said. No one did.

Then a detective who had kept silent during everything, just listening, said quietly, "He's at the State Theatre, backstage."

"How do you know so much?" one detective kidded.

"Because I've been following him for almost twenty-four hours. Hogan's orders," Shipley said.

With just a short time to get ready, Yuri Ivanov kissed the hand of a plump matron, lingering a little on the huge ruby ring, and then dashed to his dressing room to get dressed and do a warm-up. There were sighs and gasps from the women present. He was dressed in a tuxedo, his unruly tawny hair slicked down, and on his face was an impish smile. Yuri was as important to a gala as were the two bars at either end of the Promenade.

He preferred to take longer getting dressed, with more time to relax and warm up, but he also enjoyed being the center of attention. In his dressing room, putting on his makeup, he thought of Jennifer. Then he did something he hadn't done since he defected from Russia. He said a little prayer.

Pretty soon they would have to go out front to their seats. But they lingered, tensely, reluctant to go, still waiting, still watching Lieutenant Fazio for something to hang onto. Mr. and Mrs. North had been backstage at many ballets before. Ever since their daughter had given her first recital so many years ago. Mrs. North often worried that Jennifer was so intense about ballet, she might miss out on a normal life. Then she glanced up at Richard, pacing up and down. Jennifer did want to marry this young man who seemed to care deeply about her. Mrs. North didn't know what to make of him. But she knew Mr. North liked him.

She peered over at his parents. Mrs. Kupperman had wanted to be in the Promenade for a while and had just joined them. Mrs. North liked him, but not her. She seemed snooty, somehow, as if Ohio wasn't New York or Great Neck, Long Island. As if Jennifer wasn't good enough for her son. Oh, God, she wished Jennifer would show up. Pretty soon they'd all have to go back to their seats.

Richard kept up his pacing. He thought if he didn't, he would either pick a fight with someone or start clawing at the scenery. Where the hell was she? If only he could think of something, a link, a clue to help. She had never mentioned Max Forrest, except in passing. It was nothing important. They gossiped more about other people in the company. Where could she be? Was it his fault? If anything happened to Jennifer and he never got a chance to tell her how much he loved her, he'd never forgive himself. Never.

Fazio stood a little apart from the group. Just observing. He was hoping, too, that Jennifer would show up. Much as he wanted to prove his theory that the Ballet Killer was missing, he didn't necessarily want to prove it with a victim. Especially this girl.

The dancers were quieting down backstage. They had stopped their warm-ups and their good-luck taps. Some were doing yoga exercises; others did a final, favorite quiet stretch. They could hear the tune-up of the string instruments in the pit.

Fazio was standing next to Richard's father, watching the dancers, when an idea occurred to him. He whispered, "You're an orthopedic surgeon, too, aren't you, sir?"

"Yes. But I'm going to teach in the fall. My son will be taking over much of my practice."

"Let me ask you something." As Fazio talked, his eyes never stopped scanning the area looking for any sign of Jennifer, or anything out of place. "Is it possible for a person to limp some of the time but not limp all of the time?"

"Well, yes, in a way. If someone limps, that person will always limp. A limp is really the foot slapping against the ground."

"So a person always limps," Fazio repeated, disappointed.

"Well, you see, there are rare cases, oh, such as shattered nerve endings resulting from something like a car accident, in which a prosthesis can be made to give support to the foot and stop the slapping. In that case, if the prosthesis were covered up, it would look like the person didn't limp."

Fazio was beginning to feel more parts of the jigsaw puzzle fall into place. "Wait a second; then I was right. Someone could have a limp but not limp. You put a brace on his . . . or her . . . leg and there's no limp."

"Prosthesis, Lieutenant. And when worn, it would

stop that slapping motion. In fact, the one I'm thinking of is very light and made of polyethylene. It spirals around from under the foot and fastens at the knee. It's easy to slip in and out of. Really a modern-day miracle, though they've been available for about twenty years, I believe."

Fazio mimed a fake demonstration. "Just pull up your pants, unfasten it, and it's off."

Dr. Kupperman added, "Put it on under your socks and no one can see it."

Fazio stood in the semi-dark, thinking. So, Max Forrest could limp. Anyone could limp. But did Forrest know something about Jennifer? Or, worse, had he done something to her? He decided that if the girl didn't show, he would go with Moskowitz and track down the man.

Outside in the Promenade, ladies were disappearing into the powder room to fix their faces. Waiters were taking away the trays, and before intermission the whole floor would be cleared so that people could move more freely and order quick drinks. There was something happening, though, in the middle of the room. People turned to stare. It was Mr. Zolinsky. He was hugging a tall man, showing more emotion than most people had ever seen emanate from the elegant old man. Then the crowds parted and they saw Judge Martin Cooper.

"Martin," he whispered and drew him away from the people still milling about.

"I'm so happy, so happy you could be with us. It's your gala as much as mine."

The tall, graying man still had a ghostly pallor about him, but he managed to say with some life, "Ah, but, Grischa, it's your ballet. And that's what I came to see."

"Come, come with me. The dancers must see you."

He said nothing about Heather's cremation or why no one had been invited to the service. Apparently, he had buried his daughter and come back to his senses. Work. That was the antidote. It had always been that way with him. And now his work would be so much easier with Martin around.

Two cars of off-duty detectives pulled up to the State Theatre. They passed the security guards, alarmed the elegant crowd still in the Promenade and with full authority marched backstage.

The Norths and Kuppermans were lingering, waiting just a bit longer, not wanting to go out front and see a ballet Jennifer wasn't in. Richard Kupperman had stopped pacing and stood still, unable to believe what was actually happening. Fazio was trying to figure out how to get a search warrant for Max's apartment when the answer walked in with his arm linked around Mr. Zolinsky's.

Almost seconds later eight determined detectives arrived in the backstage area and Fazio guessed they were sent by Hogan. Shit! Just when he was getting closer. Now he'd have to stop and that would be the end of his career.

Moskowitz saw them, too. He motioned for Fazio to step farther backstage into the shadows. They recognized most of the faces of the detectives. Definitely Hogan's men. Jerry Turner, happily shooting away, stepped into the shadows, also. When they came toward Moskowitz, Fazio had disappeared. And so had Judge Martin Cooper.

Out front the rows of seats were beginning to fill up. The audience was ready for the main event. They flipped through the programs and read the story line for *Artemis Visions*. They leafed through perfume and restaurant ads. They tried to ignore the mauve-colored dedication to the other young ballerina victims. It was just too awful to think about at a time like this.

One dancer stealing a peak through the curtains quipped that there might be more glitter in the audience than onstage. Bits of light coming from the chandelier and the lighting in the glowing Jewel Box Theatre struck and shimmered on diamonds, emeralds and rubies. Gowns were sequined, bejeweled, dazzling.

Upstairs in a small unoccupied dressing room, Fazio held one arm firmly against the door. Standing on the other side of the room was Judge Martin Cooper.

"I need a search warrant, Judge."

"I'm not a judge anymore, Lieutenant."

Fazio thought that if anyone could lose five pounds in the space of a day, the gaunt, tired-looking man standing in front of him had.

"But, technically, you still are, right?"

Judge Cooper nodded in reluctant agreement.

"Anyway you're the best I can come up with under the circumstances. Have you got any?"

"There might be some in my briefcase in the car. But I really don't think . . ."

Fazio shook his head. "Look, Judge Cooper, I mean I feel great that you're feeling better, but I have to tell you and I trust you because you lost your daughter—but I don't think Hogan got the right man. This is just between us. No, I don't. I have a hunch . . ."

Judge Cooper finished the sentence for him. "The Ballet Killer is still loose."

Fazio said nothing. The expression on his face said everything. He was waiting for Cooper's decision, aware of the risk he was taking.

Judge Cooper said sadly, "It's going to start again."

"Not if I can help it. I'm sure if I can just get a

search warrant for a certain suspect, I'll come up with enough evidence for it to stop."

"You're doing this alone? They'll throw it out of court."

"They would have thrown Roman out of court, eventually, too. Look, I'm liable to lose my job for this, but even if they throw it out of court on that legality, if it's the real killer—at least he'll be removed. You can't deny that. Look, Judge Cooper, did you see the papers tonight?"

"No, I didn't."

"Since Ivan Roman killed himself, another ballerina is missing. It may be a coincidence, but I don't think it is."

Judge Cooper arched his bushy eyebrows upward. "Does anyone know who she is? Our company?"

"Jennifer North."

Judge Cooper seemed to stiffen. Then he started for the door. "Come out to my car, Lieutenant. It's parked near the theater. I'm sure we'll find some search warrants."

Coming back down in the elevator, Fazio's spirits were soaring. When they got to the ground floor his spirits sank. They were met by the troop of detectives. He thought it was all over, until he caught the smiling face of Moskowitz.

"They want to help, Lieutenant."

Fazio smiled, but it was more of a sneer. "You're all full of shit. You know what the department could do to you?"

Some nodded. One said, "Screw the department. We think the killer is still loose." The others voiced their agreement.

Fazio smiled a genuine ear-to-ear smile this time. God only knew how he and Moskowitz needed help desperately. They needed a hundred more hands, eyes, ears. But eight more were enough for him.

He assigned two detectives to go with Judge Cooper to get the warrant and then toss Max Forrest's apartment. He told them what he was looking for and why. The rest of the detectives were to come with him and station themselves backstage. For the time being. The whole group assumed a different attitude. There was an out-of-school aura permeating the group as they trooped backstage. They were breaking all the rules.

Backstage the atmosphere was tense. Everyone was waiting now for the conductor to come through the series of doors that led him to the pit. Some dancers were silent, some were giggling, and some were going through the motions of warming up. It was very dark backstage and Fazio moved about stealthily, watching, waiting to see what would happen next, if anything.

He slipped in and out between heavy pieces of scenery and occasionally stumbled over a wire or stopped to look at the big steel roll-down door that let in the props and scenery from the street. Maybe something would come through that door. He had nine detectives counting Moskowitz. Perhaps he should have one guarding the door. As he started to leave, he heard a small sound like a rustling or the scratching of a cat. He turned around sharply. Silence. No one was there. Fazio walked away.

Behind a fake tree Max Forrest kept his gun aimed on Fazio as he walked. His other hand was clamped tightly over the mouth of a tied, bound, gagged, and trembling Jennifer North.

Chapter Sixteen

Limping made him feel sexy. Mama hated it when he limped. So he enjoyed his own private joke. Before each girl, just a minute before they did it, he would reach down and unstrap that contraption. They never saw. Then afterward, when they lay cold and still, he would limp around and get them ready for delivery. It was all a game. Life was a game. People who weren't rich, la-de-dah, lording it over everyone else, were entitled to their fun, too. Mama had always told him that.

IT WAS FIVE minutes before curtain when a few loud gasps, a low scream, and a very clear "Oh, my God!" were heard backstage. Then no one could see anything.

Those nearest to the crowd surging backward were asking, "What is it? What's happened?" The crowd parted a little and more people rushed forward. Jennifer North stood quietly clutching tightly to a wall, warming up.

She was dressed in a costume almost like Stephanie's, a familiar-looking costume, very close but not quite the same. She was wearing leg-warmers and a loose cardigan sweater. Staring straight ahead, woodenly, she did her *pliés, tendus* and back stretches. She smiled wanly in acknowledgment but spoke to no one.

One dancer whispered to another. "She looks funny. Spooky, somehow."

Almost everyone in the company came up respectfully and tapped her on the shoulder, whispering, *"Merde,* Jennifer." No one said anything but they all knew what they felt. Relief. Jennifer had disappeared and returned. The Ballet Killer had really been found. Stephanie stomped offstage right with a loud, "Oh, shit!"

It took a minute or two for all this to reach the little circle standing much farther upstage, almost near the entrance. Jennifer's parents rushed through the crowd. They saw her first, a silhouette, almost, going through her warm-up.

"Now, don't press her, Edith. You'll make her nervous," Mr. North whispered to his wife.

Jennifer's mother ran over and hugged her. "Oh, Jennifer, we were so worried! Darling, where were you? Are you sure you're okay? Do you really want to dance?"

Jennifer's whisper was thin and breathy. They could hardly hear her. "Mom, Dad, it's good to see you." Something caught in her throat. She said nothing else. Her parents stood there awkwardly for a second while she continued her mechanical warm-up, not even looking at them.

Mr. North said cautiously, "Well, good luck, princess. We'll be out front rooting for you." Jennifer allowed herself a half-smile as her father kissed her quickly on the cheek. The Norths left for their seats, happy that their daughter was alive and well, but they were still worried about her.

Richard studied her before he went up. He had thought that he would never see that delicate face again, never hold her. It was too dim to really see, but he could feel her, though she was standing a foot or two away. When he went up to her and touched her back, pulling her toward him, she shuddered and pulled away.

"Jennifer, we were so worried! Darling, where were you? Are you sure you're okay? Do you really want to dance?"

Jennifer's eyes were unblinking. She didn't look at him. Instead, she turned around and started warming up on the other side, her back to him.

"Jennifer!" Richard pleaded. "What is it? What's happened to you?"

Her voice was a monotone. "Please, Richard, not now. Go out front. Now. Please."

Richard stood there as if she had hit him. All the dancers were clustered close by, staring at them. Richard tried once more to penetrate the wall she was putting up. Again she turned away from him. Again that same flat, dead voice. "Not now, Richard."

The curtain was being held until all was quiet backstage. Exhausted, frustrated, Richard began to lose his temper. The other dancers stood trying not to gape, very silent, waiting.

"Not *now*? After what we've been through, Jennifer? Your parents, the police . . ." Again that slight half-smile from Jennifer. The dimmed lights touched her face as she bent into a backbend. Dark, doe-eyed ballerina makeup on a chalk-white face with brilliant spots of rouge and lipstick. And eyes that hardly ever blinked.

Fazio, watching the whole scene, stepped forward and gave Richard a slight push away.

"She said not now. Why don't you obey the lady's wishes?"

"Because she's acting childish. How dare she do this to all of us?"

"I thought your generation was supposed to be liberated," he said lightly.

Richard was stunned.

"Look, go out front like she says and get out of her way," Fazio said sternly.

Richard, not seeing the sanity in any of this, slinked away silently. Fazio stepped farther backstage into the wings and gave a signal to three detectives in the corner. The signal was to tell them to be on guard. Fazio had gotten close enough to the girl to see the symptoms. He had seen that look, the trapped expression in the eyes, the death-like voice and the guarded retreat. He had seen it in hostages.

Hogan came into his office at about five minutes before 8:00. They had gotten tied up in the Christmas-time traffic. He took one look around and then kicked a chair halfway across the room in a fit of fury. All of his things had been dumped in a corner. Fazio had not only moved in, but he had begun to work at his desk. Hogan couldn't really get angry at that; after all, it had been Fazio's office at first, but it was evident he was working to undo everything that Hogan had done.

He stepped over to the desk and glanced at some scribbled notes Fazio had made. One said, "Jennifer North always expressed a desire to go to California." Then there was a list of all the hospitals in the city with checks next to them. Another line of scribbling said, "If the press calls about Roman . . ." Hogan studied the line carefully, turning the pad of paper upside down and around, but it was never finished. It ended in doodles.

While Hogan was taking off his trenchcoat and summer hat, he noticed something strange. He lit a cigar and tried to figure it out, puffing furiously to get it started. Two plain suits hung on wire hangers with shirts and ties. They were hanging on a hook in the back of a door. Had Fazio and whoever else he had

helping him changed clothes or something? A disguise?
Maybe they were impersonating patrolmen.

He paced the office trying to figure it out. Then he
spun around and snapped his fingers. Of course! The
clown had gotten dressed up and gone to the gala. He
was looking for action at the State Theatre. All he
needed was another phone call from Shipley to give
him that information, but Hogan wasn't there to answer phones. He didn't have to wait for Shipley.

Quickly Hogan reached in his drawer. Within five
minutes he could mobilize his best men and they
would come, even though they were off duty, even
though it was Christmastime. He could still do them
big favors in return. Hogan was sure Frank Fazio was
on to something. It had something to do with the gala
and the case. Well, if he was wrong, Hogan would
crucify him. But if he was right, he could step right in
and take over. Fazio was always good for doing the
dirty work first.

It was Christmas Eve at Manhattan State Hospital.
Volunteers had donated a Christmas tree and the occupational therapy lady had made sure that every
hand fumbling from medication made some sort of
ball or ornament to hang on a branch. The Christmas
tree, already a little lopsided from patients stumbling
into it, remained off in a corner, a study in confused
color and form with no presents underneath it.

In the nurses' room, Nurse Johnson was holding
court. Most patients had gone somewhere for the long
weekend, but some of her favorite babies had nowhere
to go. For them she provided a Christmas party complete with special refreshments and little boxes of dusting powder from the dimestore. For herself, a good,
thick helping of Irish whiskey buried in a cup of tea.

They had just finished singing a round of a cappella

Christmas carols. Now they were gossiping about the people in the ward. There was Christina, a former child model whose mother had taken her paychecks and left her alone and sick with nothing to show for all her years of work. Christina was sixteen years old and was growing up in Manhattan State Hospital. When she was old enough and well enough, she would find some sort of little job and commute to the hospital. Christina loved Nurse Johnson and basked in the attention she showered on her. Then there was Irma, eighteen, whose parents were punishing her for having too many catatonic trances. They said since she hadn't perked up and taken part in any activities, she couldn't have Christmas with their large Italian family. And there was Dulcey, who had eight children and a husband who beat her, and she looked upon Manhattan State as a rest home.

"Do you think Bernice has a good time at home? I mean, can she tell the difference?" Dulcey asked.

"Oh, sure," Nurse Johnson said. "She has a good time. Her parents are wealthy, educated people."

"Then how come they turned her into a vegetable?" Christina asked.

"Oh, she's better off this way. Sure, you should have seen her years before. Now, at least she knows some peace, poor child. Very violent, she was," Nurse Johnson said.

"And what about the odd one, what's-her-name? Oh, yeah, Charlotte. She went home for Christmas," Irma said.

"Charlotte's okay," Nurse Johnson said. "You know I read her records. She used to dance. Ballet dancing."

"Oh, c'mon," Dulcey laughed. "Her? She's such a . . . slob." Christina laughed, too, secretly wondering if everyone laughed at her behind her back when they found out she had been a child model.

Nurse Johnson immediately rose to the defense of her children. "Not true. Ever seen pictures of ballet dancers? Look at her face sometimes. She's got those high cheekbones." Nurse Johnson picked up the flab on her face to demonstrate.

Dulcey laughed. "Well, she's also got a fat ass."

They all laughed at that.

The audience was getting politely restless. You could hear the rustling of programs, the coughing. The conductor was waiting for a signal from the stage manager, who motioned that there was some kind of confusion backstage. Everyone was waiting for the curtain to go up. But things hadn't quieted down backstage.

"Why should she be allowed to sneak in at the last minute and go on?" Stephanie complained tearfully to Yuri, who liked to use this time to compose himself.

"It's her part, Stephanie; she can do whatever she likes. One day your time will come."

"It's not fair!" Stephanie was standing with clenched fists, tears streaming down her face.

Yuri nodded gravely. She definitely had to go, and soon. He glanced over at Jennifer. She looked pale under her makeup, but she was warming up. He hoped she was feeling well enough to dance the ballet the way it was supposed to be done. He might have to talk her through it.

"Why don't you go to Mr. Zolinsky?" he said at last to the girl who was glaring at him as if it were his fault.

"Good idea! That's just what I'll do!"

She clattered off, her pointe shoes hitting the floor as if to punish it. Yuri closed his eyes and settled into his favorite pre-performance exercise. The one he saved for last. Just basic head rolls. It would help take care of the tension she had just dumped on him.

"Have you seen Mr. Z.?" Stephanie asked another dancer.

"He's watching from out front, like he usually does for openings."

Stephanie started to walk offstage. The stage manager gripped her by the arm. "Hey, wait a second! Where are you going?"

"I wanted to try to . . ."

He held her wrist firmly. "Stay right here. We might need you. Jennifer looks a little green around the gills, if you ask me."

The doorbell rang in David Funke's apartment. He was practicing. He ran out into the hall. "Yes? Who is it?"

"It's me!"

He couldn't believe it. Olive! On Christmas Eve? He almost galloped down the stairs to get her. Her cheeks were flushed and she was breathless. She was smiling even before she saw him. When she did, she started to kiss him sloppily, almost drunkenly. David backed away.

"Olive, not here. Let's go upstairs. How did you get away?"

She laughed. "Oh, I told Edwin I had to make a charity call to Miss Murphy. He thinks I'm at the hospital holding her wrinkled hand. It worked. He thought she was one of the best teachers we had." Olive laughed again. David thought her laughs were sometimes somewhere between a grating giggle and a climbing hysteria. He was noticing that more and more lately. Truthfully, he had been quite content to stay at home alone and work on his Bach.

When they were inside the apartment, Olive slyly latched the chain lock and stood with her back to the door as if she were guarding it. David had to admit he had never seen her looking better. She was wearing a long, black dress almost like a concert gown and a long coat of burgundy velvet. Her hair was up in a bun, which he knew he would soon unravel, and she had on her long gold-and-diamond earrings, which he knew she would take off so she didn't lose them.

"Take off your clothes," she commanded jokingly.

To his surprise, David found himself blushing. "Olive, I . . ."

"Oh, c'mon, David, I only have tonight, and then a whole long week without you."

"But, Olive, I'm not a machine."

Olive had already wriggled out of her gown. He stood there and gaped. She wasn't wearing a stitch of underwear. "C'mon Davey, that's why I love you. You're nineteen and strong and healthy and you know . . ." She laughed again. "You know what to do with your equipment."

David smelled the liquor on her breath. He felt . . . but that was the trouble lately. He didn't know what he was feeling. All he knew was he had to get out of his clothes as fast as he could and put her on his highrise bed.

It was now close to 8:15 and the curtain hadn't gone up. Jennifer knew Max was behind her with a gun and she kept up her silent warm-up. She also knew he couldn't see the tears running down her heavily made-up face. They had given her a bath, this wild old lady scrubbing her all over. All the time she thought she was going to drown because she couldn't stay awake.

Then they had made her eat. It was horrible. And all the coffee she had drunk. Still she wanted to curl up on the floor and go to sleep. Terror kept her awake. She just kept repeating her warm-up, knowing that somewhere in the shadows Max was watching her every move, a gun in his hand. A fresh tear started when she thought of Richard. God, what must he think? But Max said he would shoot her and anyone else standing close enough if she talked too long to anyone. Why wasn't she clever enough to give someone some sort of hint? She had tried to think, but her brain was so fuzzy. Besides, Max would know. He was smarter than she was.

Now she was in a costume that didn't even look right on her, waiting to go on that big stage and dance. Dance? She could barely do her warm-up. But if she didn't do it right, he said he would kill her.

Olive was nibbling on David's ear like it was a potato chip and running her fingers through his thick, curly hair. "Give me a Christmas treat, hmm, darling?" She snuggled closer, wrapping herself into his hard, firm body. She giggled. "Remember the time you wore your hat to bed?"

"No." David Funke didn't know what was the matter with him, but he didn't think he could get it up. God, this would be the first time anything like this ever happened in his life. And then she touched him perfectly in the right spot and he knew that wasn't one of his problems.

"But, Davey, it was right before you lost your last one. You wore it to bed, remember? Right around the time you subbed for the New York Center's class because they needed extra help." She giggled. "Before I made it worth your while not to waste your precious talent and time away from me playing for stupid ballet classes."

"Oh, my God."

He sat up and Olive sat up on one elbow, creases in her forehead. "Davey, what's wrong?"

David kissed her on the forehead. "You have the most phenomenal memory. I never would have thought of that."

He jumped out of bed.

"Davey?" Olive asked carefully. "Are you okay?"

"Yeah, I'm okay." He was getting dressed quickly. "Lieutenant Fazio came here last night. Wanted to know about my hat. Now I understand why. And then the Ballet Killer kills himself. And I have the answer."

"Davey, you're being foolish again. Come back to bed. C'mon, now. Don't get yourself involved."

"Yes, but Olive . . ." He was putting on his socks and shoes. "The Ballet Killer wasn't the Ballet Killer. The hat I lost was the one this man they think is the killer was wearing. And if that's the case, Olive, he works for New York Center! He has to be a member of the company."

"Oh, that's preposterous!"

David Funke was already running for his checkered cap and his jacket. Olive, lying naked on his bed, looked at him hard and said, "Davey, if you leave this apartment now, I'll never take you back again."

David looked at her. He had a funny, little crooked smile on his face. Then he turned around and walked out quickly, slamming the door behind him.

Max was dressed all in black, moving quickly from one piece of scenery to the next, covering himself with his gun. When the curtain opened, Jennifer started to shake uncontrollably. Fazio was moving in the darkness backstage, too. He had a hunch Max Forrest was somewhere close by. The stage manager yelled, "Curtain going up!"

"Curtain!" echoed the whispers of a confused, nervous cast. They smiled and arranged themselves in the positions of their dances. Fazio kept moving softly downstage. As the curtain went up, he could hear the thunderous applause, but he couldn't see the dark form that wasn't a shadow.

Chapter Seventeen

"Mama, mama, please can I take ballet lessons?"
"Ballet lessons? We ain't got no money for that. Shut up!"

But she got them. When she was eight years old she started. For a long time her father didn't know that her mother took the money out of the food budget. When he found out he beat her up so hard she couldn't take ballet for a week. But she continued. When she went to them and told them she was going to have a baby, they called her a whore and kicked her out. Told her never to come back. Sometimes she wondered what ever became of her parents. Not that she really cared.

THE APPLAUSE FOR the set continued for about three minutes while the corps, poised and pointed, waited to begin. The stage was awash with gold and pink and green. A huge replica of a Greek temple rose majestically in the middle. On either side were urns. In center stage was a golden altar with real smoke curling up.

As the applause began to die down, four girls and boys jetéed in perfect unison. They circled the stage, leaping, twirling, seeming to chase one another. Then Yuri Ivanov, playing the part of Achilles, leaped in and the audience went wild with applause. He leaped again, soaring over the smoky urn, beating his feet in midair, landing flawlessly, his feet in fifth position. The corps, as the Greek chorus, swayed and flowed lyrically.

Someone tapped Jennifer on the shoulder gently. Like a graceful robot she moved toward the wings, waiting to go on. She knew there was a gun pointed at her back. She couldn't scream. She couldn't run. She had to do what she had been told. But at least she knew her solo.

Fazio studied her carefully. A pretty young girl, but she didn't match the pictures he had seen of her. There was no vibrancy, no sparkle. He guessed she had been heavily drugged. She also had the nervous, guarded look he had seen on hostages before. There was nothing to do but wait.

The music hit a crescendo. Fazio turned his eyes to the stage. Jennifer entered doing the little mincing steps that began her solo. She had the sweet smile of a ballerina on her face and her arms opened graciously as if to welcome the audience to her little world.

Jennifer had a magical stage presence. Even when she was in the corps she stood out. Now the chorus swayed to and fro in the background, the music a delicious andante. And Jennifer started her important solo in allegro with very fast, peppy *fouetté* turns. A girl in the corps tripped she was so surprised. The conductor stepped the tempo up a beat to even out what everyone onstage was doing. Nothing matched.

Backstage someone whispered loudly, "My God, she's gone crazy! She's doing a solo from *Petroushka!*"

Someone else shouted, "Get Mr. Zolinsky, for God's sake!"

The stage manager yelled back, "Someone just ran out front to see if we should pull the curtain!" He knew that if they pulled the girl off, they'd have to start over.

Stephanie stood there pointing and flexing her feet, itching to have the curtain come down and the ballet resume with her doing the solo. If she had any sense,

she thought, she would just push Jennifer off the
stage and go on. Now everyone would know that part
should have rightfully been hers.

Onstage Yuri lost his cool composure. "Pssst!" he
whispered from upstage to Jennifer, who was dancing
downstage. "Wake up!" But Jennifer paid no attention. She just repeated the same turns and spins and
steps, oblivious to everything.

The audience began to twitter. From out front it
looked like a silent-film comedy. The whole cast was
smooth and lyrical and that girl was spinning like a
top. It was out of sync. And she wasn't even that
graceful. She kept stumbling like a broken wind-up
doll. Twitters and whispers gave way to laughter
throughout the audience. Some couldn't help it. It
was just one of those things that was so funny to
watch.

As Jennifer tried harder to balance on pointe and
execute the usual flawless turns she was accustomed
to doing, she heard the laughter coming from the audience. Tears rushed down her face but she kept on
going. If her mascara ran, then she would have trouble with her contact lenses, which were already beginning to burn in her eyes. No more crying, she told
herself, but her diaphragm was heaving with suppressed sobs. She was making a fool of herself. She
was ruining Mr. Zolinsky's beautiful ballet. And all
because she was trying to stay alive. Oh, those idiots!
Couldn't they close the curtain? Then she thought
that might be worse. Because then Max could spring
from backstage quicker and kill her and anyone else
who got in his way.

She overheard one boy in the corps forced to take
part in the charade whisper, "Is she drunk? Bananas,
maybe?"

Then she heard the others.

"This is terrible. Should we stay on?"

"Keep dancing until Mr. Z. blows his stack and pulls her off."

Jennifer held her breath. She had to keep on. She prayed Mr. Zolinsky would call a halt so she could stop and at the same time prayed he wouldn't, not knowing what would happen if she stopped dancing.

Abruptly, Yuri turned and leaped offstage, leaving the tipsy, twirling Jennifer on her own. The audience was getting impatient. Almost everyone realized now that the girl wasn't part of the ballet.

David Funke came dashing through the stage entrance. First he had gone to the Twentieth Precinct out of breath and almost out of money. He had taken one of the only cabs he had ever paid for in New York City.

"Please, I've got to see Lieutenant Fazio," he had said to the sergeant at the desk in the main room.

"Sorry, I think he's off duty. Can someone else help you?"

"Noooo!" said David Funke, exasperated.

Another officer who heard them had called upstairs. He said finally, "Not there. But someone thinks he might have gone to the State Theatre. There's a ballet there, big gala or something."

David Funke broke out of the room in a fast run. He had taken another cab, telling the cabbie it was a matter of life and death.

"I have to see Lieutenant Frank Fazio!" he yelled to the security guard. "Where is he?"

"Who? Everyone's backstage." David started for an elevator and the man yelled. "You can't go back there! There's a performance going on!"

David Funke ran into an elevator which opened conveniently when he pushed the button. The doors closed, but right behind him was the security guard and right behind him was the cab driver.

David was biting his fingernails in the elevator. Getting off, he heard the music and started to run in that direction. He saw or thought he saw Fazio pacing in the wings, stage left. He tapped him on the shoulder and Fazio turned around in a split-second.

"Shh!" David Funke whispered. David grabbed Fazio by the sleeve and pulled him outside in the hall. As he looked up he saw the security guard and the cab driver coming out of an elevator.

The security guard tried to pull him away. "C'mon, kid, let's go. Sorry about this," he mumbled to Fazio.

But Fazio said, "No, it's okay. He's a friend of mine." The security guard raised his eyebrows, stood there for a few seconds, and then left.

The cab driver who had followed the security guard angrily yelling about a ten-cent tip after having gone through a red light for the kid was now acting comically delicate, realizing he was backstage at a ballet. He held the dime in his hand and said through clenched teeth, "You call this a tip? You know how hard I work. . . ?"

Fazio flashed his shield, handed the man a dollar, and pushed him toward the door before he had a chance to say anything else. Then he turned to David. "What is it?"

David Funke had now caught his breath. "It's my hat. Remember when you were trying to find out about my hat?"

Fazio nodded.

"Well, I finally remembered where I lost it. Right before Heather was murdered. You know where I left it?"

Fazio shook his head and David Funke touched his with his forefinger as if to indicate his stupidity. "I

left it on a piano bench in the rehearsal studio upstairs. I subbed for a class. So whoever took my hat
didn't just find it on the street. And if it's the same
person you saw and that was my hat, then the killer
could be someone who works for the company!"

But Fazio wasn't listening. Someone who uses the
piano bench. It all fit. His eyes flickered back to the
stage. He turned to David Funke. "I really appreciate
this, Mr. Funke. Really, I . . ." Just then he heard
another wave of commotion from the audience. His
eyes, which had left the stage for a half-second, flickered quickly back. Someone had come onto the stage.
It wasn't Yuri. It wasn't a member of the company.

Fazio started walking quickly. Then he was running
toward the stage to get a better look. There was an
old woman. Oh, wait a second, maybe she was
really middle-aged. It was hard to tell. Then he came
closer. Whoever she was, dancing on stage like that,
she looked gross, grotesque. The woman wore a big
net ballet costume. Her legs were fat and so were her
arms. In her gray-blonde hair, which looked drab
under the lights, was a red plume-like hat. She looked
like a geriatric cocktail waitress disguised as a ballerina. He squinted his eyes to get a better look as she
turned. Her makeup was dark, her rouge overdone.
But still, Fazio thought, she couldn't be that old. It
was like watching something in an amusement park
fun house and finding yourself shocked and sickened,
rather than amused. Or maybe it looked so godawful
because she was dancing next to that lovely young
ballerina. Fazio shook his head. What the hell was
she doing there?

The audience spoke in hushed tones as they watched
the exquisite but slightly sloppy young ballerina
cover the stage shadowed by the strange woman. It
was like a hideous reminder of age, a parody of the

shortness of a dancer's life. Some people in the audience covered their eyes so as not to see the two stumbling dancers on stage. Some had hoped it was a joke. Another modern ballet they had to get used to. But it wasn't long before everyone realized the spectacle was no joke and had nothing to do with the performance. Something frightening was happening. It was ugly. But there was more. An agonizing shout filled the theater and everyone became quiet. Not a member of the audience dared to open his or her mouth. That voice held them in silence.

Chapter Eighteen

He always knew what he and his mama did was wrong. But who was to say what was right or wrong? Them? The people in power who have everything? He knew they did anything they wanted and never thought twice how it might affect other people. Anyway, he knew Mama had never actually . . . well, once she had. That's how he had come into the world. He was different, though. He had done it and he had enjoyed it. Eleven times.

MR. ZOLINSKY HAD stood up and was waving his arms like a conductor trying to stop an orchestra. "Enough!" he roared, and the music stopped. "My ballet! You're ruining my ballet! Get that woman off the stage! Who is she?"

The dancers huddling in the wings were trembling. They had heard of Zolinsky's legendary temper, but they had never really seen it. Now it poured out and rumbled into the theater like thunder.

Jennifer kept on dancing. She kept on going like a mechanical wind-up doll. The stage manager was confused as to what to do.

Then there were two voices. The second was soft at first, and then it overrode Zolinsky's. Some looked around before they could figure out where it was coming from. Then the woman, the woman they could hardly bear to look at, who was stuffed into that tasteless costume, strode downstage center.

"Mr. Zolinsky, don't get so excited. Like you used to say, 'listen to what an artist is telling you and you will find out everything you need to know.' People have quoted you."

Her voice was raspy but clear. Everyone in the audience heard it. The top balconies were empty. At two hundred fifty dollars a seat, people filled the orchestra and the first few tiers. People turned to those around them to find out what was going on. After she spoke there was a chorus of "shh!s." Everyone was trying to find out what was really happening and what would happen next.

Mr. Zolinsky's chin dropped at the audacity of the heavy woman who had sabatoged his stage. "Close the curtain!" he demanded. "I say close the curtain this minute!" The curtain was just about to be closed when loud, piercing screams were heard coming from the audience.

"My God!"

"Up there!"

"He's got a gun!"

"We're all going to be killed!"

But no one rushed for the open exits. Some ducked, using the seat in front as a shield and peeking cautiously over the top. All eyes peered upward to the balcony that went around the top of the stage. Somehow, someone had opened enough of the curtain so everyone could see the ledge where the ballet scenery was hoisted down from the top. There was a gasp like a roar when the man standing up there aimed his gun squarely at Zolinsky. The man was wearing a black hood with slits around the eyes. He motioned for the conductor to start the orchestra again.

Jennifer did a turn and spotted him up there alone on the balcony. Her whole body started to tremble, but she kept going. She was really stumbling now, but she couldn't help it. It was hard to swallow, her throat was so dry. Her breathing sounded like she was having an asthma attack. But she had to keep going. The gun could go off if she didn't. It was pointed at Zolinsky, but a bullet would pass straight through her body first.

Fazio and the other detectives who had drawn their guns kept out of sight. People in the top tier, peering through cracks in seats, fumbled for opera glasses for a desperate look at the man who had turned a gun on the audience. Or so it looked from farther away.

Max laughed but no one saw it. Just at the last moment he had unstrapped his leg. That was unplanned, but it felt good, free, right.

She had always hated the sight of his foot. Always tried to pretend it had never happened. Then when that contraption was designed for him, so no one could tell he limped when he had it on, she believed it never happened. Until one day when he was playing the piano too long again. She was angry and drunk. She took his prosthesis, which he had off, and carved it up with a knife. It took two weeks at least to make up a new one. No one had ever seen him limp. He faked a sprained ankle and used crutches. No one ever guessed the truth. After that he made a point of walking without his foot strapped at home. He didn't know why. Just a little game he played with Mama. It made him feel sexy to limp. He liked it when she was angry, too. Especially now that he was too old to hit.

The woman onstage seemed much bolder. Mr. Zolinsky, his face crimson-red, heart thumping as if he couldn't get enough air, couldn't sit down. It was too dangerous to move.

"Remember when you did *Petroushka?*" she asked him.

Zolinsky stared at her. He had always done it. Sometimes he dabbled with the original Fokine choreography. Was she crazy, this woman?

"I want an answer." There was a soft murmur in the audience. The man on the ledge wiggled his hand, the one holding the gun. Zolinsky gulped and nodded. This was insane.

The woman didn't say anything more but danced around, doing what looked like drunken turns and almost bumping into Jennifer, who hadn't blinked her eyes in thirty seconds. Fazio went into a huddle with his other detectives. They decided not to do anything just yet. If they fired, the man on the ledge might shoot Zolinsky and/or Jennifer or even hit someone in the audience. Instead, they quietly formulated a plan.

The woman came spinning clumsily to stage center and again addressed herself to Zolinsky as if they were having a cozy chat and were the only two people in the theater. "When you did *Petroushka,* I had a solo. The same solo your lovely young ballerina is doing now."

Zolinsky sputtered as if he had choked on a glass of wine. An elegant, bejeweled hand from behind floated a lace handkerchief his way. He didn't see it.

"But I wasn't what you see before you, Grischa, my dear, when I had that solo. Oh, no. *I* was a ballerina. I was seventeen when you took me into your first company."

Mr. Zolinsky winced. How could he remember? Even if it were true. There had been so many girls over the years. But the way she talked to him. It was preposterous. Only good, good friends or lovers felt free to use his name that way.

"I never got to do my solo!" she suddenly screeched. "Do you remember why?"

Suddenly he began to remember, but he resisted it. The threads of the past were hanging. He couldn't sew them together. And he could remember nothing that would link him to this diabolical woman disgracing his ballet and hijacking his stage.

"You fired me," she reminded him. "You wouldn't let me do my solo." Sprawled on the floor, taking quick glances to look between seats, were reporters writing down word-for-word notes. Some were holding cigarette lighters to see.

Mr. Zolinsky took a cautious step toward the stage. It was hard to make out her face in the dark. She had also applied unnecessarily heavy stage makeup. Who was she? Seeing him staring at her so intently, she began to dance around. The audience watched mesmerized as the strange duo onstage danced in weird patterns, almost oblivious to one another.

Someone bumped Fazio on the shoulder. He jumped. "Someone should sneak up to the balcony and take him from behind. I will do it." Fazio never took his eyes off the scene onstage. His gun was poised. But he knew the voice was not one of his detectives. It was Yuri Ivanov's.

"Don't be ridiculous," Fazio whispered out of his mouth. "How can you take him from behind? You don't have a gun. I have to send a detective."

"You don't understand. My strength is in my legs. I can leap on him, knock him off guard, and then your detectives can take over."

Then another voice. Also not one of his men. "I'll help him."

Oh, yes. Dr. Richard Kupperman. Can't keep a

good man out front. That's all he needed right now—these two well-meaning helpers to botch up an already impossible situation. An unbelievable situation.

"Both of you, go stand in the wings," he ordered in a voice that no longer resembled Lieutenant Fazio, understanding listener, Mr. Nice Cop.

"But aren't you going to do anything? You can't just wait for him to shoot!" Richard pleaded.

"Yes, we're going to do something, and soon. But you two go far back into the wings and do nothing. Understood? That's the best way to help." His eyes were still onstage.

They disappeared.

"Who was the woman? Fazio wondered. What was the connection between her and the man on the balcony, who he knew had to be Max. He gave a quick nod to a detective nearby.

The man nodded back, knowing what he meant. Fazio whispered, "Be quiet or the audience might say something. It will be bad enough when they see you. We'll have you covered from all sides."

He pointed to another man, who also nodded. He would be the back-up. The two detectives left soundlessly to go up the same way Max had gotten there. By elevator. They planned to take him from behind and shoot quickly.

The woman was still dancing. She stopped, surprisingly, almost in perfect balance. One chunky leg was high up in the air, her foot exquisitely pointed. Those in the audience who really knew about ballet suspected that at one time she probably had danced. Maybe she wasn't making it all up. The woman stood in first position and opened her arms, talking to Zolinsky. "I did my solo for you in a private room. That's as far as my solo went. You wouldn't let me perform it. I was finished before I started."

Her voice was lower now. Missing was the mocking hilarity of before. "Do you remember now?" she said, almost in disgust.

Zolinsky put his hands on his head, as if to help his memory. He was now oblivious to the crowd that surrounded him, stared at him. He was getting a headache. A name. Charlotte. Yes. That was her name. But which Charlotte? His mind traveled clumsily over many years. There had been many Charlottes in his companies.

The perplexing question seemed to linger in the air, teasing him, as she began again to dance even more awkwardly around the stage. If she knew her solo and was a ballerina, as she said, why couldn't she do it? But that was the reason for Jennifer, Zolinsky thought. She was young. She could perform it. Zolinsky studied the woman as she posed and leaped in a dance style more reminiscent of the old Isadora Duncan way of moving rather than classical ballet. Yes, she had been a dancer. He could see that. But now she was like an old jalopy that could still run but not like it did when it was brand new.

"I did much more for you than dance, didn't I, Grischa, darling?" She was speaking again. The audience leaned forward to listen better. The reporters wrote furiously. Fazio was thinking of the two men. They must be on the elevator now. It shouldn't be that hard to surprise and overtake Max. Still, Fazio gritted his teeth. He would never underestimate Max Forrest. Only a fool would do that.

Just then he heard a bellowing voice being hushed up. He didn't have to turn around. The voice came closer. He knew who it belonged to. Captain William Hogan and a herd of detectives resembling a self-righteous posse had finally come. Fazio thought about it. He didn't really give a shit anymore.

"Shoot him!" Hogan commanded in a stage whisper. "You've got your gun out. Shoot the man. What's the matter, chicken? Who is he, anyway? And what's going on here?"

Fazio sighed and said nothing, never taking his eyes off the scene. He calculated that the detectives should just be getting their bearings on the upper floor by now.

"That's an order!" Hogan practically shouted. He signaled to his men to come closer. "If you don't shoot, we will."

Just then there were two crackling gunshots. The audience almost leaped from their seats. It had happened between blinks of an eye. When the smoke cleared, everyone looked up. The two detectives Fazio had sent. Max had seen them and fired. But they were getting away. Max had missed because the detectives saw Max first and ducked out of his eyesight, below the slits in his hood.

Hogan gave an order for his men to start shooting. Fazio said through tight lips, "Can't you see that if you attempt to fire, he'll kill whether you succeed or not?"

Hogan said, "He fired at police officers." But Hogan's men knew Fazio made more sense and lowered their guns.

Fazio said, "You want to know who that is? That happens to be the Ballet Killer. Not Ivan Roman, *Captain* Hogan." Fazio underscored the word "Captain." While he was talking, he was trying to figure out his next move.

"Prove it," Hogan hissed. His men had walked away from him and were standing near Fazio's detectives. Fazio didn't reply. Hogan disappeared into the shadows.

There wasn't a sound in the theater, except the occasional hard clopping of Jennifer's pointe shoes as she did the solo over and over again. No one seemed to be breathing. The woman continued to dance. She seemed less shaky, more accustomed to the stage. It seemed she was enjoying it or really believed she was a ballerina. Suddenly, she stopped again, laughing. She pointed to Zolinsky, still standing. "So . . . after all these years, you really don't remember."

Zolinsky stared at her, seeing her and yet seeing through her. Snow! Charlotte Snow! That was her name. He remembered now. But that was a phony stage name. Remembering her real name somehow came easier. The years folded away now. So many years. So that was who she had been. Charlotte Grabinsky. A little Polish girl from his original company. She had made the corps at seventeen. She was right. But what he remembered was not so much the person, but the dancer. She was brilliant. Fiery. She had quick, lissome movements, almost like a bird that never touched the ground. She could have been a Zolinsky dancer. She had that certain special look he chose in his ballerinas. Why hadn't she been? How strange.

Then he remembered. His voice came rumbling out of him before his mind had a chance to censor it. "You were a lush," he said accusingly. "I fired you because you drank." Then he fell silent. He was going to say she could have been a great ballerina.

"Oh, yes, you remember my last dance, Grischa, darling, don't you? You took me into a little room. I thought you were going to promote me to full soloist, or even principal. I wasn't drinking then. No, I was on the wagon. You're wrong. You said I had gotten sloppy. You never gave me a chance. But I know why you really fired me. You didn't want me around anymore. You had to get rid of me." Her voice rose in fury, getting louder and louder. Everyone was tense, waiting for some sort of explosion. One reporter had run out of paper and was writing on the margins of a program and then on matchbook covers.

She stopped for a while, as if to get herself into control. When she spoke again her voice had lost some of its feverish pitch.

"You gave me something, though, to remember you by." There was an air of coquettishness about her now.

Mr. Zolinsky bowed his head. He didn't want to look at her. He had remembered everything. Now she would publicly embarrass him. Well, everyone would think the woman was crazy. He swayed a little. Would she go so far as to have that hired henchman shoot him because of a meaningless little affair years ago?

"You gave me a baby, Grischa, dear. A fine, bouncing little baby boy. So that I never could work again at the career I was suited for. I had your baby and starved. I tried to work again, tried to teach, but no one would have me. They called me a lush, too. You ignored my calls and letters so I couldn't tell you. Tell you that you ruined my life."

Charlotte was almost crying now. Mr. Zolinsky's head was turned down toward the floor. He hadn't known there was a child. He had wanted her out of the way, yes. But . . . he had a son? It was possible. None of his wives had wanted children.

Tears were slipping down Charlotte's cheeks. Sweet revenge. At last. The truth. In front of all these people who could condemn him as she had all these years. She would never forget this moment. Her moment of triumph. But there was still more.

Charlotte aimed her tear-streaked face directly at Mr. Zolinsky and then tossed her head up to the ledge. "That's your son, Grischa, my darling." The man on the ledge took off his black hood as if on cue and grinned. There was an audible gasp from the wings, where dancers were hanging around the fringes, and also from the musicians in the orchestra pit.

"A son," Charlotte went on, now almost raving. "A beautiful son. Max Forrest. Maximillian Forrest. I named him after your middle name. His last name comes"—she threw up her arms—"from the phone book.

"Meet your son, Grischa." She started walking up and down the stage and then spun around. "But the best part I saved for last. Your son, Max Forrest, is the Ballet Killer, Grischa!" She cackled loudly and started to move around the stage again. Mr. Zolinsky stared long and hard at the aged ballerina galloping so pridefully on his stage. Then he passed out.

Fazio, his gun still aimed, ready to fire, realized his mouth was open. He had been right. Not only that Forrest was the Ballet Killer, but that he had a real motive.

The two women were dancing a macabre duet. That girl was going to drop any minute. He was close enough to hear her loud, labored breathing and see her glassy stare. What now? A getaway? He couldn't give Max Forrest an edge. He made a split-second decision to shoot and kill before Max had a chance to do anything. Other guns were raised, waiting for Fazio's signal. But Max was pacing up and down that balcony. The limp was evident. Fazio knew there was too much danger in attempting to shoot that moving target. Even if they all fired at the same time, he could still get trigger-happy and manage to shoot someone.

Up on the balcony Max was feeling a sudden agitation. He had been watching the two dancers. Everything had been going so well. Soon he could get them both away, holding everyone at gunpoint, shooting if he had to. Now everything was all mixed up. Mama was dancing beautifully. As he had always remembered she could. But who was that old hag ruining her lovely solo? What was she doing onstage with Mama? He had to get her off. This was Mama's crowning moment. She had waited years for this. He saw her with her lovely blond hair and those exquisite feet, finally dancing onstage again, finally showing everyone. Beautiful. Delicious. Except for that ugly old lady who was fat and couldn't dance at all. Well, there was only one thing to do. He aimed his gun and fired.

Everyone was screaming. Looking down, he saw the men with guns rush onto the stage, aiming up at him. He pointed his gun at them. Mama had stopped dancing. She was lying on the ground with the old lady. Then he screamed. The old lady *was* his Mama. Not the other one. He had shot his mama and she was lying in a pool of blood. "Maaa . . ." he screamed and fell off the balcony, his hideous scream lost in midair as he plunged to the ground.

Fazio never let Max finish. He shot and hit him almost before Max landed. Now there were two pools of blood on the stage floor and they were running into each other like a river into an ocean. Richard had dashed onstage with Yuri, and together they picked up Jennifer, who had fainted. The curtain finally closed and the audience stampeded to the exits. Ambulances were called for Mr. Zolinsky and Jennifer. Max Forrest, the Ballet Killer, and his mother were dead.

Michael ran into the kitchen, where the rest of the family was doing the dishes. "Come quick! The television! Daddy!"

Connie, Theresa, and her husband, Rick, dropped everything, literally, and a plate went clattering to the floor, shattered. They ran into the living room.

An announcer with a microphone was standing in the lobby of the New York State Theatre at Lincoln Center. People were rushing by and making so much noise it was hard to hear what he was saying.

"What is it, Michael?" Connie said.

"Special bulletin. They interrupted the program with . . ."

The harried announcer was now almost getting swept away by the swarms of people trying to get out. "Stay tuned for the eleven o'clock news. To repeat, just minutes ago a man was still holding the audience of the State Theatre at gunpoint. The man was shot by Lieutenant Frank Fazio. The man and his mother, both now dead, took a hostage, Jennifer North, who is believed to be in satisfactory condition at Roosevelt Hospital. The man, Max Forrest, who was a pianist with the New York Center Ballet Company, killed his mother after she confessed he was the Ballet Killer. Again, there's a lot to this story. More details on the eleven o'clock news. . . ."

Fazio's family sat in front of the television set, open-mouthed. Michael was jumping up and down, squealing. That was his father. Rick and Theresa were clutching hands in midair. Connie silently crossed herself. She remembered his promise to her. That they would spend Christmas together.

The announcer was now fading into the crowd with his microphone. The last words they heard were: "Captain William Hogan, head of the task force on the Ballet Killer case, has not been reached for comment yet." Then the screen switched back to the Christmas special and the announcer was replaced by three rock musicians dressed as the Three Wise Men.

Two men sat somberly around the bed of Grischa Zolinsky, who had been taken to Roosevelt Hospital.

It was 9:00 the next morning, Christmas Day. Judge Cooper had slept on a chair in the corner and Yuri Ivanov had been summoned. Mr. Z. wanted to talk.

His face looked chalky against the pillows. He had had a weak heart, which he had kept hidden from everyone, for many years. The doctors had told him he was lucky he didn't have a heart attack. The two men sat at his bedside and listened carefully.

"I was awake at four this morning," Zolinsky began. "I was thinking and thinking. Max, the Ballet Killer. The son I never knew. . . ." He shook his head. "I still cannot believe it." He looked past the two men and stared at the wall as if it could give him answers. Then he announced suddenly, "I am retiring."

Both men were shocked.

Judge Cooper spoke first. "That's impossible. You said you'd never retire. You were the one who told me to keep on working."

"This isn't the same thing, my dear Martin. I'm living on borrowed time. I have the property in Paris, the apartment in New York. I have plenty of money. I want to paint, cook, maybe write my memoirs. Watch out," he said with a twinkle, and then he remembered and his impish smile faded into a grim look of horror.

There was an awkward pause.

Yuri Ivanov said hesitantly, "But who will run New York Center? You are the company."

Zolinsky sank deeper into the pillows. Then he said in Russian, "You will stop jumping like a trained seal and choreograph. Yurek Ivanov, you will be the artistic director."

Yuri stared at the older man in disbelief. Judge Cooper understood immediately what Zolinsky had said, though he didn't speak a word of Russian.

Then Yuri was smiling broadly but saying, "Oh, no,

I couldn't do it. I couldn't fill your place. Besides, I have years left to dance."

Zolinski smiled. "You can dance. Give yourself any part you please. But you really want to choreograph; I can tell. And you only have a few more years, if that, before you begin to land from one of those thrilling leaps like a wobbly bear. The audiences won't stand up and applaud and scream for more then."

Yuri hung his head.

Judge Cooper looked from one to the other. He didn't want to lose Grischa, but somehow he knew it would work with Yuri. Both men studied Yuri, who took a deep breath as if he were gulping air.

"Da!" he said finally, laughing.

In a room on another floor of the hospital, baskets of fruit and flowers were arriving by the ton. Jennifer kept fingering the diamond earrings she was wearing. Richard's Christmas present from Tiffany's. She was too tired to read all the cards. But she was touched that many were from members of the company. Others were just well-wishers, strangers who had read about it in the paper or seen TV and felt like wishing her something, maybe because it was Christmas.

Everybody was talking at once, except for Richard, who just sat beside her bed, holding her hand and smiling like a kid who'd just found a lost toy.

"I'm sorry. About the tour, I mean. I guess I've changed a lot since this happened. Listen, Jennifer, you can dance in Iceland if you want. If that makes you happy."

"And I've changed, too," Jennifer said, fighting back the tears. "To hell with the tour. Just put some pointe shoes on me and let me dance. Anywhere."

"Hey, let's get married!"

"When?"

"As soon as you get out of here!"

"Where?"

"Someplace exotic!"

Jennifer giggled and nodded happily. Then she closed her eyes. It could have been the other way around. Oh, there could have been flowers and cards, but there would have been tears, as well.

Just at that moment, there was a knock at the open door. Jennifer's face lit up. Though she had seen him only from a distance, she knew who he was. It was Lieutenant Frank Fazio, and he was carrying a bouquet of flowers.

He walked right over to her bedside and handed them to her. "I believe ballerinas get flowers after a performance, and that was some performance you gave, lady." He smiled down at her. "We've never really met. I'm Lieutenant Frank Fazio, Sixth Homicide Division."

Jennifer took his hand and held it a moment. "Lieutenant, I heard what you did when everyone had given up. . . . I . . . I don't know how to thank you. . . ."

Fazio smiled. "Don't," he said simply. He was on his way now to the deputy inspector's home to discuss a promotion. In Max's apartment the detectives had found all the evidence they needed: camera, typewriter, and that damning string of pointe shoes. Fazio had heard that Hogan had cleared everything off his desk and crept back to Manhattan South.

"You're not going to want to thank me," he said to Jennifer, "not after you get through answering all those questions for the records. Listen, don't let those cops bother you."

Jennifer wasn't really listening. She was thinking. "Isn't it funny that Max was the real Ballet Killer all along?" she said. "He was the last person in the world anyone would have suspected."

"That's how it works sometimes," Fazio commented dryly.

"Why?" she asked Fazio, looking at the papers spread out on her with the blazing headlines like: REAL BALLET KILLER KILLED AFTER KILLING MOTHER. Everywhere were pictures taken by that photographer Zolinsky had kicked out of the theater. Jerry Turner. "Why did he have to kill? My God, millions of kids are illegitimate."

Fazio thought for a moment. "We'll never have all the answers, you know. But I guess it's like when someone puts a piece of paper on top of a stack of papers and walks away. One little piece of paper can cave the whole pile in."

Jennifer blinked. "I don't think I understand that."

"Oh, it's easy. Mr. Zolinsky thought nothing of dumping Charlotte. Men do it all the time. But he didn't know she was having his kid. Then look what happened. All that resentment and hatred built up over the years and it eventually backfired on Zolinsky. A lot of innocent girls got murdered because when he was younger he was a ladies' man."

Jennifer nodded. "But why was Max like two people? Charming, and then a raving maniac."

Fazio shook his head. "That I can't answer. Too bad Max didn't live to get his brain picked by the shrinks. My theory on Max Forrest, though, is simple. You can't look at a thirty-year-old man who was a killer and who lived with his mother all his life without taking a closer look at the mother. Maybe he merely carried out her bidding. I've seen all kinds of bizarre emotional involvements. Max was a killer, though. A twisted one, if you ask me. More sick than evil. And the mother had a real beef. Then, again, I think a man like Max secretly hated his mother. Hated all women. He didn't have to be coaxed to kill. But, of course, we'll never know the whole story now. Not from Max and not from his mother, and certainly not from me. I'm no psychiatrist," he added quickly.

There was still so much they couldn't solve, Fazio thought. Like why did Charlotte Forrest have a filled hypodermic needle pinned to the inside of her ballet costume? The lab said it was filled with liquid Thorazine, a powerful tranquilizer. Fazio could only guess. Perhaps they planned to kill Zolinsky and take Jennifer as a hostage. A very sedated hostage. The very quality that made Max such a successful killer finally ruined him. His madness. What could have been going on in his mind when he shot and killed his own mother?

At Manhattan State Hospital, Nurse Johnson, who had stayed with her girls all night, was holding a memorial service for Charlotte Forrest. The wooden couches and stiff-backed plastic chairs were arranged in pew formation. Mrs. Johnson gave the eulogy in the ward room. Some patients were sobbing, some were yawning and some were sleeping.

"Since Charlotte Forrest will not get the decent funeral she deserved, we offer this memorial service for her soul," Nurse Johnson droned, her voice husky. Outside the winter sun was melting the glistening snow around the edges of the windows.

"Charlotte Forrest was a lamb who came to our flock." Nurse Johnson's glasses slipped down her bulbous nose. "We never really knew her. Never knew she had been a famous ballerina. But even though she was talented and beautiful . . ." A few coughs drowned her out for a minute. "Even though she was all that, she knew the two P's we are all familiar with.

Pain and poverty. And she knew them well. Life was not kind to Charlotte Forrest. Her only son, whom she devoted herself to, sacrificed herself for, shot and murdered her in cold blood."

There were some nose-blowers, and a patient sleeping off her morning medication burped. "There is no one else to pray for Charlotte Forrest, and so we are today. May this unfortunate soul find a better place in heaven. Amen."

The little group bowed their heads. Most were thinking it had been a nice way to kill time until they could stand in line and wait for lunch.

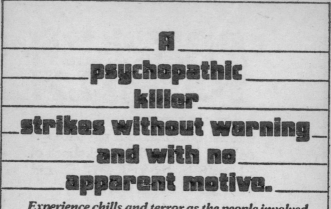